THE
KHAN DILEMMA

THE
KHAN DILEMMA

RON GOODREAU

iUniverse, Inc.
New York   Bloomington

iUniverse books may be ordered through booksellers or by contacting:

iUniverse
1663 Liberty Drive
Bloomington, IN 47403
www.iuniverse.com
1-800-Authors (1-800-288-4677)

Because of the dynamic nature of the Internet, any Web addresses or links contained in this book may have changed since publication and may no longer be valid. The views expressed in this work are solely those of the author and do not necessarily reflect the views of the publisher, and the publisher hereby disclaims any responsibility for them.

ISBN: 978-1-4401-5123-1 (sc)
ISBN: 978-1-4401-5125-5 (dj)
ISBN: 978-1-4401-5124-8 (ebook)

Printed in the United States of America

iUniverse rev. date: 06/17/2009

This novel is for Mary.

CHAPTER 1

———•———

Bernard Harris thought he heard a scream from the home two doors down from his own on a quiet cul-de-sac, but he wasn't sure. It was late, well past midnight on a chill October night in Northern California. Harris was walking his nervous Fox Terrier past his mysterious neighbor's residence when he heard the guttural cry through a lighted, upstairs window. The strange noise made Harris pause in his tracks, exchanging curious looks with his dog, Scout. A louder, more distinct yell rang out and Scout flinched, his head darting about in confusion. Harris had no time to react when a body suddenly crashed through the window, landing headfirst on the cement driveway below with a sickening thud.

Scout yapped and dashed away, yanking the leash out of Harris's hand. Scout's owner was stunned, gazing without comprehension at the heap in the driveway. More noise emanated from the home, a persistent rumbling drifting through the damaged blinds of the shattered window. It sounded like somebody was rushing out of the room, slamming into things along the way. Then Harris heard the gunshots, four of them in rapid succession, followed by a faint, prolonged crashing, something falling down the stairs.

The living room area erupted with a series of loud noises, quickly replaced by a furious jiggling at the knob of the front door. Harris was situated just down the walkway from all the commotion when it occurred to him that whatever was causing the disturbance to the quiet night was heading in his direction. Curiously, the door didn't open right away. Instead, the doorframe shook violently; somebody was desperately tugging at the unyielding door, but failing to budge it. Harris heard the scratchy fumbling of locks coming undone before the door flew open.

A dark, crazy eyed man in tattered clothing occupied the threshold, his

1

mouth a grimace, panting like a cornered animal, his frantic gaze settling on Harris. The killer clutched a gun in his hand as he bolted at Harris, screeching unintelligible words.

Panic gripped Harris and he reached for the sap tucked in his waistband. He'd barely managed to pull it out when the maniac was upon him and Harris swung reflexively at the man's forehead, connecting with the temple. The man's hands clutched at Harris's clothing and his putrid breath filled Harris's senses when he swung the sap two more times into the man's skull, driving him to his knees. The man yanked pathetically at Harris' trousers when Harris knocked him a final blow on top of the head, sending the attacker crashing to the pavement.

Dale Cox clutched the woman of his dreams, an exotic, dark-skinned beauty with the face of an angel and the body of a centerfold. They were in the frenzied throes of making love on a sun-drenched beach in Hawaii, Cox quivering with ecstasy, when a phone began ringing in the distance. The sound panicked Cox for some reason, but he ignored its persistence and continued his blissful endeavor despite the sudden emptiness washing over him. The phone grew louder in his ears, causing the nameless beauty in his arms to slowly fade into the sand they were lying on. Soon the sand faded too and the ringing phone overpowered the sunny beach, turning it black as night.

Cox groaned from deep within his throat, the sound transforming into a whine of bitter disappointment when he realized he was sleeping. The phone on the nightstand persisted in pulling him from his slumber, until his lids fluttered open, and the cramped confines of his tiny, darkened bedroom came into focus.

It was the work cell phone, the one Cox carried when he was on call. The luminous numbers on the alarm clock by his head indicated it was a bit past one in the morning. "Dammit!" Cox snapped groggily, tossing aside the covers and sitting up as an overwhelming sense of emptiness washed over him. His feet clunked heavily on the carpet as he slammed his hand on the cell phone and lifted it to his ear. His thumb hit the receive button just in time to keep the call from going to voicemail. "What is it?" he barked irritably, rigorously scratching the back of his scalp.

"Detective Cox?" a voice inquired.

"Yeah, yeah, that's me. What're you wakin' me up for?"

There was a short pause. "I've got you on the roster as the on-call homicide detective. Is that right?"

Cox breathed deep through his congested nostrils, irritated. "Yeah, I got the duty. What the hell you want?"

Another short pause before the voice spoke again, the tone testy now. "This is Officer Royer. I gotta double residential homicide here. A passing neighbor heard the whole thing when he was walkin' his dog, and he managed to smack down the perp when the guy attacked him on the sidewalk."

Cox stopped scratching his head. "Whadaya saying? You got two people killed and the suspect in custody?"

"Kinda, yeah. The paramedics are getting ready to load him in an ambulance. They're takin' him to county. The witness got him good, used an illegal sap. By the way, you want me to cite the witness for that?"

"Don't do anything till I get there," Cox said sternly. "It's my crime scene and I don't want nobody screwing things up. Are we clear?"

"Whatever, detective," the officer replied, making no attempt to mask his sarcasm. But the hostile tone went unnoticed by Cox.

"I'll be there in twenty minutes," Cox said. "You got the area cordoned off?"

"Yeah, everything's in order."

"Good. Keep all witnesses secured at the scene. I'll want to talk to them when I get there."

"Sure thing, detective."

Cox was about to make more commands, but the officer abruptly ended the connection. Cox pulled the phone away from his ear and studied it curiously before setting it on the nightstand, his mouth still agape with the words he was about to speak.

Dale Cox didn't like getting roused from sleep, but he did appreciate the stature of being in charge, being in control. It was a sense that eluded him in his personal life now that the remnants of his third marriage were unraveling after a span of only nine months.

Cox stumbled into the bathroom and flicked on the fluorescent light over the wash basin. He splashed cold water on his face and dried it with an old, used towel snatched off the shower door handle. He dropped the towel to the floor when he was done and studied his reflection in the grimy mirror over the sink. His face was wide, with pock-marked skin and a thick, crooked, boxer's nose. His eyes were beady and dark and there were puffy bags beneath them. Cox raked his fingers through the scraggly strands of his graying, brown hair, pushing back the greasy locks until he felt his coif was sufficiently presentable.

Okay, so maybe he didn't have the best looking mug, but it was handsome in a rugged way, or so he liked to think. Stepping back, Cox hunched forward, cocking his slightly bent arms away from his body before bringing his bunched fists together at his waist. He flexed every muscle in his upper torso area, presenting the best body-builder pose his stocky frame could muster. Then he frowned, not quite seeing what he'd pictured. He still had muscles, but their outlines were soft and elusive, almost flabby. Cox also hated how bronzed his arms and neck were in contrast to the rest of his torso, which was pasty white beneath a wiry mishmash of dark hairs. His latest marital disaster had distracted Cox from taking care of himself and he silently vowed to increase his gym visits in the near future, until he restored the awesome physique he once carried.

Snapping to, Cox pushed aside his vain musings and took a piss, splashing the seat with his heavy stream and forgetting to flush. He returned to the bedroom, where he threw on a rumpled shirt and slacks, attached his gear to his belt, and put on a tweed jacket. He was in a foul mood when he snatched his keys and cell phone from the nightstand and headed out the door.

When Cox radioed in, he learned that the murder he was on his way to investigate had occurred in the Pleasant Oaks subsection. It was a fairly new neighborhood in the city of Las Cruces that had been developed less than five years ago for the more upper crust of local society. A gated community, it was supposed to be a refuge from the incessant crime infesting the small California city, but a double homicide in one of the town's more exclusive areas was going to rip that illusion to shreds.

Cox rolled up on a fairly active scene when he pulled his car to a halt at the mouth of a cul-de-sac. A cluster of black-and-whites had descended on the spot and were parked haphazardly in the center of the circular street, their blue and red lights silently flashing in the darkness. Yellow tape was strung along the perimeter of the residence involved in the incident all the way to the sidewalk. Gaggles of neighbors stood clumped to either side of the taped perimeter, bleary-eyed in their night clothes, gawking at the lifeless body still crumpled at the top of the driveway. Officers held back the onlookers, answering a flurry of questions from concerned neighbors who wanted to discern what had happened.

Approaching the commotion, Cox passed a car parked just in front of his own. Looking into the blackened interior, he made eye contact with two clean-cut Caucasian men in suits. They bore placid expressions and returned his gaze with coldly professional disinterest. Cox debated stopping, but one of the milling officers called to him, diverting his attention and compelling him forward.

"Detective Cox?" the burly officer inquired.

"Yeah, you the one that called me in?"

"I'm Royer," the officer responded, extending a hand.

Cox ignored the outstretched hand and stepped closer, showing the younger man who was boss. "How long you been with the department? I haven't seen you around too much."

"I got hired on after the academy about six months ago. It's nice meetin' you. Some of the guys around the station have said good things."

"So what's the status of everything?" Cox asked, ignoring the suck-up and swiveling his head about.

Blood rushed to Royer's cheeks and his complexion darkened. He took a moment to swallow the rage that boiled inside. "We got two dead, like I told you on the phone, one inside and one on the ground. We got a witness, Harris, who says the one on the driveway got thrown out the second story window. Looks like he was stabbed first, then thrown."

"I'll tell you what, officer; you should let me draw the conclusions. I'm the detective, right? Your job is just to tell the facts."

Officer Royer's faced turned all shades of crimson, and he lapsed into a stony silence. Cox took no notice of the insult his arrogance had wrought and moved toward the driveway, assuming that Royer was following.

Evidence technicians were snapping pictures of the body when Cox squatted and gave it a once-over. The corpse was once a young white male, dressed in tan slacks and a white dress shirt. The body lay face down, the head crooked at a weird angle. The neck showed heavy swelling and had some lividity, probably snapped during the fall from the window. A pool of blood had collected in the torso area and Cox placed his hand on the dead man's shoulder, giving it an easy push so he could get a look at the abdomen. "Looks like he took a couple punctures below the chest," he said, craning his head for Royer's response. That's when he realized no one was there.

Cox removed a pen and leather bound notebook from his breast pocket and jotted down a few details before moving into the house. Royer followed as Cox scribbled more observations and proceeded toward the foot of a staircase. While evidence personnel bustled about, their camera flashes frequently lighting the room, Cox squatted on his haunches and studied the decedent by the stairs. Another well-dressed white male, he noted, this one wearing a tie. His feet were elevated on the steps, head pressed against the wall at the foot of the landing. "Four shots in the torso, and then he falls down the staircase," Cox mumbled, his brows furrowing. "This doesn't make sense. Why would the burglar be shooting a resident who's going up the stairs? Shouldn't the resident have been coming down when he heard the break-in? This don't add up." He turned to Royer. "We got any ID on the victims yet?"

"That's the funny thing," Royer responded hesitantly. "I did a cursory search of the place, looking for some kind of indicia and can't find nothing. They may have IDs in their wallets, but I didn't want to disturb the bodies. Far as the house goes, you'd never know anybody lives here, except for the few pieces of furniture. There's no pictures, no bills, no books or magazines, no nothing."

Cox stood up and looked around the living room. He saw that Royer had a point, although he'd never admit it out loud. Cox had gotten the same queer feeling when he entered the home, a sense of emptiness, a lack of occupancy. Scanning the surrounding walls, Cox confirmed the points Royer had made. No pictures, no decorations, no knick-knacks adorning the fireplace mantle or end tables. And why were the victims so dressed-up around midnight? Did they come home late and surprise the intruder? The homicides looked fairly straightforward, but Cox could see a few loose ends that needed tying off before he could close the case.

When Cox finished scrawling his latest observations, Royer led him up to the bedroom where the body had been ejected. Once again Cox noted the sparseness of the furniture. The room contained a single bed, dresser, end table, and an overturned tower lamp. Scattered about the hardwood floor were dishes and a serving tray. From the looks of it, somebody was eating fried chicken, macaroni and cheese, and a glass of milk when a struggled ensued.

"Evidence techs been here yet?" Cox asked.

"They took pictures. Other than that, nothing's been touched," Royer replied.

Cox noticed a bloodied butter knife next to the shattered window, where the blinds were wildly askew. Stepping carefully toward the object, he bent forward and studied the piece of silverware. It was a standard butter knife with a rounded tip, curved upward at the end. The dull blade was covered with blood.

Cox frowned and straightened, staring through Royer as the cogs in his mind kicked into gear. Why the hell would a burglar use a butter knife to attack a victim if the perp was packing a gun? Did he break in and surprise somebody eating a meal? Maybe they began struggling before the perp could get the gun out. Why would the victim eat a meal in the bedroom? Cox looked around. No TV. No phone to talk on. It wasn't right. And how could the intruder get upstairs to the bedroom while the other victim was downstairs? It was obvious—from the position of the other body on the stairs—that the second victim was coming up when he got shot dead. He must've heard the commotion.

"Where's the gun?" Cox asked.

"Secured in the trunk of my car," Royer replied. "It was a nine millimeter Glock automatic. The suspect dropped it on the ground when the witness clobbered him. Harris said the suspect ran at him with the gun after hauling ass out the front door. You can talk to Harris if you want. We let him return to his house a couple doors down."

"He said the perp ran at him with the gun?"

"Yeah."

"Did you check the gun? Did it still have rounds?"

"One in the chamber and four in the clip."

"Why didn't the perp shoot Harris? He blows away the guy on the stairs; why not open up when he sees a witness in the street?"

"You're the detective; I guess you'll figure that out, right?"

Cox shot a look at Royer, angered by the smartass remark. He was ready to chastise the rookie when the window drew his attention. Through the wrecked blinds, he caught sight of the dark car with the two mysterious occupants down below, the ones he'd passed earlier. For some reason, the sight of them made Cox feel uneasy. The strangers remained motionless, watching the activity of the crime scene with an odd passivity. "Hey, Royer, take a look at this," Cox said, motioning for the officer to join him. "You see those guys earlier?"

Royer stepped to the window and parted a portion of the blinds. "Oh yeah, they rolled up not long after I responded to the scene."

"Did you talk to them? Who are they?"

"I asked what they were doing here, figured they were our boys, but they told me they're feds."

"Feds? You mean FBI?"

"Yes sir, showed badges and said they were special agents from the Sacramento office."

"Why do they care about some local homicide? This ain't their jurisdiction."

Royer stretched his lips and shook his head. "Don't know; they didn't tell me nothing else. Didn't ask questions. Didn't get out of the car. They been sitting there like that this whole time. Weird stuff."

The faces of the FBI agents loomed ghostly behind the windshield as they watched Cox approach. The one in the driver's seat had short-cropped, rusty colored hair and a long nose over thin, cruel lips. His eyes were dark and lifeless, like a shark's, studying Cox with cold detachment. The driver's window made an electric hum, sliding down smoothly when Cox reached the car.

"Evening, gentlemen," Cox greeted, bending and getting a good look at the passenger and the car's interior, a reflex from his field training. "Something I can do for you?"

The driver had a leather wallet in hand and flipped it open, revealing a badge and ID. "I'm Special Agent Ross with the Federal Bureau of Investigation. This is my partner, Agent Frazier. We're watching your response to the crime scene."

"So I noticed. Mind telling me why? This isn't exactly your jurisdiction, is it? Why does the FBI care about a burglary-homicide in Las Cruces?"

Ross's cold eyes rolled away from Cox and surveyed the activity in the cul-de-sac before coming back to Cox again. "Are you the detective in charge?"

"Dale Cox, at your service," Cox replied, feeling a bit unnerved. There was something scary about Ross.

"We'd like to talk to you about what's going on here. Maybe we can buy you a cup of coffee somewhere and discuss the case when you wrap your investigation for the night."

Cox considered the request momentarily, pretending nonchalance, but feeling a sudden current of excitement coursing through him. "Sure," he said, casually, "I wouldn't mind helping the FBI."

"We'll be happy to fill you in about what our interest is," Ross responded, flashing a fake smile that quickly withered. "The bureau chiefs back in Washington will be very pleased that your department is cooperative."

"Don't worry about a thing, I'll make sure my superiors fall in line," Cox said a bit too eagerly. He was lousy at containing his awe. "I don't know if it makes a difference, but I attended your academy in Virginia last year, the one for advanced training of local law enforcement. I got the certificate mounted on a frame in my office. Finished third in my class."

Ross raised his brows in mock appreciation and turned to his partner, slowly nodding his approval. "That impresses us a lot," he said, turning his attention back to Cox. "In a way, that makes you part of the brotherhood."

"That's the way I see it," Cox beamed. "Everybody in law enforcement's joined in one way or the other. It don't matter what level, we all need to work together."

"I like that. Glad we're on the same page," Ross said, trying another phony smile that faded almost instantly. "We'll talk in a bit then.... And Cox?"

"Yeah."

"Keep this very quiet, even from your coworkers, right?"

"Right, Agent Ross, you can count on me. I'm your man all the way."

Chapter 2

---◆---

R ICHARD DANKO, THE CLAY County District Attorney, stood in his seventh floor office in the courthouse building staring at the troubled sky hovering over the city of Las Cruces. The low hanging clouds looked like a canvass painting, a series of staccato gray smudges with white tips scattered amidst patches of blue. He'd never quite seen the sky look that way. It seemed to mirror what he felt inside.

Danko's pale, almost nonexistent reflection came into focus after a while, overlaying the sprawling, dingy city below. There was something symbolic in the image, he thought. This was his town and his spirit watched over it. He was a large man in his early fifties, his hulking body still formidable looking, a tribute to his college football days. Most of the muscle that once adorned his frame was gone now. Years of high living and innumerable martini lunches had caused his physique to go to seed, but he preferred to think he still cut an impressive figure.

Danko's suit jacket hung on a coat rack while he stood before a large set of bay windows in a white shirt and tie, his bright red suspenders adding a splash of color to offset his otherwise conservative attire. Danko kept his hands thrust in his pockets, his fingers nervously jingling loose change while he brooded over the reason the visitors in the reception room had come to see him.

"They got a lot of nerve dropping in like this," he growled. "After everything that went down last year, what could possibly give them the confidence to waltz into my office?"

"Take it easy, Rich," Danko's second in command said. He was sitting in one of two leather backed chairs fronting Danko's desk. "We don't know why they're here. It could be any number of reasons. I doubt they came

9

because of that probe business; they wouldn't dare. Besides, they have Detective Cox with them. He wouldn't have anything to do with their investigation."

"Don't be too sure," Danko said, turning away from the windows. "They'll use anybody to nail me. Christ! I have turncoats in my own organization."

"You're getting paranoid, chief. It's been ten years since you've set foot in a courtroom. Cox is homicide. You haven't dealt directly with him in a decade. He can't possibly be linked to anything concerning you."

"You may be right, but I wouldn't bank on it. This community is so small it's like living in a closet. Everybody's in bed with everybody else. You can never be sure who's connected."

Danko turned back to the windows and resumed staring at the clouds. Bernie Sims, his second in command, looked on. He was tall and lean to the point of being skinny, the physical opposite of his boss. Sims had soft, almost effeminate features, neatly combed brown hair and brown eyes that peered inquisitively at the world from behind a pair of wire-framed spectacles. He was the perfect number two for a strong-willed man like Danko, quiet, obsequious, unobtrusive, bright, but lacking a single original thought of his own. Sims was the pilot fish swimming alongside the killer shark, the kowtowing servant at his master's beck and call. When necessary, he was the consummate hatchet man, performing whatever dirty work the boss wanted done at a second's notice, without question or reservation. Sims got down and rolled in the mud when he was told to do so, absorbing the grime to keep the boss' image clean. But Sims had failed over the past year.

"What should I do?" Danko asked, abruptly breaking away from his perch and striding toward his jacket.

"Talk to them, see what they want," Sims replied. "What can it hurt to learn why they're here?"

"Okay," Danko said, slipping his big arms into the jacket, "but I want you here when they come in. If things get dicey, I want you to run interference."

"Be happy to, boss."

Danko went to his desk and buzzed the secretary in the outer office. "Julie, send in Detective Cox and the agents." Danko sat down and Sims automatically rose, circling the desk and taking a position to the left of Danko's chair.

Julie, the white-haired secretary, opened the double wooden doors and ushered in the DA's guests. Once they were inside, she pulled the doors shut.

"Detective Cox, to what do I owe the pleasure of this visit?" Danko inquired, the stony set of his expression belying the pleasantry of his greeting. He remained seated and didn't offer to shake hands with anyone.

"Good to see you, Mr. Danko, Mr. Sims," Cox responded unsurely. He appeared worn out, having been without sleep all night. "I have a couple agents from the FBI with me. This is Special Agent Ross and Special Agent Frazier."

"What's this all about?" Danko asked sharply, turning a hostile glare on the agents.

"We came to discuss a homicide," Ross answered coolly, seemingly oblivious to the tension in the air. His thin lips bore a slight grin as he surveyed the DA.

"That's right," Cox added. "We had a residential homicide in the Pleasant Oaks neighborhood this morning. Looks like a burglar broke in and murdered two occupants. I picked up the case and the agents contacted me at the scene."

Danko's heavy gray brows furrowed. "What's the FBI's interest in a local homicide? Don't tell me I'm implicated in that now?" The DA was turning red in the face, his blood rising.

"Not at all," Ross soothed, still smirking.

"No, sir," Cox said, "this has nothing to do with that nonsense that's been in the newspaper the last few months. Our friends here have an interest in the suspect."

"His name's Raheem Khan," Ross cut in. "He's been a person of interest to the bureau for some time. I'm not at liberty to disclose the full nature of our interest. Suffice it to say we consider him to be a very dangerous individual."

"No kidding," Danko said sarcastically. "Like a double homicide don't bear that out?"

Sims chuckled.

Ross proceeded without any reaction to the comment. "Khan is a member of your local Pakistani community. We've kept tabs on his activities, along with various other members of a certain group associated with him."

"Hold it!" Danko exclaimed. "Stop right there. Don't come at me with this terrorist crap. The FBI dumped a case on us last year concerning one of our local Muslims. You told us he'd attended training camps in Afghanistan and that he was promoting terrorist endeavors throughout Northern California. My office took the case when the boys in the U.S. Attorney's office refused to touch it. Then we took it to court and got caught with our pants down. The FBI suddenly decided our most vital evidence was classified and couldn't be released for trial. What was that guy's name? Jinnah?"

"Ahmed Jinnah," Sims echoed.

"Yeah, Ahmed Jinnah," Danko continued. "We lost that case because of your bureau, went down in flames. And what did I get for all my troubles? Outrage from the Muslims when they screamed racism, protests and a bunch of bad press accusing me of a rush to judgment. I lost political clout on that one, along with your damned corruption probe that's never gone anywhere, by the way. Now you come to me with this can of worms?"

"It ain't like that," Cox intervened. "You're wrong on this one, Mr. Danko." He was going to say more when Ross raised his hand. Cox shut up immediately and lowered his head.

"That probe is bad business," Ross calmly stated. "If it's any consolation, Mr. Danko, I can tell you I have no part in it. My department works on counterintelligence, not criminal matters."

"You're confusing me," Danko said. "If criminal isn't your bailiwick, why are you sticking your nose in a local killing?"

"The FBI's interest in last night's events is strictly discretionary."

"Discretionary?" Danko repeated.

"Yes," Ross replied. "You mentioned opening a can of worms. The truth is we want the opposite. We want your office to handle Khan's case as routinely as possible; keep it under the radar, so to speak. Khan breaking into that home and getting apprehended is a boon to our investigation. We've been trying to compile enough evidence to move on him for quite a while, without much success. He's a very discreet operative. Taking him off the streets, parking him in a prison cell, suits us fine. It'll isolate Mr. Khan and force whatever contacts he's got to reach him inside a controlled environment that we can monitor.

"I'm here, Mr. Danko, not to ask you to make a big deal out of this matter. To the contrary, the federal government wants to keep this as quiet and routine as possible."

"What are you asking?"

"Simply to keep Detective Cox as the primary investigator on the case and assign an attorney who'll get a conviction in a quiet and expeditious manner. Also, the bureau would like to be kept abreast of all developments, nothing more than that."

Danko studied Ross. He didn't like the man. There was something about him that gave Danko the creeps. "Okay," he said after a bit, "there shouldn't be any problems with what you're asking. You may want to advise your superiors of my spirit of cooperation. They should give it very serious consideration."

Ross nodded, a trace of a smirk returning to his mouth. "I agree," he responded, appreciating the implication of the comment. "I'm sure it'll be given the consideration it deserves."

Prick! Danko thought, gritting his teeth and trying to pass it off as a smile. Ross's last remark could be taken any number of ways. Danko was sure Ross meant it to be ambiguous. "You and Agent Frazier should leave your cards with my secretary on the way out. Feel free to contact me in the future if you need anything."

"Certainly," Ross responded, understanding that the DA was pronouncing the meeting over. "We'll be in touch."

"What a snake-oil salesman," Danko said when he was alone with Sims again. "Does he really expect me to buy that load of crap that they came from Sacramento just to ask me to handle a case that's none of their business?"

"Beware of feds bearing gifts," Sims said amiably, dropping onto one of the chairs facing Danko's desk.

"There's something much bigger going on than what they're telling me," Danko said, peering ahead with steely concentration.

"What are you thinking, Rich?"

"I don't want another mess on my hands like last year. We barely got things squared away since that Jinnah prosecution. I don't need to be on the losing end of another intrigue by the feds. Why are they bringing this to me?"

"Good question; the U.S. attorneys never run from a sure thing. They like the glory."

"Exactly. The only time they pass a case off is when it's going south. What stinks about these murders?"

"I can try to find out. Cox seems to be in tight with this Ross fellow. Maybe I can pick his brain and elicit more information."

"Good idea," Danko said, springing from his chair and returning to the bay windows. He kept his back to Sims when he spoke next. "Contact Detective Cox and flesh this story out. Get every last detail you can milk from him, and then get back to me. Maybe we can figure the angle. After that, we'll assign a deputy to charge and handle the case."

"Shall I coordinate with the homicide chief?"

Danko was about to reply when a thought struck him. Cocking his head, he slowly turned to his assistant. "No," he said, "we're not giving it to homicide. After we talk again, I want you to give the case to Max Siegel."

"Max Siegel? Are you joking?" Sims had been draped in his chair, but now he sat upright, staring disbelievingly at his boss. "You can't be serious."

"Oh, I'm deadly serious."

"That doesn't compute. You just put him out to pasture with the Insurance Fraud Unit. Why pull him back in the game, especially after what's happened over the past year? Word's leaked out lately that he's contemplating a run against you in the next election. Do you really want him back in the limelight?"

"Call it a hunch, but I have a feeling on this one, Bernie. I'll know better after we talk later." Danko walked away from the windows and Sims could see that he was fired up, his large frame vibrating with nervous tension as the machinations of his mind kicked into high gear. "Trust me, I don't like Siegel any more than you do. He's been a thorn in my side for as long as I can remember. If not for civil service, I would've fired his ass years ago."

"Then why assign him to Khan?"

"Because it stinks and I want Max Siegel right in the middle of it. If this turns out to be another mess like Jinnah, I want Siegel's name all over it."

"I see," Sims said thoughtfully, his tone laden with doubt.

"Do you see where I'm going? If the case is routine, then we get a quick conviction and I send Siegel packing back to Insurance Fraud and bury him under a ton of paper. But if the case turns into another big controversy, then Siegel suffers all the bad press. We'll give him total control right from the charging stage. My differences with him are well documented. If the case goes bad, I get to point a finger and call him a rogue DA. He'll act as my buffer from all the muck. I come out ahead no matter what."

"And Mr. Goodie-goodie, Max Siegel, gets a big smudge on his pristine image," Sims said with a grin. "That's absolutely diabolical, chief."

"I know," Danko beamed. "That's what keeps me where I am, Bernie, and don't forget it."

Sims rose from his chair. "Okay then. I'll mosey on over to the police department and visit Cox while he's writing his reports. I'll discern what I can and get back to you before I make a trip to Siegel's office."

"Good … and, Bernie, let's keep tight lips on this, okay?"

"Sure thing, Rich."

After Sims left, Danko strolled toward the bay windows and thrust his hands in his pockets, rocking slightly on his feet as the yellow rays of the rising sun shed light over his city. It was always going to be his city, Danko thought.

CHAPTER 3

———◆———

M AX SIEGEL SAT AT his desk feeling despondent. Piled before him were reams of civil paperwork relating to a nasty lawsuit against the local branch of a national insurance company. The business had bilked hundreds of thousands of dollars from Clay County policy holders over the past few years under what it perceived to be loopholes in regulatory laws. The DA's office, along with some consumer groups, disagreed with the interpretations, which were too ambiguous to be considered criminal, so the office had opted for a civil suit instead. That meant tons of litigation against a bank of corporate lawyers that could drag on for years without end. It was poison to a criminal trial attorney like Siegel. He was too dynamic for such drudgery and couldn't imagine slogging through the suit for the next couple years, steeped in every conceivable sort of boring minutiae. Siegel thought he was lucky not to own a gun. Otherwise, he might put it to his head and shoot.

The phone rang and Siegel had to push stacks of paper aside to find it. "Max Siegel," he answered.

"Hello, my handsome darling," his wife, Irina, said. "I am calling to say how much I love you."

"That's nice to hear," Siegel responded, pushing aside some papers so he could see the picture of his wife that was on his desk. "I need all the love I can get right now."

"Why? What's wrong?"

"Aw, nothing, I'm just not enjoying this assignment they dropped me into. I've been doing homicides for ten years, and now this?" Siegel studied the picture as he spoke to Irina. Her dark, flowing hair framed a flawlessly beautiful face. Most striking were her eyes, pale blue to the point of being almost translucent. He always felt as if he were looking into them, not at them. Even staring at them in a picture made him go all warm inside.

"Keep your head up, my love. I'm sure something good will come of this assignment eventually. You are too great a man to have to suffer so."

Siegel grinned. "Do you really mean that, or are you trying to butter me up?"

Irina laughed. "I am not spreading butter on you, silly man," she replied in her thick, Russian accent. "Is there something wrong with trying to lift the spirits of my husband when he is in the dumps?"

"Not at all, I appreciate it very much. But, sweetheart, I wish you'd take me off the pedestal you have me on. I don't know how much longer I can stay there before you realize I'm nothing special."

"Such talk, ha! Remember when I started working at the coffee shop near the courthouse two years ago? So many men, all the time they want to speak to me, they want my attention. Lawyers, cops, judges, criminals, businessmen, they all came around and asked me out. So many, and yet the first time you walked in the place I felt my heart stop. I could see nobody else. You are the most beautiful man I have ever known."

"Stop! Enough already," Siegel begged, chuckling. "If my ego gets any bigger I won't be able to fit my head through the door to get out of the office."

Irina laughed. "Okay, so now you feel better? You need no more cheer?"

"I feel much better, thank you. Now I can get through the rest of the day."

"Good, then I will go back to my studies. The test for court interpreter is coming soon in two months. I must get more serious about studying these legal terms if I am to pass."

"You will, don't worry. Your English is excellent and you're twice as smart as me. If I can remember all the terms, it ought to be a breeze for you."

"You're too sweet. Hey, I am going to work in an hour. Will I see you there later?"

"Yeah, after I read through some of this stuff on my desk. It might take a whole pot of coffee to keep me awake."

"Good. I will see you in a few."

"Bye, sweetheart."

After Siegel hung up, he took Irina's picture and held the frame with both hands. Shaking his head, he studied her demure beauty, still not believing—despite all the time that had passed—that she was his. Irina was eleven years younger, a year shy of her thirtieth birthday. She was slim and stunning looking with her pale blue eyes and taut, curvy figure. She'd stopped Siegel dead in his tracks when he walked into Starbucks two years ago. He'd taken nearly five minutes to fumble a bill out of his wallet while she watched him with those jewel-like eyes at the register, an amused grin parting her painted red lips. Then she spoke and the Russian accent did him in, adding an exotic touch to her physical perfection. Siegel's attraction to Irina was instantaneous.

Siegel went to Starbucks frequently throughout the following weeks, turning to jelly whenever he spoke to Irina, becoming more captivated with each snippet of conversation. Every encounter increased their familiarity, until they settled into a comfortable acquaintance and Siegel summed up enough courage to ask Irina out. One date followed another and Siegel gradually got to know Irina on a more intimate level. She bore an intellect too advanced for someone who spent time sliding cups of coffee across a counter. This intrigued Siegel and piqued his curiosity about her past.

She lived with her sister in Las Cruces for four months before beginning work in the coffee shop. Prior to that, she'd resided in Sacramento under murky circumstances that were never clarified. Siegel figured it had to do with a relationship gone badly and he didn't press for more than Irina was willing to tell. She was equally reticent about details concerning her life in Russia, except to reveal that she'd had a decent upbringing in Moscow and immigrated to the United States after completing a degree in engineering at a university. Eventually, the passion for her field of endeavor waned and she took to doing translator work for the courts in Sacramento. She aspired to pass a test to fully certify her in the business and wanted to make it a career.

Siegel had never been married. Though he'd had long term relationships and gotten engaged once, he'd never strolled down the aisle prior to meeting Irina. The knowledge that he was approaching forty, combined with falling under Irina's spell, had persuaded him the time was right to make a lifetime commitment. Siegel proposed on a cold, wintry night while they snuggled in front of a fire, sharing a bottle of pinot noir. She accepted immediately, amidst an explosion of tears and gasps and kisses and hugs. The marriage happened less than a year later.

Siegel still clutched Irina's picture when Bernie Sims appeared in the doorway. "That's quite a lady you have there," he said.

Siegel looked up, surprised, and set the picture on his desk. "Bernie, what brings you by?"

Sims sauntered into the room, giving the place a once-over. "How do you like your digs?"

"Okay, I guess. We're seven blocks from the courthouse. I don't imagine it'll be too pleasant traipsing over there when the winter rains set in."

"No, I don't imagine it will," Sims replied distractedly.

"What are you doing here? I know it isn't for decoration ideas."

"No, of course not," Sims said, flashing a plastic grin. "The big man sent me to talk to you."

"You mean Danko?"

"Yes, mind if I have a seat?"

"Go ahead."

Sims dropped into a chair fronting Siegel's desk, casually draping an arm over the back. "I don't know if you heard, but we had a double homicide in Pleasant Oaks early this morning."

"No, I hadn't heard. I've been pouring over discovery all morning; no time to read the paper."

"Yeah, it's a nasty scenario. Some Pakistani kid broke into a home and killed two young businessmen. Surprised one in an upstairs bedroom, killed him with a butter knife of all things, and then tossed him out a window. Shot the other victim dead with a handgun. A Samaritan caught the suspect when the killer ran from the home and attacked him."

Siegel leaned forward, intrigued. "A butter knife?"

"Yes, can you believe that?"

"Actually, no. In a decade of doing homicides, that's the first time I've heard of a butter knife as a murder weapon."

"I'm with you. It's an odd detail."

Siegel frowned. "And a Pakistani? Since when do they venture past the east side of town? They always stay to themselves in their tiny enclave over there. This is out of the ordinary."

"I agree, and it comes on the heels of our disastrous prosecution of that Jinnah fellow last year. He's one of the biggest leaders in the community. Another Pakistani going to trial so soon after all the controversy will be like ripping the scab off a wound for the Muslims. We anticipate a lot of political fallout."

"I imagine so," Siegel said, eyeing Sims suspiciously. "But what does any of this have to do with me? You should be jabbering at the homicide boys, not me."

"Still smarting over losing the homicide chief position, aren't you?"

"You don't have to be Nostradamus to come to that conclusion," Siegel replied bitterly.

Sims pulled his arm off the chair and leaned forward, resting his elbows on his knees and loosely clasping his hands together. "I think Rich is feeling some remorse lately. You're a great attorney and a strong leader.

He recognizes that your departure has left a void in the homicide division. I think he's regretting his decision."

"What a pile of horseshit, Bernie. Please don't sit there and try to play me for a fool. Danko's hated me since he was elected DA. We've been sparring for years and I know he wants me out the door."

Sims lifted his hands and waved his palms at Siegel. "Okay, okay, it's no secret that you two have differences. You're both headstrong, if you want my opinion. But don't forget that Rich Danko is still a professional with enormous responsibilities sitting on his shoulders. He recognizes talent when he sees it. All personal feelings aside, he knows you're one hell of an attorney."

Siegel twisted his mouth to one side and shook his head. "You've blown enough smoke at me. What's Danko got on his mind?"

Sims shifted further forward in his seat, his brown eyes gleaming behind his glasses. "He wants you to handle the case."

"What?"

"That's right. He's bringing you back to homicide. Who knows, he may even make you chief again."

"Why would he want me? This case sounds as straightforward as it gets. Anybody in homicide can handle this one with no problem."

"True, but, as I mentioned, there's a political element involved. A bomb could explode in the Muslim community if the case isn't handled properly. Rich wants it prosecuted quickly and efficiently, with as little fuss as possible. However, if emotions start getting charged up, he wants somebody who can handle the fallout. Rich needs an experienced political veteran with a deft touch and he thinks you're it."

Siegel studied Sims, trying to discern his real intentions, but the man's grinning visage was an impenetrable mask. "Nice pitch," he said, "but I don't believe any of it. I've known Danko too long not to understand that there's always an agenda behind everything he does. This generous offering reeks of something underhanded."

Sims chuckled. "Oh, Max, you're too suspicious," he said, swatting the suggestion away with a wave of his hand. "For the sake of humoring you, let's say the boss has bad intentions underlying the decision. Why not take advantage of it anyway? You'll get out of Insurance Fraud and back to Homicide, like you want. If it's all a trap, it sure is a screwy way to get you. I mean, my God, he's handing you everything you want."

The skinny bastard was right, Siegel thought. Regardless of what Danko intended, the assignment was a plum—at least on the surface. Why turn it down?

Sims noticed the change in Siegel's expression and grinned. The bait worked. The fish was hooked, but he wanted to play Siegel some more. Sims rose to his feet. "Look, if you'd rather stay with the insurance fraud business, that's fine by me. I'll get out of your hair and let you work. Danko can assign the case to somebody else." He started toward the door.

"Wait," Siegel said, hating himself. "You win, I'll take it."

"Good," Sims gushed. "That's the smart move. You'll be glad you made it."

"I want total control, no interference from you or Danko."

"Of course. Rich said you can have that."

"Who's the investigating detective?"

"Dale Cox. He responded to the scene when it happened."

Siegel frowned.

"What's wrong?" Sims asked.

"I don't like Cox. We never got along during my homicide stint. His ethics stink."

"There's nothing we can do about that. He's with LCPD and it's their call."

"Then give me one of our guys from DAI."

"Who'd you have in mind?"

"Rappaport."

Sims appeared troubled. The request caught him off guard. "He's one of our best investigators."

"A pit bull, and that's why I want him."

"For what? Our personnel are steeped in a mountain of cases right now. I don't know that we can afford to give you anybody, especially on such a routine matter. Cox is adequate."

"You told me I can have what I want and I want Rappaport; otherwise it's no go. I'll stay here with my paperwork."

Sims was hesitant. What's the deal, Siegel thought? I'm asking for a homicide investigator on a murder case and they're balking. There's some mud behind this rosy picture they're painting.

"Okay," Sims relented, "I suppose we can spare Rappaport for a while, if you think it's necessary."

"I do."

"Then we're set. Reassign your cases and come to the office tomorrow. We'll clear a space for you somewhere."

"Just make sure it isn't the broom closet."

"You're such a card, Max. We'll get you a decent spot."

"By the way, what's the defendant's name?"

"Khan, Raheem Khan. The Samaritan he attacked brained him pretty good and he's presently in a coma over at county. The police have custody and got him checked in under a John Doe, which is probably a good idea for the time being. So keep the name under your hat and hold off filing charges until he comes to. That way we won't have pesky family members hiring a lawyer while he's in the hospital. It'll give us a chance to question him when he wakes up."

"Good thinking. Do we have a prognosis?"

"His condition appears to be temporary. Cox is in contact with the doctors and he can fill you in better than me. Give him a call when you get a chance."

"I will."

Sims started out the door. "Good luck, Max," he said. "Let me know if you need anything."

Siegel watched Sims vanish and gazed at the empty doorway for a long time after he was gone. What just transpired was strange business and Siegel's instincts were in overdrive trying to figure the angles. Danko was up to no good, Siegel would stake his life on it. But what exactly he had up his sleeve was anybody's guess. It would be good to be teamed with Rappaport on this one; he and Siegel always worked well together. More importantly, Siegel could trust the man. He'd need somebody like that on his side if he was going to survive Rich Danko's latest scheme to destroy him. The DA was a viper.

CHAPTER 4

D ALE COX ARRIVED AT Starbucks toward late afternoon. His mood was surly from not sleeping and spending the better part of the day doing what he hated most: writing reports. His documentation skills weren't very good, and he suffered for it time and again in the past when defense attorneys called him to the witness stand. They treated his reports like sacred scrolls, pouncing on him whenever the facts he testified to differed from what he'd transcribed. Cox tended to make a lot of mistakes when he wrote, and he couldn't stand the humiliation he suffered under questioning by smarmy defense lawyers who constantly pointed out the errors. Okay, so maybe writing wasn't his forte. His strengths lay in cracking tough cases and busting skulls, not scribbling words on paper. Compiling reports was torture for him, always leaving him in a foul disposition.

Irina Siegel manned the counter when Cox approached and that lifted his spirits. Those electric blue eyes met his before suddenly averting away—like always—as she pretended to be absorbed in waiting on the customer ahead of him. It was their usual game—or at least hers—of pretending not to know each other, denying the courthouse gossip mongers sustenance. In fact, they knew each other very well, something her pretty boy husband was oblivious to. Max Siegel carried himself like such a smart guy, but the highbrow attorney didn't have a clue. Cox often wondered what Siegel would do if he ever discovered the secret Cox shared with his gorgeous wife.

Cox was next at the counter, and he grinned when Irina finally looked at him. "Hi, beautiful," he greeted.

Irina's cheeks enflamed, the pale skin reddening as she glanced about nervously. "What are you doing here?" she asked in a hushed tone. "You told me you were not coming around for a while, that you would give it a break."

"It's been a while, dear. I ain't come around for nearly two weeks. How long do you expect me to stay away?"

"What do you want?"

"You."

"Stop it! I told you not to talk to me in such a way."

"I love that Russian accent. Have I ever told you that?"

Irina huffed. "Are you going to order?"

"My, my, all business today, aren't we?"

"Please, other customers are waiting."

"Fine, if that's how you want it. Give me my usual. You know what it is."

"Grande house special with plenty room?"

"Bingo."

Irina turned and poured Cox's order, filling the cup two-thirds full and handing it over with downcast eyes. She also rang him up without looking at him and pulled her hand away when he tried to touch it while receiving change. Cox chuckled when Irina looked over his shoulder and spoke to the next customer. She always played so hard to get at work, but they both knew better.

Cox took a seat at a small, round table next to the window, almost directly across from the cash register. He'd dumped enough cream in his cup to fill the beverage to the brim. Then he added his usual five packets of sugar, while keeping a visual on Irina. The place was busy and she paid him no mind as he briskly stirred his coffee with a flat, wooden stick, carelessly sloshing the liquid onto the table. Cox became irritated by the continuous lack of attention, and he thoughtlessly took a sip from the cup. The hot coffee scalded his tongue and dribbled over his chin. A few patrons glanced pensively his way as he cursed and sputtered, dabbing a paper napkin at the breast of his rumpled shirt.

Cox expected Irina to come around and offer assistance, but she remained at her station. He got to his feet and grabbed more napkins from the condiment stand, cleaning himself as best he could before returning to his table and resettling into his chair in a sullen funk. He sat stewing gloomily until the real reason for his being there walked through the door.

Max Siegel cut a sharp profile with his well-tailored, blue pinstripe suit and neatly trimmed salt-and-pepper hair, which was combed straight back. Cox waved to him, but Siegel's attention was instantly drawn to his wife. They exchanged smiles and Irina noticeably brightened. The sight caused Cox's spirits to sink into his bowels. Siegel was moving toward the counter when he noticed Cox. He raised a finger at Irina and mouthed something before changing direction and heading Cox's way. Irina kept Siegel in her sights, trailing him with her eyes until he sat at Cox's table.

"Hey, detective," Siegel greeted, "thanks for meeting with me."

"No problem, my shift's not officially over for another hour. I suppose we should touch base before I go home and get some shut-eye."

"Looks like you could use some," Siegel said. "You look like shit." Siegel had a big grin when he made that last remark and Cox wasn't sure how to take it.

Siegel saw Cox's discomfort and had to work to hide his amusement. They'd always had an undercurrent of animosity in their relationship, and Siegel felt no compulsion to dispel it. Cox looked like hell and that was a fact. He was unkempt, his hair scraggly, his clothes wrinkled and stained—as if he'd slept in them—and he needed a shave. From where Siegel was sitting, he also noticed that Cox didn't smell too good either. The detective was a mess, all in all.

Irina came by and set a cup of coffee next to Siegel, who thanked her. He saw Cox giving Irina the once-over but pretended not to notice. It made Siegel's blood boil, but he was determined to keep his relationship with Cox civil, at least for the time being.

"Where do we stand on the Khan case?" Siegel asked.

"Looks good, I'm still writing the reports. They'll be ready in a couple days."

"Do you have anything preliminary right now?"

"Nah, there's no rush. Khan's at county with a brain injury. The doctor says he'll be asleep for another two days or more, so we can take our time."

Siegel took a breath. "I'm not trying to push you, detective, but, regardless of Khan's condition, I need to get familiar with the facts so I can prepare the charging document."

"C'mon, what charges are you gonna struggle with?" Cox asked, leaning back in his chair and smiling with condescension. "We got residential burglary with two murders attached. I know I'm not a highly educated attorney like you, but I don't need a law degree to tell me this case is about as routine as they get. You got a cherry here, counselor."

"Yes, your legal analysis is probably right, but I still want to play it by the numbers. I don't like taking anything for granted. Even the best cases can go south when things aren't done correctly."

"Wait a minute, are you saying I'm not handling this the way it should be?"

"No, no, take it easy, Cox; I'm not implying anything. Lack of sleep has made you cranky."

Cox studied Siegel's expression, trying to cool off while attempting to get a read on the lawyer. He couldn't tell if the DA was playing or not, but Cox was ready to blow if he determined that Siegel was screwing with him. It had been a long night and Cox wasn't in the mood to take grief from anybody, especially Max Siegel. Lifting his coffee cup, Cox took a gulp, wincing when the bitter sweet beverage scorched his throat. "Sorry if I'm touchy," he said when he recovered. "I been up all night and I'm dead tired. How 'bout I give you an overview?"

"I'll take what I can get."

Cox went into a rendition of all that he'd derived from the crime scene, describing what he'd observed and summing up his conclusions about how the murders went down. He omitted mentioning his meeting with the FBI agents and concluded by describing how Bernard Harris brained Khan with a sap when the killer tried to make Harris victim number three.

Reaching into the vest pocket of his tweed jacket, Cox produced a sap and crudely dropped it onto the table, causing some of Siegel's coffee to spill. Siegel picked up the weapon. It was long and stiff and slender, widening at one end in the shape of a beaver's tail with a large lead bump in the center. The sap was made of tough, black leather with a strap attached to the slim handle. The strap allowed the user to slip his hand through for a better grip when wielding the instrument. Siegel was surprised by how heavy the sap felt.

"Ain't that a beauty?" Cox asked, grinning like a proud father. His teeth were yellow and his eyes had turned to tiny slits. "I ain't seen one of those in years. We used to carry them on the force until the mid-eighties. These babies carry a helluva punch."

"I'll bet," Siegel said. He slapped the tail of the sap onto his palm and winced at the shock of pain it produced.

"See what I mean?" Cox said gleefully. "Can you imagine that slammin' your head a few times? I'm surprised Khan took as many whacks as he did before he went down. He must have one thick skull."

"What was the witness doing with this?" Siegel inquired. "They're illegal."

"Yeah, well, you know, lots of things are illegal. Bernard Harris, he's a good guy, an upstanding citizen. He's a retired truck driver, and the sap is a remnant of his trucking days. He carried it on long hauls for protection from hijackers and crazy whores. The guy's old school, so he can't part with the thing. And it's lucky he didn't, 'cause there'd be three dead victims and no witness otherwise."

Siegel set down the sap and gazed thoughtfully out the window. "What was Khan doing in the house?"

"How's that?" Cox asked.

Siegel turned his attention to Cox. "Why would Khan enter a home in the wee morning hours, knowing that it was occupied and that people were up and about? The lights had to be shining through the windows when he approached. He'd know the residents were walking around inside. Why choose that home? Burglars rely on stealth, especially when they're entering an occupied dwelling. Other homes in the neighborhood must have had the lights off at the time. Why choose the one that didn't?"

Cox's expression sobered, his mirth draining away. He appeared nervous. "That struck me, too," he said. "It didn't make much sense at first when I assessed the crime scene, but then I figured what if it was some sort of home invasion? Khan had a gun, a Glock. What if the fact that people were up was exactly what he was looking for? He could just break in and commit a stickup, you know? Where's the money and valuables and all that? The victims were dressed like businessmen. Maybe they got in late and Khan happened to spot them when they were pulling up the driveway. It might have been a crime of opportunity while he was casing the area. He coulda followed the poor bastards inside."

Siegel thought about Cox's scenario and saw some plausibility to the theory, but it was still troubling. And why did Cox appear so uncomfortable all of a sudden? Shifting in his chair, he looked like the kid who just got caught stealing a cookie. His behavior was odd.

"You might be onto something," Siegel conceded, "but I still don't quite see the pieces fitting together."

"What's bothering you?"

"He gets inside and goes upstairs while the other victim is milling around the first floor? Let's say you're correct and it's some kind of one-man home invasion. Wouldn't Khan go after the downstairs occupant first and get control of him before heading upstairs to confront the other guy?"

"True," Cox agreed, scanning the table as his mind searched for an answer. "But this is a target of opportunity, and Khan doesn't have time to lay out a plan. He gains entry and he's nervous. Maybe victim number two is downstairs, but he doesn't realize it. He hears movement on the second floor and heads straight up to do the robbery."

"Okay, if that's true, then he should have the gun in hand. Why does Khan waste time killing the victim upstairs with a butter knife, of all things? He had no problem shooting the downstairs victim. With the element of surprise on his side, why didn't he shoot the first victim?"

"You know how it is when crimes are committed, counselor, lots of details don't make sense. Maybe the upstairs guy heard Khan coming and jumped him before he could use the gun. It could have been any number of factors. The investigation's still in its infancy; these are details that can be fleshed out in time. Stop worrying so much. It's gonna be a cake walk."

Siegel was gazing into the distance, locked in concentration. "The man upstairs is eating dinner when Khan makes contact. Victim's home long enough to prepare a meal. How does that jibe with your theory that Khan followed the men inside? He would've had to wait a while after they went in before making his entry."

"You're killin' me with these questions so late in the day," Cox said, attempting to be humorous, but showing irritation. "I've had a long day already, counselor. Maybe we can pick through this more thoroughly tomorrow."

There was an edge to Cox's tone and it snapped Siegel out of his reverie. "Oh, I'm sorry. You're right, the investigation's only beginning, and there are tons of questions that will probably sort themselves out as time goes by. You've been awake all night and here I am peppering you about inconsistencies. I must be driving you nuts."

"That's right," Cox responded in another transparent attempt at humor. He snatched the sap from the table and waved it at Siegel. "You got me wanting to use this on you, you're irritating me so much." Cox tried to chuckle, but it came out more as a huff, a tight grin fading from his mouth as an angry glint touched his beady eyes.

An awkward silence ensued, Siegel meeting Cox's stare with an ambiguous one of his own. Wanting to end the moment, Siegel lifted his cup. "Thanks for your time, detective. Go home and get some sleep and we'll talk tomorrow. Better yet, I'll have my investigator contact you, and maybe the two of you can run through the facts together."

"Investigator?" Cox repeated defensively. "What investigator?"

"I'm pulling one of our boys from DAI. I'm bringing Franny Rappaport on board."

"What the hell for?" Cox asked, jumping to his feet. He still clutched the sap and he caught the nervous attention of some nearby customers. "I have everything under control, and it's a simple case. Nobody else needs to butt their nose in."

Siegel was losing patience. His blue gray eyes took on a steely glint. "This isn't a request, Detective Cox. He's my guy and I'm bringing him in."

Cox continued to lock gazes with Siegel, but eventually averted his eyes and slipped the sap back into his vest pocket. When he spoke again, his demeanor was more contrite. "Okay, whatever you say, Mr. Siegel. You're the lawyer and I guess I gotta to along with your decision."

Cox appeared unhappy. He'd lost the battle of wills and Siegel could see that he was filled with resentment. They weren't off to a good start, so Siegel thought he'd offer an olive branch. "Look, detective, this isn't anything personal against you. We've worked a lot of cases together and I know you always do a good job. But it never hurts to put as many resources as you can into an investigation and the office is letting me tap Rappaport, so why not? I'm sure you have other work occupying your time. Rappaport can handle the small details, so I don't always have to bother you."

"I suppose," Cox relented, an undercurrent of resentment in his body language. "I'm happy to work with him," he added, without appearing happy at all.

"Good man," Siegel said. "Let's talk tomorrow after you've had some rest."

Irina watched Cox storm out of the coffee shop and could see his agitation. She'd kept a vigil on him and Siegel while they spoke and could see that the tension between them was obvious, especially when Cox was waving that object at her husband. She noticed Siegel's subtle movements when it was happening, the squaring of his powerful shoulders beneath his suit jacket, the slight shift in his chair. For a moment, she thought the encounter was going to get violent, but Siegel managed to control his self. There was an explosive side to his personality that few people knew about because of his predominantly cool exterior. Irina was sure Dale Cox was unaware of it. The cocky detective had no idea how close he'd come to getting slugged. Luckily, Siegel was able to reign in his darker side.

Siegel strolled to the counter after Cox was gone.

"What was that about?" Irina asked.

"Nothing, just cop-DA stuff. Cox got his ego bent a bit."

"I don't like that man," Irina said with a tinge of venom in her tone.

Siegel studied his wife with curiosity. "What's with you and Dale Cox?" he asked.

"Huh? What?"

"You and Cox, you're different whenever he's around. He acts strange, too. What's with you two?"

"There is nothing between me and that man," Irina responded defensively. "Why do you say such a thing?"

"Hey, take it easy," Siegel said, raising his hands in surrender and laughing. "You're such a spitfire. I'm not implying anything."

Irina's anger melted and her red lips parted over gleaming white teeth into an easy smile. "I'm sorry," she said, touching her forehead with a light slap of her fingers. "I do not know what gets into me."

"It's that Russian temper of yours, sweetheart. But don't change, 'cause I like it."

"You're so strange, Max," Irina said, playfully slapping Siegel's shoulder. "I don't know why I love you so much."

An older woman was standing behind Siegel and he turned to her. "Can you believe this clerk? She talks to all the customers like this."

The woman grinned and Irina laughed. "Get out of here, Max," she said. "Let me serve my customers."

"Okay, see you later."

Siegel was in good humor when he left through the exit, but all that faded when he turned to look at Irina through the glass window. He stood watching her for a minute—his expression contemplative and serious—before walking away under a moody sky that was turning into evening. Dark thoughts were trying to enter his head, but he brushed them aside and moved on.

Dale Cox had just entered his tiny apartment when the cell phone on his belt buzzed. Groaning, he pulled it off his belt, but changed his demeanor when the display screen showed that Agent Ross was calling.

"How did your meeting go with the DA?" Ross inquired, dispensing with any pleasantries.

"Good, I suppose, but I'm not completely happy," Cox replied.

"Why's that?"

"He asked too many questions, punched holes in everything. He's the wrong prosecutor for the case. I don't know why Danko assigned him to it. Siegel's never been a team player."

"Do you think he could be a problem?"

"I don't know, maybe. He's bringing in another investigator, a guy named Franny Rappaport."

"You know him?"

"Yeah, we ran patrols together years ago when he was still with the department. He's the best. This could spell trouble."

"We can't let that happen," Ross said icily. "This incident must be contained at all costs. Am I clear on that?"

"Crystal."

"We're relying on you to keep the situation under control, that's why we gave you total access to the facts. Agent Frazier and I will be hanging in the background and monitoring events as they unfold. You're the point man. Don't let us down."

"I'm your man, Agent Ross. Whatever you need me to do, I'll do."

"That's what we want to hear. For now, simply watch over things and keep me abreast of any developments."

"Can do. Shouldn't we have told Danko more about what's happening? Maybe if he understood the whole scenario we could get him to yank Max Siegel off the case."

"The DA has all the information he needs. We'll fill him in as it becomes necessary, *if* it becomes necessary. No, Detective Cox, aside from us, you're the only person in Clay County who knows everything."

"Not the *only* one, Agent Ross. There's one other person lying on a hospital bed, remember?"

"Oh, I remember. That one will be dealt with in the very near future, detective. Don't give it another thought."

Chapter 5

————— • —————

THE WIND WAS BLOWING cold in the parking lot next to the airstrip at the Las Cruces Air Club. Siegel leaned against his car, hands tucked in his armpits as he braced himself against the chill breeze. He was still wearing his suit and hoped his wool jacket would keep him warm, but the cold seemed to pass right through the material.

Sunlight was fading from the sky, coloring the choppy clouds bright orange, topped with streaks of crimson, the undersides black. Siegel heard the droning whine of a single-engine plane somewhere overhead. Squinting, he managed to locate its tiny silhouette almost directly above him. Siegel estimated the plane's altitude at about twenty thousand feet, its tiny form passing in and out of patchy clouds as it traversed a perfectly straight trajectory.

Siegel scrutinized the virtual speck of a plane intensely and saw something drop from it. His heart quickened with excitement as he strained to focus on the object, watching it increase in size until it took on the distinct form of a person in freefall. The figure grew rapidly larger in a frighteningly short time, until Siegel could clearly make out the goggled features of a skydiver's face and the details of a colorful, blue and white jumpsuit.

It wasn't until the skydiver drew dangerously close to land that the parachute deployed, just as the diver's body appeared to accelerate in its plunge to earth. Dark material shot straight up from the diver's back, instantly snapping into the shape of a large, oblong canopy. The jumper tugged at control cables while drifting rapidly toward a weed infested field next to the airstrip. A final tug at the cables when the diver was barely thirty feet up slowed the descent enough to let him land heavily on his feet, his knees buckling slightly with the impact. Wind blew the ungainly canopy sideways and the jumper had to run behind it until the silken structure collapsed, crumpling in fits to the ground.

Siegel freed his hands and rubbed them together briskly for warmth, tramping toward the jumper in the field. The diver was gathering together the chute and the lines attached to it and bundling them against his chest when Siegel reached him. Franny Rappaport caught sight of his friend and smiled warmly. "What are you doing here?" he asked.

"I heard the death cheaters club was meeting today. Thought I'd come by and see what a suicide attempt looks like."

Rappaport's smile broadened as he pulled off his crash helmet and goggles, piling them on top of the bundled silk and tangled lines. The fair skin of his weathered face was slightly tanned and the hair atop his head stuck up in short, sweaty blond spikes, with shaved sides that gave the investigator a military look. He was in his mid-forties and the lined features of his face were beginning to show the ravages of age. But he had bright blue eyes that managed to maintain a boyish curiosity, which skimmed off some of the years. "You need to come out here and try this sometime," he told Siegel. "You need other distractions besides hanging around that boxing gym, pounding on heavy bags."

"I like hitting bags. It staves off aggression and keeps me from punching irksome defense attorneys and irritating bosses."

"Jumping's a better way to manage stress; there's nothing else like it."

"Manage stress?" Siegel repeated incredulously. "You consider bailing out of a perfectly functioning plane and pulling a ripcord ten seconds before plunging to your death stress management?"

"Halo dives are the best," Rappaport said wistfully. "I always like to see how close I can get to the ground before breaking the fall. Believe me you're never so alive as when you're staring death straight in the eye. The feeling afterwards is soothing, better than sex."

"That's your opinion. I'll stick to the bedroom for all my thrills, partner."

Siegel followed Rappaport across the field to a hangar where Rappaport spread out his gear and repacked it before stowing it into a large private locker. There was a small mom-and-pop diner near the edge of the airstrip and the two men retreated to it after dark to get out of the cold. The place was warm and cozy and they sat in a booth next to a window. Rappaport ordered a beer that he drank from the bottle, while Siegel opted for hot tea.

"So what's up?" Rappaport asked after taking a sip of his beverage and belching. "Why is the esteemed Max Siegel coming to the edge of Booneville on a cold October night to talk to me?"

"I need your help on a case."

"Sorry, Max, I don't do white collar stuff. I'm a homicide investigator, remember?"

"I'm not talking about insurance fraud. Danko's assigned me a double murder."

"What?" Rappaport had the bottle of beer to his mouth, but checked that and set it on the table. "Danko banished you. Why would he bring you back?"

"Don't know. That's why I want you with me. Something fishy is going on and I need someone I can trust to help me get to the bottom of it."

"What case are we talking about?"

"Hear about the Pleasant Oaks killings last night?"

"Yeah, there was some talk about it in the office this morning. The details are sketchy."

"That's the one I got."

"Why? The homicide team's not impacted. Why would Danko want to revive your career?"

"Exactly my question. The man hates me. Worse yet, he knows I'm contemplating a challenge for his job next election. The last thing he needs is me making a splash in the papers on what might be a high profile case. So the same question's floating around in my mind, why's he doing this?"

Rappaport took a long swallow of beer and set the bottle down, swiping a dribble of foam from his upper lip. "Danko never does anything without a reason, so there has to be bad intentions behind this assignment."

Siegel smiled broadly. "You see? That's why I want you on board. If he's trying to take me down, I want an ally I can trust watching my back."

"Who's the local detective?"

"Dale Cox."

"Ooo," Rappaport responded, baring his teeth and sucking in air. "You'll definitely need backup with him on the scene. Dale's a good point man for anything dirty. It's bad news if he's teaming with Danko. Sorry I can't help you though."

"What are you talking about?"

"Max, I'd love to assist, but I have three other killings to work on. My plate's full."

"Don't worry about it. I'll get you pulled off a couple."

"Yeah right, I wish you had the juice. Are you suffering from delusions of grandeur or something?"

"I'm not delusional, buddy. Sims balked when I requested you, and then did a complete reversal when I threatened not to go with the program. They'll do whatever it takes to keep me on the case."

Rappaport shook his head. "Unbelievable," he said. "This is some weird juju."

"I agree. So don't worry, I'll make a call to Sims tomorrow and get your caseload freed up. You'll piggyback Cox's investigation. He says his reports will be ready in a day or two. Before then, I figure we can do some preliminary investigating of our own. Let's look at the crime scene and have a talk with the sole percipient witness, a fella named Harris. Maybe you can case the area for any witnesses that were missed last night."

"What do we have so far?" Rappaport asked. "Other than the office gossip, the blurb in the paper this morning didn't say much, just two residents killed and the suspect in the hospital because this Harris person knocked a dent in his skull. They didn't even print the perp's name."

"That's because we're not releasing it yet. He's over in county under a John Doe for now. His name's Raheem Khan. Ever hear of him?"

"Can't say that I have; doesn't register."

"He's Pakistani, from the east side. I never heard of him either. I'll have the secretaries run a rap to see if he has a criminal history."

"Pakistani, huh? That can't be good after the Jinnah thing last year."

"Exactly what Sims and Danko think. Ostensibly, it's the reason they're dropping the case in my lap. They want me to run interference for Danko if it takes a political turn."

"I don't think so," Rappaport said with a sardonic grin, reclining in his chair. "It's more like you catching the flak if the shit hits the fan."

"Very perceptive. See why I want you?"

"Alright, I'm sold. Who can resist the intrigue? It'll be interesting to see where this leads."

"Hopefully not to my neck in a noose," Siegel said, lifting the teabag from his cup, winding the string around it, and pinching out the remaining moisture. He dropped the spent bag on the table and took a tentative sip of the hot brew.

"Don't worry about a thing," Rappaport reassured. "You're a survivor, always have been. I'm sure you'll avoid whatever trap Danko's devising for you, especially now that I'm involved. We're invincible, the dynamic duo. That bloated football player won't stand a chance against the two of us."

"I hope you're right, Franny."

Siegel took a sip of tea while Rappaport swigged his beer and the two lapsed into a comfortable silence. Outside, the darkness increased and specks of rain began to fleck the window. Siegel stared vacantly into the emptiness beyond the diner as a multitude of thoughts traversed his mind.

When Rappaport finished the last of his beer, Siegel escorted him to the parking lot. He noticed Rappaport's limp as they walked. The hard landing and moist weather had made it more pronounced than usual. Most of the time Siegel could barely tell Rappaport had it. The majority of those who associated with the investigator—who weren't old school—weren't aware of his slight handicap. Rappaport concealed it well.

Rappaport had enlisted in the army in his early twenties. He travelled the world and was an enthusiastic recruit, applying for Special Forces when it came time to re-up. Accepted into the elite fighting cadre, he underwent intense, excruciating training, graduating near the top of his class. When Iraq invaded Kuwait in the early nineties, Rappaport's group was among the first deployed behind enemy lines prior to the large scale counter-invasion by the United States. He served with valor and distinction, receiving numerous decorations when the brief conflict came to a close, then went into the reserves when his second enlistment ran out. Like most young soldiers at the time, he wrongly surmised there'd be no more wars in the near future and decided to give civilian life a try.

Rappaport joined the police department in Las Cruces when he got back to the world and reveled in the quasi-military structure of his new occupation. He excelled, in fact, moving through the ranks quickly and establishing a reputation for dedication and integrity. But a part of him always longed for adventure and the intense adrenaline rush of being in the midst of life-or-death situations. Like a junky, he was addicted to the stimulation that only armed conflict could bring. For that reason, he remained with a reserve Special Forces unit and trained on weekends and two weeks a year, constantly in a state of readiness for the next big conflict.

Rappaport was on a training mission in Panama when the accident that nearly killed him occurred. It was an insertion and survival mission where a handful of Green Beret's were required to make a low altitude jump into dense jungle in the dead of night. It was a halo dive and the commandos had to rely on specially equipped altimeters to tell them when to deploy their parachutes on what turned out to be a moonless, overcast night. Bailing out under those conditions was like falling into an inkwell, even with the infrared goggles each troop wore.

Rappaport never hesitated jumping through the open cargo door of the C-130 transport plane that flew him and his comrades over the drop zone. He fell silently through the humid air, frightened, disoriented, but carrying a soldier's faith in the technology he possessed. Unfortunately, his piece of equipment proved to be faulty, a fact he didn't realize until he was already crashing through the trees. There was no time to react and his life flashed before him as he thudded into a particularly thick branch that sent a shock of pain through his body and propelled him into a wildly haphazard spin. It lasted barely a second, but felt like a lifetime before the final impact came and the lights went out.

It took search and rescue teams a day and a half to locate Rappaport's near lifeless body embedded in a partial crater on the banks of a riverbed. The rescuers thought he was dead, and were astounded when they detected a faint pulse in Rappaport's carotid artery. Speculation was that hitting a series of branches, followed by a landing in the soft, muddy gravel of the riverbank, had broken the soldier's fall enough to allow life to remain in his shattered body.

Rappaport was airlifted to a hospital in Panama City, where his condition was stabilized before a second airlift took him to Walter Reed Hospital in the United States. He made a miraculous recovery and was on his feet in little over a month. A series of operations and rehabilitative therapy followed, lasting approximately a year before Rappaport could return to his civilian duties with only a slight limp discernable from his extensive injuries.

Not long afterwards, Rappaport received a medical discharge from the reserves and desk duty in the Las Cruces Police Department. It was a double whammy from which Siegel thought his friend never fully recovered psychologically. Not able to cope with the downgrading of his once glorious career as a street detective, Rappaport opted for a transfer to the District Attorney's office as an investigator. The slightly elevated prestige of the position somehow seemed to make the bitter pill of a diminished street career easier for the former soldier to swallow. The high risk jumps from airplanes at the Las Cruces Air Club began during the second invasion of Iraq by U.S. forces. Siegel wondered if the activity stemmed from a feeling of being left behind, or was some kind of prolonged suicide attempt.

"Who are the victims?" Rappaport asked when he reached his pickup truck. "The paper didn't say."

"I don't know. Cox should have that information in his reports."

"I'll get with him tomorrow and see if he's finished writing them. Meantime, I'll head to the crime scene first thing in the morning and check it out."

"I'll join you. I'd like to get a look at it, too. Let's rendezvous there at nine."

"Alright. I take it the papers listed the right address?"

"I haven't read them yet, but I imagine so. In any event, it'll be the nice house in Pleasant Oaks with lots of yellow police tape around it." Siegel grinned and Rappaport chuckled as he got into the driver's seat of the pickup. "And, Franny, thanks for joining the case. I have a feeling I'll need you on this one."

Rappaport pulled the door shut and slid the driver's window open. "Sure thing, buddy," he replied. Even in the darkness, he could see a shadow passing over Siegel's expression. "You know you can always count on me."

CHAPTER 6

———◆———

THE SUN ROSE GLORIOUS in a cloudless blue sky the following day, a stark contrast to the previous day's stormy demeanor. It had rained hard throughout the night and the lawns and pavement outside the murder scene home were still wet when Siegel pulled his car to a halt behind Rappaport's pickup. Rappaport was casually leaning against the truck sipping hot coffee from a Styrofoam cup when Siegel joined him.

"How long you been here?" Siegel asked.

"Not long, about ten minutes or so. Just getting the lay of the place."

"Nice area, isn't it? Doesn't seem like the kind of neighborhood a Pakistani kid from the east side would wander into to commit a residential burglary. He'd stick out like a sore thumb in these parts."

"True," Rappaport said, dumping the remainder of his coffee on the sidewalk and tossing the cup into the bed of the pickup. "But everybody blends in late at night. And if you're going to steal, the money's in the nice areas, not the slums."

"Maybe you're right. I'm running a rap on this Khan kid today so we can get a handle on his background, if there is any."

"Shall we proceed?"

Siegel and Rappaport approached the home and ducked under a yellow piece of police tape stretched haphazardly across the stoop before the front door. It was a nondescript residence, a two-story structure of faux Italian design with stucco walls painted beige with white trim, resembling every other home on the cul-de-sac. Siegel checked the door handle and found that it was unlocked, so he pushed the door open and went inside.

The living room was sparsely furnished with cheap furniture and a noticeable lack of the little touches that made a home appear lived in. Siegel and Rappaport spread out, the investigator drifting down a short corridor leading to the kitchen, while Siegel remained in the living room, picking at magazines and newspapers scattered about the room. Checking the dates on old copies of the *Las Cruces Times*, Siegel noted that they dated back no more than two weeks previous.

"This has to be a bachelor's pad," Rappaport said, reemerging into the room. "The cupboards are nothing more than cans and frozen foods and packages of instant everything. They even had a box of instant potatoes. I didn't know people ate that stuff anymore. Whoever lived here wasn't fond of cooking."

"Decorating either," Siegel observed, slowly surveying the room. "Look at these walls, everything's whitewashed. Furniture's nothing spectacular, bunch of magazines and newsprint cluttering up the place, no kind of housekeeping going on."

"Reminds me of my hovel," Rappaport said. "Nothing but a place to pull off your shoes and flop your head when you need some sleep."

The men moved toward the staircase, studying the chalky outline of the body found on the landing. Dark bloodstains were soaked into the hardwood of the stairs and the markings extended three steps above the landing. Rappaport squatted and studied the markings, stroking his chin as he did so. "They've got the head of the corpse at the foot of the landing. So the victim was climbing the stairs when he died. Maybe he was in the back of the house when he heard something that drew him to the stairs. The killer's coming down and plugs him."

"That's what Cox theorized. What's the matter?"

"Khan comes in while people are about? He has to hear whoever's in the kitchen. Why go upstairs and leave someone in your rear? The resident's bound to hear something upstairs and either come running or call the police. You'd want to take care of the ground floor guy first."

"I was bothered about that, too," Siegel said. "But you know how it goes, criminals always do dumb things. That's how we catch them. The smart ones get away."

"Yeah, you could be right, but this scenario's a no-brainer."

There was the sound of movement above, the creak of loose floorboards compressing. Siegel and Rappaport exchanged wide-eyed looks as the investigator reached into the flap of his jacket and pulled out his service weapon, a Sig Sauer nine millimeter automatic. Rappaport pursed his lips and raised his index finger in a shushing gesture. Siegel nodded and followed Rappaport when he began a stealthy climb up the staircase.

With Rappaport in the lead, the two men carefully ascended the steps. More sounds carried down to them, and Siegel's heart thumped hard in his chest. He agonized over every squeak their footfalls produced. As they gained the second floor landing, Siegel saw a flickering shadow through an open doorway to the right. The intruder was in the bedroom that sat over the garage, the place where the first murder occurred.

Rappaport signaled for Siegel to stay put, and then clutched his weapon with two hands and pointed it toward the open doorway. He was ready to move into the room when Dale Cox loomed into view. He was rolling up a plastic bag and sucked in a terrified breath when he saw the gun barrel pointing at him, his eyes as big as saucers. "Jesus!" he exclaimed, retreating a step. Then he let out a sigh when he realized who was there and stepped back onto the threshold of the doorway. "You two scared the shit outta me. I didn't hear you come in."

"Sorry about that," Rappaport said, lowering his weapon. "I was outside for a bit and didn't notice your presence either."

"What're you doing here?" Siegel asked.

"Investigating," Cox replied with some irritation. "Better question is what are you guys doing in my crime scene?"

"You mean *our* crime scene?" Siegel corrected. "We're investigating, same as you."

"Yeah ... right," Cox said, somewhat chastened.

"What you got there, Dale?" Rappaport inquired, holstering his gun. He was referring to the bundled plastic bag Cox clutched in his arms.

"This? Aw, nothing, just some trash left by the lab techs. They dropped a real mess in there."

"So you're house cleaning?" Rappaport asked with a good-natured grin.

"I suppose I am. I brought this from home to bag any evidence that might have been overlooked, but all I found was a bunch of crap. Thought I'd get rid of it."

"It always helps to give a location a second going over, doesn't it?" Rappaport offered. "It seems no matter how thorough people are, something always gets missed."

"That's my feeling."

"So you find anything?" Siegel asked.

Cox locked onto Siegel with momentary disdain. "No, I didn't," he said defensively. "It's like I said, just a bunch of crap."

An awkward, tension-filled silence ensued as Rappaport and Siegel faced off with the detective. Cox was being territorial and it was obvious he didn't appreciate the intrusion into his investigation, but that was too bad, Siegel thought. As the assigned DA, it all belonged to Siegel now. He'd steer any further progress toward proving Khan's guilt. Cox was going to have to get used to his subordinate role, like it or not.

Rappaport looked from Siegel to Cox and could clearly see the animosity between them. He decided to intervene and soothe the situation. "Hey, Dale," he said, "mind if I get a look in that room? I'll wait if you need more time."

"Sure, go ahead. I'm done." Cox stepped aside. "I gotta go downstairs and dump this stuff anyway." Cox knew Rappaport was trying to play him, so he thought he'd go along with the charade for now, especially if it convinced these two clowns that they were getting the upper hand.

Cox bumped Siegel's shoulder when he made for the stairs. Siegel and Rappaport exchanged amused grins as Cox clumped heavily down the steps. Then they moved into the bedroom.

There wasn't much to see aside from dried blood and food particles that had been trampled into the hardwood floor by a multitude of feet. Furnishings consisted of a double bed and a small dresser with a walk-in closet nearby. It was a simple room, all in all. A food tray with dishes sat on top of the dresser, all stained with dark powder used to lift fingerprints. The butter knife had been removed and bagged for evidence, Siegel surmised.

The single window in the room was wide and occupied the center of the wall next to the bed, which protruded into the middle of the floor. Siegel was drawn to the window, while Rappaport went to the dresser on the opposite side of the bed and began opening and closing drawers. Siegel's shoes crunched on tiny pieces of broken glass as he carefully moved the mangled blinds and peeked at the street. Cox was staring up at him from the driveway below, the detective's expression perturbed. Cox shook his head with apparent disgust before turning toward the street and stomping off, angrily crumpling the plastic bag in his hands.

"That man's due for a psych eval," Siegel remarked. He turned and caught sight of Rappaport dangling a pair of boxer shorts in his hand over an open dresser drawer, studying the garment with great interest. "Maybe you're due for one, too," Siegel quipped. "What's with the fixation on men's undershorts?"

Rappaport glanced at Siegel and didn't respond. Dropping the shorts back into the drawer, he sifted through the remainder of the contents. When he finished, he slammed the drawer shut and proceeded to the closet and sorted through the garments hanging there. Siegel stepped behind him and watched Rappaport pushing through clothes on the rack.

"What's so interesting, Franny?"

"Look at these shirts; they still have creases."

"Yes they do. What's your point?"

"They look brand new. Same with the clothes in the drawer; they're pristine. Who's living here? Men aren't this tidy. This place appears to be every bit the bachelor pad, and yet the clothes are so clean they seem unused."

A thought clicked in Siegel's mind. "Cox was just up here with a shopping bag. You don't suppose..."

"Why would he stage the scene?" Rappaport asked, catching the drift. "That makes no sense."

"Maybe we should ask him," Siegel suggested. He frowned when he heard the sound of a car engine starting. Siegel went to the window in time to see Cox pulling away from the curb in an unmarked car. "What the hell's going on?"

"I don't know, but it's something funny."

Siegel turned away from the window. "Let's go through the rest of the place and see if we can find some indicia of who the victims are. We'll check the garage, too. We can take down the VIN and plates on the car that's parked there and run them through DMV. I need to know who these guys are."

Siegel and Rappaport separated and meticulously searched the remainder of the home, coming up with nothing but the bare essentials of what someone needed to occupy a residence. Even the medicine cabinets in both bathrooms, up and down, seemed barren, sporting tooth brushes, toothpaste, a can of shaving cream, and a few disposable razors. The downstairs bathroom had some empty prescription pill bottles in the trash, but the labels were removed, rendering them useless. It was also odd that the razors and shaving cream were located in the downstairs bathroom, as opposed to the master bathroom upstairs where one would expect them to be.

The two men reconvened in the attached garage, which housed a fairly old Ford Taurus sedan and a lawnmower. While Rappaport jotted down the VIN and license plate number of the car, Siegel scanned the surrounding area. The walls were unpainted, streaked with criss-crossed etchings of spackle where the cracks had been filled in. "This is one of the most unoccupied occupied residences I've ever seen," Siegel remarked. "If I didn't know better, I'd swear somebody just moved in. Broke college students live better."

"I'll run these numbers when I get to the office," Rappaport said. "That should give us something to go on. I'll also drop by the PD later and retrieve Cox's reports; see what he has to say about everything."

"I'll tag along."

"No, you got his feathers ruffled for some reason. It's better if I go alone. Maybe I can get Dale to open up about his insights into some of the strangeness that's going on."

"You're right. I should go to the courthouse and check out where they're posting me. I need to stop playing cop anyway and get a grip on what's happening in the office."

"Don't worry, we'll fill in the blanks soon enough. Cox is no brain trust. Whatever he's up to will come spilling out in no time. He's never been good at keeping things under his hat."

"I hope you're right," Siegel said, walking to the garage door and grasping the handle at the bottom. "I'd say we're done here." He pulled the door up and it made a racket as the rollers slid in the metal tracks. "Whadaya say?" he asked Rappaport as sunlight flooded the room.

"I'd say we're not quite ready to leave yet." Rappaport replied.

"Why's that?"

Rappaport looked over Siegel's shoulder and raised his chin. Siegel turned and saw a large, older man walking a Fox Terrier along the sidewalk.

CHAPTER 7

———◆———

THE COUNTY HOSPITAL WAS located on the outskirts of Las Cruces. It was a collection of pillbox shaped facilities sitting on a few acres of flat, sunbaked land. The buildings weren't pretty, adobe-like in appearance, nondescript, blending in with the endless, dusty expanse of brown grass and dust bordering the paved parking lots that surrounded the medical center.

Cox had driven to the hospital after leaving Siegel and Rappaport because he wanted to check the status of the suspect. Raheem Khan was being held in a special lockdown section of the facility where inmates were taken when they needed medical care. Presently, he was the only patient in the ward, occupying a bed in a barracks style room on the opposite side of a glass walled nurses station. He remained in a coma and Cox was anxious to learn when the doctors thought he might recover. Cox hoped never, but—given the prognosis—he knew he was wishing for too much.

While traversing the enormous parking lot toward the entrance, Cox spied a couple of men in suits between a row of cars speaking to a Mexican woman wearing scrubs. The men appeared familiar and it piqued Cox's attention, so he veered in their direction. When he got close enough, he recognized his new friends from the FBI, Ross and Frazier. Cox was overjoyed. He continued in their direction, but checked his advance when he realized the woman was sobbing. She constantly dabbed at her eyes with a tissue while Ross and Frazier looked on coldly through their dark sunglasses. Instinct told Cox that he should lay back and he ducked behind the cab of a pickup truck to conceal himself.

The Mexican nurse, if that's what she was, appeared extremely upset. Cox couldn't hear the conversation, but he saw her hunched shoulders quivering as she sniffled into the tissue. Ross did all the talking, his thin lips barely moving as he spoke. His silent partner, Frazier, stood close by, a looming presence. Ross's features were placid, supremely bland, a diametric contrast to the affect his words were having on the nurse. Whatever she was hearing, the news wasn't good.

The Mexican was cute, at least from a distance. Something about her apparent vulnerability stirred Cox in a way that aroused him. But the stimulation was more predatory than empathetic. There was something deliciously amusing about the reaction Ross's banal words were evoking in the woman. Ross was exercising control and Cox was a big fan of control.

When the FBI agent's lips stopped moving, the nurse's head lowered and nodded rigorously while in that position. Ross's mouth cracked into the semblance of a grin, but it lacked mirth, seemed mechanical. He pressed a hand against the woman's upper arm, but she shrugged it off. The agents exchanged looks as the nurse rushed toward Cox's position, getting into an old Honda Civic a few rows from his location and driving off in a hurry. She was weeping as she guided the car out of the lot.

The agents peered in Cox's direction and he stepped from his hiding place and waved to them, conjuring the most beguiling smile he could muster. Ross and Frazier gave no indication they recognized Cox as he approached, their expressions remaining blank behind their dark glasses. "Gentlemen," Cox greeted when he was close enough.

"Detective Cox," Ross said without emotion, "what brings you here?"

"I'm guessing the same as you. I came to see how our boy Khan is faring."

"We've already been inside," Ross said. "He's still unconscious."

"I suppose that's a good thing for now, isn't it?" Cox ventured. "Keeps anybody from having to act."

"It won't last forever, detective. That's why it's important you do your part and help us contain the matter."

"I'm on it, don't worry. Tell your bosses back in Washington that the bureau has my support 100 percent."

"Good," Ross said, trying on a plastic smile. "Our superiors will be glad to hear that."

"So, ah, you recrutin' some hospital personnel to keep tabs on the patient?" Cox asked slyly. "I saw you talkin' to that Mexican senorita and I'd be happy to act as a liaison with her if you want."

Frazier's blond brows rose slightly above the rims of his sunglasses.

"No, that's quite alright," Ross said. "There's nothing going on between us and any member of the hospital staff. Whatever you think you saw, you should forget."

"Right," Cox responded, grinning and winking. "I never saw a thing."

"You're a good man, Detective Cox," Ross said after a pause. "I think we made the right choice coming to you with our problem."

Cox straightened and threw out his chest. "Like I said, I'm with you all the way. And, just to let you know, I just left the crime scene. I took care of those little details we discussed before."

"Perfect."

"But there's one thing."

"What's that?"

"The DA assigned to the case, Max Siegel, I caught him and an investigator snooping around the place."

"Don't worry about that," Ross said, "everything's covered. Go ahead and release your reports if you like. He won't learn anything. Right now our only focus should be on Raheem Khan. He might cause complications when he wakes up. We'll need you to stay close and keep matters under control until we can take him off your hands."

"Consider it done. The investigator with Siegel is an old buddy of mine. I'll use him to keep tabs on whatever the DA's up to."

"Excellent," Ross beamed. He felt his cell phone buzzing, probably his section chief from headquarters. Ross had to take the call, but not in front of Cox. "Frazier," he said, a crack showing in his cool façade, "why don't you take the detective for a cup of coffee? I'll join you after I talk to headquarters."

Frazier's brows rose again. "Sure," he replied in a voice that was surprisingly deep. "We'll see you inside."

Ross pulled the phone from his belt and walked away from Frazier and Cox as they strolled toward the hospital entrance. He flipped open the phone when he felt he was at a safe distance. "Yes, chief?"

"I'm calling for a progress report."

"Subject is still unconscious, but all indications are that his status will change soon."

"That's very disconcerting."

"I agree, sir."

"I just emerged from a meeting with all the Washington brass, Ross, department heads from all the relevant bureaus *and* the chief of staff. People are worried. The anxiety level is high in the administration, although POTUS doesn't want to be directly involved. You have a tremendous responsibility sitting on your shoulders. This assignment can make or break you."

"I'm firmly aware of that, sir. Everything's been done to control the damage, but a lot of variables are floating around. It's going to require a fluid situational response."

"We understand that; it was all explained to the chief of staff. I expressed a lot of confidence in your ability to handle the fallout. You were handpicked by me, so don't screw it up. My reputation's on the line alongside yours. If you go down, you'll pull me with you."

"I'm determined not to disappoint you sir, but I'll need to exercise a wide range of discretion if I'm going to avert disaster. Do I have your blessing to improvise as I see fit?"

"Absolutely, the director has ordered the Sacramento office to give you full support. Their resources will be available to you without question for the duration of this crisis. We don't want any gory details. In fact, the less you tell us, the better. If the worst case scenario comes about, deniability will be paramount. Nothing can go past my level. And, Ross, I'd prefer it not reach me either."

"I'll do my best, sir. I have the lead detective onboard. He's my new lap dog. I've curried his loyalties through certain vague promises."

"Whatever they are, keep them exceptionally vague. What about the prosecutor assigned to the case? Will he play?"

"His boss will. The name's Richard Danko. Justice has his file. Danko's been the subject of a public corruption probe for about a year, so he's in our pocket. I gave him a partial sketch of the problem and he appears amenable to helping, though I'm sure he'll expect a favor in return."

"I'll have to read his file. Clear any deals you want to make through me first."

"Yes sir. The actual deputy assigned to handle the prosecution is Max Siegel. I don't know much about him except what I read in Danko's file. Siegel testified to the grand jury relating to our probe a few months ago. The attorneys apparently can't stand each other and might soon be political rivals. I think Danko handed Siegel the case because he smells a rat and wants to leave himself an escape hatch."

"Hmmm, Danko sounds like he should be here in D.C. What exactly do we know about Siegel at this time?"

"Nothing much. He's a standup attorney, no smudges on his past, at least that I'm aware of."

"Well, let's not guess. Detach some of our agents from Sacramento and have them ram a probe up his ass. We may need leverage later if he doesn't cooperate. He has to have something in his closet, everybody does."

"I'll get right on it."

"See that you do. We're holding a bomb here, Ross, and we don't need it blowing up the administration, especially with an election coming around next year. I shouldn't have to point out the dire consequences our national security will suffer if we screw this op."

"Not at all, sir, that's why I've been all over this from the start. I'll do whatever it takes to minimize the damage. I appreciate the stakes involved."

"Fine. I'll let you do your work then, but keep me posted about any substantial developments."

"I will, sir."

The chief hung up and Ross flipped his phone shut, reattaching it to his belt. Running a hand through his slicked-back hair, he took off his sunglasses and closed his eyes, tilting his head back. The sunlight felt warm despite the cool chill in the air. Ross took a deep breath, expelling it through his mouth. Then he opened his eyes and lowered his head, twisting his chin from side to side to work out the kinks in his neck. Using both hands to deliberately replace his sunglasses, he dropped his arms slowly and scanned the parking lot.

This was it—a major career opportunity that could advance him at least two ranks if he succeeded. Ross wondered if the chief understood the ramifications of what he and Frazier might have to do to successfully conclude matters. The chief was giving him wide latitude to approach the situation as he saw fit, but did his superior grasp what that meant? Ross intended to be ruthless in his quest. Everybody would be expendable, everybody but himself.

CHAPTER 8

———◆———

BERNARD HARRIS HAD AN old fashioned percolator. Siegel and Rappaport sat in his tidy kitchen, watching steam spurt from the pot's spout in orgasmic puffs, the rich aroma of Columbian roast filling the air. Harris busied himself pulling coffee mugs from the cabinets and searching for a bottle of Bailey's Irish cream to add to the brew when it was ready. His Fox Terrier, Scout, flitted nervously between the feet of the two strangers.

Harris was a large man. Siegel estimated his height at six feet four inches, maybe 250 pounds. He was solidly built, with a large head, weather-beaten features, and grayish-white patches of bristles where his hair should be. His skin was heavily lined, the rear of his neck crisscrossed with deeply etched fissures and colored a permanent ruddy red from years of sun exposure. He wore a short-sleeved, cotton shirt, exposing massive arms dotted with brown sunspots. Surprisingly, Harris's movements were somewhat dainty as he navigated the room, a sharp and perplexing contrast to his otherwise burly appearance.

The percolator announced its business was finished with a long sigh, expelling a final column of steam from its spout before going dormant. Harris had the mugs ready and filled them halfway with coffee, following with generous portions of Bailey's until the cups were full nearly to the brim. He stirred each cup rigorously with a teaspoon before setting them on the small table where his guests sat.

"Nothing like a good cup of Bailey's and coffee on a brisk morning to get ya going," Harris happily announced, taking a seat at the table. Scout immediately went to him and stood with his forepaws pressed against Harris's calf. The dog wagged his tail excitedly when Harris reached down and scratched him between his ears.

"It's nice of you to let us in your home, Mr. Harris," Siegel said, lifting his mug hesitantly and toasting Rappaport before trying a sip. "Hoo, that's good!" he said after the fluid scalded his mouth and plunged like a burning freight train down his throat, exploding in his stomach.

"You like it?" Harris asked gleefully.

"Oh yes … yes, I do," Siegel said, setting the cup down and sucking air.

Rappaport chuckled.

"Thirty-five years pulling long hauls and this is how I always got my engine going," Harris remarked with a wink, slurping his concoction.

"I like your place," Rappaport offered.

"Yes, it's a jewel, ain't it?" Harris responded proudly. "Me and the wife traded the old homestead and upgraded to this one about three years ago after the last of the kids left the nest. It's smaller and in a nicer subdivision. We thought it would make a good retirement spot."

"Where's your wife?" Siegel asked.

"In Nebraska visiting her sister; been there a week now. I woulda gone with her, 'cept I don't like the cold weather they got this time of year. No, I'm not trading good ole California sunshine for nothing. Besides, it's better she wasn't here to see that incident the other night. It woulda freaked her out."

"You haven't told her yet?" Rappaport asked.

"No, I'll wait a while before I break the news. The whole reason for us choosing this area was to get away from the crime. What's she gonna say when I tell her two of our neighbors got murdered no more than two doors down?"

Siegel perked up. "That was some terrible business, wasn't it?"

"I'll say," Harris replied. "I still don't believe it happened. I'm definitely not telling the wife about my involvement in capturing that maniac. It'll put her in the ground for sure. She won't let me and Scout out the door again."

"Must've been frightening," Siegel offered. "Did you know your neighbors well?"

"What, the men that got killed?"

"Yes."

"Hell, I didn't know them at all. I wasn't sure anybody was even livin' in that house till the night the killings happened."

Siegel exchanged looks with Rappaport, who leaned forward and rested his elbows on the table. "How's that?" Rappaport asked.

"How's what?"

"How is it you weren't certain whether the home was occupied?"

"I dunno, I never seen the neighbors around much. Couldn't tell you what anybody looks like that ever ran in and out of there."

"What do you mean?" Siegel inquired.

"Sighting them neighbors was a rare occasion. There weren't no wife and kids, I can tell you that much. No kids in the street, no wife pullin' shopping bags outta the car. The only time I did see anybody was usually at night. A businessman in a suit, that's all I ever spotted. Never had a chance to chat 'im up neither."

"How long has it been like that?" Siegel asked.

"Since I been living here. This is a cozy little cul-de-sac, Mr. Siegel. Nobody comes down the street that don't live here or have some kinda business. I spoke to all the other homeowners around here except for whoever lives in that house where the men were killed."

"What about yard work?" Rappaport asked. "The place has great landscaping. Ever spy the neighbors working in the yard?"

"Mexicans," Harris replied, lifting his mug and taking a number of swallows. "A crew arrived like clockwork every Saturday and took care of the cutting and raking and pruning. I think they used a lawnmower from the garage. I saw them going in and outta there sometimes. But if the owners were home, they never poked their noses outside."

Rappaport removed a notebook and pen from inside the vest of his jacket. Opening the notebook, he began scribbling on a blank page. "Ever get the name of the landscaping company off the work truck?"

"No, sorry, never paid that much attention. I figure everyone has the right to their privacy and I try not to stick my nose where it don't belong."

"Sounds like you should live next to me," Siegel quipped. "My neighbors are so into my business that I'd swear they lived in the other room."

Harris cracked a wide, yellow-toothed grin and released a raspy laugh, his bloodshot eyes crinkling into slits. Siegel waited until Harris was done, and then leaned toward the trucker and fixed him with an intense gaze. "Mr. Harris, what about that night?" he asked. "Can you describe in detail what you saw and heard when your neighbors were murdered?"

The lightheartedness drained from Harris and his expression sobered. "It was a strange evening, Mr. Siegel. I remember feeling it the minute I stepped out the door to take Scout for his walk. It's hard to describe, sir, but the air had a chill in it that went right through me. I'm not a superstitious man by nature, but I swear somethin' evil was afloat the night I passed that house. That feeling was kickin' around in me for days."

"Was it something you saw or heard?" Siegel pressed.

"No, can't say it was nothing particular; just a strange sensation, you know? Like an instinct, but I never saw anything. That home was always dormant. The lights came on at night, but the shades was drawn tight and you never saw no signs of life inside."

"What's the first thing you heard when you realized something was wrong?" Siegel asked.

"It was those damned bloodcurdling screams," Harris replied, his expression becoming dreamy as he relived the memory. "They sent a chill through me, the most god-awful sounds of agony from the upstairs. Then that body comes flyin' through the glass and lands headfirst on the pavement. I almost crapped my pants right there."

"Did anybody come to the window?" Siegel inquired, enraptured by the narration.

"No, nobody come to the window. All I heard after that was all this noise, like somebody getting outta that room in a hurry. Then I heard gunshots. I guess that was when the other feller was killed on the stairs. I froze stiff with fear at that point. I hate to admit it, but I was scared. My knees got weak, and I couldn't budge from the spot where I stood. Little Scout here was flustered himself, running away like a puppy." Harris reached down and scratched the attention-starved dog behind the ears.

"All that's very understandable," Rappaport soothed. "Hell, I'd be scared, too. You don't expect that kind of drama when you're taking your dog for a midnight stroll in a nice subdivision."

"Exactly!" Harris said. "One minute I'm looking at the twinklin' stars poking through the overcast, next I'm watchin' dead bodies flying through the air and seeing some berserk maniac chargin' at me."

"How did that come about?" Siegel quickly inquired, suppressing the excitement welling in him. "Give us the details of your encounter with the killer."

"Well, let's see…. I heard him comin' through the house, and he thudded against the door when he got to it, like maybe he was trying to run right through it. Then I hear fumbling at the locks for what seemed like the longest time. I'm sure it wasn't really that long, but when it happened it felt like an eternity."

"What do you mean, fumbling at the locks?" Siegel asked, grasping Harris's forearm that was resting on the table.

Harris looked at the hand uncomfortably, but Siegel didn't appear to notice that he had the trucker in a death grip. Rappaport smirked. "I mean the killer had a hard time gettin' out the door because it was locked tight," Harris said.

Siegel looked over at Rappaport, who was still smirking. Rappaport surreptitiously dropped his gaze to the hand clutching Harris's arm, and

Siegel felt embarrassed when he realized what he was doing. He released his grip on Harris while Rappaport rolled his eyes and tried not to laugh.

"That point you make about the front door is very interesting," Siegel said.

"How so?" Harris asked.

"It has to do with a theory we're developing," Siegel replied. "Nothing you need to worry about. Tell me what happened next."

Harris drank thirstily from his mug, draining it and setting the cup on the table with a satisfied "Aaah!" He wiped his mouth with the back of his hand and continued the narration. "Needless to say, the killer finally got the door open. And, brother, I'll never forget the sight of him standin' there looking like a crazy man, eyes all ablaze, his color darker than the night. I seen he had a gun in his hand and I knew I was in for it."

"Did he point it at you?" Rappaport asked.

"Not really, now that I think about it. He kinda held it down towards the floor. I don't think he was expectin' to see nobody when he came out. But he focused those dark eyes on me immediately. They honed in on me like laser beams. That's when I reached for my sap."

"The weapon you always carry?" Rappaport prompted.

"Yeah." Harris suddenly appeared nervous. "I carry it for protection since my trucker days. A sap's a good little item to have when trouble's brewin'. I suppose I never got outta the habit of having it on me, like another appendage." Harris paused, peering apprehensively at his guests. "That Detective Cox took the sap away for evidence. He said it was illegal. You don't suppose I'm gonna get in hot water for it, do you?"

Siegel smiled reassuringly. "Don't worry, Mr. Harris. I'm the DA on the case and I don't plan to press charges. It's a minor infraction compared to the murders."

"Whew!" Harris said. "What a relief. Can I get it back when the case is over?"

"No, sir," Siegel replied. "It's still against the law. We'll keep it."

"Too bad," Harris said dejectedly, appearing crestfallen.

"Please continue with your story, Mr. Harris," Rappaport urged. "We need to wrap this up."

"Sure thing, Mr. Rappaport. I don't know what more I can say, 'cept that the dark-skinned man ran straight at me, jibber-jabberin' away, smelling like a pile of used socks. I was so damned scared that all I could do was wail away at his head with my sap. I kept hitting him till he was down for the count."

"Do you remember anything he said before you knocked him unconscious?" Siegel asked.

"Not a thing. I was so panicked at the time I couldn't tell you if he was speaking English or some other language."

"That's a harrowing tale if ever I heard one," Siegel said. "Is there anything else of note about what happened? Anything you think we need to know?"

Harris lifted Scout into his lap and thought for a bit. "Not that comes to mind, other than this is the strangest experience I've had in my life."

"Murder usually is," Siegel said.

"What do you think?" Rappaport asked when he and Siegel emerged onto the sidewalk outside the Harris home.

"We need to go back to the crime scene and search for signs of forced entry. If you're right, the second victim was in the rear of the home when the first victim got killed. That would suggest our perp walked through the front door. Only now Harris tells us that Khan was struggling to undo the locks before he ran outside. What did he do when he came in, lock the door behind him?"

"Very unlikely."

"Extremely so…. No, I'm beginning to think that Khan was in the house all along, but why? Who are the victims? And who is Raheem Khan? Why's he hanging around with a couple white guys on the wrong side of town? This straightforward case has an awful lot of complications coming to the surface."

"Did Danko throw you a curveball?"

"Buddy, that's the only pitch he knows. He's got another thing coming if he thinks he'll get over on me. I'm making it my mission to get to the bottom of this riddle. Danko forgets, I may be a lot of things, but stupid isn't one of them."

CHAPTER 9

A FTER PARTING WAYS, SIEGEL met his wife for lunch, while Rappaport retreated to his office and got on the computer. They agreed to meet again at the county hospital after hours to check on the prisoner. Meanwhile, Siegel spent the remainder of the workday transferring old cases and relocating to the courthouse.

Returning to headquarters was depressing. Although Siegel hadn't enjoyed being relegated to the backwaters of Insurance Fraud, the physical separation from the main office was nice. Headquarters was a political snake pit, full of tension, intrigue, and backbiting. Siegel had relished being away from all that, sitting in the confines of the branch office seven blocks away, planning his run at the top job like a jungle insurgent. Siegel wanted Rich Danko's job and the boss knew it. Danko probably had other reasons for wanting Siegel back at headquarters, most likely to watch his maneuvers. Siegel was going to need to be vigilant during the Khan case. In some instinctual way, he was certain Danko meant for it to be his downfall.

Bernie Sims, Danko's parrot, fluttered into Siegel's new office two or three times throughout the day, ostensibly checking on Siegel's progress. His manner was relaxed and friendly on the surface. He'd casually saunter into the room bearing an easy smile, hands in his pockets, lightly bantering while trolling for information. He was transparent as glass, his eyes always giving him away. They were bright and cunning, intent, scrutinizing Siegel through the lenses of his wire-rimmed glasses. No matter how hard Sims tried, he couldn't mask the hostility he harbored, and his false attempts at civility left Siegel cold.

Getting away from the main office was a relief, Siegel thought, as he drove to the county hospital in the twilight of day's end. Danko had passed him twice in the halls back at the courthouse without so much as a flicker of acknowledgement. Combined with Sims's slithering visitations, Siegel had more than his fill of the schizophrenic atmosphere of the office for one day. It felt good to escape.

The cafeteria at the hospital was subdued and antiseptic, deserted during the early evening hours. Lighting was dim, giving the spacious, rectangular room a certain grim feel. Acoustics muffled the muted conversations of leftover visitors and a scattering of exhausted workers waiting to finish their shifts.

Siegel bought an orange juice and wandered over to an isolated table next to a plate glass window that overlooked a cement patio. He peeled the lid off the plastic container and casually watched the attractive Hispanic female in scrubs nervously pacing the length of the patio while she puffed away at a cigarette. Her face was beautiful, dark eyes, perfectly plucked brows, and a full, sensuous mouth that puckered intriguingly around the butt of her cigarette. Her body was curvaceous beneath the smock she wore, her full, round breasts straining against the material of the garment. She appeared to be having a bad day, and Siegel wondered what was going through her mind. Then Rappaport materialized at his side.

"What would Irina say if she saw you checking out that Mexican babe?" Rappaport asked.

"You here to meet me, or to start World War Three?" Siegel asked, feeling his face flush with slight embarrassment at being caught admiring another woman. He thought Rappaport looked tired.

"I suppose I'm here to meet you," Rappaport said, sinking into a chair across from Siegel. "We'll leave Anglo-Russo relations alone for now."

"You have a few extra circles under your eyes since this morning. Been busy?"

"That I was; collecting information on the case so I could have something good to tell you when we met."

"What do you have?"

"Well, Cox's reports for one. After the way he acted at the crime scene, I thought he was going to jerk me around, but he was surprisingly compliant, almost friendly when he handed them over."

"That definitely makes for a twilight zone moment."

"I'll say."

"Anything new in the reports?"

"Just the names of the victims." Rappaport pulled a notebook from his vest pocket and flipped through it. "Here it is: Robert Zimmerman and Morton Shultz."

"Who are they?"

"Good question. The short answer is: I don't know. Zimmerman has a California driver's license, but Shultz's ID comes out of Washington State. I used that information and their socials to obtain some background, but I keep drawing blanks. It's like they don't exist."

"What do you mean?"

"I mean I've been on the computer all day and, other than their IDs, I can't pick up any traces of them. It's very unusual in this age of information. I couldn't even score a Google match."

"Strange, did you talk to Cox about it? They must've had other things on them, credit cards, business cards, phone numbers of friends or relatives...."

"I tried reaching him after poring over the reports, but he never answered his phone. I paged a few times, but still no luck."

"Maybe you can catch up to him tomorrow. What about Khan? What do we have on him?"

"Turns out he's a local kid, just like we thought. Twenty-three years old, three siblings—all girls—still living with his parents. Father's a merchant, owns an east side liquor store. Mother's a homemaker. The suspect's been attending Las Cruces Community College for the past four years. Aside from general ed courses, he appears to have a penchant for computer programming. No criminal record whatsoever, not even juvenile. An unremarkable kid, all in all, not somebody you'd picture committing residential burglaries in occupied dwellings."

"Which goes back to why he was in the home to begin with. The theory that he was an inside man when the killings happened just gained some ground."

"What do you think, Max, this some kind of homosexual situation? Maybe Khan was a pickup in a bar that went wrong?"

"It's possible, but who knows? The best way to get a handle on it is to talk to the only survivor, and that's Khan himself."

"He needs to wake up soon."

"Real soon. We'll get the staff to update us on his condition when we check him out in the custodial ward."

Siegel took a sip of his orange juice and peered through the glass at the Mexican woman. Her agitation seemed to have increased. She flicked her cigarette to the pavement and it exploded into a cascade of orange sparks. Then she pulled a cell phone from her smock and tapped out the numbers with her thumb.

"Hey, chica, how you doin'?" the Mexican woman said.

"Leticia? Is that you?"

"Yeah, who else? How you doin'?"

"Just started my shift. What you up to?"

"Nothin' much, I'm at the hospital."

"What? You don't come on till tomorrow morning. Why you wanna be here?"

The inquiry made Leticia nervous and she paused for a moment. A good looking white man in a suit was looking at her from inside the cafeteria. She met his gaze full on and he looked away. "Y-you know how it is," she stammered. "Me an' Carlos are fighting again."

"Oh, shit, is he actin' up? It's like I told you before, *hermana*, you need to borrow a scalpel and cut it off when you catch him steppin' out on you again."

"No, it's not like that. We're just fightin' over general stuff, you know? He's drivin' me crazy tonight."

"That's too bad, Leti, but I can't hang with you right now. I gotta work my shift."

"I know, *tonta*, that's why I'm here. What if I come by and check you out at the station for a while? We can shoot the breeze for a few, keep you from dyin' of boredom."

"Are you serious? You're off the clock and you wanna spend it at work? And you're calling me stupid?"

"C'mon, I don't know what to do. I'm upset and you're my best friend. Where else can I go for Carlos therapy?"

Leticia's friend laughed. "Aye, chica, come by if that makes you happy. The killer is still out anyway. I could use the company."

"Okay, I'll be there in a few. I'm gonna have another cigarette to steady my nerves, and then I'll be right over."

Leticia reached into her smock and dumped the cell phone, exchanging it for her crumpled pack of cigarettes. The pack was nearly empty. She extracted a cigarette and tapped the tip on the back of her hand before putting the filter in her mouth and pulling a lighter from her other pocket. She took a long draw when the cigarette was lit, sucking the nicotine deep into her lungs and leaning her head back before expelling a geyser of blue smoke into the air. Her eyes dropped while her head was still tilted and she caught the gringo in the cafeteria watching her again. Slowly, deliberately, she brought her chin down and turned toward the man. Leticia felt a rush of liquid warmth flooding her body, especially her lower regions, as a knowing smile parted her full lips. The man in the suit returned the smile with just a trace of a grin before he resumed talking to his friend, but his gaze had lingered long enough to tell her he was interested.

Leticia studied the man while he pretended not to pay attention to her. He was good looking, a little older, but with strong features. He was wearing a sharp suit and appeared fit beneath the material. Three years working as a nurse had taught Leticia a lot about body types and she could discern a good physique no matter how dressed up it was.

Leticia felt her cheeks flush and she turned away from the window to face the patio wall. What was she doing anyway? If Carlos caught her flirting with an older white guy he'd hit the roof. He was so jealous all the time, so insecure. But it would serve him right to see his woman taking an interest in somebody else. He spent half his time working cars at the garage and the other half hitting the bars and chugging beers with his loser friends. Maybe he needed to know he had competition in the world. The revelation might make him more attentive.

Leticia took another puff of her cigarette and found herself slowly turning around again. The gringo was engrossed in conversation with his companion, this time making no pretense of ignoring her. She wondered what was so important that he talked with such intensity. He probably had a relative, or somebody close, undergoing surgery or something. Leticia puzzled over whether he had a wife. This is so damn silly, she thought, catching herself. She needed to get her head on straight and concentrate on what she had to do.

Another long draw on the cigarette brought Leticia down to earth and her nerves kicked in again. In a way, the man in the cafeteria reminded her of the one who accosted her in the parking lot earlier. Only that man had a cold, empty look in his expression, like somebody had hollowed him out and taken his soul. He'd given her the chills, the type she used to feel when her grandfather sat her on his knee when she was a little girl and told her ghost stories late at night. It was the same feeling.

Leticia had no idea who the man and his friend were. They blindsided her when she was heading to her car, seeming to materialize out of nowhere. She would've thought she was being attacked if they hadn't been so well dressed. It stunned her when the cold one called her name. She thought maybe she knew him, but didn't recognize him when they approached. Then he started talking to her, saying her name and address and the names of her boyfriend and family members. This stranger she'd never met before spewed out the facts of her life like he was a computer in overdrive dumping data. And the whole time his lips were moving he had this nasty smirk on his mouth, this smug expression like he owned her.

Leticia was overwhelmed. She asked the men who they were, but they ignored the question. That's when the cold one suddenly rattled off her convictions and caused her breath to catch in her throat. Leticia's mouth hung open she was so stunned. How could he possibly know?

"Those *are* your convictions, aren't they?" the man asked in a smooth, flat tone. "One count of possession and one count of possession for sale, methamphetamine right? And all before the age of eighteen." The man pursed his thin lips and sucked his teeth rapidly while shaking his head. There was a large crease between his brows that Leticia could see despite the sunglasses he wore. "And after you're an adult you go and garner a conviction for embezzlement."

"How can you know that?" Leticia protested. "I went to court and had all that expunged. The judge said he was gonna wipe it off my record."

"Records never get completely clean, my dear. There's always a stain left over," the man calmly replied. "It's not a stain that just anybody can see. You have to wear special glasses to make it appear visible, magical glasses like the ones I'm wearing now. I can see everything about you."

"Why are you telling me this? Who the fuck are you?"

"Tsk, tsk, Leticia Angelina Cruz. You kiss your patients with that mouth?" The man and his silent partner grinned. "It's unfortunate you never told your employer about any of this. You never would've been hired had they known about your past."

"I didn't have to say anything. Those convictions were expunged."

"You keep harping on that point, but the question on your employment application asked if you'd been convicted, not if you'd been expunged. You can't parse the truth when you're applying for a job with the weighty responsibilities that a nurse carries. Do you truly believe the hospital wants a drug pusher and embezzler tucking patients in at night? Dispensing medication?"

"I don't believe what I'm hearing," Leticia said, her voice quivering, tears welling.

"But you should believe what you're hearing, because it's what I'm telling you."

"So what now?" Leticia asked shakily, the first of many tears streaming down her cheeks. "Am I gonna get fired? I need this job."

"Yes, you do, but did we say anything about getting you fired? Did I say that?"

"N-no."

"Stop jumping to conclusions, princess. We're not here to get you canned."

"You're confusing the hell outta me."

"I'm sorry about that. It's not my intention to confuse you, Leticia. To the contrary, we're here to have a frank discussion about important matters, matters you must clearly understand. Throwing out your past was a means of getting your attention. Do we have it?"

"Totally, but who are you, mister?"

"We're your friends, that's all you need to know, not our names, not what we do for a living, not what planet we come from—"

"Huh?"

"Shut up now. Listen to what I say. Are we friends?"

"What?"

"I asked, are we friends? If we are, then your employers don't need to know about your past. It'll be a deep, dark secret, but only if you acknowledge that we're friends. Are we?"

"Sure, anything you say."

"Good," the man said, smiling in a mechanical way that had no warmth. He reminded Leticia of a crocodile. "I'm glad we got that squared away. Let's get down to business. I want you to do me the smallest favor. Since we're friends now, I expect you won't turn me down."

"What is it?"

The man leaned close and spoke in a whispery voice, like an intimate lover, but what he said wasn't close to what a sweetheart would say….

Leticia was looking into space, her hand propping a lit cigarette in front of her mouth while her other arm protectively encircled her waist. She snapped out of her reverie, recalling the creepy conversation with the stranger earlier, and felt a cool chill in the air that made her shiver. She was staring at the two men in the cafeteria and she shook her head angrily, dropping the half-smoked cigarette to the cement floor and stubbing it out. Life is a trip, she thought before walking briskly toward the door of the cafeteria.

Leticia crossed the dreary room and headed for the lockdown section.

Chapter 10

---•---

THE LOCKDOWN SECTION OF the county hospital was housed at the end of a long corridor that had whitewashed walls. The double metallic doors enclosing the section were also whitewashed, each sporting a thin strip of reinforced, shatterproof glass for windows that looked directly into the ward. In a corner of the ceiling above the doors hovered a tinted bubble that housed a security camera monitored by a sheriff's deputy inside the ward. It reminded Leticia of a zit, a big blackhead growing out of the white ceiling. She glanced briefly at the object before punching in a code on the keypad next to the door handles. The buttons made a series of beeps as she pressed them, followed by an electronic buzz and a loud click when the locks came undone.

Leticia opened the door and passed into a large, dimly lit sitting room where a small nursing station was located. Her friend, Juana, stood behind the work desk in the middle of the room, while a mounted television blared noisily from a corner that was furnished with nondescript sticks of hotel-style furniture. Across from the station was a glass enclosed office where a sheriff's deputy sat at a desk. Beyond that was the darkened patient ward.

Juana was engrossed in a show playing on the television. She was a heavy-set, dark-skinned Mexican girl in lavender scrubs with thick lips that parted into a smile when Leticia came through the door. "Hey, girlfriend," she greeted, running her fingers through her long brown hair that was streaked blonde. "Get over here, you crazy girl."

"Hey, chica, how's it goin'?"

"Fine, now that I got a friendly face to look at." Juana leaned across the counter and lowered her voice. "I got the Ku Klux Nazi lady pulling guard duty tonight," she said, referring to the rotund young sheriff's deputy with frizzy hair sitting in the security room. She was reading a magazine at the desk, but her cold blue eyes shot a look at the nurses when Juana spoke about her. Busted, they turned away, giggling. The deputy curled her upper lip and resumed reading her magazine. "Bitch," Juana whispered.

The nurses shared a conspiratorial laugh, briefly clasping hands across the counter. "I still can't believe you showed up tonight," Juana said. "I don't want nothing to do with this place when I'm off the clock. I'd be at the bars right now if I wasn't pulling this shift."

"Go then," Leticia invited. "I'll do your shift for you."

Juana tilted her head back, studying her friend warily, not quite sure if she was joking. "You're crazy, girl. What's up with you anyway? You're acting all weird, like nervous and stuff."

"I'm fine, just shaken up over Carlos."

Juana continued to gaze skeptically. "I don't know. Something's not right with you."

"Look, I came to keep you some company, okay? Can't you appreciate that I'm here with you?"

"Sure, sure, take it easy," Juana said with a trace of concern. "I'm glad you came over."

Leticia tried to smile but the gesture withered on her lips. She craned her head around and peered past the lighted security booth into the dark ward beyond. Raheem Khan's prone body appeared as a shadowy lump on a raised bed surrounded by monitoring machines that blinked with tiny flashing lights. "How's the patient doing?"

"Fine," Juana replied, still studying Leticia with a critical eye. "His brain activity's been fluctuating for the past few hours. I think he's regaining consciousness."

"That's good," Leticia responded emptily, enthusiasm clearly lacking in her words. "When's the last time you monitored him?"

"What are you, a supervisor now? Why you asking questions?"

"I'm sorry, girl. I was watching him earlier and I guess I can't stop being his nurse."

"You got it bad, don't you?" Juana said, a revelation dawning on her. "Now I know what's going on. Carlos nothing, you got the hots for the patient."

Leticia was shocked. Her eyes widened as she raised her fingers to her mouth. "Oh my God, no," she protested. "Where you get that from?"

"Don't lie, chica, I know you. Somebody's gotta crush on that boy in there. That's why you're showin' up at work during time off actin' all outta sorts."

"You're crazy, Juana."

"Hey, it's okay. He's not bad looking. I understand the attraction. He's got that barrel chest and that dark skin ... whew!" Juana feigned a shiver.

"Stop!" Leticia said, slapping her friend on the shoulder. "It ain't like that."

"Mm-hmm, sure. It's your man, Carlos, that's got you here, like you said. I'll go along with that if it makes you feel good."

"You're such a troublemaker," Leticia said, the cylinders in her mind spinning. Juana had come up with something Leticia hadn't expected. Maybe she should run with it. A supposed crush would give her the perfect cover. Leticia decided she'd go along with the misperception, especially if it alleviated her friend's relentless suspicions.

Leticia took another look into the ward before turning to Juana with a conspiratorial grin. "It's probably been a while since you checked his vitals, right? Why don't I take a look for you? I'll update his chart if you want."

"Uh huh," Juana said with a nod and a knowing look. "You wanna check his vitals, huh? Go ahead and knock yourself out. I have some paperwork to take care of anyway."

"Okay."

"You're so bad," Juana said.

Leticia grinned broadly, but her expression lost its humor almost instantly when she turned away. If Juana could have seen her face at that moment, she would have seen fear.

The deputy barely paid attention to Leticia when she passed into the patient area. A brief, almost imperceptible sneer, and then the deputy resumed reading her magazine. The patient's bed was next to the window where the deputy sat, the only occupied bed in the long, darkened room. He lay motionless, a dark, husky man, his barrel chest slowly rising and falling amidst a tangle of tubes and sensors attached to his body. Although he'd been unconscious from the time he was admitted, a silver handcuff attached his right hand to the metal bed frame.

Leticia pressed against the bed, her back to the window, and pretended to check the readings on the heart monitor next to the patient's head. Her own heart pounded uncontrollably while she studied the man's broad, whiskered features for signs of awareness. His countenance was lifeless. Were it not for his breathing, and the steady beep of the EKG machine, Leticia would have thought he was dead.

Nervously, Leticia glanced around to check her rear. She was startled to see the deputy staring at her. Leticia used every ounce of self-control to appear calm. She nodded to the deputy, who ignored the gesture and redirected her attention to her magazine. Leticia kept watching, and then shot a look at Juana, who was engrossed in paperwork at the station.

Leticia fumbled in the pocket of her smock for the syringe beneath her crushed cigarette pack. Pulling it out in a smooth motion, she kept it in front of her to obscure it from the deputy. There was a small television screen next to the deputy that showed a full view of the ward from the perspective of the rear of the room, but the quality was bad in the dark. Leticia could see the screen through the glass partition. Her image was a smudgy shadow hovering next to the patient's bed.

Another brief glance to ensure the coast was clear and Leticia pulled the safety cap off the needle. Fighting a wave of panic, Leticia struggled to control her shaking hand as she guided the point toward the patient's exposed forearm. She was about to plunge it in when a loud buzzing erupted outside.

The deputy rose abruptly, looking toward the entrance as Juana pressed a button under the counter and buzzed in the visitors. Leticia contemplated completing the injection, but her nerves gave out and she swiftly replaced the cap on the syringe, almost sticking herself in the process.

Siegel and Rappaport stepped into the ward and Siegel spied the nurse he'd seen on the patio earlier. Looking past the hostile glare of the overweight deputy, he was struck by the odd expression the attractive Mexican woman bore. The deputy directed her bulk into the station area with the pretty Mexican nurse trailing behind. They arrived at the counter together.

"May I help you gentlemen?" the heavy-set nurse at the counter asked. Her makeup was garish.

"I'm Max Siegel, with the Las Cruces District Attorney's Office. This is my investigator, Francis Rappaport." Siegel removed his wallet from his back pocket and displayed his ID, while Rappaport flashed his badge. The fat nurse gave the items a perfunctory look before saying, "Okay." Siegel was in the process of returning the wallet to his pocket when the deputy spoke up, her tone indignant. "Um, I need to see them too guys," she said with barely contained hostility.

Siegel and Rappaport exchanged glances before redirecting their credentials to within a few inches of the deputy's sneering face. "Looks to be in order," she declared after studying each item for an inordinate amount of time. "What do you want here?" she demanded.

"I'm the DA assigned to handle the case involving the patient," Siegel responded. "My investigator and I thought we'd come by and get a prognosis." Siegel glanced at the pretty Mexican and smiled. She offered back a blank stare, almost like she was in shock.

"Nobody cleared this contact with me," the deputy said.

"It's an impromptu visit," Rappaport replied, irritation in his tone. "We're just here to do a quick check and be on our way."

The deputy turned a venomous look toward the investigator. "You should know the protocol, officer. You shoulda scheduled this appearance in advance."

"We don't mean for it to be a problem," Siegel cut in quickly. He could see Rappaport's hackles rising. "I'm going to file charges when the patient regains consciousness. We just want an update and then we're out the door—with your permission, of course."

That did the trick. The deputy's hostility began to thaw when she was vested with the respect her insecure personality craved. Her cold, blue eyes darted between Siegel and Rappaport while she debated the request over which she exercised complete authority. "Okay, I can let it go this time, but you need to play by the rules in the future."

"Absolutely," Siegel said.

Rappaport rolled his eyes.

Khan appeared almost peaceful as he lay comatose on the hospital bed. Siegel and Rappaport stood to either side of him, studying his features. The nurses and the deputy were back at their stations, leaving the attorney and investigator to go about their business alone. The heavy nurse had briefed them about Khan's condition while the pretty one looked on apprehensively. An East Asian male in his early twenties, he'd suffered a major concussion with some swelling of the brain. All vital signs were good and his lack of consciousness was expected to change soon.

Siegel was impressed by the hospital staff's accuracy regarding Khan's age, even though he was still listed as a John Doe. He watched the interaction of the nurses through the glass while Rappaport read the chart.

"Why do you keep mad-dogging that Mexican girl?" Rappaport asked without looking away from the paperwork.

Siegel grinned. "What are you talking about?"

"Don't play dumb, you're no good at it," Rappaport said, lifting a page from the clipboard and reading the next sheet.

"Okay, so you got me, but it's not what you think. I'm getting strange vibes from her. Something's going on in that nurse's head."

"That's her wondering why you keep staring at those thirty-eight Ds. The vibe is her discomfort in being visually undressed. Can we get to business please? I have places to go."

Siegel shook his head. "Such a cynic. You should know I love my wife to death."

"No doubt," Rappaport replied, lifting another page. "But everybody knows you DAs are just like cops; no matter how much you love your wife, you love a piece of strange better."

"You're projecting, pal, but I'm not going to argue with you. I know how you get when you think you're right."

"Good," Rappaport said, folding the chart cover shut. "Now that I've won another debate, can we look this man over and get out of here?"

"Sure," Siegel replied. "Anything interesting in the chart?"

"Other than the fact that I can't decipher half of what's written in it, no. Head trauma's the general consensus, like the nurse said."

Siegel looked Khan over. What he saw was a short, powerfully built young man with a wide face and bull neck. "Athletic looking, isn't he?"

"I'll say. Looks like he carries refrigerators around for a living. Doesn't appear he'd have much trouble chucking a dead guy out a window."

"No, I wouldn't tangle with him. I don't see any bruising or swelling in his facial area, so I'm guessing the upstairs victim didn't give him much of a fight."

Rappaport lifted the breast of Khan's hospital gown and peeked inside. "No bruising on the torso either. You're probably right. He must've gone straight for the butter knife on the dinner tray and got down to business when he entered the room."

"Yeah, but you'd think there'd be a tussle before the killer gets the knife. The victim presumably has it, so Khan has to wrestle it away. Where are the signs of struggle?"

"Let's see," Rappaport said, examining Khan's left hand.

Siegel followed suit, scrutinizing the right, which was handcuffed to the bed rack. He noticed some scraping and discoloration about the wrist. "They've been winding the cuffs too tight. Look at this," he said, taking hold of Khan's thick hand and rolling it.

Rappaport looked over. "You're right. His circulation was cut off here and there. That's the kind of injury a prisoner suffers when the cuff exerts too much pressure. Rookie cops tend to cause that a lot. They get overzealous with the bracelets."

"How about old timers?"

"Only the mean ones. It doesn't take long to learn the proper technique. Believe me, the custodies let you know when it hurts. If veterans do it wrong, it's because they want to."

"What about the uniformed Nurse Ratchett behind you?" Siegel asked, referring to the deputy. "She look like a candidate for sadistic cuffing?"

"You need an answer to that?"

"You're right, stupid question."

Rappaport examined the other wrist. "We got the same thing happening over here," he said. He turned and peeked at the deputy. "Sweetness back here doesn't have qualms about screwing with unconscious prisoners."

"Should we talk to her supervisor?"

"I'll drop by the department tomorrow. I know some good people in the sheriff's office. I'll pull somebody aside and give him a heads up."

Siegel and Rappaport finished looking Khan over and found nothing else remarkable. They thanked the staff in the ward and departed. Siegel's attention lingered on Leticia when he left. All Rappaport's kidding aside, there seemed to be a lot of tension balled up inside her and Siegel wondered why.

A lone figure stood leaning against the wall at the end of the corridor outside the security wing. He was tall and lean, with brown, scraggly hair and a floppy mustache. His attire consisted of blue jeans, pointy-toed cowboy boots, and an open blue and white flannel shirt over a brown turtleneck. He had one leg crooked, resting the bottom of a cowboy boot flush against the white wall, as he watched Siegel and Rappaport approach.

"Dave Langerman," Siegel announced.

"Hello, boys," Langerman greeted.

"How'd you track us down?" Siegel asked good-naturedly.

"Weren't too hard. I saw you leaving the cafeteria earlier and trailed you here."

The men exchanged handshakes, Rappaport slapping Langerman on the shoulder. Langerman was a reporter with the *Las Cruces Times*, working the court beat. He was hard-nosed, but fair. Many on the law enforcement side liked him. Sharp-minded and tenacious when on a story, he was well known for not pulling punches, for better or worse.

"What brings you by?" Siegel asked when the hand-grabbing was done.

Langerman's dark eyes twinkled. "As if you don't know," he said, lips curling beneath his heavy mustache. "I came to get the name of our mystery man in there. Two days since a murder occurs and I still can't print who's alleged to have done the deed. Care to share some enlightenment?"

Rappaport looked to Siegel.

"We'll be happy to give you the name when we learn it," Siegel replied, disingenuously.

Langerman darted his eyes from one companion to the other. "Horseshit," he said. "I caught that look between you two. You know damn well what his name is, but you don't want to share it. Same with the victims.

What are they called? I understand withholding the names pending notification of the next of kin and all, but why the mystery regarding the perpetrator? That don't make a helluva lota sense."

"Neither does your mistrust," Siegel said. "We've collaborated on a lot of cases through the years, Dave. Don't you have faith that I'll keep you in the loop?"

"I know you'll spoon feed me what you see fit, like you always do. You'll also hold out on me as you please."

"Somebody's cranky tonight," Rappaport chided.

"Sure am, Francis. I gotta murder and I gotta deadline and I don't have shit to print. What gives? Hell, I went down to the county recorder today to ascertain the name of the owner of the property where the killings happened and still came up with a big fat zero."

"How's that?" Siegel asked. "What name did you get?"

"Didn't get a name, got a corporation." Langerman's mouth curled under his mustache when he saw Siegel and Rappaport exchange looks. "Hell, you boys really don't know, do you?"

Siegel's shoulders rose and he lifted his hands to his sides, palms up. "I ain't been yanking your chain. We're as much in the dark as you are."

"I doubt that," Langerman huffed.

Siegel pressed on, unable to contain his curiosity. "What did you get off the title?"

"I didn't get anything. The title showed the home was purchased by a corporation about a year or so ago. The name was something like the Pharmagroup Corporation, or something close. I have it tucked in my notepad."

"Pharmagroup?" Siegel repeated, turning to Rappaport. "Did you know anything about that?"

Rappaport shook his head. "First I'm hearing of it."

"Well, ain't this peachy?" Langerman said sardonically. "Here I am the reporter giving out information to the DA when it's supposed to be the other way around. Are you two truly this ignorant about the facts, or just trying to get over on me?"

"Listen, Dave," Siegel said, "I have your number programmed on my cell phone. We have to get going, but—if you bear with me—I promise you'll get the scoop when I get the facts together."

"The scoop?" Langerman repeated with sarcasm. "If I wasn't the only court reporter in the only newspaper in town, that bit might actually impress me, counselor."

Time seemed to be running so slow that Leticia began to think the hands on the clock were turning backwards. Hours passed since she joined Juana at the nurse's station and she was talked out. Leticia had tried to kill time by discussing the problems she was having with her boyfriend, Carlos, both real and imagined. As the hours dragged on, they segued into talking about the job, Juana's life, the state of race relations, the entertainment world, and back again to Carlos. Finally, the conversation wound itself down until there was nothing left to say. The two friends alternated at that point between simply gazing at one another and staring off into space. Leticia eventually wandered over to the television area and slumped exhaustedly into a chair.

As she sat, Leticia inevitably reached in and out of her smock, repeatedly grasping the syringe and fiddling with it between her fingers. She was anxious and wanted to complete the task she'd come to perform, get it over with so she could go home and sleep. Her cell phone buzzed several times during the night, but she never answered it. Leticia checked the screen each time and saw that it was Carlos trying to reach her. He must've been going crazy wondering where she was.

There'd been numerous opportunities for Leticia to gravitate to the patient's bedside and do what had to be done, but guilt and fear and myriad other emotions repeatedly held her back. Leticia felt trapped in a situation that was out of control, her head continuously spinning because of the insanity of it all. What she was going to do went against every fiber of what she was about, why she was a nurse. But a stronger motivation was at work in the internal struggle raging throughout her thoughts, and that was self-preservation.

Leticia needed her job. The cost of living being what it was, Carlos's mechanic pay didn't come close to meeting their needs, especially now that she was expecting. Leticia hadn't told anybody yet, but she was informed the day before that she was pregnant. Seven more months and she'd be a mother. Leticia pitched forward in her chair, burying her face in her hands. She'd worked too hard to let everything fall apart, not for the sake of a stranger, a killer. God would forgive her.

Juana had to use the restroom and she asked Leticia to spell her while she was gone. Leticia did her friend one better, inviting her to take a lengthy break in the cafeteria. "Would you do that for me?" Juana responded gratefully. "I don't know what's with you tonight, but you're the best damn friend ever. I owe you big time, chica."

The deputy had her head down on the desk between folded arms and was snoring away. All the right circumstances had fallen into place. Leticia decided that a better opportunity to act couldn't happen, that it was now or never to make her move.

Seized with trepidation, her body and hands quivering, Leticia slowly moved past the sleeping deputy's desk and entered the darkened ward where the patient slept. She absently reached a hand into her smock and wrapped her fingers around the syringe so tight that she almost snapped it.

Leticia released the syringe when she eased next to the bed and nervously wiped her sweaty palms against her smock while watching the deputy's slumbering form through the glass. When she was certain the deputy was out, Leticia took a deep breath and tried to calm herself. Her heart was beating so hard and fast that she could literally feel the blood pulsating through the arteries in her neck. She suddenly needed to pee. Leticia couldn't believe it, but she had to fight not to let her bladder go.

Squeezing her eyes shut, Leticia steeled herself and reached blindly into her smock and withdrew the syringe. Opening her eyes again, she slid off the safety cap and readied the tip of the needle for insertion into the patient's arm. Leticia was about to plunge the needle home when the arm flexed and the patient's hand shot up, grasping her wrist in a viselike grip.

Stunned, Felicia looked into the patient's murderous eyes that were opened so wide the orbs seemed to bulge from their sockets, his gaze riveted to her with a savage intensity. She couldn't help herself. Leticia shrieked.

CHAPTER 11

---•---

M AX SIEGEL WAS HAVING a nice dream, although it instantly went out of his head when he felt Irina moving next to him. There was a shock of cool air against his naked flesh when she lifted the covers to get out of bed and he heard her softly padding into the master bathroom. Siegel was lying on his side and he slowly let his lids flutter open, blinking several times until the digital clock on Irina's nightstand came into focus. It was just after five. The alarm would go off in an hour.

Siegel heard the toilet flush and Irina's form appeared in the bathroom doorway, her taut, shapely form silhouetted inside her skimpy T-shirt until she flicked off the light. She transformed into a darkened figure with slightly tousled hair and moved toward the bed with smooth, sensuous strides.

Another shock of cool air hit Siegel's body when Irina slid beneath the covers, backing into his muscular arms while they encircled her waist. Irina let out a surprised gasp when Siegel hugged her close, pulling her firm shapeliness against him.

"You scared me," Irina whispered. "I did not know you were awake."

Siegel nuzzled his nose against the hair at the base of Irina's slender neck and breathed in her light scent. "You woke me when you got up," he said. "But that's okay. It was a nice vision to wake up to."

Irina's small hands rested on the back of Siegel's as he squeezed her. Then she maneuvered around, spinning into his grasp until she faced him, the full length of her body pressed against his, her lips parted into a grin. Siegel felt his manhood rising. "It's so nice to be appreciated," she said thickly. "I hope you still find me attractive when I am old."

"When you're old? Sweetheart, I have eleven years on you. When you're old, I'll be ancient."

"You are a man, it is not the same," Irina said, her pale blue irises sweeping over Siegel's features. "You will get better looking with age, more distinguished. Unfortunately, we women fall apart with time."

"What a myth," Siegel responded, edging his mouth closer to Irina's. "You'll be beautiful from now until the end of eternity."

"Max, you are such a corny," Irina chided playfully.

Their lips met in a tentative kiss that slowly became more passionate. Siegel felt himself getting hard as his yearning increased. His arms held Irina tighter and she sighed, her tongue invading his mouth with greater urgency. Siegel rolled on top of her and lifted himself enough to grasp the bottom of her T-shirt. Irina obligingly raised her arms so he could pull it off. Siegel tossed the garment to the floor and lowered his body onto Irina's, resuming their kiss. They moaned and writhed, stroking and grasping at each other as their passions continued to climb. Finally, Siegel reached a hand down and his fingertips felt the heat as his middle finger gently probed Irina's vagina. It was soaking wet and he knew she was ready to take him. Siegel guided his shaft into her love canal and Irina grunted, clamping her fingers onto his back, sinking her nails into his skin.

Siegel groaned.

Then the phone rang.

Siegel tried to ignore it and plunged himself into his wife over and over, but the persistence of the ringer distracted him, until he broke his rhythm and reached for the receiver.

"Nooo," Irina protested.

"I know," Siegel said sympathetically, lifting the receiver to his ear.

"Max, this is Bernie Sims," the voice on the other end of the line said.

Siegel frowned. "Kinda early for a phone call, isn't it?"

"Yes, I'm sorry, but this is urgent. Our suspect is awake in the hospital. Rich wants us all to convene in his office right away to discuss the matter."

"What? Who's all of us?"

"You, me, Rappaport, and Detective Cox."

"Why? What's the big emergency?"

"Mine is not to reason why, Max. I just do what I'm told. If the boss says he wants us in his office, I say, so be it."

Yeah, you would, you little weasel, Siegel thought. He caught the subtle admonishment Sims gave him, basically telling him not to question orders. "Okay, I'll be there in half an hour," he said, feeling the passion that consumed him only moments ago seeping away.

"What is it?" Irina asked, her voice oozing with disappointment as Siegel cradled the receiver.

"I have to report to Rich Danko's office immediately."

"But why?"

"The suspect in my murder case woke up. Danko wants us all in his office to discuss it."

"That makes no sense," Irina pouted as Siegel lifted himself off her, flipping off the covers and rolling into a sitting position.

"You're right," Siegel replied, his back to Irina. "Danko's never gotten involved in one of my cases like this before. It's not like him to micromanage."

"That is very strange, Max."

"Tell me about it. This whole case has been strange from the start." Siegel rose to his feet and strolled toward the bathroom. "I have to take a shower."

Everyone was already assembled in Rich Danko's office when Siegel arrived. Danko sat at his desk with his parrot, Bernie Sims, perched beside his chair. Cox appeared disheveled and thoroughly wrung out, slumped in one of the two high-backed chairs fronting the desk, while Rappaport reclined on a leather sofa next to the entrance. Danko's attention immediately latched onto Siegel when he came through the door. The DA's demeanor was obviously belligerent. "Mr. Siegel, so glad you could join us," he said in a sarcastic tone.

Sims covered his mouth as he smirked.

"Good morning to you, too," Siegel shot back, mimicking Danko's tone.

The two men locked gazes for a few tense moments before Danko broke the silent confrontation with a wave of his hand, like he was batting away flies. "Alright, forget all that," he said grumpily. "Take a seat next to Cox here."

Siegel complied with the request, noticing a sour odor coming from Cox when he sat down. The man's hygiene was horrible.

"Let's get started," Danko said, clasping his massive hands together. "Our boy, Mr. Khan, has come to life over at county. It's unfortunate because I was hoping the prick would die and save us a lot of trouble."

The remark surprised Siegel. Cox snickered.

"The situation's going to get ugly when the Pakistani community finds out they have one of their own facing a murder rap," Sims piped in.

"This is too close to the mess we just concluded with that Jinnah prosecution," Danko groused. "Why couldn't the kid be a Mexican or some other damn minority? With all the diversity in this town, why'd it have to be a Pakistani committing the murders?"

"Don't you think you're making more of this than it deserves?" Siegel asked. "It looks like a clean case so far. What do you think the community will have to sink its teeth into?"

Danko looked sharply at Siegel, his cheeks flushing. "Don't you get it? They don't need anything to sink their so-called teeth into. Nine-eleven, Iraq, the war on terror, the Jinnah fiasco, Las Cruces is sitting in the middle of a culture clash. Khan's people are going to exploit any weakness in the case as another instance of vindictive prosecution. The smallest discrepancy will get blown out of proportion and spark exactly the kind of unrest the city just clamped a lid on."

"You have to appreciate the delicate political subtleties we're dealing with, Max," Sims chimed in.

"Oh, I do, Bernie," Siegel replied mockingly at the condescending remark. "That's why I plan to dot the Is and cross the Ts. And while we're on the subject of doing a thorough job, perhaps Detective Cox can help clarify a few details about the victims."

Cox had appeared amused during the discussion, but, at the mention of his name, he straightened his posture and garnered an angry, defensive expression.

"What are you talking about?" Danko demanded.

"It recently came to my attention that the victim's home is owned by a corporation, the Pharmagroup," Siegel began. "Franny and I did a walk-through of the residence yesterday and noticed the place appears barely lived in. We don't seem to know anything more about the victims than their names and that one of them has a Washington State ID. We read your reports, detective, and they don't shed any light on who these men are and why they were at the murder scene."

"You accusing me of something, counselor?" Cox asked angrily.

"Not at all," Siegel replied. "I'm just wondering if you know more details than what's in your reports."

"Do you hear this guy?" Cox asked Danko, rudely sticking a finger in Siegel's direction.

"Relax," Danko said irritably, "it's a fair question. What's all this about a corporation being on the title?"

Cox shifted uncomfortably in his seat. "I'm a good detective. I put everything I knew into my initial reports."

"Nobody said you didn't," Danko said, lifting a brow. "But is there something else you know now?"

"I was gonna write a supplemental. During further investigation, I just learned that Mr. Siegel is right; the home is owned by a corporation. It's a pharmaceutical company headquartered in Arizona. They recently purchased the property to house salespeople travelling through the area. The two men that were killed were employees, using the place as a transit stop." Cox turned to Siegel. "It's no big deal. I was gonna give you that new information today, if you woulda gave me the chance."

Siegel was taken aback. He looked at Rappaport, who shrugged. Siegel returned his attention to Cox. "That explains a lot," he said, feeling deflated.

"Okay," Danko said, "now that we cleared that up, do you have any other concerns before we move on?"

"I want to know about the gun," Siegel said.

"What about it?" Cox asked.

"I take it you collected the Glock at the scene and booked it into evidence. Has there been a ballistics check yet?" Siegel inquired.

"I did that the next day," Cox replied with growing agitation. "We shot out two slugs that we'll compare with the bullets from the victim's body when the coroner releases them. I know how to do my job, Mr. Siegel."

"I didn't say you don't. Stop taking it so personally, detective. I'm only checking on the details in my case."

"It don't exactly sound like that," Cox responded. "For some reason it feels like you're questioning how I perform my duties."

"Christ! Will you lighten up, Cox?" Danko cut in. "Max is asking routine questions and you're getting your panties in a bunch."

"I want to know who the gun belonged to," Siegel continued.

"What for?" Cox asked.

Siegel was surprised by the cluelessness of the question. "Details, detective," he said. "Did the perp shoot the second victim with his own gun, or did it belong to the victims? It's another detail that needs to be filled in."

"Harris picked the gun out of Khan's hand after he knocked the bastard out," Cox said. "This was right after he heard the gunshots, and there weren't any other guns found. The Glock is the murder weapon. What does anything else matter? You're overdoing it on the details, counselor."

"Why don't you let me worry about that?"

"Your attitude is startin' to piss me off," Cox said, rising from his seat.

"Enough!" Danko barked, the force of his voice arresting Cox's motion. "Sit down and stop being so damn sensitive. And, Max, back off a bit and trust the detective to do his job. It sounds like everything's under control.

So if you girls are done with your catfight, I'd like to get to the business of why I called you here."

"Fine by me," Siegel said, studying Cox in his peripheral vision. The detective's reaction to Siegel's simple queries was odd. Siegel wondered what the problem was. It made him suspicious.

"Let's move on," Danko said. "Raheem Khan emerged from his witness-induced slumber a few hours ago. If we're lucky, we have a window of two or three hours before he contacts family and retains a lawyer, whose first piece of advice will be that Khan clamp a muzzle on his mouth. We have one shot to pry a confession out of him. That's why I got you all out of bed. Let's pounce on the opportunity. My clock says six-fifteen. I want somebody sitting at Khan's bedside in twenty minutes to take a statement from him."

"We don't really need a confession," Sims offered. "The evidence is more than sufficient to convict Khan of the murders. Talking it over, we decided that admissions of culpability from the defendant's own mouth will go a long way in keeping the Pakistanis from creating a political backlash."

"That's right," Danko agreed, scanning the room. "I want to be proactive in minimizing any fallout this case generates."

"As the assigned deputy, shouldn't you let me worry about that?" Siegel asked.

Danko's vision froze on Siegel, his heavy brows coming together over narrowed lids. "I'm top dog in this office," he growled menacingly, "remember that. Any garbage that hits the office, hits me. You're my subordinate, doing my business. I have a right to get involved in any case as I see fit. Do you have a problem with that?"

Siegel grinned. "Now that I've been verbally mounted, no," he cracked. Rappaport stifled a giggle. "I understand you're the boss, all the way to next November. After that, we'll see."

A vein appeared in Danko's forehead. He looked like he was ready to burst. The entire room remained quiet for a tension-filled minute in anticipation of the explosion, but it never came. Danko's internal struggle for control visibly dissolved as he kept an unwavering gaze on Siegel. "The election is still a long way away," he said in a low tone. "A lot can happen between now and then. In the meantime, I still call the shots, and I say Detective Cox gets to the hospital and takes the statement. You and Rappaport can go along for the ride."

"I want Franny in the room when Cox talks to Khan," Siegel demanded.

"Here we go again," Cox complained, but Danko cut him short.

"Fine, there shouldn't be a problem with that, but it's Cox's case, so he'll do the lead inquiry. He doesn't need our investigator stepping on his toes. That okay with you, detective?"

"I can live with that, long as I get to conduct the questioning my way."

"There, see? We're all in agreement," Danko said. "One big happy family. I don't care how you go about it, detective, just come back with a juicy confession in your pocket. Let's put the last nail in the coffin of this case."

CHAPTER 12

S ITTING IN THE RECEPTION area of the hospital security wing, Siegel felt like he'd never left. The nurse, Leticia, was at the nurse's station, appearing worn and worried. He tried to make eye contact with her from time to time without success. She was obviously aware of his presence, but she apparently wanted to avoid him.

Siegel craned his neck to get a visual into the patient ward Cox and Rappaport had disappeared into, but he couldn't see a thing. They were about to question the suspect—who was awake and alert—and Siegel desperately wanted in on the process. However, being the prosecuting attorney, it wouldn't be a good idea. Anything Khan told about the killings would constitute evidence, and hearing it would make Siegel a witness in his own case, subject to testifying on the stand if the defense wanted to call him. For that reason, he'd let the detectives conduct the interrogation and get their findings secondhand when it was over.

Raheem Khan watched his visitors enter the room with coal black eyes that had an intelligent, animalistic intensity. He was sitting up, slightly inclined, his shoulders and chest bulky with muscles that strained against his flimsy gown.

"Mr. Khan," Cox greeted, wearing an oily grin. "Raheem Khan, is that right?"

Khan said nothing, giving a barely perceptible nod as the detectives came alongside his bed.

"I'm Dale Cox, a detective with the Las Cruces Police Department,"

Cox began. "This is my colleague, DA Investigator Rappaport. We come to chat about what happened the other night in Pleasant Oaks."

Khan jerked his thick arm, pulling against the handcuff attached to his wrist, rattling the steel bed frame. "Why am I cuffed?" he asked in perfect English.

"You're under arrest, Mr. Khan," Rappaport replied, to Cox's obvious chagrin.

"Arrest?" Khan repeated incredulously. "For what?"

"Two counts of murder," Rappaport said.

Cox put his hand up. "Let me handle this," he insisted.

"Murder?" Khan repeated. "You're crazy! What I did wasn't murder. I—"

"Don't say anything yet!" Cox cut in. "Don't open your mouth till I give you your rights."

Rappaport gazed at Cox with astonishment, although he tried to conceal it. He couldn't believe the detective just shut up a suspect about to spill his guts regarding the crime he committed. They hadn't asked any questions yet, nothing that would elicit an incriminating response. The law didn't require cops to stop a criminal from making voluntary, incriminating statements that weren't in response to questions. Spontaneous statements were a freebie to investigators and always admissible in court. As an experienced cop, Cox knew that. So why did he interrupt a suspect ready to run off at the mouth?

"You have rights under the law, Mr. Khan," Cox announced. "Before you utter another word, I want to explain your Miranda rights."

Rappaport removed a pocket recorder from the inside of his sports jacket and clicked it on. "We'll be recording the conversation," he said.

"No we won't," Cox countered. "Put that device away."

"What?" Rappaport asked, surprised again.

"We don't need a recorder. This is just a preliminary questioning, and I want our friend here to feel comfortable talking to us."

Rappaport couldn't believe what he was hearing. He was about to utter a protest when Cox cut him off.

"I'm the lead detective," Cox announced sternly. "Your own boss said so, remember? You're here to assist while I conduct the interview, and I say no recorders. So please, put it away."

Rappaport saw Khan warily watching the exchange and he slowly complied with Cox's order, turning off the recorder and replacing it in his jacket. He could see Khan getting spooked and Rappaport didn't want to argue in front of him. He'd take the matter up with Cox later, when they were alone.

"Mr. Khan," Cox said. "I'd love to get a full statement, but I'm required to say that you have a right to remain silent. You don't have to tell us anything. In fact, whatever you do say can be used against you later in a court of law. That's no joke. You open your mouth and say something now and I guarantee you'll hear the prosecution asking me or Rappaport about it at trial when the jury's listening. Understand?"

"Yes," Khan answered.

Rappaport glared at Cox in amazement, wondering what he was pulling.

"You have a right to have an attorney present during questioning," Cox continued. "Let me tell you, that's always a good idea. Attorneys are trained to know when you're incriminating yourself and they'll stop questions real fast when that happens."

"What the hell are you doing?" Rappaport asked, unable to contain himself.

"Stop interrupting," Cox commanded. "This man has a right to know his rights under the Constitution."

"You're sabotaging the interrogation," Rappaport fumed.

Cox smiled with condescension and shook his head. "Sorry about this bickering, Mr. Khan, but you need to know that if you can't afford an attorney, the court will appoint one for you, free of charge. That's free legal advice, without paying a dime. In a case like this, with you looking at two counts of murder, you're gonna want that free advice, partner. Do you understand everything I explained so far?"

"Yes," Khan replied, "you made things very clear."

"Good," Cox said. "With that in mind, is there anything you want to say about the killings?"

Khan looked from Cox to Rappaport with quick, intelligent eyes. "No," he said. "I'm not saying a word until I have a lawyer."

"Why would you?" Rappaport muttered with disgust.

CHAPTER 13

---•---

RICH DANKO STOOD GLOWERING in front of his office window like an angry bear. He watched the tiny figures milling about the courthouse steps seven stories below like they were ants. He had his hands crossed behind him and kept curling his right hand into a meaty fist, clenching and unclenching it over and again. "Look at those bastards," he grumbled. "We don't officially file charges until Friday and they're already gathering to protest. I knew this was going to cause trouble. I could feel it."

"I counted nineteen when I came in," Sims said. "Jinnah's down there rallying them with a bullhorn. He says we're at war with the Pakistani community."

Danko hissed. "I'm surprised he didn't use the word jihad. The mayor's office is nervous. They were on the phone with me every five minutes yesterday seeking assurances that our case is sound. The Muslims are up in arms and it's not just the Pakistanis. The east side's turning into a tinderbox that's getting ready to explode. The police had to increase patrols."

"Siegel seems to have everything under control. The case is solid, even without a confession."

"Yeah, and what's up with that?" Danko asked, turning away from the window and fixing a stern gaze on his number two. "I send those three bozos over to county to extract admissions from the suspect and get zilch. They come back and tell me Khan invoked his right to counsel."

"That surprised me, too," Sims said.

"How hard could it be? The man just came out of a coma. Nobody else was around. How does he have the presence of mind to keep his mouth shut?"

"You're right, Rich. Any experienced interrogator should have walked out of the hospital with Khan's fate in his pocket."

"This whole case stinks and I still can't figure what angle the feds are playing. Something bad's coming down the pike, I can feel it."

"Best to keep doing what you're doing," Sims said. "Stay in the background, lay low, let Siegel absorb the heat."

"That's my plan, but it doesn't make me immune from the flak."

"No, not totally, but it gives you a fall guy if the situation turns bad. In the end, all you have to do if the politics go wrong is turn on Siegel, make him your scapegoat."

"Oh, I will, believe me. I'd love nothing more than to see him fry."

Siegel heard the mechanical voice blaring from the bullhorn as he walked toward the courthouse from his parking garage. Instinctively, he knew the commotion concerned him. Langerman had printed an article in the newspaper the day before, exposing the identity of Clay County's latest murder suspect. On cue, the demonstrators were materializing out of the woodwork to protest the martyrdom of another member of the Muslim community.

Siegel saw them when he approached, dark-skinned, working class men crowding the courthouse entrance. Ahmed Jinnah stood at the top of the steps next to the towering statue of Lady Justice, a bullhorn pressed to his mouth, exhorting his compatriots with fiery rhetoric. He was a small, shabby man with deep-set eyes that were too close together. His hair was short and black and he wore a cheap gray suit with a black collared shirt. He sported at least two days dark stubble and a gray and blue striped skullcap.

"We cannot let these injustices to our people go on," Jinnah said as Siegel reached the outer perimeter of a group of spectators. "They blame us for everything since the attack on the twin towers. They see us as their enemies and want to make us responsible for all bad things that happen. First they came after me, and now they are trumping up false charges against our brother, Raheem Khan."

Siegel pushed through the spectators and moved boldly onto the steps in the midst of the Muslims. Jinnah took notice of him immediately and pointed an angry finger. "There!" he thundered, drawing all attention onto Siegel. "There is the prosecutor who brings the erroneous charges against our brother. He is Max Siegel and he will seek to persecute Raheem Khan, to separate him from his family, to lock him away forever in a dungeon for crimes he did not commit."

The crowd parted to make way for Siegel, watching him with simmering hostility. Siegel pressed on, appearing oblivious to the hatred.

"There is more than one type of justice, but none more supreme than that of God," Jinnah continued when Siegel walked past. "You will pay for making a mockery of his justice, Mr. Prosecutor. His will is supreme. Let those who falsely accuse be struck down by his might. Praise be to the one true God!"

Siegel passed through the courthouse doors where a phalanx of sheriff's deputies had gathered in case of trouble. "Some excitement this morning, eh?" a burly deputy remarked when Siegel cleared the metal detector.

"I'll say," Siegel replied. "Overly dramatic, but entertaining."

"You watch yourself, counselor," the deputy said with a measure of concern.

"I always do," Siegel responded coolly, heading for the elevators.

Despite the bravado, Siegel was unnerved by what transpired. He wasn't officially filing charges against Khan until tomorrow, and the paper had yet to mention his name as prosecutor in the case, so how did Jinnah know? That was inside information that the public wasn't privy to, yet Jinnah pointed Siegel out the moment he saw him. How? It was another oddity in a strange case.

Rappaport was waiting for Siegel in the office when Siegel arrived. He was still upset about Cox's conduct during the botched questioning of Khan. He was convinced Cox purposely dissuaded the suspect from making a statement, but couldn't, for the life of him, figure out why. He discussed the matter with Siegel at length over the past few days and decided that, for whatever reason, Cox couldn't be trusted. The two made a secret pact to double-check all aspects of Cox's investigation, to not rely on him for anything, to gather the evidence themselves and draw their own conclusions about the facts.

Rappaport's latest complaint concerned one of the murder weapons: the gun. He intended to retrieve it from the property room in the police department and take it to Sacramento for a separate ballistics check, and also to trace the ownership. But when he tried to check it out, he discovered it was gone. The property clerk told Rappaport that Cox had signed for it. Rappaport couldn't discern what for.

"Cox's supplemental report says that the Glock was reported stolen from a registered owner down in Los Angeles," Siegel said. "Maybe he wanted to conduct follow-up."

Rappaport appeared skeptical and scratched the top of his head. "I don't know about that," he said. "He's already gotten the serial number and other identifying information off it. Any other follow-up doesn't require physical possession. Dale is making moves that I don't understand. He's excessively guarded about the investigation, yet he seems to be screwing it up in subtle ways. If I didn't know better, I'd swear he's trying to throw a wrench in the case."

"Why would he do that?"

"I don't know. That's what's driving me crazy. I've known him for years. We started as rookie cops together. He's not the best cop in the world, but working cases has always been his ego trip. He always wants to do the best job possible, even with his limited mental resources. What he's doing lately doesn't compute."

"What should we do about it?"

"Watch him, maybe it will help explain why he's acting the way he is."

"Okay, but keep it on the down low. We don't want LCPD getting up in arms if they find out we're surveilling one of their own."

"Don't worry, I know how to hug the shadows."

Raheem Khan was released from the county hospital and transferred to jail, which meant it was time for Siegel to file charges. The suspect could only be housed in the jail for two business days without charges, and then good cause would have to be shown to hold him without a complaint. Siegel had already filed the paperwork with the court. Khan would be arraigned on murder charges the following day.

Siegel worked late getting his case ready. He lost track of time, not noticing the sun had set until he looked up from his computer, where he was typing away. That's when the phone on his desk rang.

"Siegel," he answered.

"Why are you still at work?" Irina asked.

Siegel glanced at the clock on the wall and was surprised that it was ten past seven. "Jeez, I didn't notice the time."

"You were supposed to be home an hour ago. I am worrying about you. And you don't call me."

"Sorry, honey, I'm preoccupied. We're arraigning the murder tomorrow and I was prepping the case."

"Forget court, you need to get home. Your dinner is getting cold. I made a nice stroganoff and it is going in the garbage if you are not here in fifteen minutes."

"Yes, sir, ma'am. I'll be right there."

Irina laughed lightly. "Don't call me ma'am. That's for old ladies."

"Your vanity is out of control, my dear. We'll talk about that later."

Aside from a few straggling attorneys, the office was dark and deserted when Siegel passed through on his way to the elevators. The click of his heels on the marble floors echoed loudly in the empty corridors when he emerged from the elevator and made his way toward the exits. The nightshift guard broke away from his portable television to unlock the doors. Siegel thanked him and thrust his hands into the pockets of his trench coat as he walked quickly in the chill night air to the parking garage.

Devoid of residences and popular night spots, the area around the courthouse sported little traffic and a minimum of street people at night. Siegel could feel the emptiness as he traversed the two blocks to his car's location. The garage entrance was well lit, but the glass enclosed ticket-taker box was empty. Siegel thought it odd as he passed the booth and climbed the cement stairwell to get to the fifth level.

His mind was wandering over the events of the day when he reached the third level, and then it dawned on Siegel that he was hearing faint footsteps below. Siegel halted and listened, but heard nothing. After a few seconds, he continued his climb, straining to hear any telltale sounds other than his own. Siegel arrived on the fourth level when he caught a noise. He stopped again, hearing nothing but silence and the distant hum of car engines in the street.

Siegel leaned far over the steel railing next to the steps, peering down the winding stairwell for signs of someone else, his heart beginning to pound and his scalp becoming itchy with the first prickly sensations of fear. The thought occurred that the garage worker might be making rounds. "Hellooo," he called, his voice sounding hollow in the emptiness. Nothing came back.

A cold rush of air blew against Siegel and he shivered slightly, his breath quickening and his heart racing even faster as tension filled his body. He straightened and resumed climbing the stairs, abruptly rushing to the rail when he thought he heard another sound. This time he caught the trace of a shadow moving deliberately away from the edge of the stairs one landing below. "Who's there?" Siegel demanded.

No response.

The awful realization that he was truly in danger began creeping into Siegel's consciousness. Somebody was there and he sensed it was a malevolent presence. The worker being absent from the booth now seemed ominous. Somebody was stalking him.

Siegel turned and ran up the remaining steps, trying not to panic, as he distinctly heard the following footsteps. When he gained the next landing, he spotted his car parked alone about forty feet away. He sprinted toward the car as the sound of rushing feet continued on the stairwell behind him.

Siegel's mad dash was interrupted when he detected movement below his car and he stopped instantly. Pounding footsteps approached from the rear and Siegel wheeled around, shocked to see a dark-skinned man charging him, the glint of a sharp blade flashing from the intruder's clenched hand.

There was no time to think. Siegel pivoted, dodging left as the man lunged past with the blade extended, a primal scream emanating from the deranged man's throat. Siegel's long coat wasn't buttoned and he hurriedly removed it as the attacker checked his charge and spun around. The man looked like one of the Pakistanis from earlier in the day, and he turned wild, hate-filled eyes on Siegel, his lips bared over white teeth in a snarl as he readied to lunge again.

"Who are you?" Siegel asked in desperation, a sense of disbelief gripping him.

The question went unanswered as the man made another charge, the knife thrusting directly at Siegel's chest. Siegel dodged away on reflex, swiping at the extended arm. The trench coat twisted and flew into the attacker's face, covering his head as he passed. Seeing his chance, Siegel threw his arms around the man while he was tangled in the coat. The attacker was strong and he strained against Siegel's desperate hold, his muffled cries coming through the material. Siegel rushed the struggling bundle forward, pushing his assailant smack into the concrete wall with all his might.

The attacker grunted and went slack, the knife clattering to the floor. Taking no chances, Siegel palmed the round head that bobbed inside the coat and shoved it into the wall three times, until the man collapsed, sprawling onto the hard floor.

Siegel tugged the trench coat off the incapacitated attacker, who groaned in semi-conscious misery, his head slowly bobbing from side to side. A red pool quickly formed on the gray cement beneath the man's hair.

Siegel panted, relief beginning to wash over him despite the adrenaline surging through his body, when he detected a sound to his rear. Turning, he noticed movement on the far side of his car, a shadowy form ducking below the trunk. Siegel rushed forward and saw a dark-skinned man materialize, rising from the car. He circled the vehicle and Siegel lunged into him, causing both men to sprawl over the trunk before rolling onto the cement floor in a heap. The new assailant landed on top of Siegel and horror contorted the man's features. Peering with fright at something under the car, he screeched and scrambled to his feet. Siegel expected him to attack, but instead the man took flight, jabbering in a language Siegel didn't understand.

Looking to see what had scared the assailant, Siegel saw a device with protruding wires sitting beneath the engine block. He heard a hissing sound and—in that terrible moment—realized it was a bomb. A jolt of sheer panic streaked through every fiber of Siegel's body, and he sprang instantly to his feet, bolting toward the stairwell as fast as he could when a thunderous explosion went off. He felt its concussion ripping through his body. Then everything went black.

CHAPTER 14

———•———

IRINA SIEGEL HURRIED INTO the emergency ward of Mercy Hospital and immediately spied Franny Rappaport and two uniformed officers speaking to a doctor. Rappaport turned and opened his arms as she rushed toward him, tears streaming from her eyes. She'd been holding her emotions in since getting the call about Siegel, but the dam burst and she started crying when she pressed her face against Rappaport's chest. She couldn't hold it in any longer, her tortured mind envisioning the worst during the frantic drive over.

"Everything's alright," Rappaport soothed, hugging Irina tight and gently stroking her hair with an enormous hand. "He's going to make it. The doctor's right here and he says Max is more shaken up than anything else. His wounds are minor."

Irina pulled her head back and looked at Rappaport through tears that were streaming down her cheeks. "What happened?" she croaked. "Who tried to hurt Max?"

"We don't know yet, Max just came out of it. There was an explosion in his car at the parking garage and it knocked him out, but he'll be okay."

"Where is he?"

"Examination Room C," the doctor volunteered. He was a young man with dark hair and hazel eyes. "I'm Doctor Latimer," he said, "Mr. Siegel's attending physician."

Irina let go of Rappaport and dug a tissue out of her purse, dabbing at her eyes and wiping the tears from her cheeks. "I'm sorry, doctor, I am a mess." She extended a hand and the doctor clasped it. "I am Irina Siegel. How is my husband?"

"It's like Investigator Rappaport says. He's fine, just slightly disoriented, but that should clear up soon. We took X-rays and found no internal damage. There's no brain injury of any sort. Other than a few contusions and some bruising, your husband's in excellent condition."

"Thank you," Irina sighed, dropping her head and dabbing at her eyes again. She let go of the doctor's hand and smiled. "This is a shock to me. It's a relief to hear that Max is okay. May I see him?"

"Certainly," Doctor Latimer replied. "Why don't we give him another ten minutes to orientate before you go in? I'll give him another examination, just to make sure he's still alright. After that, he should be able to go home, barring any unforeseen complications."

"Thanks, doc," Rappaport said.

As the doctor left, Rappaport took Irina by the elbow and steered her toward an empty corner of the visitor's room. The uniformed officers followed.

"What is it?" Irina asked.

"Nobody's had a chance to talk to Max about what happened," he said. "A passing motorist heard the blast in the garage and phoned it in as an anonymous 911 call. These officers responded. When they got there, they found Max lying on the ground with his car in flames."

"Oh my God!" Irina exclaimed. She felt herself weakening and her head began to spin, but she somehow willed herself to hold it together until the fainting sensation passed.

Bernie Sims came into the emergency ward wearing a trench coat over casual attire. His weak chin somehow appeared weaker without a suit and tie. "How's Max?" he asked Rappaport.

"Fine, we're waiting to see him when the doctor clears it."

"Irina, I came as soon as I heard the news," Sims said. "You should know that the office is with Max 100 percent. We'll find whoever perpetrated this cowardly act and prosecute him to the hilt. No one messes with our deputies like that. I spoke with Rich Danko and he sends his regards also."

"Not coming himself?" Rappaport asked wryly.

"No, he sent me in his place. You know how it goes, he's a busy man."

"Right," Rappaport muttered with disgust, "a 100 percent, like you say."

"I was attacked," Siegel said to his surprised audience. He was seated on the edge of an examination cot, his arm around Irina, a hospital smock draped loosely about his heavily muscled chest and shoulders. His body was wracked with pain and a searing ache was throbbing in his skull, but Siegel suspected a good night's rest would put him right. Rappaport, Sims, and one of the uniformed officers were crammed into the tiny room with him and Siegel was doing his best not to appear as wrung out as he felt.

"That's incredible," Sims remarked with automatic concern. "Do you have any idea who it was?"

"One of them came at me with a knife while I think the other was planting the bomb," Siegel said.

"Max!" Irina gasped, squeezing him tighter.

"A knife?" Sims repeated incredulously.

"I think I interrupted them while they were trying to place the device. I managed to put the guy with the knife down. I was struggling with the other one, after that, when he suddenly broke away and tore ass outta there. That's when I saw the bomb and tried to do the same. I suppose I didn't run fast enough."

"Apparently you did," Rappaport said.

"They looked like the protestors in front of the court today," Siegel said. "I don't mean I recognized anybody in particular, but they appeared to be Jinnah's people."

"Would you recognize them if you saw them again?" the uniformed officer asked. "If so, we have mug shots you can view."

"I'll do that tomorrow after the arraignment," Siegel replied. "I think I can recognize them."

"Well, the stakes have certainly risen in the Khan case," Sims said. "We'll arrange protection for you, Max, until this matter gets resolved."

"I'll be alright on my own," Siegel said. "Thanks for the concern. I'll let you know if I change my mind down the road."

"Okay then," Sims said. "I'll get out of here and leave you alone with your wife. I'll brief Rich on what happened. You have an open line if you need anything from us, Max."

"I appreciate it," Siegel said, blinking wearily.

When Sims was gone, Siegel gave a statement to the officer about what occurred while the officer dutifully took notes. A detective was going to be assigned to the case for follow-up and the officer said that Siegel would be contacted Friday afternoon to look at mug shots. Siegel thanked him, and then the officer left.

"Are you sure you'll be alright?" Rappaport asked, concern etched in his expression.

"No, but I don't intend to live in a state of fear," Siegel answered. "I'll be careful about where I go and what I do from now on."

"Why can't you withdraw from the murder case?" Irina pleaded.

"It's my job, darling. I've been doing this for years. I can't run and hide whenever trouble happens."

"You call this only trouble? Are you a madman? You can get killed," Irina declared, her voice nearing a hysteric pitch.

"Shall I leave the two of you alone?" Rappaport inquired.

There was a knock at the door before Siegel could answer and Dave Langerman walked in. "I heard you were over here," Langerman said. "How are you, counselor? Folks?"

"Hi, Dave," Siegel greeted.

"What brings you by," Rappaport asked with a smirk.

"You're a funny one, aren't you?" Langerman quipped. "I just came from the parking garage by the courthouse where somebody tried to remodel the fifth floor with a car bomb. I talked to a few of the police boys that responded and heard them dropping Max's name all over the place. Imagine my surprise. It weren't hard to track you down for my exclusive after that."

"How's my car looking?" Siegel asked, a wan smile parting his lips.

"Not as good as you, I can tell you that. Funny thing, I was by the courthouse steps this morning taking notes on Ahmed Jinnah's gabfest. You didn't spy me, Max, but I heard him calling down the wrath of God on your head when you were going through the doors. Low and behold, your car's blowing up the same day, and almost with you in it. Care to comment on any linkage between the two events?"

"Wish I had something for you, but I'm not sure what's happening myself," Siegel responded.

"Yeah, yeah, I know, another 'I'm walking in the dark' statement," Langerman said. "You promised me a scoop not too long ago, but all I'm getting is the poop."

Rappaport laughed. "Take it easy on Max, will ya? The man got blown up. He's still trying to get his head on straight."

"Shucks, Max, I don't know if you realize how fortunate you are that we can joke about your situation," Langerman remarked.

"What do you mean?" Siegel asked.

"I heard the bomb squad talking about your predicament. Sounds like you shouldn't be alive. The bomb that went off was crude, but powerful. It was to go on the undercarriage of your car, designed to blow up, rather than out. When it went off, your car absorbed most of the blast. That's the reason you're alive to discuss what happened."

Irina broke from Siegel and put her palms to her temples, her fingers clawing at her hair. "This is insanity!" she declared, and then spun on Siegel. "What if this happens again?" she asked. "Will I be a widow next time?"

"It won't happen again," Siegel assured her without conviction.

"How can you say that?" Irina queried angrily. "You have no control over these people that want to get you."

"I'll watch over him, Irina. Don't worry," Rappaport offered.

"Like you did tonight?" Irina asked pointedly. "Two men tried to kill my husband today. Were you there to protect him?"

"That's enough," Siegel interrupted, getting stiffly to his feet. "You're upset, sweetheart. Franny means well and I'm sure he'll do everything he can to keep this from happening again. I'll be more careful in the future now that I understand the danger that's out there. It's been a long day, so why don't we all go home and get some rest? There's a lot to do tomorrow."

Siegel put his arms around Irina and she wearily rested her forehead against his chest. He could feel her collapsing weakly against him, her entire body trembling slightly with fear and tension. The three men exchanged looks when she clamped her lids shut. Everybody appeared concerned.

CHAPTER 15

---◆---

SIEGEL WAS TAKEN ABACK when Irina dropped him off at the courthouse the next morning. A phalanx of news reporters and camera crews were milling about amidst a cluster of haphazardly parked vans. He hadn't gone three steps when the reporters swarmed like locusts. Microphones thrust at his mouth and questions came in staccato bursts. News of the car bombing had gotten out, along with the implication that it was connected to the Khan murder prosecution. The linked events had created a media frenzy, with Siegel in the eye of the storm.

He fought through the gaggle of desperate reporters hungry for sound bites as camera lights blinded him, their lenses mere inches away. His movements were stiff and somewhat labored, though he did his best to conceal that from the newsmen. "I have no comment at this time," was Siegel's mantra as he pushed through the mob and into the courthouse.

The office was no better. Siegel was beset by secretaries and colleagues the moment he buzzed through the security doors. A nervous excitement rippled through the ranks of the employees as they voiced concern over Siegel's narrow brush with death and pressed him for details. The excitement was more than Siegel could bear first thing in the morning. Eventually, he retreated to his private office and slammed the door shut.

There was a knock a short time later and Rappaport entered, carrying a cardboard tray with two coffees. "I figured you needed one of these," he said, closing the door again.

"You're a lifesaver."

"Can you believe the circus out there?" Rappaport asked, handing over a coffee. "I saw an NBC van pulling in."

"Bombing a DA about to start a murder case is always a publicity enhancer. It doesn't happen every day, thank God."

"So you think there's a connection between Khan and what happened last night?"

"It's one hell of a coincidence if there isn't."

"I checked with LCPD, no leads so far. Whoever tried to take you out is still a mystery, at least the actual perpetrators are. As for the mastermind, if it ain't Ahmed Jinnah I'll eat my shirt."

"I'll help."

"Don't worry, we'll lean on him, apply a lot of pressure. Maybe we can piece some evidence together and take him down."

Siegel took a sip of his coffee, before setting it down with a long sigh. He reclined against the back of his chair and rubbed his eyes. "You know, Franny, I was awake half the night thinking about what happened. I'm still freaked out. They had me, do you understand that? After the bomb went off and I was sprawled unconscious on the cement, they could've returned and finished me off. I was out, defenseless; it would've been easy."

"Lucky for you they were amateurs," Rappaport said. "They obviously panicked and fled when you walked in on the job. If they were professional hit men, you're absolutely right, I'd be making funeral arrangements rather than getting ready for court. But that's karma. It wasn't your time."

"Like you say, lucky. Being alive because of sheer luck gives me pause. It's made me reflect long and hard on my short life and how much more I'd like to live it."

"Been there myself," Rappaport said somberly.

Siegel snapped out of his musings and peered hard at his friend. He felt badly, so absorbed in self pity that he'd forgotten about Rappaport's life-changing ordeal. "That's right, you know all about this position, don't you? I'm sorry. I didn't mean to dredge up bad memories."

The courtroom was filled to capacity when Siegel and Rappaport entered. They were there for the arraignment calendar. The room was long, with a divider running down the center to the swinging gates in order to separate the prisoners from the audience. The inmates sat on rows of wooden benches after being led in from an adjacent holding cell. Opaque, plastic windows kept the prisoners from seeing into the audience and vice versa.

In front of the swinging gates were the bench, lawyer's tables and bailiff's desk. A jury box stood against the right wall, crammed full of reporters and news cameras that pointed toward the prisoner section. Siegel strolled along the narrow path dividing the audience from the inmates and pushed past the swinging gates into a sea of dark suited lawyers that were milling about the tables and jury box. Some attorneys were appearing on their own matters, but many others were there out of curiosity, wanting to experience the vicarious thrill of a high profile case.

Attention was clearly focused on Siegel by other attorneys and by the cameras in the jury box, some of them swinging toward Siegel as he received handshakes and backslaps from his colleagues. While mingling with the mob of prosecutors and defense lawyers, Siegel chanced a look at the custody area where the benches were nearly full, but saw no sign of Raheem Khan. The prisoners were still being ushered in by bailiffs through a side door.

"See Jinnah and his boys in the back row?" Rappaport whispered.

Siegel switched his attention toward the spectators in the audience. Through a multitude of faces, he quickly spotted Jinnah. He was seated in the very last row, flanked by followers, and he kept a steadfast gaze on Siegel.

"He has some nerve" Rappaport said bitterly. "Tries to kill you yesterday, and now he's here mad-dogging you. This is a blatant attempt at intimidation."

"It won't work," Siegel responded, turning slowly away from the audience. "But what can we do about it anyway? There's no proof he ordered the bombing and he has a constitutional right to attend a public forum and stare at me if he wants."

"It irks the hell out of me, all the same."

"Me too, but don't let him know he's getting under your skin. That's exactly what he wants."

Khan's stocky form appeared in the doorway of the holding area, his hands shackled, wearing an orange, jailhouse jumpsuit. An immediate murmur rippled through the courtroom and the jury box came to life. Cameras whirred, flashes went off and soundmen swung their foamy microphones in Khan's direction. Reporters scribbled furiously into notepads as Khan nervously scanned the room while shuffling to a bench at the front of the custody box. Since his presence was garnering so much attention, his case would be called first. The hope was to winnow away spectators and allow business to return to normal after he was gone.

"All rise!" a bailiff called when the door to the judge's chamber opened. The judge stepped briskly into the courtroom in a flowing black robe and strode to the bench. He was a balding, middle-aged man with a firm jaw and nondescript features. "Department 31 of the Clay County Superior Court is now in session," the bailiff announced, "the honorable Harold Grafton presiding. Please be seated and come to order."

As the audience resumed their seats and the lawyers herded away from the tables and swinging doors, a clerk handed Judge Grafton a file and he called the first case.

"People of the State of California versus Raheem Khan," the judge announced. "Will the defendant please rise and stand where the bailiff directs?"

Khan rose to his feet as more camera shutters snapped and stepped tentatively along a short path inside the box that left him standing alone near the bailiff's desk. The sheriff who led him there handed him paperwork and stood beside the box.

"Are you Raheem Khan?" the judge inquired.

"Yes, I am," Khan replied in a timid voice.

"You've been handed a copy of the complaint against you. Please look at line thirteen and tell me if your name's spelled correctly."

Khan bowed his head and scanned the document, noticeably trembling. "Yes, it is," he replied in barely more than a whisper.

As more flashes lit the room, Judge Grafton read each count in the complaint, which alleged murders, residential burglary, several enhancements, and a special circumstances allegation that he explained made the defendant eligible for the death penalty. An audible gasp rose from the audience when that last pronouncement was made and a woman lapsed into a bout of sobbing. Some of the video cameras in the jury box swung in her direction, zooming in on her face.

"Let's have order," a bailiff barked.

"Mr. Khan, do you have enough money to afford an attorney?" the judge asked.

"If it pleases the court, I will act as Mr. Khan's attorney," a voice said. It came from a swarthy-skinned man in a richly tailored dark suit, who stepped forward to the defense side of the lawyer's table.

"Who are you?" Judge Grafton asked. "State your name for the record."

"Certainly. I am Saddam Gul, practicing out of San Francisco. I've been retained by acquaintances of Mr. Khan to act as his defense counsel."

Khan looked at the attorney with confusion. Judge Grafton noted his discomfort and knitted his brows. "Does the defendant have knowledge of your hiring?" he asked.

"Not yet," Gul replied. "I was contacted a few hours ago. I have just arrived from the Bay Area."

"Hmmm, this is unusual," the judge remarked. "Mr. Khan, are you willing to accept the appointment of Mr. Gul as your defense attorney?"

Khan hesitated, scanning the audience for support. Siegel looked back at Jinnah, who was concentrating intently on Khan, his head nodding almost imperceptibly.

"Mr. Khan?" Judge Grafton repeated. "I need an answer."

"I don't know," Khan said. "I guess so."

"I take it that's a yes, Mr. Khan?" the judge pressed.

"Yes, sir, I'll accept Mr. Gul as my attorney."

"Fine," Judge Grafton said as Gul stepped closer to Khan. "Mr. Gul, how does your client plead to the charges that have been brought against him?"

"Not guilty," Gul announced to a disruptive smattering of voices from the audience and more clicking cameras.

A bailiff called for order and Siegel saw Jinnah's lips part into a self-satisfied grin.

Saddam Gul had a broad face and a bald skull, except for the neatly trimmed ring of black hair that circled his scalp. He had piercing brown eyes and thick brows that arched high over thick lashes that didn't appear natural. Judge Grafton had sent him and Siegel into the hallway outside the judge's chamber to confer on a date for a preliminary examination that would be convenient for both parties.

"Who hired you?" Siegel asked.

"That's a confidential matter," Gul replied in a baritone voice.

"Was it Ahmed Jinnah by any chance? What's his involvement in these matters?"

"Once again, Mr. Siegel, my employers will remain undisclosed, nor should it concern you. Suffice it to say that I have been paid a hefty retainer and plan to be involved in the Khan case over the long haul. He has quite an interesting defense to the charges fabricated by your office. I believe the public will be shocked when the true details come to light."

"Is that so? Care to enlighten me about your mystery defense?"

"All in good time," Gul replied. Then his eyelids suddenly fluttered and his features contorted, as if in pain.

Gul pitched forward slightly and Siegel placed a steadying hand on his shoulder. "Are you okay?" he asked.

Gul didn't reply, instead digging hurriedly into his pocket and producing a pill bottle. He shook a tiny tablet onto his palm and pinched it between a thumb and forefinger before placing it under his tongue. Gul squeezed his lids shut and screwed the cap back on the pill bottle, replacing it in his pocket. Silence ensued while Gul waited for the medicine to take effect. Siegel watched Gul's discomfort gradually melt away, until he finally opened his eyes again. There was a thin sheen of sweat on his lined forehead.

"Do you need an ambulance?" Siegel asked with concern.

"No, I'll be fine," Gul replied in a raspy voice. He removed a handkerchief from his breast pocket and mopped his head with it.

"Nitroglycerin?" Siegel volunteered.

"Yes," Gul sighed.

"How long have you had a heart condition?"

"Not long, perhaps six months since it was first diagnosed. I require an operation, but, due to certain health concerns, the doctors are unwilling to chance a surgery at this time."

"Sorry to hear that," Siegel remarked with genuine sympathy. "Why would you take on a case of this magnitude under the circumstances? Won't the strain be too much for you?"

"Perhaps," Gul conceded, appearing very drawn, "but it's a chance I'm willing to take."

"Why? What could possibly make it worthwhile to jeopardize your health like this?"

"It's a matter of justice, Mr. Siegel. There's a great wrong here that I intend to undo." Gul took a deep breath and dabbed at his forehead again. "Also, the money is tremendous."

CHAPTER 16

D ALE COX SAT IN Starbucks nursing a mocha while engaging in his favorite pastime, watching Irina Siegel work. She was the most gorgeous woman he'd ever seen, slim and shapely, well-endowed. But it was the shiny, dark hair, coupled with those pale blue eyes, that did him in. He'd loved her from the first time he saw her working the counter. It was like a lightning bolt struck. And she'd felt the same about him, at least until Max Siegel showed up one day and spoiled everything.

Cox hated Siegel. It grated on him whenever he had to talk to the man, which, lately, meant frequently. Siegel was on him a lot since the arraignment, demanding this and that, treating Cox like a personal assistant. The preliminary examination was set thirty days out and Siegel wanted Cox at his beck and call, as if Cox had no other cases to investigate.

Attorneys were such prima donnas with their sharp suits and college educations. They thought they were the shit. But none of them had an ounce of common sense. They knew nothing about the real world, sitting in their ivory towers, spewing bullshit crime theories gleaned from textbooks. The real education came from the streets; any cop worth his salt knew that. It's where reality lay, in the muck and grime of the gutter, something the pretty boys in suits could never understand, especially Max Siegel.

How would Siegel react if he ever discovered the truth about Khan? How shocked would he be? Cox doubted Siegel could grasp the overall implications of what had to be done and why. For all his education, Siegel was too naïve, too much of a Boy Scout to be trusted with reality.

Cox was sitting near the concession stand when Irina came along to wipe the counter. She avoided looking at him. "Hi, honey," he greeted.

"I told you to stop calling me that in the store. People will hear."

"I haven't seen you in a while. I miss you, dear."

Irina huffed. "Please shut up."

"Does Max know about us? Did you tell him?"

"There is nothing to tell. Leave me alone now."

Cox grinned, wrinkles forming on his pock-marked face. "You love playing hard to get, don't you? Max is gonna hafta know the truth one of these days. It's inevitable, sweetheart."

"Don't call me that," Irina said with marked irritation. Then she moved away.

Cox took in Irina hungrily as she maneuvered past customers and took a position by the cash register. Stirring the remainder of his mocha, he tipped the cup to his mouth and thirstily drank the remnants, wiping foam from his lips with his hand. He attempted to get Irina's attention when he walked to the exit, but she was busy and didn't notice him.

Walking along the street, Cox was surprised by a car swerving to a stop at the curb beside him. He sprang back a step in near panic until he saw the passenger window slide down then regained himself. Ross studied him through dark sunglasses. "Get in," he said. "We need to go for a ride."

Cox looked around before opening the rear door of the sedan and getting inside. He didn't notice Rappaport sitting in a car half a block away.

"You two scared the hell outta me," Cox said as the engine gunned and the car sped off. "You coulda called first if you wanted a meeting."

Ross turned in his seat while Frazier drove. "Matters are approaching a critical juncture," Ross said. "The parties have set a preliminary hearing a month from now and that won't do."

"How do we stop it?" Cox asked. "The wheels are already in motion."

"There are ways and there are ways, detective. We need to improvise. That hearing can't take place."

"It ain't my fault it got set. I did everything you asked."

"And you've done a fine job, we're not complaining. Your level of commitment has been exemplary. Officials in Washington are well informed about your cooperation."

"They are?" Cox beamed, a surge of pride welling inside.

"Absolutely," Ross replied, attempting a smile that didn't quite happen. "It's our good fortune we contacted you the night of this inconvenient incident. You're an asset that the bureau cherishes."

"Glad to hear that. It means a bunch to me."

"I like your attitude. We just wanted to tell you what good work you've done, but it's time to increase our efforts."

"Just say what you want done. I'm your man."

"Excellent! First, have you turned over the gun to the investigator yet?"

"I have it. I was gonna do that today."

"See to it. It's important you appear cooperative. It helps allay suspicions, delays pesky inquiries about apparent inconsistencies."

"Consider it done."

There was a pause in the conversation that turned into a lengthy gap as Ross studied Cox through his dark lenses. The silence lasted long enough that Cox began to feel uncomfortable under the scrutiny. A thin smiled stretched across Ross's lips, but it wasn't friendly. "We saw you speaking to Max Siegel's wife in the coffee shop."

Cox felt unnerved that he'd been under surveillance. He didn't know what to say.

Ross's smile grew. "We conducted a background investigation of our dashing prosecutor and his wife. It's uncovered some interesting details regarding Irina Siegel's past."

"I'm not following," Cox mumbled, feeling uncomfortable.

Ross produced a manila envelope and handed it to Cox. "They say you should never judge a book by its cover. In the case of Mrs. Siegel, that's especially true. She's an intriguing woman in more ways than one, although I don't need to tell you that, do I?"

"You're not making much sense, Agent Ross."

"Oh, come come, detective, it doesn't take a Sigmund Freud to discern your interest in Max Siegel's wife. It's quite obvious."

"That's getting a little personal, ain't you?"

"Yes, I am. That's the nature of my work, yours too, detective. We probe people's personal lives to find information helpful in obtaining what we want. It's not hard to discern what you want, Detective Cox. What's in that envelope may help you. Consider it a gift from your Uncle Sam."

"I don't get it."

"Read the information in the envelope. That should enlighten you. Use it. Ultimately, I think what you do with it will benefit both our desires. The clarity will come when you peruse the documents."

Cox clutched the envelope, twisting it around unsurely. He almost fell sideways when the sedan pulled to an abrupt halt at the Starbucks. They'd driven in circles. "Here you are," Ross said. "We'll be in touch."

Ross faced forward, as if suddenly oblivious to Cox's continued presence. Cox took his cue and opened his door and got out. The sedan sped away immediately after he slammed the door shut.

"This is unacceptable," the chief said, no mistaking his displeasure.

"Yes, sir, I agree completely," Ross replied into his cell phone. He was walking in the middle of a park, his wing tipped shoes sinking into the cold, wet grass.

"You have a mission: containment. That's why we sent you there. I put my reputation on the line by specifically choosing you. So imagine the disbelief when Las Cruces made it into the national spotlight? All the major networks are buzzing about a DA nearly getting blown up in what should be an obscure double homicide. How could you allow it?"

"I'm sorry, sir, it was out of my control."

"How can that be? You're pulling all the levers."

"Not quite, sir; rogue forces are at work."

"The president has gone through the roof. The chief of staff went ballistic on the director, who, in turn, gave my ass a good chewing. They called an emergency meeting of all the agency heads and there's one question we need an answer to: can the situation be salvaged?"

"It's not too late; there's still time."

"Are you sure? The panic button's ready to be pushed on this end. Walls are going up and all the chiefs are diving for cover. The news has the whole town on edge. What can you do to keep the powder keg from exploding?"

"Do you truly want to know, sir?"

There was a thoughtful pause. "No, I suppose not," the chief replied. "You're a highly competent professional. There shouldn't be a need for me to guide your every move."

"Absolutely not, sir."

"You know what the bottom line is and how to achieve it."

"Correct."

"That settles it then. I'm giving you full discretion to proceed as you see fit. Whatever restrictions you thought you were under are lifted. You have total decision-making capability. Understand?"

"Yes, sir."

"In fact, I don't see the need for any further communications about the matter, do you?"

"No, sir."

"Good, then it's your ballgame. You're completely on your own."

"Thank you for your confidence, sir. I won't let you down."

"I hope not, because if you do, it's the end for both of us. Are we clear?"

"Crystal, sir."

Ross flipped his cell phone shut and slipped it into his vest pocket.

Taking a deep breath, he expelled it slowly and saw white wisps fluttering into the cold air. Frazier made his way toward Ross in the middle of the grass field. "You don't look happy," Frazier observed.

"That's because I'm not. The chief's upset and apparently so is everybody else in the capital, including POTUS. Heads are going to roll soon, unless we can bring matters under control."

"That's a tall order under the circumstances. We got into the matter too late to sanitize it."

"Yes, we did, but that's the past. We need to concern ourselves with the future, ours in particular. We're in the center of a potential catastrophe that's about to do us in."

"Did the chief give any instructions?"

Ross turned his full attention to his partner. He'd previously been staring off into the distance. "He's done quite the opposite," he replied. "The chief is standing down. I have absolute discretion."

Frazier's brows rose. "Is it that critical?"

"Unfortunately, yes. Can't you smell the desperation? They want the problem solved and they don't care how we do it."

"How much further can we go? We already stepped way over the line."

"We've stretched the rules alright, but not enough. The chief's sudden absence is a signal that it's time to break a few. This is a golden career opportunity. If we pull this off, we'll have the gratitude of every power player in Washington, including the top office. They'll give us the world if we succeed."

"Yes, but if we screw it up…," Frazier said, letting the thought fade.

"If we screw it up, *we're* screwed," Ross said. "All I need to know at this time is whether you're with me. I plan to take actions to whatever extreme required to handle this situation successfully. Can I count on you to go along?"

"You have so far. I don't see any reason to change my attitude now. I'm with you, Ross."

"Good," Ross said, grinning like a mannequin.

CHAPTER 17

---•---

DARK CLOUDS MOVED IN over Las Cruces before nightfall and a light rain was falling by sunset. Normally, Siegel would have gone to his boxing gym for a workout he performed three times a week. Since his body was still wracked with aches and pains from the bombing, the thought of exercising didn't appeal to him in the slightest. The fact was he felt like a rodeo clown that had been stomped repeatedly by a rampaging, half-ton bull. Circumstances being what they were, he decided to skip the workout and meet Rappaport for a drink instead. Given his profession, Siegel usually avoided the local neighborhood bars when he wanted a stiff drink. Too many former defendants were wandering the streets of Las Cruces for Siegel's comfort, most of them inevitably landing in the popular watering holes. Siegel liked to avoid unnecessary confrontations whenever possible, so he chose to meet Rappaport at a Hilton hotel. It was out of the way and catered to an affluent clientele.

Siegel arrived at the bar first and sat at the crook of a horseshoe counter while a musician played tunes nearby on a baby grand piano. He ordered a Bloody Mary, spicy, and was stirring it with a swizzle stick when Rappaport took a seat next to him. His friend was limping slightly more than usual because of the cold, wet weather.

"I hope you don't mind, but I invited Dave Langerman to join us," Rappaport said.

"That'll be fine."

"I bumped into him on my way over and made the invite. I didn't think you'd care."

"Not at all, it'll be good to see Langerman."

"What'll you have?" the blond, female bartender asked Rappaport. She was young and pretty and scanning him with appreciative green eyes.

"I'll take a Heineken," Rappaport replied, oblivious to the attention.

The bartender gave him a lingering gaze when she returned with the beer and poured him a glass from the bottle. Rappaport thanked her and sipped the foamy head as she moved away.

"What's the matter, your radar switched off?" Siegel asked.

"Come again?"

Siegel leaned in close. "That bartender was checking you out and you're acting oblivious."

"She is?" Rappaport asked, genuinely surprised, his cheeks flushing red.

The bartender gave Rappaport a fetching smile, which he shyly returned before lifting his glass and taking a long swallow.

Siegel had seen it before. Rappaport was a rugged, generally good-looking man who lacked an ounce of self-esteem when it came to women, especially since his divorce. Siegel attributed it to Rappaport's injury. His limp was barely noticeable, but it wreaked havoc on his confidence. He'd been in and out of relationships since his wife left him, most of them killed quickly by Rappaport's insecurities. He was drifting toward middle-age alone for the most part and Siegel was beginning to think his friend preferred it that way.

"Cox dropped the murder weapon by my office earlier," Rappaport related, apparently wanting to change the subject.

"Just like that, huh?"

"Just like that. One minute he's stonewalling, giving me a hard time, next thing I know he's cooperating and being sweet as can be."

"He's a strange duck, isn't he?"

"That he is."

"What did you do with the gun?"

"I got the serial number off it first thing and ran a trace. It's like Cox said: the Glock was stolen during a residential burglary down in LA about six months ago. Either Khan was involved in that or, more likely, it made its way here and got sold in the streets."

"Let's not jump to conclusions."

"Oh, I never do, that's why I drove the gun up to Sacramento for a separate ballistics test. Before that I ran by the coroner's office and signed out one of the slugs they dug from the victim's body. I took the added measure of obtaining one of the bullets Cox was holding in the evidence room at LCPD, the one he had his ballistics people fire for comparison with the victim's slugs. I know the clerk over there and she let me borrow it on the QT."

"Why'd you do that?"

"Why not? I figure we might as well be thorough, since we're running a guerilla investigation."

Siegel raised his glass to Rappaport. "That's why you're one of the best, pal. You leave no stone unturned."

Rappaport lifted his glass and clinked it against Siegel's. He appeared thoughtful after taking a sip. "You know, I normally would have ignored taking the slug from Cox's evidence locker, but I saw something today that made me believe we should scrutinize his actions."

"What's that?"

"I started keeping tabs on him, like we talked about. Today I saw him leave Starbucks and take a ride with a couple of suits that picked him up at the curb. They drove around and eventually deposited him the same place they started from."

"Who were they?"

"It was hard following the car. I tried hanging back as much as I could. I almost couldn't get a plate number because whoever was driving engaged in counter surveillance tactics."

"But you obtained the plate number?"

"Barely."

"Who'd it trace to?"

"It was blocked on our CLETS system when I tried to punch it into the computer. When I made the trip to Sac later on, I took a detour to the Department of Motor Vehicles and talked to a few friends."

"You have acquaintances all over, don't you?"

"That I do, and it's a lucky thing, otherwise I wouldn't know that the Samaritans who provided chauffer service to Cox this morning are FBI."

"FBI? Why would he be talking to them?"

"Good question. The kind of contact I saw today is similar to how we handle confidential informants. They're talking to him without wanting people to know."

"Regarding our case? Khan?"

Rappaport shrugged. "Who knows? He's got a case load. He could be consulting the feds on any number of things."

"But he's been acting hinky on Khan, so has Danko. I was wondering why the boss pulled me out of Insurance Fraud to handle a homicide. He must be in on it, too. The feds must have talked to him about Khan and then he suddenly puts me on the case."

"And Danko doesn't like you."

"Not at all. He's certainly not throwing any peaches my way. So we have a murder that the feds are interested in. They're talking to the DA and the investigating detective about it, but trying to keep it secret from everybody else, including me—the prosecuting attorney. Why?"

"It might be something ominous, Max, but it could also be because that's how the feds operate. They're super secretive about everything they do. Those guys are full of themselves."

"No, it's more than that, Franny. If it was just an ego exercise, they'd let me in on the secret. What we're dealing with is more substantial. Let's put the pieces together. Khan kills two traveling salesmen and the FBI's all over it, but they don't take it to the U.S. Attorney. They cuddle up to the people controlling the case, but they want it hush-hush. Ahmed Jinnah—a person we spent most of last year trying to nail as a terrorist sympathizer—is imposing himself into the picture, apparently backing Khan. They're both Pakistani and both from the same neighborhood. On top of that, some high-priced Bay Area attorney is showing his face at arraignment—apparently unknown to the defendant—crying about righting some injustice. What's it add up to?"

."Khan and Jinnah are connected," Rappaport ventured. "Do we have a terrorist cell that the FBI's watching in our area?"

"That's what I'm thinking, and maybe they don't want to step in directly because they don't want their investigation compromised."

"Or maybe it's something more."

"Right, it could be."

"Why would Danko want to involve you?"

"Isn't it obvious? Last year the feds handed him a case on Jinnah that burned him. He doesn't trust them. Danko probably suspects a repeat, so who better to put in the middle than the attorney he most despises? I'm making noises that I might run against him next election, this is a chance to smear me if this case turns into a disaster."

"Maybe not the disaster he bargained for. Now you're a hero, a martyred DA who almost got blown to smithereens."

"It does raise my profile in the public eye, doesn't it? Danko couldn't have foreseen that. But I can do without any more publicity boosters."

"Here here," Rappaport said, raising his glass and draining the beer.

The bartender came right over when Rappaport set his empty glass down. "Get you another, honey?" she asked.

"Sure."

The bartender reached under the counter and produced another Heineken. She pressed the top against a bottle opener attached to the counter and popped the cap off, and then refilled Rappaport's glass. Siegel saw her looking at Rappaport while she finished the pour, attempting a silent flirtation, but his friend kept his vision directed at the glass, as if afraid to meet her eyes. The bartender was visibly disappointed by the snub and moved away dejectedly. Siegel shook his head and took a sip of his Bloody Mary.

Dave Langerman appeared at the entrance, a long, lean form, and sauntered to the bar, taking the stool next to Siegel. "Hello, boys," he greeted in his deep voice.

Siegel and Rappaport returned the salutation and the bartender approached to take Langerman's order. He gave her an appreciative look that made her blush, slowly rolling his eyes up and down, a devilish grin curling beneath his mustache. "Aren't you the gorgeous one," he commented. "I come to a classy bar to get service and find a Cosmopolitan cover girl manning the counter. I must've stepped into a slice of heaven."

The bartender pushed a strand of hair behind her ear, smiling broadly. "Oh oh, we got a charmer here," she said.

"I do try, darlin'."

"What can I get for you, cowboy?"

"A gin and tonic would do me fine, with a twist of lime if you don't mind."

"Coming up," the bartender said, reaching for a glass that she filled with ice. The two shared playful looks while the bartender prepared the drink. Siegel turned to Rappaport and grinned. "Writers," he said after the bartender walked away, "they'll do it every time, the romantic bastards."

"Sorry, am I stepping on somebody's toes?" Langerman asked.

"You're stepping on something, but it's not Franny's toes, big guy," Siegel replied.

The men shared a laugh.

"I suppose you two owe me, since I'll be doing some investigating for you over the weekend," Langerman declared after a bit.

"What are you talking about?" Rappaport inquired.

"I'm flying to Phoenix, Arizona, this evening to visit with family for a couple days."

"And?" Siegel prompted.

"And if you look at the title for the property where the murders happened, you might notice that the company claiming ownership is based in Phoenix."

"Pharmagroup," Rappaport offered.

"Very good," Langerman said. "Since I'll be in town anyway, I figure it wouldn't hurt to swing by the headquarters and see what they're about. It might not amount to anything, but what the hell? Never hurts to check, right."

"Not a bad idea," Siegel said.

"I'll look you fellows up when I get back Monday," Langerman continued. "I can tell you then if I find anything of interest."

"Thanks, Dave," Siegel said. "I'd appreciate any insights you produce, as long as you don't get the idea I owe you special treatment on the Khan case."

"Oh, hell no," Langerman chuckled. "I've finally come to realize that you're a miser without a conscience."

The men shared another bout of laughter that came to an abrupt end when three men entered the bar. One of them was Ahmed Jinnah. The two Pakistanis with him bore fierce expressions.

CHAPTER 18

A PERVASIVE QUIET SETTLED over the room when the three men wandered inside, Jinnah staring unabashedly at Siegel as they passed. The two men with Jinnah exchanged menacing looks with Rappaport, who rose slightly from his stool until Siegel put a restraining hand on his forearm. Jinnah and his crew proceeded to a booth at the far end of the room opposite Siegel's party. Jinnah sat on the bench facing Siegel and kept his attention riveted on the prosecutor from a distance.

"Do you believe this jackass?" Rappaport said, starting to rise again, ready to explode.

"Take it easy," Siegel soothed, despite the uneasiness growing in his gut. "They have a right to be here like anybody else."

"They're sending you a message, Max," Langerman noted in a low voice. "Showing up in this out-of-the-way spot tells you they know how to find you."

"That goes both ways," Rappaport said, his attention not wavering from the strangers, his jaw muscles visibly clenching with tension. "Right now we know where they are, too. If that ugly little bastard doesn't stop looking over here, I'm going to—"

"Do nothing," Siegel interrupted, his own heart racing. "Calm down, Franny. Don't let them see that they're getting to you. That's exactly what they want."

"Max is right," Langerman agreed. "Don't play into their hands."

"Okay," Rappaport relented, breaking the visual contact and sipping his beer. He was breathing hard and his cheeks and ears were bright red. Rappaport's blood was way up.

One of the men came to the bar and requested three orange juices, giving Siegel sideways glances while the bartender filled the order. Siegel alternated between watching him and Jinnah, whose beady eyes scrutinized Siegel with unshakeable intensity. Jinnah exchanged some remarks with his companions when the drinks were brought to his table, and then he resumed staring at Siegel.

"I believe our friend over there wants a parlay," Langerman observed.

"You may be right," Siegel agreed, rising from his stool. "Stay here, Franny."

"Are you sure?" Rappaport asked anxiously.

"I'll signal if I need anything."

Siegel proceeded boldly to the booth, where Jinnah and his cohorts registered slight surprise at his approach. Jinnah appeared small at close range. "Is there something you'd like to say to me?" Siegel asked.

"There are many things I'd like to say to you, Mr. Siegel. Perhaps a chat is in order."

"Fine with me, Mr. Jinnah."

"Is it possible that we could retire to the lounge, just you and me? I'd like to speak privately."

"Let's go."

The lounge near the concierge desk was quiet and dimly lit. Siegel and Jinnah left the bar and walked there alone, leaving the others inside. They found a set of comfortable chairs in a secluded corner and sat across from each other.

"May God be praised to find you in such good health after your recent ordeal," Jinnah began.

"Thank you. Since we're on the subject, maybe you can explain why I don't have a work car any longer."

Jinnah placed a gnarled brown hand against his chest. "You think *I* have knowledge about this incident?"

"You mentioned the wrath of God coming down on me and the next thing I knew two Pakistani-looking men attacked and blew my car apart. Yes, I'd make the assumption you know about it."

"You assume too much, Mr. Siegel. All I know of the attack comes from reading the newspaper and watching television. Despite the accusations your corrupt law enforcement agencies have leveled against me, I assure you I am a man of peace. I deplore violence, except at unfortunate times when it is necessary."

"When do you consider it necessary?"

"In self-defense, of course."

"How about in defense of your friend? Maybe you see me as a threat to Raheem Khan's life?"

"That you most definitely are. I am no lawyer, but I understand that California has the death penalty, which applies firmly in cases of murder with special circumstances. But I respect you as a servant of the law and would not resort to violence to stop my brother from being unfairly condemned. I choose to oppose you in other ways."

"Like in hiring a lawyer for Khan?"

"Yes, with donations from concerned members of the community."

"And some of those members are so concerned that they're willing to kill the prosecutor in the case?"

Jinnah closed his eyes and lowered his head. "Once again, Mr. Siegel, let me tell you that I had no hand in that violent act."

"Who did?" Siegel demanded, already becoming tired of Jinnah's smug game-playing.

Jinnah casually shrugged. "I wish I knew. Your office has accused me of leading a terrorist cell for quite some time. You have vested me with the powers of a puppeteer, the notion that I somehow control all Muslim people in the local area with a kind of absolute power. I wish you could see how untrue that is. I would love to have such authority. Unfortunately, it's only an illusion created by your leader, Richard Danko. My people are a headstrong and independent group, and individuals are quite capable of devising their own course of action."

"Are you saying it may have been Pakistanis who tried to kill me?"

"I don't know. It could be as you say, or it could be enemies from other matters you are handling. One can only guess. I imagine you create many grudges in your line of work."

"That I do, but nothing happened until I took on Khan's prosecution."

"Then perhaps you should take that as a warning," Jinnah said, his expression hardening.

"Are you threatening me?" Siegel asked defiantly, fighting hard to keep his anger in check.

"Not at all, I'm trying to help."

"I'm not stupid, Jinnah. You sit here playing cute games that are transparent as glass. I know you had a hand in the attempt on my life, and now you're trying in a roundabout way to tell me to get off the case."

Jinnah lifted a palm toward Siegel, his lids scrunching shut. "Please, Mr. Siegel, you are misinterpreting me." When he opened his eyes again, there was a peculiar, penetrating urgency in their depths. "I don't blame you for not believing my words, for reading bad intentions in my actions. These are strange times and truth has become clouded with confusion. But I am not lying when I say I want to discover who tried to kill you. I don't like shouldering the blame for something I didn't do."

"Okay, let's say I give you the benefit of the doubt, will you share any information you learn with my office? If you produce a name, will you relay it to our investigators?"

"That I can't do, I'm afraid. When I resolve the mystery, it will be dealt with in a way of my own choosing."

"That's what I figured," Siegel said with disgust. "This talk is nothing but a smokescreen, a chance for you to play twisted little games."

"We're getting nowhere with this discussion."

"I couldn't agree more," Siegel sneered.

"What a pity, I hoped we'd reach an understanding. I wanted us to have an accommodation."

"What accommodation? Raheem Khan murdered two men in cold blood and for that he's going to be convicted, end of story. This isn't a persecution, or some type of government conspiracy to punish people for 9/11; it's a murder case, pure and simple."

Jinnah's brows rose as Siegel spoke. He appeared surprised by Siegel's words. "Are you truly so sure of yourself?" he inquired. "Can such an educated man as yourself really be so naïve? The case against Raheem Khan is far from simple. You have unwittingly wandered into a murky realm of illusions, where nothing is quite what it seems. You're an intelligent man. I can't believe you haven't noticed the inconsistencies that are rife in this matter. Have you found nothing troubling since you took on the prosecution?"

"What are you getting at?" Siegel asked, beginning to feel unsettled.

Jinnah's expression became eager, as if he were on the verge of revealing something, until a sudden invisible wall went up and he emitted a sigh. Jinnah's chest deflated, his shoulders sank, and he collapsed into the backrest of his chair. "I've said too much. I can go no further in this discussion."

"You were going to tell me something. What is it?"

Jinnah's attention wandered and he became uncomfortable, obviously wanting to disengage. Siegel kept his gaze fixed on the man with steadfast determination, refusing to let the question go adrift. As if giving in to Siegel's will, Jinnah refocused on Siegel, but there was an exhausted, defeated look to him. "I can say nothing more at this time," he said. "We're not enemies, despite what you believe. I'm merely playing my role, as you must play yours."

"What roll? What are you talking about?"

"We all have roles to play, Mr. Siegel, and we conform our actions to the ones we have been assigned. 'A poor player that struts and frets his hour upon the stage and then is heard no more.' That's what Shakespeare said."

"This is gibberish."

"Perhaps," Jinnah sadly conceded, rising slowly to his feet. Siegel did the same. "I have done what I can," Jinnah said. "The rest will be God's will. It would be wise if you remove yourself from Raheem Khan's prosecution. You're a good man and I don't want to see evil befall you."

"Thanks for the concern, but I'm going to stick with it. And if any evil should befall me, I hope you're not connected to it, because if you are—"

Jinnah raised a hand. "There is no need for threats," he said, cutting Siegel off. "I promise I will have nothing to do with any violence against you. Go with God, Mr. Siegel." Jinnah's dark eyes locked onto Siegel's with an ominous coldness that was unsettling. Then he averted his gaze and proceeded to walk away with a slow deliberation.

When they returned to the bar, Jinnah collected his companions and they left without touching their drinks. Jinnah kept from looking at Siegel as he walked out, but the other two weren't shy about giving the lawyer hard, murderous stares. Rappaport sprang to his feet, ready for a brawl, but Siegel held him back again.

Langerman took off a short time later in order to catch his flight. He was eager to hear about Siegel's discussion with Jinnah but disappointed when Siegel kept mum about the details. Langerman shook his head while departing, his mouth stretched to one side in disgust, but he left the subject alone.

"Okay," Rappaport said, leaning into Siegel, "now that Jimmy Breslin's gone, mind telling me what the hell you and Jinnah talked about?"

"Nothing that you wouldn't expect," Siegel responded. "He denied involvement with the car bomb and claimed he wished me no harm."

"What a crock," Rappaport spat.

"Yeah, so I thought," Siegel replied, his attention noticeably drifting off.

"What is it?" Rappaport asked.

"I don't know," Siegel said, lifting his drink and draining it. "A few things Jinnah said bothered me."

"Like what?"

"Maybe not so much what he said, but how he said it."

"What are you getting at?"

"Franny, you were in the arraignment today. You've been a cop for a long time. You know how to size up criminals, right?"

"I hope so. I wouldn't be worth much in this business if I didn't have those instincts."

"You saw Khan in the courtroom. What was your impression?"

"Come again?"

"Forget the case and all your preconceptions about his guilt. If you were in that courtroom, seeing Raheem Khan for the first time and didn't know squat about him, what would your impression be?"

"I don't get it," Rappaport said stubbornly. "This isn't a mystery we're trying to solve. Two victims got killed and Khan was caught red-handed. He ran right into Bernard Harris immediately after the act. Why are we discussing his demeanor in court? What difference does it make?"

"I've tried a lot of homicides," Siegel said, undaunted. "I've spent years watching killers parade in and out of court. One thing that's always struck me about every one of them is that certain look they have, especially in the eyes. Some are angry. Some are scared. Some don't have any emotions at all, but what they all share in common is that look, that emptiness inside that they can't hide. It takes a certain soullessness to kill in cold blood, and the people who possess that quality can't escape that look."

"What are you getting at?" Rappaport asked suspiciously.

"I didn't see it in Khan today. It wasn't there. And I didn't see it at the hospital either. It's a detail that's been nagging me since this whole thing began."

"You're overanalyzing, counselor," Rappaport declared with a forceful tone. "Fact: Raheem Khan did it. We have no dispute about that. Fact two: you're no psychic. With all due respect to your powers of observation, Max, you're only human. Even you can be wrong once in a while. I don't care how much experience you have. Don't go getting all mystical on me, buddy.

"Maybe Khan's not a cold-blooded killer," Siegel ventured. "Maybe he only intended to boost a few items and got caught in the moment. Defendants kill for lots of reasons, you know how it goes. Khan might not have realized anybody was in the house and panicked when he found out otherwise. He killed his first victim with a butter knife, Franny, and then tossed him out the window. That's about as personal as it gets. Why didn't he just use the gun? The pieces don't quite fit, amigo. You have to see that. We're missing something that fully explains what happened that night, but I have no idea what it is."

Rappaport lapsed into silence, reluctantly conceding that maybe Siegel had a point.

CHAPTER 19

———◆———

DURING HIS DRIVE HOME, Siegel couldn't shake the sense that he was being followed and it made him tense. He kept the radio turned off during the trip so he could concentrate. All he heard—besides the motor—was the beating of the wiper blades against the windshield as he traveled along darkened streets in the rain. Siegel constantly checked his mirrors, thinking from time to time that he spotted a suspicious car, only to see its headlights turn off onto another road. By the time he reached home, Siegel had chalked his nervousness up to paranoia, concluding that he'd been spooked by Ahmed Jinnah's ominous warning.

Siegel parked his car beside Irina's Lexus in the attached garage and walked into the adjoining kitchen as she was setting the wireless phone on the counter. She appeared stricken, her skin the color of alabaster, her pale, blue eyes reflecting hurt and fear.

"What's wrong?" Siegel asked, rushing over and grasping her shoulders.

"Max, you're home," Irina responded shakily, her eyes misty.

"What is it?" Siegel reiterated. "Who were you talking to?"

"It's nothing," Irina quickly replied, sniffling and obviously shaken.

"What do you mean nothing?" Siegel asked impatiently, extending his arms, pushing Irina away so he could study her. "You're upset about something. Tell me what it is"

Irina turned her face from side to side, trying to escape Siegel's scrutiny. Overcome with emotion, her throat was tight when she spoke. "Please believe me when I tell you it's nothing, a silly spat between women."

"Who was on the phone?" Siegel pressed with growing concern.

"An old friend from Sacramento," Irina replied, her features contorting.

"I didn't think I would hear from her ever again, and then she called and..."

"And what?" Siegel implored.

Irina broke away from his tight grip. "Oh, Max, can't you leave me alone?" she pleaded and rushed from the kitchen when the tears began to flow.

Siegel considered going after Irina, until he heard her sobbing in the bathroom. He was plunged into confusion by her strange behavior and stood helplessly for a few minutes, wondering what he should do. Feeling like a spy, he checked the wireless phone to get the number of the last caller, but saw it was restricted. Siegel became more unsettled, knowing something was terribly wrong but unable to do anything about it. He went into the master bedroom while Irina remained sequestered in the guest bathroom and changed out of his suit and took a shower. After toweling off, he dressed in night clothes and made his way to the living room, where he found Irina curled on the edge of a sofa blankly watching the television. She looked up at him when he approached, her lashes matted together in tiny points, still wet from the tears she'd shed. Irina gave Siegel a wan smile and wrapped her arms around him in a tight embrace when he sat down, burying her face against his shoulder.

"Better now?" he asked, gently stroking her flowing hair.

"A little," was her muffled response. "Please give me time, darling."

They sat in silence for a while, Irina resting her head against Siegel while the television droned unintelligibly. Irina's breathing became steady after a bit and Siegel realized she was sleeping. Not wanting to wake her, he remained still and listened to the deep sounds of her slumber while thoughts swirled in his mind.

Irina's odd behavior had stirred something in the depths of Siegel's psyche, dredging up a host of doubts he'd carried into their marriage. From the day Irina strolled down the chapel isle and they'd exchanged I dos, Siegel had always wondered whether they'd rushed into their union.

After years of bachelorhood, Siegel was captivated by Irina, but at times he found her inscrutable. Her actions tonight, along with her murky past, made Siegel wonder just how well he really knew his wife. The air of mystery he used to find so intriguing about Irina, now scared him. He loved her, truly and deeply, but nagging doubts were beginning to surface in some ways.

Siegel let Irina sleep until late into the night, and then he turned off the television and woke her, escorting her to bed. Not a minute ticked by before Irina resumed her heavy breathing, lying on her side near the edge of the mattress, her back to Siegel. He tried to snuggle, but Irina was unresponsive. Feeling rebuffed, Siegel eventually moved to his own side of the bed and drifted into a fitful slumber.

Irina was still remote the next morning, although she did her best to pretend otherwise. It was Saturday, and Siegel took her to a local eatery where they had breakfast before deciding to drive into San Francisco. During the ride, Siegel attempted to broach the subject of the previous evening, but Irina deflected his queries with noncommittal comments. Mostly, they discussed the insurance claim he filed regarding his blown up car. Luckily, they had three. The one they lost was paid off and used strictly for commuter purposes. Throughout the conversation, Siegel noticed a vacancy in Irina, like she was preoccupied. He decided to avoid probing what was bothering her for a while, concluding that she'd eventually open up when she felt the time was right.

They spent the day strolling the piers and ducking into shops when the brisk ocean breezes blowing in over the water got too cold. At times, Irina would relax and had brief episodes of normalcy, only to lapse time and again into moody silence.

Occasionally, Siegel felt himself peering over his shoulder, or studying passing faces when they walked through throngs of people, as an uneasy sense gradually occurred to him that he was being watched. He never detected anything suspicious, but he couldn't shake the feeling once it took hold. Whenever he and Irina passed a shop or restaurant, he scanned the reflections in windows, searching for signs of stalkers, but never seeing anyone. Eventually, Siegel decided he was just being jumpy. Silently chastising himself for his edginess, Siegel attributed the nervousness to his recent brush with death and his talk with Jinnah. He tried to divert his thoughts by concentrating on Irina, but his trepidation was stubborn and refused to go away.

When it grew dark, Siegel and his wife wandered into the North Beach area and had dinner at an Italian restaurant. They drank red wine with their meal, but stopped when Irina complained of a headache. After supper, they decided to drive home.

It was pitch black on the Altamont Freeway. The dark sky was overcast, cloud-cover blocking out everything but a sliver of moon and a few stars. Siegel wondered if they'd be caught in a downpour before they reached Las Cruces. He hoped not, because visibility was horrible and the traffic was thick. Rain would make the driving miserable.

The weather didn't burst until Siegel was piloting the car down his street. Then the rain came in an onslaught of heavy droplets that pelted the windshield in a watery deluge. Siegel eased into the attached garage of his home and cut the engine. He was surprised when he and Irina were getting out of the car and he caught sight of another car at the foot of the driveway. It was barely rolling along when the automatic door of the garage shut tight and obstructed Siegel's view. He rushed nervously to the door and pressed his hands against the wood, peering through a small square of glass, his heart suddenly thumping in his chest.

"Max, what is it?" Irina called out.

The car came to a complete stop, its headlights cutting a swath in the night. Siegel's home was built on a grade, so he looked down on the car, an old model Mercedes sedan. Its windows were blackened and he could barely make out the shadowy features of the driver. Siegel sensed more people were in the car, but he couldn't be certain.

"Max, tell me," Irina said, starting toward him.

Siegel stretched a hand at her. "Go inside, honey," he said.

"What is it?"

"Do what I say, please!" Siegel implored, urgency in his tone. "Give me a second."

As Irina reluctantly opened the interior door to the house, Siegel dashed in her direction, hitting the button by the doorjamb. Irina hesitated and he gave her a push through the kitchen door, pulling it closed behind her. The gears of the garage door sprang to life and it slowly opened. Siegel rushed toward the moving door and waited until he had a clear view of the Mercedes—which was halted in the road—before starting down the driveway. His senses came alive in that moment, a heightened state of readiness pervading him in anticipation of the potential danger he was plunging toward, fear mixed with an odd excitement. Before he could get to the street, however, the car's engine suddenly revved to life and it peeled off, tires squealing. Siegel ran after it in a futile sprint, his legs pumping desperately as he tried to get a read on the license plate while the Mercedes accelerated away. The rain drenched him, thoroughly soaking his clothes, as the car turned a corner and vanished before Siegel could make out anything.

He remained in the middle of the street after the car was gone and scanned the surroundings while the rain continued to wash over him in sheets. The droplets were cold and stinging and he began to shiver. Starting back toward his home, he saw Irina's silhouette appear at a window and Siegel stared at her form while he climbed the driveway. The shadow disappeared before he made it into the garage and closed the door.

"What was that about?" Irina asked with deep concern when Siegel entered the house. "Look at you, you're dripping wet. What happened?"

"I don't know," Siegel replied. "Maybe it's nothing, or maybe we were followed."

"What?!"

"I saw a car outside. It stopped in front of the house."

Irina's hand flew to her mouth in fright. "My God, Max, what are we going to do? Is it the same men that tried to hurt you?"

Siegel crossed the room to Irina and took her by the shoulders, pulling her to him. "It's a mystery to me who it was," he said. "For all I know, it was somebody looking for an address and I spooked him. My nerves are on edge since the attack. It's possible my imagination's running wild."

"Should we call somebody as a precaution?"

"And tell them what? That I saw a car stop by the house and take off again? That isn't enough to sound an alarm."

"Max, I'm scared."

"Don't be, everything will be alright. I'll lock up and set the alarm. Let's not call anybody unless something substantial happens. We'll just be very careful, very vigilant for a while, until this case is finished."

"I don't like what is happening."

"Neither do I, but we'll get through it."

Irina peered deeply into Siegel's eyes. "I hope you are right," she said desperately.

Siegel studied her cautiously, suddenly wondering if they were talking about the same thing.

"Oh!" Irina exclaimed. "You're making me all wet. Take these clothes off and get into something dry before you get sick."

"Yes, mama."

Irina smiled a genuine smile that made her eyes crinkle. For a moment, she was her old self again. Siegel kissed her and she returned the kiss with urgency before breaking away and tugging at his jacket. "Let's get you changed," she said, the forlorn mask beginning to settle over her features again like a falling curtain.

Siegel awoke early Sunday morning after a restless night of frequent trips to the window to peek through the blinds. When he did manage to drop off, his sleep was plagued by phantom noises that continuously roused him awake. But all he ever detected as he lay in the dark was the pitter-patter of falling rain.

He felt exhausted when he crept out of bed in the twilight of semidarkness and heard the storm continuing outside. Irina remained asleep while he gathered his gym gear and quietly made his way to the garage. He paused at the bottom of the driveway after backing his Honda

Accord out and didn't drive away until the garage door was firmly shut and he was convinced the coast was clear.

Siegel's boxing gym was located in what used to be a warehouse on the outskirts of town. It was a square, concrete building set in the midst of weeds and scrub grass at the edge of a two-lane highway. The gym had a nondescript façade, except for the faded painting of a pair of red boxing gloves above the metal entrance doors. It was a no-frills place from the old era, before workout facilities became sheik, and that's what Siegel liked about it. The equipment was ancient, the punching bags patched and sagging, the wooden floor full of splinters, and the walls colored prison gray. The air inside was always thick, smelling of blood and sweat and toil. It was where hard men came to work to exhaustion, where bone and muscle were forged into steel.

Siegel arrived at the gym and said hello to the old man with one cloudy eye, who sat behind the counter. There were only five other clients working out at the time, so Siegel had the run of the floor. He went back to the locker room and changed, stuffing his clothes into his tall metal locker and padlocking it. Then he returned to the gym floor and pulled a jump rope off a hook and started working.

Siegel did a full routine, skipping rope for half an hour to get a good sweat going, then putting on a pair of gloves and working the heavy bag for another twenty minutes. He spent some time doing alternating sets of push-ups and sit-ups and finished with fifteen minutes on the speed bag. A husky young Mexican challenged Siegel to a sparring session, but Siegel was spent and declined the invitation.

He didn't bother showering, preferring to do that at home. Siegel went to his locker and gathered his things, folding them and carefully placing them in his bag before heading back out to the gym. He saw more gym-rats crowding the floor and maneuvered through them to the exit. Waving good-bye to the cloudy-eyed, old man, Siegel went outside where the rain was still falling. Gray clouds covered the sky and cast everything in semidarkness, despite the time being near noon. The rain actually felt good to Siegel as he packed the trunk of the Accord. His body was overheated from exertion and the icy droplets soaking into his gym clothes felt refreshing. Slight, steamy bands of vapor rose from his shoulders when he scooted into the driver's seat of the car.

The vehicles in the unpaved lot were parked haphazardly. Siegel had to steer carefully when backing away from the building in order not to hit any of the zigzagged cars in his path. Shifting into drive, Siegel pointed the Accord toward the highway and prepared to navigate to the road.

His foot on the brake pedal, Siegel lifted a water bottle from the center console and unscrewed the cap, fumbling it between his fingers until the cap fell onto the floorboard. Siegel leaned over to retrieve it and heard a bang on the windshield, followed by a tinkling sound. He rose slightly above the dashboard and was surprised to see a round hole in the glass over the steering wheel. Looking ahead, he saw a shadowy form in a crouch, about fifteen feet in front of the car. In a split, horrifying second, Siegel realized the figure was pointing a gun. Stunned, Siegel dipped his head toward the passenger seat and heard two more loud bangs, followed by more tinkling as bits of glass fell onto his face and scalp.

Reacting quickly, his mind ablaze with disbelief, Siegel steeled himself and hoisted up enough to push the gearshift on the console into drive. With his left hand on the steering wheel, Siegel jammed his foot on the gas pedal and headed straight toward the shooter in a desperate move to slam into him. He heard more pops above the roar of the engine and peered over the dash in time to see a man cartwheeling away from the hood of the car. Siegel sprang upright as the car bounced onto the highway, shooting across the road while brakes screeched from oncoming vehicles. Siegel's Accord continued forward, bouncing again when it left the asphalt and plowed through a field of wet weeds. His body jerked violently forward when Siegel slammed on the brakes, his chest compressing painfully against the steering wheel. Gripped with panic, his skin prickly with extreme anxiety, Siegel whipped around and looked through the rear window after skidding to a halt.

Through the rain, Siegel saw the car he'd nearly hit stalled on the shoulder of the highway. Across the street, he detected the shadowy form of a man limping hurriedly to a waiting Mercedes—the same car he'd seen the night before—that peeled off down the road once the man jumped inside. Patrons emerged from the building, attracted by the commotion, and the driver of the stalled car was getting out when Irina leapt into Siegel's frenzied thoughts.

Realizing that his wife was home alone, Siegel felt a fearful shock ripping through him. Spinning the steering wheel, he gunned the engine, fishtailing the car onto the highway. Tires screeching against wet asphalt, Siegel accelerated down the road, the driver from the stalled car chasing behind him on foot. Siegel watched the figure shrink from view in his mirror, and then concentrated on the road ahead, grimly determined to protect his wife from the danger heading her way.

Irina was in the kitchen pulling a cup of hot water from the microwave when she heard a crash at the front door. The noise startled her and she dropped the cup to the tiled floor and it shattered, spraying her ankles with scalding liquid. Irina shrieked in pain as a heavy rumbling came through the house. Turning fear-filled eyes toward the doorway, she saw Siegel emerge in the opening, hair and clothes askew, a feral look contorting his features.

"Irina!" Siegel shouted when he saw her squatting on the floor. "Are you okay?"

"Max?"

Siegel rushed to Irina and lifted her to her feet by the shoulders with powerful hands. "Did somebody hurt you?" he roared, looking wildly about. "Is somebody here?"

"No … Max … I … I just dropped a cup when I heard the door."

Siegel clamped his hands to Irina's ears and studied her closely, relief seeping into his features. "You're okay, then?" He hugged her to his chest. Irina could feel the thumping of Siegel's heart against her cheek. "My God," Siegel sighed, "I thought they got you."

Irina drew her head back, pushing away from Siegel. "Who are you talking about?"

Siegel slid his hands to Irina's shoulders and held firmly. "It happened again, baby," he said breathlessly, his palms quivering with nervous energy against her flesh. "They tried to kill me!"

"No!" Irina gasped. "Not again."

"We can't stay here," Siegel declared. "Gather your things together. We're getting a place where they can't find us."

"Max, will we be safe?"

"Hurry, there's no time to waste!"

CHAPTER 20

———◆———

RICH DANKO WAS IN a high state of agitation. He was in his office on Monday morning pacing by the bay windows while reading the newspaper. He couldn't believe the headlines: "Clay County DA Attacked Second Time." Max Siegel's picture was plastered on the front page above a harrowing account detailing how the prosecutor managed to avoid another narrow brush with death less than a week after the first attempt on his life. The story was heavy with implications that Siegel's stalkers were somehow connected to the Khan murder case and finished with a quote from Siegel about how nothing was going to sway him from seeking justice in the Pleasant Oaks slayings.

Danko treated the paper roughly while paging through the story, crumpling and stretching it in hands that shook with barely contained rage. When he finished reading the account, he returned to the front page and held it taut, glaring at Siegel's bigger than life, handsome features, a headshot of him peering off camera with a steely look of determination in his blue, blue eyes. Danko couldn't hold it in any longer, frantically shredding the paper apart with his hands and letting the strips fall to the floor.

Storming to his desk, Danko snatched the receiver from the phone and jabbed a finger at the intercom button. "Yes, sir," Julie's voice responded.

"Where's Sims?" Danko demanded. "I sent for him fifteen minutes ago."

"Coming through the door now."

On cue, the door opened and Bernie Sims stepped tentatively over the threshold.

"Get in here and close the door," Danko growled unceremoniously. "Do you see this?" he asked, indicating the pile on the floor.

"It's a mess. Do you want me to get a janitor?"

"Have a seat, smart guy," Danko ordered.

Sims obediently squatted in one of the chairs fronting Danko's desk. Danko's coat was off, his white shirt rumpled, his red suspenders tight against massive shoulders. He was moving about like a caged bear. "Max Siegel's all over the news again," Danko announced. "We stuck him on this case so it could be his undoing. Instead, he's turning into a goddamned hero figure! How is this happening?"

"I heard he abandoned his home," Sims said. "He and his wife are staying in some undisclosed location for safety's sake. The police are pissed. They're planning to roust the east side with a mass of warrant services and probation and parole searches. It's going to stir up a hornet's nest."

"Who's going after Siegel? They're the most inept assassins walking the planet!"

"You sound disappointed, Rich," Sims said, watching the DA warily.

Danko stopped pacing and glared at his assistant. "Two times now the bastards have made their play. You'd think they'd learn how to shoot straight."

"Boss, you have to be careful with what you say."

"Careful!" Danko bellowed. "Siegel wants to cut my balls off in the next election. His star is on the rise and you're telling me to be careful?"

"Don't get me wrong, I'm with you all the way. But you can't forget that you're the DA and Siegel's one of your deputies. The man's being victimized in a murder case and you have to appear to be standing by his side."

"Are you serious?"

"Don't let personal feelings get the better of you. Siegel's in the spotlight at the moment. The best way to deal with it is to soak up some of the light for yourself. It'll go over well with the public."

"Yeah, I see your point. I'll call a news conference later and express solidarity with my poor, beleaguered deputy," Danko said with disgust.

"Now you're talking."

Danko turned toward the windows and clamped his hands behind his back. Sunlight was peeking through a dissipating cloud cover. He stared contemplatively at shafts of light radiating through breaks in the gray cumulus. "This is the second time the feds have stuck me with a dud, and they still haven't mentioned any deals about calling off that bullshit corruption investigation they're running against me. This Khan thing was supposed to be a blessing. Instead, it's turning into another curse. Somehow or other, we have to figure out a way to turn the situation in our favor. I don't care what we do to pull it off, but the Khan case needs to end with Siegel's head in a basket, not mine."

"Have faith, Rich," Sims soothed. "There's still a lot of road to travel before the case is over. You should go along for now, while we sit back and wait for an opportunity. One's bound to happen sooner or later. When it does, we'll pounce."

Danko turned slowly to his number two, a vicious grin on his mouth. "You're a devious son of a bitch, aren't you?"

"All to serve you, boss," Sims replied obsequiously. "I'll do whatever you want to take down Max Siegel."

Siegel was busy at his desk when there was a knock at the door. Rappaport poked his head inside. "You busy?" he inquired.

"Not anymore. Come in."

"How goes it?" Rappaport asked, limping into the room.

"I'm about as well as can be expected for someone surviving another assassination attempt," Siegel replied sullenly, his body filled with aches and pains that seemed to be pinning him to his chair.

Rappaport eased into a seat in front of Siegel's desk. "That's what I wanted to touch bases about, to let you know we're not laying down on this matter. LCPD and the sheriffs are conducting sweeps throughout the east side as we speak. Ahmed Jinnah and his boys are going to be put through the wringer until we catch your would-be killers."

"Will it work?"

"It's worth a try."

"I don't know, pal," Siegel said doubtfully, slowly shaking his head. "This could stir up a lot of simmering tensions in the Muslim community."

"To hell with that!" Rappaport declared angrily, his complexion reddening. "They tried to kill you twice. Those people need to know who calls the shots around here. What they did can't be tolerated."

Siegel was thoughtful, pausing for a few long seconds before he spoke again. "That's true only *if* it's them, Franny. We don't know for certain."

"Maybe you don't, but I do!" Rappaport replied, incredulous at what his friend had said.

"Easy, buddy, I'm the one who almost got executed, remember? You're more out of sorts than I am."

"Sorry, Max, guess I'm getting thin-skinned in my middle-age."

Siegel looked at his friend with concern. Rappaport was wound tight, but Siegel could see it had to do with more than the latest incident. For all his attempts at pretending otherwise, Rappaport had unresolved issues surrounding his disability. The fall from the plane years ago had wrought profound changes in his personality, creating a permanent edginess that was never there prior to the accident.

"I want you to relax, Franny," Siegel said. "Everything will turn out for the better. Whoever those guys are, they're obviously amateurs. They took their best shot twice and missed both times. I appreciate your concern, but you don't need to worry so much. I can take care of myself."

Rappaport looked sharply at Siegel. "You can't possibly be this cool, not in your position."

Siegel held Rappaport in a stern gaze that eventually cracked, melting into a helpless grin. "You're right," he conceded. "Truth is I'm scared out of my wits, but I'm trying hard not to show it."

Rappaport smiled, the tension visibly draining from him. "That's more like it. You had me going there for a while, Charles Bronson. I was beginning to think you were more macho than me."

"No, your macho creds are still intact," Siegel reassured.

"How's Irina?"

"Okay. She was pretty shaken up when I told her what happened. After I got home, we spent about twenty minutes packing before we hightailed it out of town. We're staying in a motel for now. Irina's taking the day off to look for an apartment we can lease until the case resolves."

"Sounds drastic."

"What do they say? 'Drastic times call for drastic measures.' I don't know if it was necessary to take this step, but I'd rather be safe than sorry. Somebody followed us home the night before last. I'll feel a whole lot better if no one knows where we're sleeping in the future."

"We can get you protection, if that's what you need."

"No, I prefer to handle this myself. Playing by the numbers means too many people having access to where I live, including Danko and friends. I'm not sure I'd like that."

"You don't trust our own people?"

"What do you think? The man pulls me away from Insurance Fraud and suddenly hands me a homicide case that's possibly responsible for two murder attempts on my life in less than a week. On top of that, he knows I plan to dethrone him come next election. If you were in my shoes, would you trust him with your secret location?"

"No, I suppose not."

Dave Langerman stood outside the crime scene house watching the yellow police tape that was stretched across the entrance bouncing raggedly in a stiff breeze. He'd been back from his trip for a few hours and felt compelled to have a look inside the home. Images of Arizona flitted through his mind, especially the sunbaked plot of land he'd stood on at the end of a dusty road outside Phoenix. It was considerably warmer there than in California, and Langerman remembered feeling the heat from the sun slightly scorching the back of his neck as he stood outside his rented car staring at the emptiness around him. Hands wedged into back pockets, Langerman walked about the shoulder of the road, twigs and gravel crunching underfoot.

A lone, dusty car had sped by, its engine a far off buzz as it approached, gradually morphing into the noise of a roaring engine that subsided again once it gained distance. Langerman figured he must have been a peculiar sight, a lone man standing by the road in the middle of nowhere. A hawk circled overhead in the sundrenched blue sky. It let out a fearsome cry and Langerman squinted as he watched it flying in languorous, twists and turns....

Back in the present, Langerman scanned the quiet cul-de-sac and saw that nobody was about. When he was satisfied that the coast was clear, Langerman walked toward the front door, ducking beneath the yellow police tape, and opened the unlocked door. Grinning as he passed inside, Langerman never ceased to be amazed at how unsecure secured crime scenes were. Once the initial investigation was over, locations tended to be an open house that anyone could wander into.

He stepped tentatively into the empty home, calling out a hello while strolling through the living room. There was no response. Langerman wandered into the kitchen, continuing to call out until he was satisfied he was alone. Then he felt free to roam and search at will. He covered the entire residence, looking into and around every cabinet, every piece of furniture, every nook and cranny. Langerman wasn't sure what he was searching for, or if he would know what it was when he found it. He was running on instinct, a gut feeling that there was something to uncover.

Saving the bedroom for last, Langerman entered and had a look around. The place was a disaster and he felt the first pangs of disappointment that he was possibly wasting his time. The floor was littered with trash and remnants of macaroni and cheese that was ground into the woodwork.

After a cursory search of the room, including the closets and dresser, Langerman checked the bed, lifting the top mattress from each corner and sliding his hand over the surface of the box spring. Still nothing. Langerman stood and gave the room a last look, pinching his lower lip with a thumb and forefinger. The reporter felt foolish. He'd come to the crime scene on a vague hunch and gotten nothing.

Langerman was on his way out of the room when the filthiness of the floor caught his attention. It occurred to him what a mess it must have been on the evening of the killings. Langerman looked at the bottom of the bed and an idea came to him. Choosing a clean side of the bed, he got delicately to his knees. Pressing his ear to the floor, he scanned beneath the bed until he caught sight of a metallic glint toward the area of the headboard. Langerman's heartbeat quickened when he reached a hand toward the object, stretching his arm as far as it could go. The tips of his fingers touched the object and clawed at it until it came into his grasp. When he had it fully in hand, Langerman pulled the object out and rose to his knees.

He'd found something important.

CHAPTER 21

———◆◆———

DALE COX ENTERED AHMED Jinnah's small variety store with a contingent of uniformed city police officers and sheriff's deputies. Jinnah was behind the counter with a worker when the cops came through the door and dispersed throughout the narrow aisles.

"What is the meaning of this?" Jinnah demanded. "Why are you coming into my store?"

"Relax, Jinnah," Cox said, sauntering cockily to the counter. "We're here on legitimate police business."

"Your men are entering the back room!" Jinnah noted excitedly. He started to come around the counter, but Cox and another uniformed officer blocked his way.

"Stay where you are," Cox directed. "We're searching the premises."

"By what right?" Jinnah asked, his color darkening.

"You can thank your boy there," Cox replied, indicating the young man next to Jinnah. "Mohammed Iktar is on probation for misdemeanor receiving. One of his conditions of probation is a search waiver that we're invoking."

"That's ridiculous. He's only a worker here. This is my store."

"The condition extends to his place of business or surroundings. While he's here, that puts us within our rights to search. Why don't you chill and let my men do their job?"

"This has been happening all day to the people of this neighborhood," Jinnah stated heatedly. "Do you think I am stupid? You're retaliating against innocent people for the trouble caused to that lawyer in the DA's office. This is the height of racism. We have done nothing and you are treating us like a pack of criminals."

131

"Settle down, Mr. Jinnah," Cox said, smirking slightly. "We're doing no such thing. Since you bring it up though, maybe you can tell us something about the persons assaulting Max Siegel. The perpetrators looked a lot like your people."

"My people? What are you talking about? I cannot believe the prejudice I am hearing."

"Prejudice ain't got nothing to do with it," Cox replied, obviously enjoying the exchange. "You're the one that stood on the courthouse steps making all sorts of incendiary statements about the DA. What do you expect to happen when that's followed by a car bombing and shots fired at the man later on?"

"You believe this is funny, officer, but I am not laughing."

"Detective."

"What?"

"I'm a detective, not a patrol officer."

"I don't care what you are!" Jinnah snapped. The young man next to him looked on fearfully. "This is all a joke to you because you have the power, because we are helpless to respond to your show of force. But we are not a helpless people as you believe."

"Careful, Jinnah."

"No, you be careful … detective. I am warning you that we cannot be treated like this. There will be consequences for these actions and you can arrest me if you want for saying it. I don't care."

Cox glared murderously at Jinnah, his pock-marked face flushing a bright shade of red. Without thinking, he reached into the breast pocket of his sports jacket and pulled out Bernard Harris's sap. Clutching it tightly, he dropped the hand to his side, while his other hand balled into a fist.

"What is that?" Jinnah shouted, pointing at the weapon. "Are you going to assault me?"

Cox was gritting his teeth, incensed at having his authority challenged. His anger was boiling and about to overflow. Cox tensed for action and Jinnah's orbs bulged when he perceived the violence about to erupt.

"We didn't find anything," an officer announced to Cox, who remained fixated on Jinnah. "Detective Cox? Did you hear me?"

The spell snapped and Cox turned to the officer, a bead of sweat rolling down his forehead. "What was that?"

"The area's clean," the officer said. "We didn't find any contraband."

"Fine," Cox responded. "Let's pack it in."

"Sure thing, detective."

Cox calmly, deliberately replaced the sap in his pocket while wearing an oily grin. "Looks like you lucked out," he said to Jinnah, "at least this time. We'll be back, though, you can count on it, over and over again until we find the murdering bastards that keep trying to kill one of our precious DAs."

Jinnah was speechless, peering at Cox in disbelief as the detective followed the other officers out of the store.

Ross and Frazier were parked slightly down the street from Jinnah's store. Cox spied them when he emerged onto the sidewalk. After ordering an officer to proceed to the next location, Cox crossed the street and contacted Ross through the open passenger side window of the vehicle.

"I didn't know you were coming by," Cox remarked nervously.

"It's important to monitor the progress you're making," Ross replied. "It's good to see Ahmed Jinnah squirm. He needs shaking up."

"Is he another target of your investigation?"

"Policy forbids commenting on who we're probing. Suffice it to say that if Raheem Khan is a small fish, then Jinnah is a whale. He's an extremely dangerous man."

Cox smiled conspiratorially. "Gotcha," he said.

"This is good work, Detective Cox. Keep the pressure going. Jinnah needs to understand where the true power lies."

"My thinking exactly!" Cox exclaimed, slapping a hand on the roof of the car.

Ross nodded to Frazier, who immediately started the engine. "We're at a critical juncture, detective."

"How so?"

"Unfortunately, we can't apprise you of all the details, not yet anyway. We require your patient and continuing cooperation, however."

"Count on me all the way, Agent Ross."

"Good attitude, I like that," Ross said with a plastic smile. "Keep in touch and let us know of any developments."

"I will," Cox replied, and was cut short when the car lurched away from the curb. Cox straightened and stared dumbly after the departing agents, feeling a tinge of fear in the pit of his stomach. Normally, he would be offended at receiving such an obvious snub, but he was in such awe of Ross that all he felt instead was an unquenchable desire to please the FBI agent.

Rappaport arrived at his cluttered office in the courthouse early. He had a lot of work he wanted to crank out on the cases he was handling before meeting Siegel for lunch to discuss the Khan matter. There was a message on his voicemail that he listened to while sipping a hot cup of coffee he'd gotten from a McDonald's drive-thru.

"Franny, this is Jack at DOJ. Hey, I finished the ballistics analysis on those items you provided and they don't seem to pan out. I wrote down the results and you can download them off our Web site. Just so you know, I took it upon myself to double-check the tests to make sure everything was kosher. The results are accurate.

"I packaged the gun and slugs you gave me and sent them to your office by courier. You should get them before the day's out. Let me know if there's anything else you need. And good luck, okay?"

Rappaport frowned. What did Jack mean by the results not panning out? It was supposed to be a routine check confirming the analysis Cox provided that said the bullets in the victim came from the gun recovered at the crime scene. Rappaport wasn't sure what could be wrong.

It took a while for the computer to come on line. When it did, Rappaport went to the DOJ Web site and punched in his access code, bringing up the report Jack had talked about. He clicked the print function and scanned the report while the laser printer spit out the pages. Rappaport couldn't believe what he read. Siegel would be equally astonished. The Khan case just kept getting stranger by the minute.

At a deli near the courthouse, Siegel had just taken his second bite of a bad ham and cheese sandwich when a document landed beside his elbow. He looked up and saw Rappaport standing next to his table.

"What's this?" Siegel asked.

"Another headache to deal with," Rappaport replied, taking a seat across from Siegel. He lifted the other half of Siegel's sandwich from the plate next to the paperwork. "You gonna eat this?"

"Not anymore," Siegel replied, grinning.

Rappaport bit ravenously into the sandwich while Siegel turned his attention to the report in front of him, picking it up with his free hand and reading.

"Let me save you the eyestrain," Rappaport said between chews. "It's a DOJ ballistics report that says the gun we sent doesn't match the bullets dug out of the corpse at the Khan murder scene."

"What?"

Rappaport swallowed. "It gets better. The bullet I copped from the evidence locker at LCPD, the one that Cox had *his* ballistics expert fire from the murder weapon, that one does match the slugs from the corpse." Rappaport took another bite from the sandwich.

"I'm not following," Siegel said, confused.

"The gun Cox gave me isn't the murder weapon. Cox's ballistics expert had the real thing when he performed *his* test, but Cox switched guns before he handed it over to me." Rappaport resumed chewing.

"You're going to choke," Siegel said.

Rappaport pointed to the half-empty bottle of Sprite next to Siegel's glass of soda and lifted his brows. "Sure, go ahead," Siegel said. Rappaport put the bottle to his mouth and took generous swallows, continuing to chew until the remnants of the sandwich were gone.

"So Cox switched guns on us?" Siegel asked.

"It appears so. His expert used the real gun in his test, but for some reason Cox felt the need to give us a phony."

"Why?"

"Good question. I can't figure it out. There's no reason he should have done that."

"Obviously, *he* thinks there's a reason. Maybe I should call him to my office and ask about the discrepancy."

"Hold off on that. If he's getting cute and playing swapsies with the murder weapon, we shouldn't alert him that we're on to his game until I get the real gun in my hands."

"How do we do that?"

"I know Dale very well. I partnered with him a long time ago and I know all his bad habits. One of them is that he likes to misappropriate evidence."

"What do you mean?"

"It's a quirk he has. He's been disciplined for it more than once. Cox likes to personally hold onto evidence, especially if it's something that tickles his fancy. He's very sloppy about that aspect of the job and it's come up in chain of custody issues in court a few times in the past. Instead of properly booking items into the evidence room, he tends to keep them for one reason or another."

"I see what you're saying. When I first met with him on this case he had Bernard Harris's sap. He pulled it out of his jacket. I thought that was odd."

"Exactly, it's his habit."

"You think he has the actual murder weapon in his possession?"

"It's a long shot, but it could be. He'll either carry it around, or have it stowed in his place. I can take a look and see."

"You're not saying what I think you are."

"I am."

"Franny, if you get caught breaking into Cox's home, that'll cause a lot of trouble. You could get fired."

"Then I won't get caught. Don't worry, Max, I'll take full responsibility for my actions if it goes bad. I need to get to the bottom of this. Something fishy's going on and I'm tired of the smell."

"Be careful."

"Oh, I will."

Rappaport was sitting in a car outside the Las Cruces Police Department when Cox emerged and got into his own vehicle. Rappaport had parked in the street a few car lengths from Cox's spot and he eased into traffic after giving Cox a bit of a lead. Fortunately, it was midday and the streets were congested, making it easy to stay out of sight while the cars navigated the surface streets to the edge of town. It surprised Rappaport when Cox entered the on-ramp to the freeway. He hadn't expected Cox to travel away from the city during work hours, but it intrigued him.

They were almost to Jefferson, the next town over, when Cox abruptly veered off the freeway at a truck stop complex. It was an area in the middle of nowhere. A large diner sat in the center of a virtual graveyard of long haul big rigs, next to which was a cluster of service stations, convenience stores, fast food restaurants, and a motel. Rappaport hung back once Cox's car entered the bustle of activity at the stop. Rappaport eventually parked next to a McDonald's restaurant when he saw Cox breaking to a halt at the motel's registration office.

"Extracurricular activity, huh?" Rappaport said out loud as he watched Cox cautiously glancing around before entering the office. "I wonder who the unfortunate victim is. She must not know anything about you, my friend … or, is it a he? Oh, wouldn't that be a hoot?" Rappaport grinned mischievously and slid down slightly in his seat.

Cox came out of the office a short time later and drove along the length of the motel, parking near the end of the building. He had a cell phone pressed to his ear when he got out of his car, unlocking the door to his room and going inside.

Rappaport started his engine after the door closed and coasted into the motel portion of the parking lot. He nestled the car into a cluster of vehicles a few rows from the building, where he had a fairly clear view of the room Cox occupied. Rappaport felt a sense of amusement while he surveilled the motel. He'd always thought of Cox as a buffoon, a Neanderthal with a slight spark of intelligence that was just enough to keep him bumbling through his profession. The behavior Rappaport was witnessing now, a secret liaison during duty hours, was typical of what he expected from the man who carried his morals in his shoes. Rappaport couldn't help musing over who'd be foolish enough to take Cox seriously. The answer arrived twenty minutes later.

Rappaport saw a black Lexus roll slowly, tentatively into the parking lot and pull into the spot next to Cox's car. A slender woman emerged from the vehicle, wearing a long, dark coat, headscarf, and sunglasses. Her expression was deadly serious as she looked around the parking lot before closing the driver's side door. She appeared tense and nervous, Rappaport thought, as the first pangs of familiarity crept in. Then the woman pulled off her sunglasses and Rappaport was struck with a jolt of disbelief when he recognized her. It was Irina Siegel!

CHAPTER 22

RAPPAPORT WAS DAZED AS he drove back to Las Cruces. He couldn't believe what he'd seen. In fact, if anyone told him Irina Siegel was clandestinely meeting Dale Cox in motels, he would've never bought it. It was too incredible, and Rappaport found it impossible to get his stunned mind around it.

By the time Rappaport pulled into Cox's apartment complex, his confusion had morphed into a simmering rage. Max Siegel was a good friend, perhaps the best friend Rappaport had, and the thought of Cox banging Siegel's wife was more of an outrage than Rappaport could stand. He felt even more anger at Irina. How could she? Rappaport was introduced to her not long after she and Siegel started dating. She was unbelievably gorgeous. On top of that, she was sweet and sensible, with a warm and loving personality. She had a beauty that emanated from within, as well as without. From the beginning, Rappaport always held her in the highest esteem, on a pedestal almost. And now, with the image of Irina slinking into a cheap motel room to have sex with a lowlife like Cox searing his thoughts, Rappaport's image of Irina came crashing down. He was suddenly disgusted with her and didn't think he'd be able to treat her with anything amounting to respect ever again. He hated her.

Trudging up the stairs to Cox's apartment, Rappaport snapped out his ruminations and checked the area for onlookers. When he didn't see anyone, he removed a set of master keys from his jacket pocket and began trying them in the door lock. The fourth key did the trick and he was able to open the door. Another check to make sure the coast was clear and Rappaport moved inside, slamming the door shut.

Cox's apartment was what Rappaport expected: a dump. Sparsely furnished, cluttered with discarded newspapers, magazines, clothes, and various other miscellaneous items accumulated from daily living, the place resembled a disaster area. A stack of porn videos adorned the television stand in the living room and a table in the adjoining dining area was littered with dirty dishes and remnants of food and wrappers of all sorts. The kitchen was equally dirty with dishes overflowing the sink and encrusted pots and pans sitting on top of a grease-covered stove. A faint, musty odor hung in the air and Rappaport grimaced with disgust.

Cox was a slob. It was no wonder he didn't have Irina come to his place, which made it all the more confounding as to why she had any interest in him at all. Rappaport couldn't figure it.

After making a cursory search of the immediate areas, Rappaport proceeded into the bedroom. Despite his purpose for snooping, Rappaport felt a stab of guilt for prying into the detective's most intimate living area.

Like the rest of the apartment, the bedroom was largely devoid of furniture, but heavily cluttered. It sported a double-sized bed, a lamp, a nightstand, and a single tall dresser. Piles of filthy clothes, along with stacks of documents, were scattered everywhere.

Swallowing a tiny bit of remorse, Rappaport rummaged through the nightstand and dresser, finding revealing items of interest, but not what he was searching for. Moving to the walk-in closet, Rappaport pushed through clothing and shoeboxes and more piles of junk that were crammed on top of the overhead shelf. He came upon a small .22 revolver, but not the Glock.

Discouragement sunk in as Rappaport started running out of places to probe. Reemerging from the closet, he placed his hands on his hips and let his eyes rove about the tiny room. He'd been fairly thorough in his quest for the missing gun, but his options were quickly dwindling.

Heading into the bathroom, Rappaport checked the cabinets with no luck. His confidence dropping, he returned to the kitchen and went through all the cabinets there, discovering little more than the fact that Cox was overstocked with a ridiculous amount of Hamburger Helper.

Perspiration was forming on Rappaport's forehead when he checked his watch and noted that nearly an hour had elapsed since he entered the apartment. His comfort level was dropping as time passed. Not knowing anything about Cox's staying power, Rappaport had no idea how much longer he'd be safe from interruption. If the detective's romantic prowess matched the rest of his lack of character, Rappaport estimated his window of safety was going to vanish quickly.

Not wanting to admit defeat, Rappaport returned to the bedroom and dropped to his hands and knees. He found a leather travel bag under the bed and felt a jolt of excitement when he dragged it out. The bag was heavy, weighted with bulky items.

Rappaport unzipped the main compartment and threw aside the flap. What he found was a trove of weapons, some with evidence tags still attached. There were two handguns, a Beretta and a German Luger, along with a pair of nunchakus, a K-bar knife, and a Japanese short sword in a sheath. The investigator shook his head in wonderment. The bag was a virtual evidence locker. Rappaport was astounded that Cox could get away with misappropriating so much material from the police department. It was crazy, unprofessional in the extreme. Rappaport puzzled over Cox's mental stability as he went through the remaining compartments, finding ammunition, empty clips, and more girly magazines.

Frustrated by his failure, Rappaport carefully replaced the items in the bag and slid it into its original position under the bed. Consulting his watch again, he felt a sense of urgency to get going. Rappaport was ready to get off his knees when the mattress caught his attention. It was the last option.

Without much enthusiasm, Rappaport pushed his hand between the mattresses and moved it from side to side. Failing to feel anything, he stood on his feet, crouching over, and pushed both hands in, sidestepping his way toward the headboard. He detected a heavy piece of metal near the nightstand. Both hands closed on the object and Rappaport felt the distinct shape of an automatic weapon.

"Please be it," Rappaport pleaded out loud, pulling the gun from its hiding place. Then he smiled with delight, recognizing a replica of the Glock Cox previously provided him. "Aren't you beautiful?" Rappaport said, rolling the gun over in his hands.

The satisfaction Rappaport felt was short-lived when the doorbell rang, cutting crisply through the air. Rappaport froze, not sure what to do. The doorbell went off again, followed by a loud, rapid pounding. Rappaport cursed under his breath and limped stealthily into the living room. The blinds on the window next to the door were drawn and Rappaport tiptoed across the room without the intruder outside detecting him.

Pressing his eye to the peephole, Rappaport felt a surge of relief when he saw the brown, uniformed visage of a UPS delivery man. The worker was looking around, his expression already showing signs of resignation. Rappaport remained still until the deliveryman eventually gave up and left, clunking down the steps. Rappaport opened the door a crack and poked his head outside, making sure the deliveryman was gone before leaving himself. He went directly to his car, locking the gun in the glove compartment before driving out of the complex.

Later in the day, Rappaport sat in his office looking blankly into his computer screen, the Glock resting next to the keyboard. He'd just gotten off the phone, having spent hours running the serial number on the gun and tracing its origin. The results surprised him. He needed a few minutes to gather his thoughts before calling Siegel with the news.

His mouth was dry so Rappaport unwrapped a stick of spearmint gum and chewed it as he reached for the phone. Taking a deep breath, he released it slowly while the ringtone buzzed in his ear.

"Max Siegel," the voice on the receiver answered.

"This is Rappaport. We need to talk."

"What do you have for me?"

"Not over the phone. In fact, I don't want to talk about it in the office either. Can we meet someplace?"

There was a pause. "I just got off the phone with Langerman and he said the same thing. What's going on with you two?"

"Langerman? Why is Dave calling you?"

"Don't know. We hung up right before you called. He was all cloak-and-dagger like you and said he wanted to talk away from the office. We're supposed to meet at Lyman's Bar and Grill in half an hour."

"I don't have a clue what Dave wants, but we need to speak immediately."

"Why don't you join us at Lyman's? We can all get a drink and a bite to eat."

"What I have to discuss is private. I don't want a newsman privy to the content."

"I'm not sure what revelations either of you wants to make, Franny, but I have a feeling they're connected somehow. I want Langerman there. He's trustworthy."

"Have it your way. I'll see you guys in thirty."

Rappaport locked the gun in a desk drawer after he hung up the phone. Resting his elbows on the desktop, he made a fist and clasped it with his other hand, pressing both against his mouth. What a head trip, he thought.

Rappaport was hoping to catch Siegel alone when he arrived in the dimly lit eatery, but Siegel and Langerman were already sipping drinks when Rappaport strolled through the door. "Hey, Franny," Siegel greeted as Rappaport approached the table in the mostly empty restaurant. "Great timing, Dave just got here. Have a seat."

Rappaport pulled out a chair and sat down. He ordered a beer from a waitress that came by and the men instinctively refrained from talking until she returned with the beverage and moved away again.

"Okay," Siegel started, "you sounded sufficiently mysterious on the phone, Franny. What have you got?"

Rappaport looked warily at Langerman. "Nothing personal, Dave, but I don't feel comfortable giving Max the news I have with you hanging around."

"Does it relate to Khan?" Langerman asked, grinning slightly. "Because if it does, I have my own tidbit of information I'd like to share."

"Is it Khan?" Siegel queried.

Rappaport nodded.

"There you have it," Siegel said, "we're all on the same page. We all have new facts to share. Why don't you start off, Franny?"

Rappaport hesitated.

"Come on," Siegel prompted, "Langerman has a sense of discretion, buddy, otherwise he wouldn't be meeting me in secret like this. I'd be reading about whatever he has to tell me in the *Las Cruces Times*. He's shown sensibility so far, so I think we can trust him. Right, Dave?"

"Absolutely, Max. Franny's lucky I'm not thin-skinned, because I'd be feeling a world of hurt at this snub if I were."

Rappaport smiled and raised his palms in surrender. "Okay, you win, Max. It's your case, so I guess it's your call."

"Glad we cleared the air on that," Siegel said. "What do you have?"

Rappaport glanced around, and then leaned over the table toward the others, who followed suit. "I have the gun, the actual gun used in the murders."

"Where'd you get it?" Siegel asked, eyes beaming with sudden excitement.

Rappaport gave Langerman a nervous look. "I went into Cox's apartment and found it stuffed under his mattress."

"Amazing," Siegel remarked, shooting Langerman a look. "Where was Cox when you perused his place?"

The question unnerved Rappaport and it registered to his companions. "He wasn't around and let's just leave it at that," he responded testily.

"Okay," Siegel said, frowning, "but how do we know this is the right gun?"

"Instinct," Rappaport replied. "I know it in my gut, but, of course, I'll have it tested at the lab to confirm it. But there's no doubt in my mind it's the one."

"What more do you have?" Siegel asked, studying Rappaport shrewdly.

"What makes you think there's more, boss?" Rappaport responded, smiling grimly.

"Because it's written all over you. Also, because you wouldn't be meeting me in secret like this if that was all you had."

"You're smart, Max, I'll give you that. You sure you want Dave hearing what I'm about to tell you?"

"There he goes again," Langerman said, feigning hurt.

"He's here for better or worse," Siegel replied. "Spill the beans and let me worry about the rest."

"It's your funeral," Rappaport said with resignation. "I ran a trace on the serial number off the gun. It came up blocked. I spent the rest of the day making phone calls and bypassing authorizations before I could find the origin of where the Glock came from."

A heavy crease formed between Siegel's brows. "Are you saying it was government issue?"

"Yep."

Langerman stirred in his seat, his expression showing intrigue.

"Which branch?" Siegel asked.

"The feds," Rappaport replied. "I had to pull a lot of favors to narrow down the department, but I finally got an answer."

"FBI?" Siegel suggested.

Rappaport shook his head. "CIA," he retorted, and then reclined and let the letters hang in the air while surprise washed over Siegel's face.

"Hot damn, that makes sense!" Langerman ejaculated, slapping a hand on the table.

"Why does that make sense?" Siegel inquired.

"I told you I was taking a trip to Phoenix," Langerman began. "Well, I did like I said and brought along the address for that Pharmagroup Corporation so I could pay a visit and see what they were about. A peculiar thing happened on the way to the headquarters, the road petered out and I wound up standing in the wilderness. Turns out the building housing the company doesn't exist, not unless the CEO and board of directors are a bunch of snakes and scorpions."

"A front," Siegel said absently, his thoughts swirling.

"Exactly the conclusion I came to," Langerman continued. "I decided that matters were shady, but I wasn't sure what was causing all the darkness. It piqued my interest enough though that when I got back I decided to visit the crime scene and see what I could find. I've witnessed lots of investigations during my career and I've come to learn that no matter how thorough detectives are, something always gets missed."

"We went over every inch of that place," Rappaport interjected indignantly.

"I don't doubt that you did," Langerman quickly added. "I'm not trying to cast aspersions. We're all only human, even experienced veterans like yourself. Sometimes items get overlooked by the best of us, until some dumb cowboy happens to stumble over it."

"What did you find?" Siegel asked impatiently.

Langerman leaned sideways and dug an object from his pocket, slapping it onto the table with a heavy thud. "This," he said. When he took his hand away, Siegel and Rappaport stared in amazement.

"Handcuffs," Siegel observed.

"That's right," Langerman replied.

"You found them at the crime scene?" Rappaport asked dejectedly.

"Uh-huh."

"Where?"

"Under the bed, pressed against the wall where the headboard was. My guess is that they might have been kicked there during a struggle. You found corpses on the stairs and in the driveway, and the alleged killer was apprehended running from the scene. With the facts appearing so straightforward, I'm supposing nobody ever thought to peek under the bed. I almost didn't myself except for a last minute hunch."

Rappaport's cheeks noticeably reddened with embarrassment.

"Sure," Siegel said, emerging from a deep thought. "That explains what we saw on Khan when we went to the hospital, Franny."

"What are you getting at?" Rappaport asked.

"Remember those marks on Khan's wrists, the ones we thought were made by the sadistic deputy? Maybe we assumed too much. Maybe he had those before he got admitted."

"At the house?" Rappaport said. "Oh my God."

"Oh my God is right," Langerman reiterated. "We have the CIA in a safe house with a Pakistani national. We have handcuffs and apparent marks on the wrist suggesting Khan was being held against his will. Then he goes running amok and slaughtering those CIA boys. Even a dumb, Okie reporter like me can see that you fellas have a nasty little incident on your hands."

"That attorney from San Francisco, Gul, he came into court crowing about a defense at arraignment," Siegel said, his excitement growing as the pieces of the puzzled snapped together in his mind. "I couldn't understand his confidence at the time, but now I get why he was so cocky. He's going for self-defense."

"Sounds like a highly reasonable assumption under the circumstances,"

Langerman agreed. "As the prosecutor, you're going to be standing before a jury attempting to explain why two CIA case officers were holding this Pakistani defendant in a safe house on American soil. Last time I checked operation statutes for our spy agencies, they're not supposed to be playing games in country. Kidnapping citizens and holding them is beyond their jurisdiction. This ain't Guantanamo anymore."

"This explains a lot, Max," Rappaport chimed in. "Like why Cox is cozy with the FBI. They must be here to perform damage control."

"But how?" Siegel wondered, still reeling from the revelations. "It will all come out at trial."

"Only if there is a trial," Rappaport countered ominously. "Now we know why Cox is playing with the evidence. Delaying reports, coaxing Khan's silence, switching the murder weapon; he's deliberately sabotaging the case so that there isn't any."

"That fits," Siegel said, the lights coming on in his head. "Gul would have run an independent test on the gun during pretrial motions. It wasn't going to match. The judge would have thrown it out. But even without the Glock, we still have a solid circumstantial shot at conviction. The evidence tampering would need to be much more substantial to prevent all the facts from getting out. They'd have to get rid of Khan himself to complete this kind of cover-up."

Siegel's last words triggered a short period of silent genuflection by the men at the table. They stared at one another in disbelief, the weight of their discussion settling in. Siegel felt himself getting the chills. "Do you suppose Danko knows what's happening?" Rappaport finally asked.

"Your guess is as good as mine," Siegel replied. "Nothing he's done so far computes. If all this is true, he'd have a lot of leverage to use against the feds to shut down the corruption probe against him. But why bring me into the picture? If he wanted Khan's case thrown out, there's a multitude of ass-kissing sycophants in the office who'd be happy to screw things up. No, Danko must be in the dark himself."

"Then we need to talk to him," Rappaport declared. "He has to be told what we've uncovered."

"I don't know," Siegel responded slowly.

"Come on, Max. He's still the boss," Rappaport insisted. "Like it or not, we don't have a choice."

CHAPTER 23

---•---

Rich Danko arrived at work early, anticipating his scheduled meeting with pent up agitation. He'd been reeling ever since Siegel and Rappaport had dropped their bomb on him. He knew something was fishy when the feds handed him the Khan case, but he'd taken the bait anyway. His experience from the previous year hadn't taught him a thing. He got suckered again.

Danko picked up the phone receiver and hit the button for his secretary. "Is Sims here yet?" he demanded.

"I haven't seen him."

"What about the others?"

"Nobody's arrived. I'll be happy to let you know when they do."

"You do that," Danko barked and hung up.

Danko rose from his chair and stripped off his coat, tossing it on top of his desk and pacing in front of the bay windows. It was a clear day for a change. The sky was blue and sunshine was spreading over the decrepit city horizon.

How could I have been so stupid? Danko thought. Letting them use me like some cheap, brothel whore. He blamed his weakness on the federal probe he was under. He'd put a brave face on the investigation, puffing his chest in public forums and pretending to be dismissive of the allegations swirling about him. But the truth was he knew the feds had him good. During his years as the Clay County District Attorney, he'd taken numerous kickbacks and bribes from local businessmen whose practices were running afoul of the law. This rang especially true with local developers and dairy concerns that continuously violated environmental codes. Danko saw the businesses as boons to the local economy and couldn't fathom the logic in hindering them with criminal proceedings that deprived the county of sorely needed revenues. Taking payoffs to quash prosecutions that arose against them seemed more like bonuses than bribes. Danko enriched himself by serving what was ultimately the public good, and he couldn't understand why the feds wanted to make such a big deal of it.

Of course, there were also payoffs from a few major drug dealers here and there. Those he couldn't so easily rationalize. But Danko convinced himself that the true drug problem lay with the street pushers who actually distributed product to the addicts, not with the wholesalers who brought it into the area. Taking down the major players would do little good, since somebody else would always fill the vacuum. As long as Danko's office addressed the scumbag pushers who polluted the streets, he could live with skimming money off the trade from quiet men who wore suits. He thought the FBI and DEA should have better fish to fry than him.

It was this vulnerability that convinced Danko to acquiesce so easily in the Khan case, when he should have been more suspicious, more demanding about why the FBI was involved. Now he was lording over a situation that had implications far beyond crime fighting in Clay County, but for some reason the feds didn't want to touch it directly. Why? What was the hidden agenda? Better yet, what was Danko's reward going to be for his continued handling of the matter? His meeting was scheduled with the feds' point man, Ross, who was going to give him answers to all his burning questions. Danko sensed a golden opportunity to reap enormous benefits from the matter at hand and he was going to press his leverage to the hilt.

Danko returned to his desk and got on the intercom again. "Julie, anybody arrive yet?"

"Yes, yes, yes," the secretary replied impatiently. "Bernie Sims just entered and he has Detective Cox and the two FBI agents with him."

"Send them straight in."

"Yes, sir!"

The door to the outer office opened and Sims preceded the others as they all filed inside. Danko was seated, his massive hands clasped tightly together, his thumbs twirling around each other. The expression on his broad face was firmly set. Danko was feeling powerful and he thought the agents looked slightly chastened as they came before him.

Julie the secretary followed the brood and stood with her hand resting on the door handle. "Will there be anything else, Mr. Danko?"

"No, Julie, go ahead and close the door. Hold all calls and don't let anybody in until I'm done with my visitors."

"Yes, sir," Julie responded, pulling the door shut.

"Come in, gentlemen," Danko commanded, his dark eyes focused squarely on Ross. "Cox, why don't you take a seat on the couch? I want our friends from the FBI to occupy the chairs in front of my desk. Sims, stand over here with me."

Sims did as he was told like an obedient servant, while the others also complied with Danko's orchestrations. Cox fidgeted when he sat, wearing the air of a child about to be scolded.

"Thank you all for coming," Danko began in a somewhat condescending manner. "Agent Ross, I appreciate you taking the time out of what must be a very busy schedule to have this meeting."

Ross's thin lips parted into a mechanical smile. "It's my pleasure, Mr. Danko."

Danko felt a stab of indignation at Ross's lack of humility and his expression instantly hardened. "Okay," he said, "let's cut through the bullshit and get straight to business. I called you agents here today, along with your police flunky, to tell you I'm onto the shenanigans you're playing with the Khan prosecution."

"Shenanigans?" Ross repeated coolly.

"You shut up!" Danko snapped, pointing a thick finger at Ross. "You walked in here a few weeks ago with a line about how Raheem Khan was a dangerous person and of interest to the bureau. Then you shoveled me a load of crap about how you were only worried about us conducting a quiet prosecution so you could monitor him and his friends."

"All true," Ross said.

"Yeah, but you left out the best part, something that would have been of tremendous interest to our handling of the case. How about the fact that Raheem Khan was a prisoner of a couple CIA case officers? I'm sorry, did I miss out on some secret piece of federal legislation that says it's okay for CIA personnel to take prisoners on the American mainland and hold them against their will in some safe house? Please tell me if I'm off the mark here."

Sims chuckled into his hand and Frazier looked at him with cold intensity.

"No, I'd say you're right on it," Ross responded calmly.

"Would you mind explaining what the hell is going on in my humble county?"

"Fair enough," Ross said. "I suppose you're owed an explanation of what we're dealing with."

"Damn right," Danko declared.

"I need it understood by everybody in this room, before I proceed, that what I'm about to say is classified," Ross said.

"Yeah, yeah," Danko replied with an impatient wave of his hand. "Get on with it already."

Ross remained unnaturally composed, calmly fixing his attention on Danko, seemingly oblivious to the rudeness. "I understand you're feeling out of sorts about the Khan matter, Mr. Danko, but I can assure you it was never our intention to be deceptive in any way. What I told you at our first meeting holds true. The bureau—and various other agencies concerned with national security—consider Raheem Khan to be a very dangerous man. We believe he's a terrorist associated with a sleeper cell that's active in your area and also that he has vast knowledge of other sleeper agents in Northern California."

"Why?" Danko asked sternly. "Nowadays, the word terrorist is a catchphrase. Anybody with rusty-colored skin and a funny last name seems to be a candidate for that label. What specifically do you have on Khan?"

Ross glanced cautiously at the others in the room before replying. "Khan is a close friend and associate of a Pakistani man named Tariq Nasir. Nasir is a follower of Ahmed Jinnah, of whom you gentlemen are very familiar. Six months ago, Nasir took a trip back to the mother country and took Khan with him. They made the journey with the blessing of their spiritual leader, Ahmed Jinnah.

"The source for this next piece of information is highly classified and won't be divulged to you. Suffice it to say that we have a very credible, very knowledgeable mole in Jinnah's organization who related that the purpose for Nasir and Khan's trip was to visit a *madrassa* run by an extremely radical cleric named Faisal Abdul. Abdul's been on our intelligence radar screen since long before 9/11. He's a well documented conduit for terrorist activities throughout the world. Our friends stayed with him for about a month before returning stateside. We kept them under tight surveillance, but, despite that, Nasir managed to run aground and gave our agents the slip in San Francisco. We believe he did that in preparation for a planned attack. The analysts aren't certain about the nature of the mission, but they're highly confident it's going to be launched in the near future."

"What about Khan?" Danko asked.

"He went to Pakistan with Nasir, stayed at the same *madrassa*. I don't think it's farfetched to conclude that whatever Nasir's into, Khan's right alongside him. Unfortunately, from a counter-terrorism, or even a criminal perspective, we have nothing solid on Khan other than a lot of speculation. One problem with plots of an international nature is that evidence tends to get sketchy. Legitimate, by-the-book procedures for getting at the crux of a potential national security threat are usually inadequate."

"So you substitute unconventional methods to make the legitimate methods adequate," Sims volunteered.

"Precisely," Ross agreed. "At least that's the way some members of the national security team see it. And that's what was done in this instance."

"You mean the CIA took custody of Khan?" Danko asked, his astonishment rising.

"Yes," Ross replied, "for questioning purposes. They wanted to debrief Khan as to what he knew."

"By what authority?" Danko pressed.

Ross remained cool. "None," he replied with a slight shrug. "They had no legal authority to do what they did."

"Incredible!" Sims gasped.

Danko's attention remained fixed on Ross, his eyes narrowing, a certain belligerence edging into his demeanor. "We have a name for that kind of stuff around here," he said. "We call it kidnapping."

"The same phrase is used in our lexicon," Ross calmly replied. "Although there are some in the community who would probably label it interventive detention, or some other such thing." He couldn't conceal the slight play of a smirk on his lips. "In any event, it doesn't really matter," Ross continued. "The case officers responsible for this transgression have paid the ultimate price for their indiscretions. Mr. Khan has seen to that."

"Where did the order for what the agents did come from?" Danko pointedly inquired.

Ross didn't try to hide his amusement. "If I could tell you that, I'd be a man of infinite wisdom and knowledge. Whether there was an order and where it came from is anybody's guess. A man of your stature can understand the extremely delicate nature of what's occurred. Instructions could have filtered down from the top, or the actions of the case officers might have been pursuant to their own decision making. None of us here will ever know for sure. Who tipped over the first domino is no longer important. What we're concerned about now is stopping the chain reaction."

"Let's cut through the bullshit," Danko said. "What were the CIA guys planning to do when the questioning was over? Khan would have run to the authorities the minute he got released."

"Our thinking exactly," Ross agreed. "Enough of a stir was already made. It couldn't be allowed to spill over into the public domain."

Danko's gray brows rose high. "What are you saying, that he was going to be sanctioned? That the government was going to kill him?"

"Nothing so dramatic," Ross said. For the first time in the conversation he was hesitant. "The consensus was that Khan had to be removed from our jurisdiction, put into the hands of people who could more effectively illicit information vital to national security."

"You can't be serious," Danko said, catching the full implications of what Ross alluded to. "And you fellows are investigating me? What you did is far outside the legal boundaries. Christ! Are you Washington people executors of the law or a Mafia clan?"

"Our local agencies should have been informed of these activities," Sims chimed in.

"A situation was created by irresponsible parties," Ross said defensively. "The bureau's interest, along with those of other departments, was to clean up the damage as quietly as possible."

"Then Raheem Khan blew those tidy plans apart with a butter knife and a Glock," Danko said firmly. "So the cat's out of the bag. How do you propose to pull off your plans now? Probably the best course of action is to designate your scapegoats and hope the congressional hearings don't dig too deep."

"All isn't necessarily lost yet," Ross said, raising a finger. "Admittedly, we began our task hoping that Mr. Khan would be so overwhelmed by events that he'd cop a plea for a good deal. If he started talking about CIA conspiracies, we felt there was sufficient cover that his allegations would be taken as the rantings of a deranged lunatic. We're not so comfortable in that assessment now."

"What are you proposing?" Danko asked suspiciously.

"That's simple," Ross responded. "My superiors in Washington believe it would be best if the case never gets to trial."

Sims gasped, while Danko looked at Ross like he was an alien from some distant galaxy. "No trial?" he repeated. "How the hell do we pull that off? Are the U.S. attorneys taking this case from us?"

"No, the federal government wants to stay out of it," Ross said. "We'd prefer it remain a local action."

"I'll bet," Danko said angrily. "You create the fiasco and dump it in our laps, and then you want to walk away and let us take the hits when the shit comes down. There's no way we can let Khan go at this juncture. He's lawyered up and apparently not planning to cop. On the flip side, our evidence is too solid to let him walk."

"You have a single witness on the street that came into contact with a man fleeing the scene of a violent crime," Ross said. "Khan could have been the killer, or then again, he might have been another victim whom the witness assumed was the killer. The facts are sufficiently ambiguous that they can easily be construed in many different ways. Perhaps your office could find—based on the evidence—that Khan is exonerated of guilt."

"After two attempts on the life of my deputy?" Danko countered with incredulity.

"Nobody knows who tried to kill your man," Ross replied. "It certainly wasn't Khan. He was in custody the entire time."

"You're crazy," Danko pronounced unceremoniously. "Say we go along with your insane scheme and let Khan off the hook, you'll be back to square one. What's to keep him from shooting his mouth off when he leaves the courthouse?"

Ross took a long pause, holding Danko in a steady gaze before slowly surveying the others in the room. "Maybe this would be a good time to make our conversation more confidential," he suggested. "Could we clear the office?"

Danko opened his mouth to speak, but then thought better of it, the idea occurring to him that a private talk could be beneficial. Danko didn't like the way the agent was studying him, it gave him the creeps, but the two of them needed to be alone. "Sims," Danko finally said.

"Boss?" Sims replied, stepping closer to Danko's side.

"Take Detective Cox and Agent Frazier out for a coffee break. I'd like a word alone with our esteemed colleague, Agent Ross."

"Sure thing, chief," Sims responded. His discomfort in conducting the others out the door was apparent.

When everybody else was gone, Ross rose to his feet and strolled around Danko's desk to the bay windows. His back to the DA, he gazed appreciatively at the expanse of the city below. "Nice view," he remarked.

"I like it," Danko said, turning uneasily in his chair.

"Of course, it's not New York City or Washington D.C., but I'm sure Las Cruces is an up and coming town. With a bit of development, it might even evolve a skyline."

Ross was still scanning the landscape and didn't see Danko's sneer. "Yeah, okay, we're not a metropolis," Danko said, "but we're no backwater hick town either." Danko lifted his bulk off his chair and joined Ross at the window.

"Funny," Ross said, "with these windows stretching to the floor the way they do, you almost feel like you're standing on top of the city as you peer down into the ragged collection of streets and buildings. I imagine you must stand here a lot—just like we are now—feeling god-like from this perspective; Zeus looking upon the earth from Mount Olympus."

"There a point to these ramblings, Ross?"

"Only that I appreciate that you're a man of power. You have every attribute of a career politician. What would you do if you lost your position?"

Danko's lids narrowed, his face flushing crimson. "Are you trying to threaten me?" he asked in a low, menacing tone.

Ross's lips cracked into a mechanical smile. "Not at all," he calmly replied. "Quite the contrary; I want only to help you."

"Get to the point," Danko growled. "I don't have time for empty sentiments."

"You made some very acute observations during our meeting, Rich. May I call you that?"

"Mr. Danko suits me fine."

Ross's mechanical smile grew. "Fair enough ... Mr. Danko. As I was saying, you're observations about our problems were on the money. Raheem Khan is in a position to cause the federal government a tremendous amount of embarrassment. People in the highest echelons of power are walking a tightrope, scared to death of falling off. And all because of some insignificant little brute with a brainwashed head full of radical, fundamentalist ideals. It would be the height of absurdity to let such a nobody bring down an entire government."

"That it would, but how do you keep his mouth sealed?"

"With your help, I believe we can pull it off. Your cooperation is the key."

"What do you expect me to do? Better yet, why should I want to help you bunch of scamps on Capitol Hill?"

"One good deed deserves another, Mr. Danko. I've been empowered by my superiors to reward you handsomely for any assistance you're willing to give."

Danko's grin exposed yellowed, pointy teeth that were grit together. "Now we're getting to it. I want that probe to disappear. It's been chafing my ass for over a year."

"The bureau's tired of filing paper on you. In today's world, they have more important matters to spend their time on than a quasi-rural district attorney who's taking kickbacks."

"You really are a prick, Ross, you know that?"

"Yes, I do."

"So do we have a deal? I find a way to get Khan off the hook and you boys leave me alone for the duration of my tenure in office?"

"As you stated earlier, we have to do more than just get Mr. Khan off the hook. We must persuade him to shut his mouth about everything that's happened."

Danko lifted a wary brow. "What's your plan for doing that?"

"Better you don't know for now, but if we get your cooperation as circumstances dictate, I believe we can bring matters to a swift and satisfactory conclusion. May we count on you?"

"For what you're offering, absolutely, but what should I do about Max Siegel? He's got wind of the facts and there's no way in hell he'll just let it go. The bastard will use it as a soapbox to stand on while he kicks my ass in the next election."

"Yes, Max Siegel is quite a thorn in your side, isn't he?"

"Lower that estimate about six inches and you'll know better where he gives me pain."

"Hmm," Ross hummed, almost switching into a genuine smile.

"How do we deal with him?" Danko pressed.

"Siegel's already been taken into consideration. He should be fairly easy to neutralize after we finish with him."

"Brother, you guys are scary. I don't know what part of Hades they recruited you from, but I'm glad I'm not on your bad side."

"Then I take it we have a deal?" Ross asked, extending an outstretched hand.

Danko grasped the hand in his own. It was cold and clammy. "You bet your ass," he said, while the two men shook hands over the City of Las Cruces.

CHAPTER 24

———————•———————

MAX SIEGEL RAPPED ON the door to Rappaport's cluttered office and pushed it open. He found the investigator glumly tapping out a report on his computer amidst stacks of files and reports. "You look busy," Siegel observed.

"Yeah, when it rains it pours around here," Rappaport replied without humor. "You know how it is."

"You seem depressed, Franny, something bothering you?"

"I'll be fine. Whadaya got?"

Rappaport was obviously down, it was written all over his expression. But if he didn't want to discuss it, Siegel wasn't going to press the matter. "I just got called by the courts," Siegel announced. "Gul put our case on calendar this morning for a bail reduction pitch. I think he wants to get into some of what we uncovered. This should be interesting, because I have to disclose everything that I know to be exculpatory. Can you imagine what I might be compelled to say in open court? You should come along and see the show."

"What? Now?"

"Yep. I didn't get the proper notice, but it's probably because Gul assumes I already know the factors he's going to cite to get the bail reduced. I'm curious about comparing notes with him."

Rappaport glanced at his computer without enthusiasm and shrugged. "Sure, what the hell?" he said. "I can take a break."

"Good, let's get going. We're on the second floor in ten minutes."

Siegel and Rappaport were walking along the corridor to the calendar department when they came upon Gul and Ahmed Jinnah having a heated argument outside the courtroom doors. The hall was packed with people, so it was hard to hear what they were saying over the echoing din of voices. But it was apparent they weren't having a pleasant conversation. Both were flushed and they were exchanging hostile glares. Siegel tapped Rappaport on the shoulder. "Let's see what they're talking about," he said. Rappaport nodded and the two drifted toward the unsuspecting pair.

Gul and Jinnah ended their argument when Siegel and Rappaport edged closer. Gul turned on his heel and stormed into the courtroom, while Jinnah started in the opposite direction, bringing him face to face with Siegel. There was fury in Jinnah's deep set eyes and his nostrils were flared. He gave Siegel a murderous grimace before pushing past and cutting through the surrounding crowd.

"What was that all about?" Rappaport asked.

"I don't know, but it appears Jinnah's not happy with how he spent his money. Let's get inside and see if we can figure out what went wrong."

The courtroom was full of activity, a swarm of well dressed lawyers buzzing about the counsel tables in front of the swinging gates. Orange, jump-suited prisoners filled the wooden benches by the holding cell and Siegel spotted Khan in their midst through the shatterproof glass as Siegel traversed the aisle next to the audience. Khan appeared stoic, shackled, his posture rigid as he gazed into space. The other inmates, by contrast, lounged casually about him, jeering, snickering, and craning their necks in futile attempts to see into the audience. Siegel couldn't tell if Khan was angry or shell-shocked.

A host of reporters and news cameras crammed the jury box again. Siegel spied Langerman with them as Siegel pushed past the swinging gates. Langerman was sprawled over the alternate juror seat at the end of the top row. He grinned lazily when he spotted Siegel, pointing at him with a forefinger and raised thumb. Siegel sidled next to Langerman at the edge of the box.

"What brings you by?" Siegel inquired.

Langerman raised his chin at the prisoner section. "Your boy over there," he replied. "Heard he's got ideas about lowering his bail, or at least his attorney does."

"How the hell did you hear about that? I only got the word ten minutes ago."

Langerman grinned mischievously. "I have my sources, counselor. You know that. Wouldn't be worth my salt as a court reporter if I didn't."

"Expecting a break in the story at a bail reduction hearing?"

"You never know. I wouldn't want to get scooped by my colleagues here. Besides, maybe I'm hoping for a green light to write about what I already fathom. I'm trying to be noble, but my typing fingers are getting itchy lately."

A nearby television reporter clutching a microphone caught Langerman's last remark and turned his blue-eyed, Ken-doll face toward Siegel, scrutinizing him through gold, wire-framed glasses.

"We should talk about this later," Siegel suggested.

"You're right," Langerman agreed, winking at the reporter. "Channel ten, aren't you?" he asked.

The reporter didn't respond, turning away and carefully running a hand over his parted, perma-pressed, blond hair. Siegel and Langerman exchanged grins.

Judge Grafton took the bench and had the clerk call Siegel's case first. The courtroom quieted and the attorneys surrounding the counsel tables stepped away, allowing Siegel and Gul to come forward. Rappaport faded into the mix and took a place by the door next to the jury box. Glancing at the audience, he noticed Cox seated in the back row next to a professional man in a suit. The man's attention was fixated on the attorneys, his thin lips clamped tightly together. He had a cruel appearance. Cox's gaze strayed toward Rappaport, the detective's features contorting into a malevolent mask.

"Mr. Gul," Judge Grafton started, "you put this matter on the docket to make a pitch for lower bail. What new circumstances have arisen that I should honor you request?"

Gul appeared uncomfortable, shooting a look at his client, who stood beside him in the prisoner box, and then at Siegel.

"Mr. Gul?" the judge repeated. "Do you have something to say?"

"Your Honor," Gul began hesitantly, "through recent discussions with my client, I have learned of facts that would more than warrant a reduction in bail if true. The problem is that the allegations my client makes are of such a fantastic nature that I am reluctant to discuss them on the record without some kind of corroboration. It would be irresponsible, with all these newsmen in the audience, to announce these facts in such a public forum."

"I don't get it," Judge Grafton said. "That's precisely why I thought you requested this event, to present facts on the record that you deem material to a bail reduction."

While cameras whirred and clicked, Gul remained with his mouth agape, contemplating words that never spilled from his lips. The judge watched with impatience. "Counsel," he said, "I'll see you both in my chambers."

A murmur arose when Siegel and Gul approached the bench, following Judge Grafton through a side door. Once inside the judge's chambers, the judge removed his black robe and dropped it on a couch. Then he circled his desk and sat in a high-backed, leather chair, while the two attorneys took the chairs fronting the desk. "Mr. Gul," the judge began, "I saw you struggling out there. That's why I called this private session, to see if we can clear the air on these allegations you spoke of. We're off the record. No court reporter. Feel free to spill the beans."

"Your Honor, I'm sorry for my hesitancy," Gul said. "I suppose I'm still trying to process what I learned over the past twenty-four hours. I'm not completely sure how to proceed.

"You can start by telling me what's on your mind, sir," Judge Grafton responded.

"Well, Your Honor, I conducted a routine visit to my client, Mr. Khan, last night at the jail. We discussed the pending case and possible defenses for the upcoming preliminary hearing. Prior to arraignment, it was hinted by the party that hired me on Mr. Khan's behalf, that a defense of false imprisonment might exist. I was told nothing more than that. Given the vague nature of the assertion, I naturally wanted to discuss it in more depth with my client. That was the reason for yesterday's visit."

"What did he tell you?" Judge Grafton asked.

"First, let me state that Mr. Khan has waived the attorney-client privilege with regard to what I am about to say."

"Understood," the judge said. "Get on with it. I have a big calendar ahead of me."

Gul took a deep breath. "In a nutshell, my client tells me that days prior to the killings, he was abducted by the two men designated as victims. He said they forced him into a car at gunpoint during nighttime, when he emerged into an alley behind the downtown restaurant where he works. He did not know these men. They identified themselves as federal agents, accusing him of being a terrorist and making numerous threats to his life and the lives of his family in a crude attempt to coerce information about his supposed terrorist activities. On the night of the killings, he was told that men were coming for him, other government agents who were going to transport him to a military base. From there, his understanding was that he would be flown overseas to an undisclosed country where he would be tortured and possibly killed.

"After learning these facts, Mr. Khan escaped his restraints during a dinner break and in an act of self-defense, killed his captors and fled. That's when he ran into the bystander, Bernard Harris, who incapacitated him."

Judge Grafton's mouth was agape. It took him a few moments to process what he'd heard before shifting his attention to Siegel. "What have you got to say, counselor? Is there any validity to the defendant's incredible story?"

Siegel was on the spot, his professional reputation hanging in the balance. He opted for objective honesty. "I don't know whether Khan's version of events is true, judge. I have my suspicions about what actually transpired the night of the killings, but I couldn't say for sure what occurred. The one hard piece of evidence I do have is that the gun taken from Khan by Bernard Harris traces back to the Central Intelligence Agency. I also know that the headquarters of the business the decedents were purported to work for doesn't exist at the location listed on the property title. That's what I know. Whether it corroborates the defendant's story and justifies the deaths remains to be seen."

Judge Grafton ran a hand over the sparse white hairs of his balding scalp. "Remains to be seen, you say? I'd say the revelations I've heard suggest a very powerful defense. If what Mr. Khan says is true, then we have an intriguing piece of scandalous behavior, perpetrated by our own government. If what he says is true, then I'd certainly be inclined to not only reduce his bail, but to suggest the charges be dropped completely. But we're getting far ahead of ourselves. The question before me now is whether I should reduce the defendant's bail as it is at present, which is a million dollars. I might be so inclined, Mr. Gul, but not in reliance on secondhand information. If this tale is going to be spun, I want a chance to assess Khan's credibility in a formal hearing, under penalty of perjury that everything he tells the court is true."

"But that would mean getting into the crux of the case," Gul protested. "My client would have to give up his right to remain silent and talk about material facts, subject to cross-examination by the prosecutor."

"Exactly," Judge Grafton said. "It's a tough call, I know, but those are the legal hoops you're going to have to jump through if you want a bail reduction. I'll leave the decision to you and your client."

"Taking the stand at this stage could greatly jeopardize my client," Gul said.

"You're probably right," the judge agreed, "but that's the best I can offer under the circumstances."

Gul remained silent for a bit. "I need time to ponder this over. I'll also consult with my client before we proceed any further."

"That's understandable," Judge Grafton said. "How much time will you require?"

"A week should be sufficient."

"A week it is."

"Excuse me, judge," Siegel interrupted. "Are we going to put any of this discussion on the record?"

"I'd prefer we didn't," Gul quickly responded.

"I'm of the same mind," the judge said. "The facts are not quite substantiated. We can all probably agree they're also quite inflammatory in nature. There's enough media frenzy surrounding this case as it is. What are your thoughts, Mr. Siegel?"

"I concur, judge. These are an aspect of pretrial negotiations that don't need to be made public right now."

"There you have it," Judge Grafton concluded. "Since we're all in agreement, I'll put the matter over one week for a hearing. I'm also going to impose a temporary restraining order with regard to statements to the press. Nothing we discussed in these chambers is to be divulged to any media sources until after the bail hearing. Is that fair enough, gentlemen?"

Both Siegel and Gul nodded their agreement and Judge Grafton adjourned the meeting.

Another murmur arose in the audience when the judge resumed the bench and announced the continuance. Ross's jaw muscles flexed when Judge Grafton pronounced the gag order. Cox could clearly see the tension in the FBI agent as the words were spoken. He followed Ross when the agent abruptly got up and squeezed along the aisle toward the exit. Ross was walking briskly along the corridor when Cox emerged from the courtroom and he had to trot to catch up.

"What's wrong?" Cox asked.

"The fools," Ross spat, not breaking his stride. "They talked about the night of the murders. They know everything."

"How can you tell?"

"The gag order says it all. Why else would the judge impose it? Our secret's out."

They stopped at a bank of elevators and Ross stabbed his finger at the down button.

"What do we do now?" Cox asked. "Game's over, isn't it?"

Ross turned a deadly cold expression on the detective. "Nothing's over yet," he said in an icy tone.

Cox felt a stab of discomfort rippling through his gut. "What else can we do at this juncture?"

"Throw a Hail Mary pass," Ross replied.

"I don't get it."

"We make the desperation moves," Ross said with chilling resolution. "It's time to stop half-measures and to act decisively. The damage must be contained at all costs. No effort can be spared."

"I'm not sure I completely understand."

"You don't need to, detective. All I want to know from you, here and now, is if you're willing to see this game through to the end. If so, I'm going to ask you to perform tasks you may not have contemplated, very unpleasant tasks. Can I depend on your cooperation?"

"I said when we first met, I'm your man all the way."

Ross smiled a mechanical smile. "Very good," he said, "because there are a few important things I need you to do. They'll require a lot of fortitude. Do you have fortitude, Detective Cox?"

"In spades. Just tell me what you want done."

The elevator door opened, and the conversation abruptly ended as Ross and Cox squeezed into a crowded compartment.

CHAPTER 25

---•---

I T WAS NEARING DUSK and the sky was clear, except for a few patches of gray clouds. Rappaport couldn't resist the opportunity to go for a jump. He and two other die-hard parachutists chartered a plane from the air club and had it take them up twenty thousand feet. Rappaport let the other two jumpers go first, waiting until they landed before taking the plunge himself.

He loved the otherworldly feel of a freefall, the cold, maddening wind rippling the features of his face, the deafening rush of air in his ears, the illusion of utter weightlessness as his body plunged toward the earth at incredible speeds. Until he touched the ground again, he was alone and free, his mind clear as crystal. He enjoyed an adrenaline surge triggered by the knowledge that he was in peril, defying death, daring it to take him should he falter in his calculations of when to pull the cord. Every jump was a test of his will to live, of his desire for continued existence. It was a question buried deep in his mind before every plunge out the plane door and he was never sure of the answer until it was time to deploy the chute.

As the tableau of green grass, dusty patches, and toylike structures rapidly grew, Rappaport made his split-second decision, tinged by a slight hesitation. His harness pulled against him when the halo chute snapped open, causing an instantaneous drag that slowed the descent. Rappaport's feet touched down quicker than he expected and his knees buckled, sending a shooting pain through his bad leg. Despite that, he managed to keep on his feet by jogging a few steps before the nylon chute collapsed over him.

Rappaport released his harness and gathered his gear together in the waning daylight. The other jumpers were already marching toward the hangar to repack their chutes and Rappaport followed at a distance. That's when he noticed a car pulling to a stop next to the runway. As Rappaport trudged through the grass, he saw Dale Cox emerge from the car and walk jauntily toward him. Cox's broad, pock-marked face bore a belligerent expression and he moved with powerful, urgent strides. Rappaport tensed when they neared one another, sensing that he should free his hands. "What's up, Dale?" he asked.

"You tell me," Cox responded angrily, coming to a halt and squaring his shoulders.

"What's this about?" Rappaport reiterated, stopping and letting his load sag.

"Did you think I wasn't gonna find out, Franny?"

"Find out what?"

"Don't play dumb. You took the goddamn gun out of my apartment and sent it to Sacramento. You broke into my home, you bastard."

"How'd you come to that conclusion?" Rappaport asked cagily.

"I have friends, too. Property told me you took one of the slugs from the evidence locker. Nobody around here had it, and calling DOJ in Sac was easy to figure out. I know about your retest. You're burglarizing my place and checking over my work. How did you think you'd get away with it?"

"Okay, you got me," Rappaport conceded. "You want to fill out a report and bring charges, go ahead. But make sure to explain why you're falsifying evidence that you turn over to the DA's office, and why you're stashing a murder weapon from a major homicide between your mattresses. Internal Affairs should make a lot of hay with that."

The words had a noticeable effect, taking some of the steam out of Cox's bluster. He studied Rappaport through narrowed lids. "You're treading in deep waters," he declared in a low voice. "Getting involved in areas far beyond you."

"Like what, Dale?"

Cox ignored the question. "I'm worried about you, Franny. Good guy like you stickin' his neck out and don't even know it. You're gonna get your head chopped off if you're not careful."

Rappaport could feel the anger welling inside. "You trying to threaten me, Dale?"

"No, I'm trying to protect you. We go way back. You're a good cop and I'm tryin' to watch your back. You and that goody-two-shoes lawyer, Max Siegel, are like a couple of kids lost in the woods, but you don't realize it yet. Night's comin' and you're fixing to freeze to death while still admiring the trees."

"Stop trying to wax poetic; it doesn't suit you. We know a lot more than

you think. How about the CIA holding Khan? How about you working
with the feds to cover it up? You're a dupe. What do they tell you, that
you're in the vanguard of national security? That you're protecting against
terrorism? Are you too stupid to see that you're only a screening action
for a bunch of sleazy politicians trying to protect their precious careers?
They're using you and you're eating it up like a clueless idiot."

"All high and mighty, ain't you?" Cox stated bitterly, beginning to come
unglued under the pressure of the truth. "Big Franny Rappaport, macho
cop, war veteran with a bum leg. Always thought you were better than me,
even when we were rookies."

"This conversation's over," Rappaport announced, pushing past Cox.
"Go find yourself a couch and a good psychiatrist."

Cox reached into his jacket and grasped the sap. Rappaport was
walking away, but the investigator could hear the menace in Cox's voice
when he spoke. "You shouldn't turn your back on me you arrogant son of
a bitch!" Cox spat.

Rappaport tossed his gear and spun around in time to raise his arm
and ward off the blow coming at his head. Cox swung the sap again and
Rappaport jammed his elbow into Cox's forearm as the sap descended. Cox
winced in pain and Rappaport gripped Cox's throat fiercely with his free
hand and planted a foot behind Cox's legs. One powerful push tripped Cox
to the ground, the sap slipping from his hand. Rappaport clenched his fists
and waited for Cox to get to his feet, his blood boiling, ready for battle, but
Cox groaned and remained on his back. The impact of hitting the ground
had knocked the wind out of him, along with any more desire to fight.

"Are we done?" Rappaport asked.

Cox nodded feebly.

Rappaport gathered up his gear. "You really should put that sap in an
evidence locker," he said. "And I meant it when I told you to get some help.
You're a mess."

Cox attempted a response but couldn't get the words out.

"By the way," Rappaport said before departing, "I don't know what
you're doing with Siegel's wife, but you better stop. If he ever finds out, he'll
kill you."

Cox wanted to respond but Rappaport didn't hang around to listen.
Cox was able to rise into a sitting position as Rappaport limped toward
the hangar. You got lucky, he thought. Next time will be different. You
and Siegel got a reckoning coming your way. We'll see who's the idiot,
Franny.

Gul was working late in his law office on Sansome Street in the business district of San Francisco. His secretaries had gone home for the evening and the outer offices were darkened. The overhead lights were also turned off. Gul preferred his desk lamp and the glow of his computer screen for illumination while he worked, the skyline of the city as a backdrop. He enjoyed the atmosphere of his office at night, the solitude after the frenetic hustle and bustle of the day filled him with a certain serenity. He was putting the finishing touches on a civil motion he was preparing to argue in Superior Court. After that, he planned to knock off for the day and drive home to his family across town.

Gul was typing away, the clickety-clack of his keyboard filling the void in the silent room, so intent on his work that the sound from the outer office almost escaped his detection. Gul wasn't sure if he'd actually heard anything and his fingers abruptly stopped. Cocking an ear toward the door—which was open a crack—he remained still, waiting for another sound. When none came, he resumed working, until a more distinct noise caught his attention.

Gul felt a sharp pain in his left arm that shot into his chest. Clutching his bicep, he leaned over in his chair, attempting to see into the other office. "Who's there?" he called.

No answer, but Gul heard whispery voices. Another thudding pain struck his chest and he grimaced and clutched tighter at his bicep, his heart pounding. "Whoever you are, answer or I'll call the police," he gasped when the pain subsided slightly. A cold sweat broke out on his forehead.

The voices in the next room became more pronounced, eliminating any doubt that there were visitors. Gul watched the doorway fearfully as shadows converged on the opening and filled the threshold. Three men emerged into his office, one of them, Ahmed Jinnah.

"What are you doing here?" Gul rasped, fighting for breath, his pain increasing.

"You don't look good, Mr. Gul," Jinnah observed coldly, his two dark-skinned companions easing to either side of Gul's chair. They were young men with angry expressions and Gul felt trapped.

"Are you having a seizure?" Jinnah asked, his tone devoid of sympathy.

"I need my medication," Gul whispered hoarsely.

"Yes, I remember that you require heart pills," Jinnah said. "Do you have them with you?"

Gul was panting. He pointed a trembling finger at the bathroom adjoining his private office. "In there … on the sink," he managed to grunt through more intense pain.

"Let me get them for you," Jinnah calmly offered. "I'll be right back." He strolled casually to the bathroom, went inside, and closed the door.

Gul looked after Jinnah with horror-stricken eyes, confused by Jinnah's actions. Gul felt light in the head, the room slowly beginning to spin. Looking at Jinnah's companions, he saw compassionless expressions. Through the door, Gul heard splashing then Jinnah urinating in the toilet. It was a heavy stream that seemed to last forever and Gul felt a sense of disbelief settling over him as the pain in his body increased.

The toilet flushed and Gul heard Jinnah washing his hands. Then the bathroom door opened again and Jinnah came out with his palm outstretched, a single white pill in its center as he approached Gul. "Sorry about the delay," Jinnah said without remorse. "I had to take care of something before I could get your medication."

Gul contemplated the pill with trepidation.

"Take it," Jinnah urged. "What do you think of me? You'll die without it."

Gul plucked the tablet from Jinnah's palm and shakily placed it under his tongue, closing his mouth and squeezing his lids shut while he waited for the pill to take effect. Jinnah and his men watched Gul with dead, unsympathetic eyes as the pain gradually subsided and a sheen of perspiration speckled Gul's forehead and scalp.

Jinnah stepped to a coatrack where Gul's suit jacket was hanging and pulled out a handkerchief, walking it back to Gul. "Dry yourself," he commanded.

Gul did as he was told, warily eyeing his visitors while sopping the moisture from his head. "How did you get inside the building?" he asked hoarsely. "The outer doors are locked and there's a security guard in the lobby."

"That's not important, Mr. Gul. I didn't come to discuss such trivial matters."

The men with Jinnah appeared restless, one of them surveying the street below through a window. Gul nervously watched them. "What did you come to talk about?" he asked.

"Your appearance in court today was very disappointing," Jinnah stated coldly. "When I hired you to represent Raheem Khan, I expected your compliance with my wishes. In our consultation, I told you not to mention his defense to the court until the preliminary examination. This case represents a delicate political dance between the government and members of the Muslim community in Clay County. Raheem was framed by officials for a crime he did not commit because he is Pakistani and a

Muslim. It is a symptom of the oppression our people have suffered, part of the racism and discrimination we are forced to endure since the attack on the Twin Towers. It is time to orchestrate a response to this blatant oppression and we are prepared to do it in defending against the false charges leveled against our brother. But it must all be done in a certain way, at a certain time. What you attempted today is premature."

"I don't understand what you're saying."

"I'm telling you not to disobey me again. Keep silent about Raheem Khan's defense until the preliminary hearing."

"But why?"

"That you don't need to know, just do as I say!" Jinnah thundered. He was leaning over Gul as he spoke, a fanatical fire possessing him.

"Mr. Jinnah, please understand," Gul feebly replied, looking nervously at the others, "I represent Raheem Khan despite the fact that you are paying my fees. I have an ethical and fiduciary duty to represent *his* interests, not yours. I must rigorously defend Mr. Khan to the best of my abilities and put his benefit above all else. I appreciate your concern about the issues revolving around the crimes charged against him, but I cannot let that sway me from the performance of my duties."

Jinnah continued hovering over the attorney, the ferocity of his expression terrifying Gul. Jinnah's teeth were bared inside his dark beard, but then he suddenly relented and stood straight up. Jinnah took a deep breath and slowly released it.

"What-what are you going to do to me?" Gul asked fearfully.

Jinnah appeared genuinely surprised by the question, spreading his hands, palms up. "What do you think of me, Mr. Gul? Am I some kind of gangster that will kill you if you don't cooperate? Is that what you believe? Do I look like a thug?"

Gul was confused and couldn't reply.

"I merely came here to ask you to help us in our struggle with an infidel society," Jinnah ranted. "I specifically chose you because you are Muslim and raised in a Muslim country with Arab peoples. I hoped you would understand our plight and aid us, but, apparently, I was mistaken."

Jinnah paused and glanced from one to the other of the men that were with him. They returned his attention with eager anticipation, causing Gul's insides to curdle.

"I'm sorry we cannot come to terms," Jinnah lamented. "We've driven all this way for nothing, but we will leave now and go home."

With a nod to his silent companions, Jinnah headed toward the door and they trailed behind. Gul watched them go, confused by their actions, listening intently as they passed through the outer office door before he sprang to his feet. Rushing into the darkened, adjoining room, he twisted the lock on the entrance door. Gul panted and sweat was rolling down his face in large droplets. Leaning his back against the door, he felt a wave of dizziness overtake him. Gul slid to the floor while his heart pounded raggedly in his chest.

CHAPTER 26

———◆———

D AVE LANGERMAN WORKED EXTRA late at his station in the *Las Cruces Times* bureau. After cranking out three stories for the day, and a blurb about the continuance in the Khan case, he typed more thorough notes about what he really knew about the Khan matter. Pausing once in a while to scan the busy newsroom, he worked feverishly, doing his best to escape the notice of nosy editors.

As fatigue set in after a long day, Langerman saved the last of his notes on his computer and stretched, his spinal column crackling as he raised his fists into the air. He let out the guttural groan that a person makes during a particularly good stretch and followed it with a yawn.

"We keeping you up?" his colleague from the next station over asked. His name was Kendrick Olsen, a relatively new hire who worked the sports desk.

"I suppose you people are doing just that," Langerman replied with a pleasant grin. "I'm getting too old for this lifestyle of chasing deadlines every day. I need to get out of the way and let young pups like you run with the torch."

"Aw, don't sell yourself short. You still have some pop left."

"That's nice of you to say. But the question is, do I wanna waste the rest of that pop on the job, or save it for something more personal?"

Olsen chuckled. "That's a good one, old guy."

"Thanks, kid," Langerman said, rising to his feet. "Have a good evening and don't work yourself too hard, partner."

"You, too. Take it easy, Dave."

"I don't know how to take it any other way, kid."

The parking lot for the newspaper sat in a fenced area under a freeway overpass in the worst part of town. It was poorly lit and full of murky patches of blackness where hordes of criminals could hide if they were of a mind to ply their trade in the area. The lone attendant usually went home around sunset, leaving the place completely devoid of any semblance of security. Langerman hated journeying to his pickup late at night. It always set his nerves on edge, until he got safely inside the cab.

After a brief look around, Langerman walked briskly across the empty street bordering the lot. The only sounds cutting through the crisp, still night came from the whoosh of cars passing overhead on the freeway. Heading toward his truck, Langerman wondered if Max Siegel could ever fully appreciate what a good friend Langerman was being. The reporter couldn't believe it himself. He had an inside scoop on a major homicide of national interest at his fingertips, and Langerman was sitting on it, all for the sake of a foolish promise to an old friend.

Langerman was dying to get the story out. It strained against every fiber of his journalistic instincts not to publish the tail. The truth was, however, he didn't know how much longer he could resist the impulse. Max Siegel was a good man and a better friend. It was hard to find persons of such high caliber in a single lifetime. The privilege wasn't to be taken lightly and Langerman weighed the idea of jeopardizing his special relationship with Siegel over a scoop worth about fifteen seconds in the spotlight.

Lost in his musings, Langerman didn't survey his surroundings before getting into his truck. He shut the door and inserted the key in the ignition, and then nearly jumped out of his skin when Dale Cox slammed into the window. "How ya doin', Dave?" Cox called through the glass.

"Jesus!" Langerman exclaimed, recoiling until recognition set in. "You scared the living daylights out of me!"

Cox tapped on the glass. "C'mon, open up. I wanna talk."

Frowning, Langerman turned the ignition key and activated the power window, sliding it down a bit. Cox grinned and stuck his cratered face into the cab. "That's better, now we can talk," he said, his stale breath reeking of booze.

"This is an unusual way of contacting me," Langerman observed. "Most people use the phone and don't take to sneaking around in dark parking lots late at night."

"Pardon the intrusion, but I felt a pressing need to have a conversation. Hope you don't mind."

"What can I do for you, detective?" Langerman inquired warily.

"Saw you in court today," Cox said, scanning the cab, "sitting in the jury box with all those other reporters covering that nothing homicide."

"I wouldn't refer to the Khan case as nothing."

"C'mon, are you kidding? This is Clay County, Dave. We're homicide central, especially in Las Cruces. Did you know we have more murders per capita in Clay County than any other county in California?"

"I wasn't aware of that. Number one?"

"Yeah, number one. So why are people so taken with this murder? Don't you have better stories to focus on?"

"This one has some excitement attached, don't you think? What with those attempts on Max Siegel's life and all."

"Max Siegel," Cox snorted. His lips were stretched tight, his head bobbing up and down. "Good ole Siegel, the Boy Scout somebody wants to kill. Spend a lot of time with him, don't you?"

"We're acquaintances."

"He's got silly ideas about Khan, dangerous, irresponsible ideas. Has he shared any with you, Mr. Star Reporter?"

Langerman felt leery about Cox, whose hostility mounted as the conversation progressed. "I'm not sure what you're talking about, detective."

"Of course not. If Siegel was sharing his stupid ideas with you then I woulda read about them in the newspaper, right? It woulda been in bold print under banner headlines: DA Sees Major Conspiracy Behind Nothing Case! How's that? Is that how you'd write it?"

"Been drinking, detective?"

Cox's bloodshot eyes locked angrily onto Langerman. "Yeah, what of it?"

"I don't know. You just seem a bit out of sorts. Maybe you should go home and get some sleep."

"I will when we finish."

"What are we talking about exactly? I'm not quite sure."

"We're talkin' about Max Siegel and his dumb case!" Cox ejaculated. "Ain't you listening? We're talkin' about him being irresponsible with the facts and how you need to exercise better judgment about what you put in print regarding Khan. I'm tellin' you this as a friend, got me?"

Cox leaned further into the cab during his tirade, his belligerence barely contained. Langerman felt pensive and paused before responding. "Thanks for that piece of professional advice," he said. "I'll be sure and remember it while I'm writing my stories."

"Good!" Cox said, pulling his head out of the cab and slamming his palm onto the roof. The noise reverberated in Langerman's ears. "I'm glad to hear that, because I'd hate for anything bad to happen to you. The fate that befalls irresponsible people isn't very good."

"What fate might that be?" Langerman asked.

"You don't wanna know," Cox replied in a low, chillingly serious tone. "But, hey, I should let you get home, huh? You must need sleep after such a long day."

"Thanks, but I'm not going home tonight. I have a couple days off and I'm heading to Arnold for some wine tasting."

Langerman regretted the words as soon as they left his mouth and silently cursed himself.

"You don't say?" Cox responded with surprise. "Arnold, huh? Going into the foothills this late at night? Isn't that a bit treacherous?"

"Not particularly," Langerman replied. "I drive real slow."

"Sure you do," Cox said, studying Langerman queerly."

There was a long pause, Langerman waiting for Cox to continue, but Cox wasn't saying anything more. He seemed content to stand next to the truck on slightly wobbly legs, something perceptively menacing in his manner. Langerman was anxious to get on his way. "Is there anything else?" Langerman finally inquired.

"No," Cox replied, appearing suddenly preoccupied. "No, sir, you have a pleasant evening, Dave. Enjoy your trip to the foothills."

"I will, thanks," Langerman said, flicking the button to slide the window shut when Cox stepped away. Cox waved as Langerman started the engine, and then walked into the gloomy darkness. Langerman wasn't sure where Cox was going. There weren't any cars nearby. Langerman thought it was strange.

Highway 4, leading into the foothill town of Arnold, was long and lonely. A one-lane highway in either direction, it stretched initially over flat, desolate land, eventually becoming interesting when snaking its way through higher elevations. There it became twisting and winding, constantly rising and falling over random hills like a ride at an amusement park. The road had little lighting, mostly passing through pitch blackness, the treacherous bounces and turns cutting through woodlands where tall trees waited to greet cars unable to negotiate the intricacies of the road.

Langerman was tired, full of second thoughts while he drove to Arnold. Perhaps he should have waited until morning to make the trip. Fortunately, there weren't many cars on the highway, only an occasional flash of headlights followed by long stretches of emptiness. The only exception was a distant pair of lights in his rear. Langerman first noticed the specks in the mirror when he was cresting a hill, but they disappeared when the road dropped and veered to the right.

The lights kept appearing and fading as Langerman piloted his car through crazy twists and turns, growing in intensity, drawing closer at a surprising rate. Langerman wondered what kind of speed demon was behind him; what could possibly be so important that a driver would take such risks on this deserted road. Help would be a long time coming if a wreck happened in such an isolated place.

Langerman nearly swerved onto the shoulder a few times becoming preoccupied with watching the rearview mirror. The speeding car was beginning to absorb all his attention, gaining on him too quickly. Langerman estimated its speed at somewhere around one hundred miles per hour. "Who is this fool?" he asked out loud.

Irritation morphed into concern when the car got close enough that Langerman could discern its make, guessing it was an older model Lincoln. He waited for the car to slow, since he was now directly in front of it, but instead the Lincoln accelerated and its headlights swelled to enormous size. "What the—," Langerman said before the car smashed into his rear.

The steering wheel jerked and Langerman had to fight to keep from flying off the highway. Instinctively, he began to slow, believing he was involved in an accident. The Lincoln's engine revved and the car came barreling at him again, plowing into the pickup and snapping Langerman against his seat as he struggled to keep from spinning out of control. Fear washed over him, a sudden hollowness inside, a thousand ants crawling through his scalp. The Lincoln backed off before closing in again. A sickening realization finally rushed into Langerman's brain and he jammed his foot down hard on the accelerator. Somebody was trying to kill him!

The pickup gained speed and distance on the Lincoln as the highway formed a series of twists and rises. Langerman felt like he was watching a movie screen as he turned the steering wheel right and left, tires squealing, trees and bushes swerving dangerously close before passing out of the way over and again.

The Lincoln struggled to keep up, fishtailing around the bends and becoming slightly airborne on the rises, shooting orange sparks each time it crashed back down onto the road. Langerman couldn't see through the car's windshield, but he sensed the driver's determination to catch him. It was a reckless desire that nearly sent the Lincoln off the road several times, but still it came on, its speed increasing in spite of the danger.

Langerman's bladder released when he saw the Lincoln bearing down on him after the vehicles swooped over another rise, a seeping warmth filling the crotch of his trousers. He was in a state of disbelief when the impact occurred, violently jolting the pickup again. The rear end of the truck swished from side to side as Langerman neared another sharp bend and he fought to keep the vehicle from leaving the road.

That's when the Lincoln's speed ramped up and, incredibly, it closed in. Langerman was in shock, seeing the headlights grow in his mirror until they were the size of two suns. The resulting crash was more than he could handle and the wheel spun out of control as a giant tree lit up and loomed large before the pickup smashed into it. It was the last sight Langerman registered before everything went black.

CHAPTER 27

———————◆———————

SIEGEL WAS UNABLE TO sleep. He lay awake in bed throughout most of the night while Irina slept fitfully beside him. She hadn't been herself lately, moody and quiet most of the time, rebuffing any attempts at physical contact. Siegel would hug her and she'd tense in his arms; attempt to hold her hand and it would slip away after barely a second. Siegel tried asking what was wrong, only to have Irina avert her eyes and mumble a despondent "nothing." Whenever he pressed the question, she'd become either irritated or sad, begging him to give her time alone. Sometimes her lids would flutter, as if she was fighting tears, and she'd rush from his presence. Siegel felt the distance growing between them with each rebuff, the cause of Irina's despondency a mystery that he couldn't crack.

Frustrated with his inability to drop off, Siegel grabbed his cell phone from the nightstand and walked into the living room of the tiny apartment he and Irina occupied. Plopping onto a cheap rental couch, Siegel rubbed his tired eyes and contemplated turning on the television. It was four in the morning. If he was lucky, watching some sappy show might make him drowsy enough to catch a good half-hour's sleep.

The cell phone surprised Siegel when it buzzed. He looked at the call screen and saw that Rappaport was calling. He flipped open the phone and put it to his ear. "Franny," he said.

"Max, you're up. I was planning to leave a message."

"What's going on?"

"I thought you should hear about it first thing, Raheem Khan's escaped."

"What?"

"That's right. The sheriffs discovered it about an hour ago."

"How did he pull it off?"

"That's the interesting part. Know how the bus transports inmates to and from the jail for court appearances?"

"Yeah."

"Yesterday afternoon, after Khan's loaded on the bus at the courthouse, word is that Dale Cox shows up and starts bullshitting with the driver and guards, distracting them. Well, the bus doesn't only go to the main jail, it also goes to the honor farm, the overload facility where prisoners are sent when the main jail's too crowded. That's for low level offenders and there's no security there. The guards sort the prisoners out between the facilities by color coded outfits, orange for the main jail and blue for the honor farm. So, while Cox is shooting the breeze with the sheriffs, Khan's in the back of the bus swapping outfits with one of the honor farm inmates. How they managed to change clothes while shackled is a big mystery. The moral of the story is that Khan ended up at the honor farm and simply walked away. The mistake wasn't caught until an hour ago when there was a bed check at the main jail and one of the jailers, who's followed this case, realized an imposter was in Khan's bed. By the time the alarm went out to the honor farm, Khan was long gone."

"Unbelievable. Any leads as to Khan's whereabouts?"

"Not that I know. I just received the call ten minutes ago. A dragnet's set up with checkpoints near the major roads and freeways. I imagine we'll be sweeping the east side later. That ought to raise another storm with the Muslims."

"Cox again," Siegel said with exasperation, swiping a hand over his face. He noticed Irina standing sleepy-eyed in the doorway, wearing a T-shirt and nothing else. She looked at Siegel inquiringly and he held a finger up at her. "Why is Cox involved in every piece of strangeness concerning this case?"

"He's in cahoots, Max, working with the feds. Their agenda is getting obvious."

Rappaport's last statement struck a cold chord in Siegel. He refused to believe what he was about to utter. "They don't want this case in court. They want Khan to disappear."

"Permanently, Max. I can smell the fear coming out of Washington all the way over here in California. Khan spewing a story about illegal CIA abductions won't do anybody any good in that town."

"We have to find him, Franny," Siegel said, feeling a touch of dread inside. "Anybody else will recover a corpse. I don't want to believe what's in the back of my mind but my gut is screaming at me."

"Me, too. I'll phone a couple of our investigators and get on it first thing this morning. Being Pakistani, there are only so many places Khan can disappear to."

"Let's hope. Call me if anything develops."

"I will."

"And keep tabs on Cox if you can. We can't let him get to Khan first."

"I'll be in touch."

Siegel flipped the phone shut and set it down. Irina was more awake now, eyeing him with concern. "What is it?" she asked.

"Raheem Khan escaped. That was Franny. He called to tell me."

"You mentioned Cox. What about him?"

Siegel frowned. "Why are you asking?"

Irina's grogginess suddenly melted away and a fearful, almost guilt-ridden expression came over her features. Siegel felt a twinge of something unpleasant as he studied her. "It's nothing," Irina said quickly. "I-I heard you mention his name. I only want to know what is going on around me. Are we safe now? Can we go home?"

Siegel saw Irina's arms folding protectively beneath her breasts, her shoulders slightly quivering, and it dawned on him that she was afraid. He rose and crossed the room, wrapping Irina in his arms. "I'm sorry, honey," he said. "I've been so caught up in what I'm doing that I haven't realized the strain this is putting on you."

Irina sighed, pressing her face against Siegel's chest. He kissed her forehead. "I have been so scared, Max," she said. "I worry every day that something will happen to you. It's good that Khan is gone. Maybe now our life can return to normal."

Siegel put his fingers under Irina's chin and lifted until her face met his. "Is that all that's bothering you?" he asked. "You haven't been yourself lately. Is something else the matter?"

"What are you talking about?"

"The distance between us, something's been bugging you for a while. You have it all bottled up inside and you won't tell me what's wrong."

Irina stiffened. "Max, I don't understand what you are getting at."

"Sure you do, Irina. I know you well enough to notice you're holding something back and it's tearing you apart. Why won't you talk to me?"

"Max, stop!" Irina pleaded, pushing away. "I keep telling you nothing is wrong. I don't know what else to say … I'm tired. Let me go back to bed."

"Fine, go," Siegel said angrily.

Irina could see the frustration in him, tinged with a hint of sadness. Something in her went soft at the sight and she wanted to embrace Siegel. But she thought better of it. He would only start asking questions again and she couldn't have that, not yet. She wasn't ready to tell Siegel what he eventually had to know. The time was not yet right.

Siegel watched Irina retreat into the bedroom, depression descending heavily upon him. Irina's behavior confused him. Siegel was certain that something was happening between them, but clueless as to what it was. The marriage was beginning to fray at a time when Siegel needed Irina the most. He couldn't escape the feeling that disaster was looming ahead. It filled him with dread.

After Siegel arrived at his office later in the morning, he put in a call to Sims and left a message concerning his trial assignment status. Now that Khan was gone, Siegel wanted to know if he'd remain in the homicide unit, or whether he was to return to Insurance Fraud.

He flicked on his computer after he hung up and brought the *Las Cruces Times* online. Siegel was taking a sip of coffee and nearly choked when he read the headline on the front page, hot fluid dribbling down his chin. It said: "Star Reporter, Langerman, Injured in Accident." Siegel read the article while dabbing at his jaw and throat with a paper napkin. The account said that Langerman had been in a single car collision off Highway 4 in Calaveras County; that he'd crashed into a tree and suffered head injuries. His pickup was found smashed into a tree by a CHP officer shortly after two in the morning. Langerman was unconscious. No drugs or alcohol were believed to be involved, although blood tests were going to be analyzed for confirmation. Langerman was taken by ambulance to the county hospital, where doctors had listed his condition as serious.

Siegel's heart raced as he called the newspaper to get more details about the accident. He was able to connect with one of the secretarial staff, who knew Siegel, and she told him that Langerman's condition was stable, and that doctors expected a full recovery. He'd suffered a concussion and would probably regain consciousness soon. Siegel felt relieved. He thanked the secretary and gave her his cell number so she could call him with any updates.

Siegel no sooner cradled the receiver when the phone rang. "Did you hear about Langerman?" Rappaport asked.

"Yeah, I just got off the phone with his people at the paper. Looks like he should be okay. I'm going to see him later. Wanna come along?"

"Maybe, but I'm wrapped up in finding Khan and might not have the time. Things are getting too weird around here."

"What makes you say that?"

"I don't know, just a feeling. First Khan gets away, and now Langerman's in an accident soon afterwards."

"You seeing a link?"

"Possibly ... I don't know, maybe I'm paranoid. Talk to Langerman when you see him—if he's awake. I'd like to know what caused the accident."

"You're scaring me, Franny."

"I'm pretty scared myself, Max. Be careful when you go see Langerman."

"Right," Siegel replied thoughtfully.

The head of the homicide unit came to Siegel's office and handed him two more murder cases without any fanfare. It was the answer to the question he'd left on Sims's voicemail. Siegel was once again a full-fledged member of the homicide team. He spent the remainder of the morning reviewing the new cases and performing preliminary workups. Then Siegel signed out for the day and headed to Calaveras County to visit Langerman.

It was late afternoon when Siegel arrived at Langerman's hospital. There was a gathering of *Times* staff in the reporter's room when Siegel checked in, so he hung back for an hour in a nearby visitor's area until the crowd dispersed. He waited until the last person left before strolling into Langerman's room.

Langerman looked beat up, his eyes blackened, bandages over his nose and around his head, his usually robust color now paled. He appeared genuinely happy to see Siegel. "Hey, amigo," he said, "glad you could make it by."

Siegel crossed over to Langerman's bed and gave him a semblance of an embrace. Langerman returned the gesture as best he could, his arms strung with IV tubes.

"How are you?" Siegel asked.

"Alive," Langerman replied, tossing a glance at the open doorway. "I'm glad you came, Max, because I want to tell you what happened. Anybody else out there in the hall?"

Siegel went and checked the corridor and saw that only hospital staff was about. "We're clear," he said.

"Good, come over here so I don't have to raise my voice," Langerman said secretively. Siegel complied and took a seat in a chair next to the bed. "I ain't told this to nobody else," Langerman said in a low voice. "My people believe I had an accident. I told them I went off the road when I took a little snooze, but that ain't it."

"What happened?" Siegel pressed.

"Max, I was run off, deliberately and coldly, by somebody who wanted me dead."

Siegel felt his heartbeat quicken. "By whom?" he asked.

"I couldn't make out the driver, but I'm sure it was Dale Cox. He was talking to me not twenty minutes prior in the newspaper parking lot. It was a strange conversation. He kept jawing about you and the Khan case, about how I shouldn't be irresponsible with the facts. Cox gave me the clear impression I was being threatened. He didn't want me writing about Khan. Then I'm stupid enough to tell him I'm heading to Arnold. The next thing I know I'm getting run off the highway into a tree."

"Are you sure you couldn't see the other driver?"

"Positive, it all happened too fast. I was so busy trying to deal with the car slamming into my tail that I didn't have time to make the driver."

"This can't be happening."

"Oh, it is. My condition is proof of that. We stumbled into a dirty situation, Max, and powerful people don't want it exposed. What happened to me is an example of how far they're willing to go to keep the lid on."

"Khan escaped yesterday. We found out about it this morning. Looks like Cox was buzzing around that event, too."

"Oh my God," Langerman said, laying his head against his pillow. "They're pulling out all the stops. Any idea where Khan is now?"

"None. I have Franny and a couple DA investigators on the hunt. I'm hoping we can get to Khan first."

"I doubt it. I hate to sound like the pessimist, Max, but I'd be deeply surprised if Khan doesn't surface as a corpse in the next day or two. This is a cover-up, sure as there is, and we're all tied into it."

"Think they're coming after us, too?"

"You had two attempts on your life and I just had one on mine. What do you think?"

"Pakistanis came after me. It's not the same situation."

"You sure about that?" Langerman queried, his brow raised. "This case has ramifications going all the way back to Washington. Don't make assumptions about what's up and down and who's on what side."

"If what you say is true, then this isn't over. Somebody will come after me again … and you."

Langerman nodded grimly. "That's what I'm saying. I got lucky this time and I'm not planning to stick around long enough to give somebody another shot at finishing the job. My editor was in here before you arrived and I told him I'm taking a leave of absence."

"Where are you going?"

"Far away from here. I've been needing a long vacation and I reckon now's a good time to take it. Some of my relatives have a spread in West Texas. I'm gonna visit them for a time to get away, Max. This story ain't worth my life."

"You feel that strongly about it?"

"I do. They say I'll be released by tomorrow, after a little more observation. I'm going straight to the nearest airport when that happens. You should contemplate doing the same, if you know what's good. You cheated the grim reaper twice now. How many more times can you expect to stay ahead of that scythe he's wielding? Take my advice, Max, get ahold of that pretty wife of yours and get out of town."

"No, Dave, I won't do that," Siegel replied, his jaw set. "It's not my style. There may be something to what you're saying, and I hope to God there isn't, but I'm not turning my back on it. Someone has to hold the line. That's my job. I wouldn't be worth much in this business if I ran at every sign of trouble."

"Then I guess that makes me a coward," Langerman lamented. "Sorry I'm running out on you, Max. I wasn't built for the thrill-seeking lifestyle."

"Don't apologize," Siegel said, resting a sympathetic hand on Langerman's shoulder. "Truth be told, I'm scared to death, too. I don't know if I'm following the wiser path, or the foolish one. I only know that I'm fed up with the intrigue surrounding the Khan case. I need to get to the bottom of it, one way or the other."

CHAPTER 28

———— • ————

RAHEEM KHAN RECLINED ON a bare mattress in a sparsely furnished bedroom. He was nervous, propped on one elbow, listening to the heavy traffic on the I-5 Freeway. The window next to the bed was crudely covered with a sheet that drooped in places. Through it, Khan caught glimpses of the dilapidated wooden fence in the yard and the grassy rise of the elevated highway. It was gray and drizzly outside, and the sound of passing vehicles was incessant.

There was no heat in the tiny, abandoned house and Khan shivered slightly in the cool, damp air. He'd been on the go for three days since his escape, moving from one house to another in Las Cruces, the police never more than a step behind as their dragnet grew tighter. Khan had barely left the east side apartment he was staying in the night before when the police came in searching for him. Informants were everywhere and Khan didn't know who to trust. Finally, he made contact with Ahmed Jinnah, his benefactor, who led him to the place where he was presently staying. He was to lay low for a day or two until arrangements could be made to get him to a safe haven.

A car turned into the driveway and Khan sprang from the mattress. Bolting across the empty living room outside the bedroom door, he peeked through the blanket-covered window as a car door slammed shut. He blew a sigh of relief when he recognized his friend, Raymond, approaching with large Carl's Jr. bags and a cardboard tray of drinks.

A blast of cold, moist air entered the room when the door flew open and Raymond rushed inside. "What're you doing by the window?" Raymond scolded, kicking the door shut. "Somebody could see you, dude."

"I'm jumpy, man. I can't help it. The cops have been doggin' my ass all over town."

"Well, you can relax, food has arrived."

"What you got?"

"Burgers and fries and some drinks. C'mon, we'll eat in the bedroom."

Khan followed Raymond into the bedroom, briskly rubbing his hands together. "It's freezin' in here," he complained.

"Stop gripin'. It's better than a prison cell, bro." There were two beds in the room. Raymond dropped a bag on one of the beds, and then sat on the other, setting the tray of drinks beside him. "Come and get it," he said.

Khan went to the other bed and tore open the bag, grabbing a bunch of fries and stuffing them in his mouth. He chewed frantically while unwrapping a burger, and barely swallowed before taking a bite of the sandwich. Raymond watched in awe. "Dang, man, you *are* hungry, aren't you?" Raymond peeled the paper off a straw and poked it through the plastic lid on one of the drinks. Lifting the cup from the tray, he handed it to Khan. "Here, you better wash that stuff down."

Khan grabbed the drink and stopped chewing long enough to take several pulls on the straw. He swallowed a few seconds later and let out a satisfied "Aaah," his eyelids drooping as he savored the pleasure of the food. "It's been a long time since I had anything to eat," he said, stuffing more fries in his mouth. "I can't tell you how good this tastes."

"That's cool, man, but try to slow down. You're gonna chew your fingers off."

"Can't help it. This being on the run is the shits, dawg. I'm not gonna sleep good till I blow this crazy town. Did Ahmed say when I can get outta here?"

"He's finalizing the details. Got you a safe place in the Bay Area. You'll take off tonight, after dark."

"Good," Khan responded, allowing himself a smile for the first time. "I can't relax in Las Cruces. This whole deal's got me stressed out."

"I hear ya," Raymond said.

Khan took another bite of burger and thought he heard the squeal of brakes outside. He froze in mid-bite, staring wide-eyed at Raymond, who also became still. The sound of skidding tires came to both of them and Raymond dropped his burger and scrambled into the living room. Khan lowered his hands and waited, feeling the bile rushing up his throat. "Oh shit!" Raymond cried. "It's five-oh!"

Khan rose on impulse and dashed to the window, spilling his drink on the floor. Pulling aside the sheet, he managed to slide the window open just as a thunderous crash exploded in the living room. "POLICE!" a voice shouted. "Stop where you are! Get down!"

Khan gripped the window frame and had one foot on the sill when two shots rang out, followed by a brief cry and a thump. His heart racing in his throat, Khan prepared to hop up and out when a powerful voice yelled, "FREEZE!" Turning his head, he saw a squat man in plain clothes with a pock-marked face, pointing an enormous handgun at him. The man looked familiar but, in his panic, Khan couldn't remember from where. "Hold it right there!" the man yelled forcefully.

Khan relaxed his hold slightly, resignation draining the strength from his limbs. He was ready to surrender when he saw a curious transformation come over the man. His stern expression melted and his lips parted into a wide, yellow-toothed grin. The man's dark eyes looked mean and sadistic and Khan realized—at that moment—that the man was going to shoot.

A surge of strength coursed through Khan's arms, and he pulled hard, kicking his foot off the floor and propelling himself through the window as the gun exploded. Khan fell face first into the muck of wet grass as the window shattered above him. Pushing himself up, Khan regained his feet and sprinted across the slippery grass toward the wooden fence. Ignoring another command to stop, he leapt onto the flimsy fence and was sliding over the top when the man fired from the window. The bullet splintered the wood beneath Khan before he dropped to the ground on the other side, scared senseless. He lay on his stomach in a wet patch of grass as two more shots rang out, the bullets passing through the wood just above his head.

Panic ripping through him, Khan rose to his feet and scrambled up the hill toward the noisy freeway. Slipping and recovering twice, he chanced a look back and saw his pursuer scaling the fence and falling clumsily to the ground with a grunt. Another uniformed officer appeared at the window of the house.

Feeling more urgency, Khan continued ascending the hill until he reached the shoulder of the freeway. Traffic whizzed past in three lanes at incredible speeds. Khan was seized with reluctance, until a patch of gravel puffed up at his feet, another shot that just missed. Looking down the hill, he saw the plainclothesman pointing a gun at him, ready to squeeze off another round.

Seized with uncontrollable fear, Khan darted into the first lane of the freeway without thinking and was sprinting into the next one over when he barely halted in time to narrowly avoid an SUV careening past. He heard the shriek of squealing tires and suddenly noticed a compact car coming straight at him. The brakes were on, but the car kept plunging forward. Sheer terror contorted the driver's face as Khan was struck, his body spilling violently onto the hood with a bone-jarring thunk. The car bucked two times more when it got slammed from behind by a couple other cars, creating an instant pileup.

Rain splattered the windshield when Khan lifted his head in a daze, pain coursing through his body, and peered groggily through the glass at the driver. "I'm so sorry!" the driver was frantically mouthing over and over while Khan stiffly lifted himself from the hood, sliding his feet to the wet asphalt.

Cars continued to squeal to stops all over the freeway, including the opposing lanes across the center divider, as onlookers gawked anxiously at the metallic mess that had spontaneously formed in the northbound lanes. Ignoring the audience, Khan spotted the shooter halfway down the hill taking a careful bead on him for another shot. Khan watched helplessly and heard the sound of more squealing tires as another speeding car careened toward the rear of the pileup, its brakes locked but the car couldn't stop. Just before the inevitable crash, the car veered onto the shoulder, overshot it, and soared like an arrow toward the shooter. The gunman reacted instantly, diving straight backward, barely in time to avoid the car as it swooped past, the shooter tumbling helplessly down the hill. In the next instant, two uniformed officers bolted over the fence to take up the chase, leaving Khan with only one last chance to act.

The driver that hit Khan was a young, red-haired kid. He was out of the car and standing next to the heavily dented hood. "Hey, man, are you okay?" he gushed in a nervous spasm.

Khan grasped the kid by the jacket, twisted hard and tossed him down the hill. As onlookers screamed, Khan jumped into the compact car through the open driver's door and pulled it shut. He was slamming the car into gear when loud thunks banged off the chassis. Khan peeled away as the uniformed officers took three-point stances from the shoulder of the freeway, firing repeatedly at the car as it fled.

"Goddamit!" Dale Cox wailed in anguish as the car sped off in the distance.

"He got away," Rappaport announced, coming unceremoniously into Siegel's office.

Siegel glanced up from the file he was reading. "Who got away?"

"Your boy, Raheem Khan."

Siegel dropped his pen, surprised. "They found him?"

Rappaport closed the door. "*They* didn't find him. Dale Cox and his posse of cowboys tracked him down. Khan was holed up in an abandoned shithole next to I-5. Don't ask me how Cox found the place." Rappaport dropped his palms heavily onto Siegel's paperwork and leaned forward. "There was some other kid in the house with Khan, unarmed, but that didn't stop Cox from pumping two bullets into him. DOA at the hospital. Then Cox tore after Khan and practically emptied a magazine at him. That's until Khan got bumped by an oncoming car on the freeway and improvised a carjacking. He got away clean."

"What the hell is going on?" Siegel asked in disbelief.

"They're not playing," Rappaport said, looking sternly into Siegel's eyes. "They mean to wrap this up, tie off loose ends, and Cox is their point man."

"How long ago did this happen?"

"A little over an hour. We received a protocol officer-involved shooting. Some of our investigators are at the scene now, documenting details and talking to witnesses."

"And Cox?"

"He's being interviewed as we speak. I was there for the preliminary statement. He was first through the door and he swears Khan had a gun. Cox claims he shot in self-defense and that Khan's associate got caught in the crossfire. The other officers came in after the fact and they don't know anything, other than Khan ran onto the freeway and got away. Cox's statement about Khan's gun can't be confirmed or denied."

"We need Khan," Siegel declared.

"Tell me about it."

"He's in a stolen car. That's bound to get spotted. We're a registration check away from catching the slippery bastard."

"Correction, Max, *Cox* is a registration check away from nailing Khan. No matter how close we monitor the police radio, it's LCPD that'll pull the car over."

"Unless Khan makes it out of town. Better yet, out of the county."

"You have a point, Max. If Khan gets stopped outside our jurisdiction, we might get to him first."

"Exactly. Let's stay on top of it. Don't just monitor the radio, send computer queries to the Department of Justice and DMV every hour or so. If we're lucky and get a hit, maybe we can get our hands on Khan before anyone else."

"Then what do we do with him? Sticking his carcass in jail will be like handing him to Cox."

"Good point, Franny. Let's agree now that if we get Khan, we'll put him on ice, take him somewhere outside the system until we figure out who to trust."

"Serious?"

"Deadly."

"Do you know what you're saying? That can be construed as aiding and abetting. We'll be accessories to escape."

"Probably, but what else is there? Something rotten's in the system and we can either stick our heads in the sand or deal with it. I don't like what's happening, but I won't ask you to go against your principles. You decide how you stand."

Rappaport stood erect. He took a deep breath and briskly rubbed the back of his head. "Okay, buddy," he said. "I don't know where this intrigue is heading, but I'm with you. God have mercy on our souls."

CHAPTER 29

---•---

THE DAY AFTER SIEGEL heard about Khan's escape, he was in Starbucks talking to Irina, when he saw a man in a suit smiling at him from a corner table. The man was well dressed, professional looking, with thin lips and cold eyes. Despite the smile, the man appeared cruel, although Siegel couldn't specifically discern why. The man's fixation on Siegel was deliberate. He made no attempt to look away whenever Siegel glanced at him. Instead, his gaze became more fixed and his smile broader, until it was obvious that he wanted contact.

Siegel broke away from Irina when a customer approached the counter and carried his coffee to the man's table. The stranger watched Siegel as he drew closer, appraising him coolly, like he was sizing up an opponent. "Excuse me, do I know you?" Siegel asked.

"No, but I know you. Max Siegel, deputy DA."

"And you are?"

"Special Agent Ross with the FBI," Ross replied, without extending a hand. "I've wanted to meet you for some time. Care to join me for a few minutes?"

Siegel set his cup on the round table and sat down. "FBI?" he repeated. "I take it this regards the Khan matter?"

"Very perceptive," Ross said, his smile expanding. "That's exactly what this concerns, Mr. Siegel."

"Call me Max."

"Okay, Max. I've been in the area for a while, ever since this unpleasantness began. My partner and I have kept a low profile, working behind the scenes with your Detective Cox."

"Why's that? Why the secrecy?"

"Don't be disingenuous, Max, you understand precisely why we're low-key. We're aware that you're aware of whom the victims were and some of what was occurring."

"You have the victim part right, but I'm not up on the circumstances surrounding the killings. Care to illuminate me?"

Ross looked around cautiously. The coffee shop was crowded and the ensuing buzz was enough to mask their conversation. "We should be careful how we discuss this, for obvious reasons. So I'll talk in a roundabout way."

"Fine. What was our man doing in that house with those agents?"

"I explained that to your boss, Rich Danko. Didn't he brief you?"

Siegel was surprised, but tried not to show it. "No, he didn't. Perhaps you can give me a rundown."

Ross smirked, his expression smug. "Your defendant is of great interest to us. He's a close associate of a man named Tariq Nasir. Not long ago, the two of them made a special trip to Pakistan to study at a *madrassa* run by a radical cleric. We kept tabs on both individuals, until Nasir gave us the slip in San Francisco. We formed the opinion, based upon certain intelligence, that a scheme was in the wind and action was imminent. That's when another agency decided to pick up Khan. It was a unilateral decision, quite illegal, as you are aware, but well-intentioned. Once the act was done, officials from the upper echelons decided it was best to transport the problem far, far away, to a place where information could be more lucratively extracted."

Siegel's brows rose.

"Yes, I see your reaction and I agree it was a messy action. But turning our man back out on the street—under the circumstances—seemed … irresponsible. We were between a rock and a hard place and the only logical course was transportation elsewhere. Unfortunately, Khan's move superseded our plans. Now he's on the loose."

Siegel sat back and gave a low whistle that was lost in the noisy room. "You guys really put your foot in it, didn't you?"

"Yes, we did. I hope you appreciate the stickiness of our problem."

"Absolutely, but let me ask you," Siegel leaned over the table and glanced about before continuing. "Did you help with the escape?"

Ross took a pregnant pause before answering. Siegel thought the hesitation was a bit too long. "No," Ross replied, "that wasn't our doing."

Liar, Siegel thought, straightening in his seat. You must think I'm stupid. He was irritated by the smirk on Ross's mouth. There was something condescending about his manner. "Agent Ross, why are you telling this to me now? You didn't share it with me when the case began, why when Khan's gone?"

"I'm sorry about the lack of communication, Max. Danko should have taken care of you," Ross replied without credibility. "As for why we're presently talking, I suppose it's to come to an understanding."

"About what?"

"You're a dogged prosecutor, Max. That hasn't been lost on the numerous people monitoring events. It's universally agreed that you're a good man, a good American."

"Oh oh, here it comes."

"Here what comes?"

"Anytime someone from Washington starts appealing to a person's patriotism, it's a prelude to something that stinks. Why don't you put the 'good American' crap aside and come to the point? What do you want?"

"Direct, forceful, I like that," Ross said appreciatively. "Want to know what I want? Silence, Max, blissful, deafening silence. I want Raheem Khan to disappear and no mention of this incident to leak into the public realm. And I'm not the only one. As you sit here, Max, you're not speaking to me alone, but to a round table of the most powerful people in the country, the world really. Each has a stake in the outcome of how events unfold in this backwater town. What happened in Pleasant Oaks a few weeks ago is insignificant against the backdrop of a worldwide battle against forces that have one goal, the destruction of the United States. I hope you can see the bigger picture, Max. I hope you'll cooperate and help us sweep recent events under the carpet. Go along and I believe you'll find a big reward waiting for you."

"What might that be?"

"Maybe the office you seek to win next November. We're aware you want to be DA, to extinguish Rich Danko's career. He's the target of a federal probe. If we were to step up the investigation, who knows? Perhaps he'd be forced to take his name off the ballot just before the polls. You could win by default."

"You people are beautiful," Siegel said with much sarcasm. "What did you promise Danko when you kept me in the dark? Your political situation is desperate. Officials must be scrambling to save their precious careers all over Capitol Hill. Is this really about national security, or politicians running for cover?"

"You don't get it, Max."

"Oh, yes I do. You want me to see the big picture, to understand that we're fighting an underground war against an implacable enemy. Okay, I get that. But I'm also taking a further step back, looking at an even bigger picture, the one where a democratic society, in order to protect itself, throws out the very values it swears it's defending. What about the law?

What about due process? When the government stoops to going outside the law to protect itself, it becomes no better than the enemies it's claiming to fight. That can't be, not if I have a say."

"What are you getting at?"

"There was a double homicide in this city. There's a suspect out there who's accused of committing them, who needs his day in court. Possibly the killings were justified, perhaps not; I don't know. But there's a system set up to explore those questions and the apparatus functions through a court of law, under the guidelines of due process. Unlike you, I support the process, no matter where it takes us. Tell those people I'm talking to that their positions don't place them above the law. They're subject to it the same as anybody else. If they did something wrong, they'll have to answer for it, just like anybody else. Tell them Max Siegel's not playing in their dirty little game."

"You're a fool!" Ross gasped, his composure cracking.

"Maybe so, but that's where it stands."

"You're making a big mistake, Max. This conversation is your only chance to come onboard."

"What's that supposed to mean?"

"I made my pitch," Ross replied enigmatically. The distress his expression displayed only a moment prior vanished, a curtain descending over his emotions. His gaze bore into Siegel with unnerving intensity, until Irina's voice cut through the surrounding din. She was speaking to a customer near the cash register and it tugged at Ross's attention. "Pretty wife," he remarked in a flat, mechanical tone. "Isn't her name Irina?"

"Yes, Irina," Siegel replied warily.

Ross turned quickly to Siegel. "Is that her name?" he demanded.

"Why are you talking about my wife?" Siegel asked defensively. He could feel his blood beginning to boil.

"Those recent attempts on your life must've been hard on her, and then relocating suddenly to Pine Grove."

Siegel felt a chill racing along his spine.

Ross sensed Siegel's discomfort and smirked. "Still living at the same apartment?" he pressed. "Let's see, isn't the address 1227 McHenry Place? Apartment 226?"

"How do you know that?"

"Does it matter? I'm concerned for you and your beautiful wife, the one you call Irina. Somebody's tried to kill you two times recently. I'd be concerned if they learned your new address."

"That's enough!" Siegel said sternly, his color darkening. "You try anything to harm us and I'll come after you myself, you hear me?"

Ross played at being confused, his amusement increasing. "You're taking this conversation wrong, Max. I'm not threatening you."

"Sure you are," Siegel countered, rising to his feet. Nearby patrons took notice of the abrupt move. "We're done talking."

"If you say so," Ross replied lightly, lips pursing.

Siegel stormed out of the coffee shop, paying no heed to Irina's concern as he passed. She turned her attention to the man Siegel was speaking to and felt a cold tingling when she saw the man staring at her. He appeared amused and gave Irina the creeps. A customer approached and Irina helped him. After she punched the order on the computer, she tried to chance another look at the man, but he was gone.

Siegel's mind was in turmoil. He didn't want to admit it, but Ross had unnerved him. The revelation about the victims being CIA and that they'd abducted Khan was no more than a confirmation of what Siegel already suspected. The veiled threat was a concern, and Siegel planned to change apartments first thing, but that wasn't what struck a nerve either. The remark that hit home, the one that knocked Siegel off balance, was Ross's response to the topic of Irina. "Is it?" Ross emphasized when Siegel confirmed her name. He let the quirky remark fly over his head, but in truth, it had set off bells and whistles, dredging up a host of doubts buried deep in Siegel's thoughts. Ross knew something about Irina and he'd dangled it at Siegel to torment him.

Irina was acting strange lately and Siegel wondered if what Ross alluded to had anything to do with it. Siegel had only known Irina for little more than a year when they got married. Her prior life in Sacramento was a mystery, not to mention Russia before that. After talking to Ross, Siegel realized the mystery didn't sit well with him. He'd subconsciously avoided probing its depths, but he didn't know why. Perhaps it was because he'd found an island of happiness in what had been an unsettled life prior to his marriage and he didn't want to lose it. But the time had come to confront his fears. There was a shadow in Irina's life and a light needed to be shined on it.

Outside on the street, Rappaport was pulling to the curb near the courthouse in his pickup when he saw Siegel coming from Starbucks. Siegel walked toward the truck and knocked on the passenger window. Rappaport unlocked the door and let Siegel climb inside. "What's going on?" Rappaport asked.

"You arrived at the right time, Franny. I was heading to your office."

"For what?"

"We have moves to make. I just had a weird meeting with a special agent from the FBI. His name's Ross."

"How'd that come about?"

"He was waiting for me at Starbucks. He knows everything about Khan, and he's working with Cox."

"That son of a bitch. I knew it," Rappaport spat. "Ross must be the same person I saw Cox rendezvousing with when I followed him."

"No doubt; this Ross is an odd character. Don't ask me to pinpoint it, but there's something wrong about him."

"What did he want?"

"Cooperation, at least that's what he claimed. He confirmed that Khan wasted two CIA spooks in Pleasant Oaks. He's in the area with the backing of the Washington top brass and his job is to clamp a lid on the killings."

"What are you saying exactly?"

"Ross has cart blanche to do whatever it takes to keep the feds' secret, that they abducted a citizen off the streets to render him out of the country. Cox talked to Langerman the night Langerman was run off the road. Cox also took potshots at Khan when he found the kid's hiding place. But for Khan snatching a car on I-5, his carcass would be laid out on a slab right now. It wasn't an accident that Ross told me he's working with Cox. He wanted me to know. Cox is his personal hit man. The partnership was announced just before Ross let on that he knows where I live."

"Did he threaten you?"

"That was the implication. It came right after I told him I wasn't playing ball. He was telling me I'd painted a target on my back, Irina too."

"It's hard to get my head around this."

"You're not alone, my friend. This whole situation is surreal, but its happening and we need to deal with it."

"What do you want from me?"

"We need to get our hands on Khan. Any info on the car he stole?"

"Yes, news came through on the computers this morning. It was found abandoned in San Francisco, the Haight-Ashbury district."

"Good. Chances are he's still there. Khan can't fly out of the airport.... Ross mentioned one of Khan's associates. What did he say the name was? Nasir, that's right. The feds were tailing him when they lost the scent in San Francisco."

"So Khan hooked up with this Nasir in the city? You think they're still bumming around there?"

"It's a long shot, but it's the best we got. They have a lot of heat on them, so they can't move around much, not if they want to stay underground.

San Francisco's a big city. It'd be easy to blend in there. Unless they already blew the country, we have a chance of finding them."

"I suppose it's worth a try. I'll grab a couple investigators and do a canvass."

"No," Siegel said quickly. "We can't bring anybody else in. Ross told me he's talking to Danko. He's also working with Cox. The feds have been inside the investigation from the start and we don't know who to trust, even from our own office. I don't know how cozy Danko is with Ross, but we have to assume anything Danko learns is going straight into Ross's ear. There's not enough time to assess who's loyal to Danko. We have to run this operation alone. Nobody else from the office gets involved."

Rappaport took a deep breath and blew it out. "Man, that's a tall order, Max. Going alone in San Francisco will be worse than trying to find the proverbial needle in a haystack."

"Understood, but we don't have a choice. There's too much intrigue surrounding the case. Who to trust is a major issue. But at least we have a starting point."

"What's that?"

"Khan's attorney lives in the city, this Saddam Gul fellow. Start with him. Pay a visit and feed him whatever information you need to secure his cooperation. Maybe he's heard from his client. He might know where Khan's hiding, or at least he can point in the right direction."

"Sounds like a solid lead, I'll try that. When should I leave?"

"When I get out of your truck. We're in a race against time and who knows what else. I'm sure the feds already have their agents swarming the city, so keep your head down."

"You too, Max. We're in dangerous territory."

"Don't worry, I can take care of myself, Irina too."

Rappaport saw a curious change come over Siegel when he mentioned his wife. "What is it?" Rappaport asked.

"Oh, nothing," Siegel replied, looking morose. "There's another matter I want you to look into when you get back, something personal. I'm asking a favor."

"Sure, Max, anything. What's it about?"

"Irina," Siegel replied, staring steadily at his friend. "I want a background check on her."

Rappaport went cold inside. He wanted to respond, but he couldn't move his jaw.

"Are you okay, Franny?" Siegel asked.

"Yeah, sure."

"Listen, I know I'm asking a lot. It's nothing to do with the job and you can turn me down if you want."

"No, that's fine, Max. You caught me off guard is all."

"I understand. It's pretty strange. Don't ask me what's wrong, or why I suddenly have this desire to rummage around in her past. I'm running on gut instinct. Something's wrong with her. Call it a husband's intuition, but since this case began, Irina's changed. I don't know why, but something tells me it has to do with her past."

"Max...," Rappaport began.

"Yes?"

Rappaport was on the verge of spilling what he knew about Irina and Cox, but discretion held him in check. "I'll take care of it," was all he said.

"Thanks, buddy."

CHAPTER 30

---•◆•---

THE RECEPTION AREA FOR the Law Offices of Saddam Gul was impressive, professional, yet not ostentatious. It contained two mahogany desks, one occupied by a slightly elderly secretary with short-clipped, gray hair. She was cleaning out her desk when Rappaport walked through the door, placing items in a cardboard box. She didn't look up until Rappaport was immediately in front of her. The secretary's heavily lined eyes appeared dull, almost lifeless. "Is there something I can do for you?" she asked in a fatigued voice.

"I'm looking for Attorney Gul," Rappaport said, already sensing a problem.

"I'm sorry, he's not here."

"Do you know when he'll return?"

"I'm sorry, I mean he passed away."

Rappaport felt an electric bolt pass through him. "He's dead?"

"Yes, it happened yesterday, I'm afraid. The firm is closed."

"Sorry to hear that, Miss—"

"Bruin, Amanda Bruin."

"Miss Bruin, my condolences. Are you alright?"

"Yes, I'm fine, thank you."

Despite the secretary's reply, Rappaport could see she was barely holding it together, obviously in a state of shock. The tragedy of Gul's death was still sinking in. Her movements were listless and mechanical. "Is there anything I can do for you, Miss Bruin?"

"No, thank you. Did you have business with Mr. Gul?"

"Sort of, I wanted to speak with him about Raheem Khan."

Miss Bruin reacted with a start, gasping slightly.

"What is it?" Rappaport inquired.

Miss Bruin's lids flickered rapidly, fighting back tears. "I'm … I'm … I apologize, it's the mention of that name. It was Mr. Gul's last call before he … *passed.*" The final word came out as a sob. Miss Bruin pulled a tissue from the top drawer of her desk and blew her nose.

"Excuse me, Miss Bruin, but could you tell me what you mean by that?"

Miss Bruin was still pressing the tissue to her nose with the fingers of both hands. "Yes," she said, blowing her nose again. She wiped firmly at her nostrils and pulled the tissue away. "It happened yesterday morning. A man who refused to identify himself phoned and demanded to talk to Mr. Gul. His voice was gruff and I thought his attitude was incredibly hostile. I almost didn't put the call through, but Mr. Gul had insisted he wanted to take all calls concerning Mr. Khan."

"What did the man say, exactly?"

"Nothing really, only that he wanted to talk about the case. It wasn't what he said that put me off, it was how he said it. He had a terrible attitude. I shouldn't have put that call through."

"Why's that?"

"Mr. Gul took the call in his office," Miss Bruin said, staring into space. "I didn't hear anything after that. I was working on the computer when I heard a thump behind the door. I paused for a second and listened, but there was nothing more, so I went back to work. Why didn't I go in and check out that noise? I could have saved him."

"Was it Gul you heard?"

"Apparently, but I swear I didn't realize it at the time. It wasn't until another call came in thirty minutes later that I opened the door and entered Mr. Gul's office. He'd … he'd collapsed in the bathroom doorway. There was nothing I could do. He was already cold when I put my hand on his cheek. He'd taken a heart pill but it didn't do any good this time. They were scattered all over the floor…." Miss Bruin's narrative broke off and she started sobbing into another tissue.

Rappaport circled the desk and put a gentle hand on Miss Bruin's quivering shoulder. "It'll be okay," he said soothingly. He froze when a thought went through his mind. "Gul took something right before he died?" he asked.

"Yes," Miss Bruin replied, sniffling, "his medicine."

"What kind of medicine?"

"Nitroglycerin pills, for his heart. He took them whenever he had an episode. He wasn't supposed to get stressed out."

"But the phone call about Khan upset him," Rappaport declared.

"I don't know. It might have. As I said, the man who called sounded belligerent and the seizure hit about the time Mr. Gul got on the phone with him."

"You don't suppose—," Rappaport started to say, and then cut himself off. "Miss Bruin, are any of those pills still around?"

"No, the paramedics collected them for analysis."

"Do you mind if I have a look at the bathroom?"

"Why would you want to do that? Who are you?"

"Please don't get upset," Rappaport said, taking out his badge and identification. "My name is Francis Rappaport. I'm an investigator with the Clay County District Attorney. I'm working the Khan case."

"I can see your credentials are in order, but I'm confused as to why you want to snoop around in Mr. Gul's bathroom."

"Please," Rappaport persisted.

Miss Bruin scrutinized him briefly before the defensiveness left her and was replaced by resignation. "What does it matter anymore?" she sighed, a slight catch in her throat. "Go ahead and suit yourself. Now that Mr. Gul's gone, I don't see what difference it makes."

"Thank you. I'll be quick about it."

Rappaport walked into Gul's office while Miss Bruin returned to emptying her desk. He wasn't sure what he was expecting to derive from the attorney's medication, but he found the timing of Gul's death suspicious. His investigator instincts wouldn't let him overlook details, no matter how farfetched they were.

The bathroom was a mess, the remnants of efforts to revive Gul spread across the floor of the tiny room. Rappaport got down on his hands and knees and rummaged through the detritus, hoping to find a pill that might have gotten missed. He was lucky, finding two small tablets pressed against the molding by the sink.

Rappaport carried the pills to Gul's desk, retrieving an envelope and dropping the pills inside. Then he folded the envelope and placed it in the pocket of his slacks. He'd drop the tablets by the DOJ crime lab the first chance he got for a confirmatory analysis of the makeup of the medicine. It wouldn't hurt to probe whether Gul was poisoned.

"Thank you for the look around," Rappaport said, reemerging into the reception area.

"Certainly," Miss Bruin responded. "Did you find anything of interest?"

"Nah, I'm sorry to intrude."

"You don't suppose something underhanded happened to Mr. Gul, do you?" Miss Bruin inquired with concern. "The case with Mr. Khan was taking a toll on him."

"No, I wouldn't be concerned about that," Rappaport soothed. "Your employer was the victim of unfortunate medical circumstances and nothing more. I'd stake my reputation on it," Rappaport lied. There was no reason to make Gul's secretary more distraught. Then a thought occurred to him. "Now that you mention it, though, has Khan contacted your office in the past day or two?"

"I couldn't say. Mr. Khan is a client and any communications with him are confidential," Miss Bruin replied, her professional persona kicking in.

"Not quite true, Miss Bruin. I don't know whether you're aware or not, but Khan escaped from custody a few days ago. He's a fugitive from justice. Anyone knowing his whereabouts and not disclosing it could be considered an aider and abettor to his continued flight. It's not covered by the attorney-client privilege. His lawyer and, by association, his lawyer's assistants are required by law to divulge any information about Khan's location. That includes you, Miss Bruin."

"Well, Mr. Rappaport, I certainly don't know anything about Mr. Khan's whereabouts and I have no desire to end up on the wrong side of the law."

"I know you don't."

"Now that I think about it, there was a call on the voicemail to Mr. Gul yesterday evening. The caller identified himself as Raheem."

Rappaport hit the mother lode. It was hard to contain his composure in front of Miss Bruin. "Did you save that call?" he asked.

"Yes."

"Would you mind if I listened to it?"

"Mr. Rappaport, I—"

"We need to ascertain whether it's Khan."

Miss Bruin pondered her next action briefly, then sighed and lifted the receiver off the desk phone. After punching in the numbers to retrieve the voicemail, she gave the hand-piece to Rappaport.

"First message was sent on Wednesday at six-fifty-three PM," the recording announced. *"Mr. Gul, this is Raheem,"* stated a voice tinged with desperation. *"Listen, I'm jammed up. I had to take a hike from the jail. People were planning to kill me! I'm in the city and I don't know what to do. I need your help. Oh, man, I'll call you again later. Please be in. I need to talk to you somethin' fierce."*

That was Khan. Rappaport felt energized when he cradled the receiver. "Miss Bruin, does this phone have caller ID? It looks like it does."

"Yes, of course."

"One last favor, could you write down the phone number for this call? Is it on there?"

Without replying, Miss Bruin punched the keys on the phone pad and watched the display screen. She picked up a pen and scratched a number on a memo slip, handing it to Rappaport. "Will that be all?" she asked. Her manner suggested she wanted Rappaport's visit to end.

"Yes, thank you," Rappaport replied, taking the piece of paper. "You've been a tremendous help. I'm sorry about Mr. Gul and I wish you all the best, ma'am."

As soon as he was outside, Rappaport used his cell phone to dial the number. It connected to a Muslim community center that a suspicious secretary said was located near Union Square. After Rappaport hung up, he drove to a fast food restaurant and ordered enough meals to keep him fed for a day. Then he located the center, a nondescript block building in the middle of a quasi-business district. After circling around for a bit, Rappaport found a parking space across the street from the entrance that gave him a good view of who was coming and going. He alighted on foot and walked the perimeter, peeking through the entrance when he passed. A group of Arab men crowded the foyer and some of them watched Rappaport warily when he strolled by.

Rappaport also cased the street before returning to his car, searching for signs of FBI surveillance teams. There were a couple vans parked nearby, possibly occupied by agents, but Rappaport couldn't be certain. The surrounding buildings were also good locations for watching posts, but the windows in the area were too numerous and opaque to clearly discern if the feds were about. Rappaport decided to proceed on the assumption that they were.

CHAPTER 31

───────•◆•───────

IT WAS CLOSE TO 9:00 PM and a light drizzle fell from a starless sky. The temperature had dropped substantially after sunset and gusts of wind were sweeping along the street as Rappaport continued his surveillance of the Muslim center. The car's interior was like a refrigerator and Rappaport had to turn the engine over from time to time to crank the heat for warmth. It worked for short spells, but never long enough to get the chill out of his bones. He spent most of the time shivering, wondering if his mission was worthwhile.

Just when Rappaport was about to admit defeat and pack it in for the night, something caught his attention. Heavily clothed men had been entering and leaving the center all day, many of them so similar in appearance that Rappaport couldn't distinguish one from another. He might have seen Khan twenty times that day and not realized it. But when the entrance door opened and two young men emerged—one with a scarf wrapped around his face—Rappaport perked up.

The two men slowly descended the few steps to the sidewalk, looking around with a wariness that appeared unwarranted. The one with the scarf had Khan's stocky build and somewhat large head, from what Rappaport could remember. The man moved in a jaunty fashion similar to how Rappaport remembered Khan moving when he stepped into the prisoner's box in court. It might be a long shot, but Rappaport decided to check out the men.

The two walked in a direction away from Rappaport's position. There was no time to start the car and hang a U-turn, so Rappaport decided to pursue the men on foot. His legs were cramped, especially his bad leg which ached in the joints because of the cold weather and prolonged lack of movement. Rappaport limped as he crossed to the other side of the road. He tried to keep a good distance from the men, hoping they'd eventually stop someplace and allow him a nonchalant approach for a better look.

The two men slowed when they came to the mouth of an alley and appeared to confer with each other, turning their heads slightly as they spoke. Rappaport was far to their rear and couldn't tell if they were sneaking glances at him, though he had a feeling they were. Before he knew it, the pair cut into the alley and disappeared from view.

Rappaport discreetly withdrew his service weapon from the belt holster under his jacket and held it low as he approached the alley. Arriving at the entrance, he saw no sign of the men, only the shadows of trash bins and scattered waste.

The alley was long and narrow, a thin sliver of random lights glimmering at the opposite end. Rappaport debated going in, wary of a trap. But he couldn't pass up the chance to get Khan, if, in fact, it was Khan he was following. Rappaport had to know, and decided it was worth the risk.

Easing his index finger onto the trigger of his Sig Sauer automatic, Rappaport limped cautiously into the alley, eyes alert, ears attuned to any sounds other than the pitter-patter of rain. So much trash lined the alley that Rappaport was assaulted by stale, rotting odors, each bin, each stack of bags looming ominously in the darkness. Rappaport felt his heart rate quicken and he had to steady his breathing, lifting the gun before him, anticipating an attack.

A form materialized a few feet ahead, stepping from behind a bin and taking a wide stance. Rappaport stopped and dropped into a crouch, leveling his gun at the figure. "Hold it right there!" he commanded, and then felt a searing pain when a metal rod crashed into his wrist.

The gun clattered to the pavement as Rappaport's attacker raised the weapon for another strike. Rappaport lifted his left arm to intercept the rod as it whizzed toward his head. Metal smacked against bone and a shock of incredible pain in Rappaport's forearm sent him reeling backward. A lashing kick snapped into his solar plexus, sending Rappaport crashing into a wall, his head smacking hard against brick before he collapsed onto a heap of trash. Pain wracked his skull and his head felt as if it were spinning as he gasped for breath, his diaphragm in spasms.

The man with the rod stepped forward, readying for another strike, his eyes blazing with hatred. Rappaport raised a feeble arm for protection, too dazed to scramble to his feet. As the attacker raised the rod for another blow, his partner grasped his wrist and arrested the motion. "Tariq, no!" It was Khan who spoke.

"Let go of me," Nasir said, fighting against Khan's grip, but unable to break it.

"No!" Khan demanded. "I want to know who he is first." Pushing Nasir aside, Khan squatted in front of Rappaport. "Who the hell are you? Why you tryin' to kill me, bro?"

"I-I'm not trying to kill you," Rappaport gasped raggedly, fighting a wave of nausea as Khan's face came into focus. "I'm an investigator with the DA's office."

"Wait a minute," Khan said, drawing closer. "I recognize you. You and another dude questioned me at the hospital. That other one tried to shoot me in Las Cruces."

Two explosions crackled from the opposite end of the alley. Rappaport and Khan looked simultaneously at Nasir, whose expression contorted, his mouth yawning into a gaping hole.

"What is it, Tariq?" Khan asked, but his friend didn't respond. Instead, he dropped the rod to the pavement and clutched at the breast of his coat, tearing it open to reveal growing red patches of blood spreading across his chest. "Oh shit!" Khan exclaimed when another explosion caused Nasir's forehead to explode, spraying blood and brain fragments into the air.

Nasir's body slumped forward in a heap, to Rappaport and Khan's horror, revealing two dark figures that were stealthily approaching from the end of the alley.

Khan was paralyzed, but Rappaport's training and instincts kicked in and he crawled toward the Sig Sauer, ignoring the pain wracking his body and head. He grasped the gun when the two figures began to charge and pointed it shakily in their direction, managing to squeeze off two shots that sent the figures diving to both sides of the alley.

Unaware if he hit anything, Rappaport forced himself unsteadily to his feet and put his free hand on Khan's shoulder. Khan wheeled around, swatting Rappaport's arm away.

"C'mon!" Rappaport urged. "We have to get outta here."

Khan stared at him with the ferocity of a trapped animal.

"I'm not going to hurt you," Rappaport assured as he saw a flash from the lower side of the alley and a bullet ricocheted off the brick wall above his head.

Khan whipped around in the direction of the shot and more explosions and flashes erupted from the walls of the alley, bullets whizzing so close that he and Rappaport could hear them cutting through the air.

Rappaport tugged at the collar of Khan's coat. "If we don't get outta here, we're dead!" he yelled. "Follow me!"

Crouching, Rappaport ran zigzag fashion toward the street, not worrying if Khan was following. The alley was like a shooting gallery, bullets pinging off metal trash bins, smacking against the brick walls. Rappaport cut sharply around the corner to his left when he reached the street, out of shooting range. Khan emerged immediately after and Rappaport pulled him against the wall beside him.

Gun raised, Rappaport peeked around the corner into the alley, ready to engage the shooters. He was surprised to see two shadowy forms making a mad dash for the opposite end of the alley. It didn't make sense.

"What's happening?" Khan asked breathlessly.

"They're leaving."

"Why?"

The answer came with a snapping sound and a spray of brick fragments in the narrow space between their heads. Khan's expression was puzzled, but Rappaport understood instantly what was happening. "Sniper!" he gasped, tugging at Khan's coat and running down the street. Khan trailed him as the side window of a parked car blew out. "Keep moving!" Rappaport urged, darting into the street to get to his car.

They were almost hit by an oncoming truck that braked to a screeching halt. Rappaport continued past the vehicle with Khan in tow, ignoring a rapping on the hood of the truck that caused a burst of steam to shoot into the air.

"Hey!" the driver cried, his voice carrying through his closed window.

Rappaport estimated the shots were coming from the building opposite them, but he had no time to pinpoint the location. When they reached the opposing sidewalk, Rappaport pulled Khan against a wall a few yards shy of his car. "The sniper's above us," he said to his wide-eyed companion. "He can't sight us as long as we stay pressed against the wall. We have to make it to my car over there." Rappaport removed keys from his trouser pocket and remotely unlocked the doors, the tail lights flashing in response. "See it?" he asked.

"Yeah," Khan responded breathlessly.

"When I say, we make a dash for the car. You get in the back on the floor and stay down until I drive away. Got it?"

"Yeah, yeah, I'll do it!"

The rain was falling harder and traffic in the street began to pile up because of the stalled truck. Horns blared and Rappaport was grateful for the mounting confusion, estimating it would give them a better chance to make it to his car. "Are you ready?" he asked.

"Yeah, man, let's get the hell outta here."

"Okay, let's go!" Rappaport shouted. He heard what sounded like a punch just as he started to run.

Khan cried out and slumped against the wall, sinking to the sidewalk.

Rappaport stopped short and retreated back to Khan. "What's wrong?" he asked, squatting down.

"I'm shot," Khan moaned, right hand clutching his shoulder, his features contorted.

Right then a piece of wall exploded over Rappaport's head, and he realized there was another sniper across the street. They were in a cross fire!

There was no time to waste, no time to think. Rappaport grabbed Khan and hauled him to his feet. Then he raised his gun and fired two shots into the air. A woman screamed and pandemonium broke out around the stalled cars. Despite the din, Rappaport heard a bullet whiz past his ear. Pulling Khan with every ounce of strength he had left, Rappaport limped and ran toward his car. Khan did his best to keep up, but Rappaport could sense Khan's ebbing strength as the shock of his wound set in.

A young male pedestrian, fleeing the sound of gunshots, crashed into Rappaport when Rappaport reached the car. Then the man suddenly grit his teeth, growling in agony when a crimson plume sprouted from his chest. He dropped to the pavement, writhing in pain as Rappaport tugged Khan over his prostrate body and yanked open the rear passenger door of his car.

Rappaport threw Khan onto the seat and slammed the door shut, ducking when he heard a bullet strike the roof. Running in a crouch to the driver's door, he pulled it open as the rear passenger window shattered in a spray of glass. All Rappaport could do when he was inside was pray that he wouldn't be hit while he fumbled the key into the ignition.

The windshield popped, a spidery crack forming over the steering wheel when the engine roared to life. Rappaport slammed the car into gear, jamming his foot on the accelerator pad. Tires squealed as two more knocks resounded off the roof. Rappaport almost sideswiped an SUV when his car tore away from the curb. Another bullet struck what was left of the rear window while he rounded the corner. Then they were home free.

Chapter 32

Siegel was surprised by the dark form sitting below the light switch when he stepped through the door to his office. He had to control himself to keep from reacting.

"Hello, counselor," Dale Cox greeted.

After steadying himself, Siegel clicked the switch by Cox's head and proceeded to his desk. "Why are you lurking around my office first thing in the morning?" he asked.

"I'm not lurking," Cox said with a smirk. "I got up early on this glorious Friday morning and thought I'd come by and have a chat."

"About what?"

"Khan."

"He's gone. What's there to talk about?"

"I hear he's not gone anymore." Cox paused and studied Siegel, trying to gauge him. The detective looked bad. His clothes were rumpled, his hair pushed back on his scalp in greasy strands, his pocked face full of stubble and his eyes lined red. "Have you heard from Rappaport lately?"

"Why do you ask? What's this all about, detective? I have work to do."

"It's about Khan, a skanky little terrorist that shouldn't be walking the planet, but he is. It's about your boy, Rappaport, having him in custody but not bringing him back to jail."

"What are you talking about?" Siegel asked impatiently. Cox's ominous words had pricked his attention and he was feeling nervous.

"You really don't know, do you?" Cox said, rising to his feet and closing the door. He sauntered to Siegel's desk and leaned over it, bracing his fists on the surface. "Franny Rappaport got ahold of Raheem Khan in

San Francisco last night. Khan was partnered with Tariq Nasir, another fugitive terrorist, who ended up dead in an alley, apparently at the same time Rappaport made contact. Very suspicious circumstances, Mr. Siegel. People are gonna want to question Franny about that. Problem is, he's disappeared with Khan and nobody knows where he is."

Siegel was sent reeling by the revelations. He did his best to maintain a cool exterior, but he could feel color coming to his cheeks. "How do you know this?" he asked.

"C'mon, I'm juiced in with the feds. They feed me. Agent Ross told me he talked to you about what's what. Apparently, you and Franny don't wanna cooperate."

"Cooperate with what exactly? What is it we're supposed to be doing with Khan besides prosecuting him? What's the federal version of justice?"

Cox stood erect, spreading his palms outward, a condescending grin stretched across his mouth. "Look, you know what time it is. The government's fightin' a filthy war with an enemy that don't play by the rules. Our cause used to be popular, but now it's got to be toned down because of the backlash by a buncha spineless, tree-huggin' liberals. But the war still drags on and the conventional rules won't let us win, so we have to tweak 'em a little here and there. Khan's in one of those here-and-there places. They know what he's about, but they can't prove it. He don't stop being dangerous because we can't prove it, know what I mean? You and Franny need to get with the program."

"And who's making all these decisions about what Khan is or isn't?" Siegel asked.

"People in a lot higher places than you and me, counselor. People at the top. People I trust."

"It must be nice to be so trusting, detective. I wish I could be as sure about things. Unfortunately, I was born with a more skeptical mind. I believe the so-called 'people at the top' are just that, people. They're human beings, just like you and me, and they're not perfect. They make mistakes, just like you and me. So forgive me if I'm not as ready to swallow whatever they're dishing out. I like to judge situations for myself and we happen to have a system set up in this country to help us parse the facts.

"Khan may or may not be a danger to society, I don't know. He may have committed murder, or he may have killed in self-defense, I don't know that either. But—unlike you and Agent Ross and all the higher mucky-mucks back in Washington—I'm willing to plug those questions into the system and let the process sort them out. That's the way it's done in a free and democratic society. That's what's supposed to set America apart from all the totalitarian regimes we're always railing against in the world.

"Am I getting through to you? Are you understanding what I'm saying?"

Cox shook his head with dismay. "You're an idiot, Siegel. They told me you were a Boy Scout that just didn't get it, and I tried to stand up for you. I told 'em they were makin' a mistake, that you were capable of seeing the light. But they had it right. Ross has got you pegged. You're hitchin' yourself to the wrong cause and gettin' ready to go down in flames. How can such an educated man be such a goddamned fool?"

"Whoever's the fool is in the eye of the beholder, detective. It all depends on your perspective. Now, unless you have anything intelligent to say, this conversation's over."

"Okay, counselor, whatever you want. I tried to help but I can see it's no good." Cox started toward the door. "I feel sorry for that pretty wife of yours. Losing you will be a tragedy."

Cox grunted when his face slammed into the door. Siegel had moved so fast that the detective never heard him coming. He'd seen a flash of blue when his nose hit the wood. Now the pain was radiating through his sinuses as Siegel pressed him hard against the door.

"Don't ever mention my wife in the context of a threat, you hear me?" Siegel hissed into Cox's ear. Cox felt a sharp pain in his lower back when Siegel punched him in the kidney. "You stay away from her. If anything happens to Irina, I swear I'll kill you! Got it, you son of a bitch?"

Cox felt another jolt of pain in his lower back. "Yes, yes, I get it!" he gasped.

"Good," Siegel said, yanking Cox away from the door and pulling it open. "Get outta here," he commanded, shoving Cox over the threshold.

Cox staggered into the corridor, the curious stares of two passing attorneys on him. He rubbed his back, wincing as Siegel slammed the door shut.

Siegel kept his ear pressed to the wood and listened for Cox's departure. He knew the detective was armed and didn't want to take any chances that Cox might retaliate with his gun. Crazier things had happened lately. Siegel breathed a sigh of relief when Cox moved away.

Siegel went to his desk and sat down, calming himself. He was surprised by his own reaction when Cox mentioned Irina and wasn't sure why it set him off. Instinctively, he reached for the phone and started to punch in Rappaport's number, then abruptly stopped.

It flashed into Siegel's mind that his desk phone might be monitored. He was familiar with a concept the FBI called "tickling the wire." It was an information gathering technique whereby an agent, or some other informant, engaged a target in a dialogue meant to provoke a reaction. The agent would then walk away, the hope being that the target would get on the phone and start calling leads that could help further the investigation. Ross and his cohorts apparently wanted to find Rappaport and Siegel was probably their best conduit.

Siegel cradled the receiver, his suspicions on high alert. The cell phone on his belt buzzed and he saw Rappaport's name on the display screen. "Franny, is that you?" Siegel asked.

"Yeah, I got Khan."

"I know."

"How can you?"

"Cox told me a few minutes ago, before I threw him out of my office. The FBI is all over it. Cox also mentioned something about Tariq Nasir getting capped in an alley."

"If they know that, then they're the ones that did it."

"What do you mean?"

"I picked up Khan and his friend's trail outside a community center last night. When I contacted them in an alley, two men took potshots at us until Nasir ended up with a couple slugs in his back. Khan and I barely made it to my car alive. Max, there were snipers firing down on us from the neighboring buildings. They had us in a cross fire."

"You're kidding!"

"I wish I was. This was Special Forces stuff, Max. These people were professionals. It was a hit team and they were on us the second Khan's ID got made."

"Did you get a look at any of the guys?"

"No, everything happened too fast. It was night and it was raining, and I was too busy trying not to get killed to stay around for a meet and greet. Khan took a hit in the shoulder, but it's nothing serious. I managed to staunch the bleeding and got him patched up with some basic first aid."

"You have him now?"

"Yes, we're at—"

"No! Don't say anything more. Let me call you back on a landline. Somebody might be tapping our call. Can you get to a payphone?"

"Nowadays, who knows? They're disappearing fast."

"Try to locate one. I'll do the same. I'll call back in an hour on your cell phone, and then we can swap payphone numbers and talk that way."

Siegel was leaving the courthouse when Ahmed Jinnah approached him on the steps. Siegel's senses were hyper alert, scanning the surrounding area for signs of Jinnah's companions.

"Relax, Mr. Siegel, I am quite alone," Jinnah assured. He blocked Siegel's path, causing him to stop short.

"What do you want?" Siegel asked.

"To talk about an important matter."

Siegel brushed past Jinnah. "I'm busy," he said, without looking back.

"You have Raheem Khan," Jinnah declared in a raised voice. "It's quite urgent that we speak."

Siegel stopped abruptly and slowly turned. "What do you know about Khan?" he asked suspiciously.

"That you have him," Jinnah repeated, his deep-set eyes darting from side to side, worried that someone would overhear his words.

"What makes you believe I know where Khan is?"

"Come, come, Mr. Siegel, we don't have time for games. Members of the Muslim association in San Francisco witnessed the strange event resulting in the murder of our brother, Tariq Nasir, and the abduction of Raheem Khan. The man that took Raheem away was described as a middle-aged white man who moved with a decided limp. That is just like your investigator, Francis Rappaport. I have seen you with him."

Now it was Siegel's turn to look around. He stepped closer to Jinnah until they were mere inches apart. "I don't know what's on your mind, but I don't have time to discuss this with you here and now. I have pressing business."

"I'm sure you do. Take my number," Jinnah offered, discreetly thrusting a card into Siegel's hand. "I wrote my personal cell number on it. You may call any time and I strongly suggest you do within the next few hours. It's crucial that you do this. Lives are depending on it."

Siegel was about to respond when Jinnah broke away, walking briskly along the sidewalk. Siegel glanced at the card before thrusting it into the pocket of his slacks. Then he went to Starbucks and found Irina at the counter.

"Max, what is it?" Irina asked, instantly reading her husband's troubled visage.

"Has anybody bothered you this morning?" Siegel quietly asked.

"Bothered me? No. Why do you ask?"

"What about Dale Cox? Has he been around?"

Siegel saw a curious flicker in Irina's eyes and it unsettled him. "No," she replied, "he hasn't come by. Why do you bring up his name? I don't understand."

"Hey, buddy, you gonna order or what?" a customer behind Siegel asked impatiently.

Siegel whipped around and gave the man a dangerous look that backed him up a step. Siegel returned his attention to Irina and led her by the elbow away from the register, ignoring the groans of waiting customers.

"Max, what are you doing?" Irina asked.

"I want you to come with me," Siegel said. "Is there somebody who can cover your shift?"

"Yes, but we are very busy."

"Don't argue, Irina. I'll explain everything when we get to my car. I don't want you here."

Irina was perplexed, but she went along with Siegel to his parking garage and barely had time to attach her seatbelt before he shifted into gear and sped through a series of winding turns and emerged onto the street. While Siegel drove through downtown, frequently checking his mirrors, he told Irina about recent events and Cox's malevolent visit. Irina grew increasingly concerned while he spoke, but her reaction was off the mark from what Siegel expected. There was something disconcerting in her demeanor, but Siegel was too preoccupied to break down what it was that bothered him.

"Are we in danger, Max?" Irina asked shakily. "Are people trying to kill us like Dave and that Khan person?"

"I can't say, sweetheart. They definitely want Khan out of the way. Where that leaves the rest of us, I'm not sure. We're in danger as long as they believe we have Khan. They'll go through anybody to get him. We're dealing with desperate individuals."

"What if you give them Khan? Won't they leave us alone then?"

Siegel shot Irina a harsh look, diverting his attention from the heavy traffic they were in. "They'd kill him for sure. We'd be handing him over to the slaughter. It would be murder."

"Why should we care?" Irina almost shouted, her voice breaking. "Isn't he just a killer also?"

"I have no idea," Siegel replied, jamming the brakes to avoid rear-ending a car. "That's what we're charging, but he's my responsibility until I'm sure. I'm not handing him over to the wrong people."

"Who are the right people? If you cannot trust the government, who is left?"

"I wish I knew," Siegel said, gripping the steering wheel harder. Irina's question went to the crux of his confusion.

When Siegel located a payphone, he called Rappaport's cell and obtained his location's number, and then hung up and called it. "We better make this quick," Siegel said. "Technology being what it is there's no telling how long it'll take to tap this call. What's the scoop, Franny?"

"That attorney, Saddam Gul, is dead, apparent heart attack, but I don't know. I managed to retrieve some pills he was popping and got them to DOJ for analysis."

"Do you have Khan with you?"

"Yes, we're tucked away in a fleabag motel off Highway 99 called the Rio Rancho. It's about five miles north of Las Cruces. Best I can tell we're the only guests in the place, if you don't count the roaches."

"What's the room number?"

"The shadow on the door where it used to hang says 3."

"Sounds like a real five-star establishment," Siegel said, jotting the information on a slip of paper. "How are you two doing?"

"I'm banged up, but I'll live. Khan's coming along. No sign of infection in the wound he got during our escape, but I'll keep checking."

"Is he cooperating?"

"For now. After what happened last night, he's flying scared; doesn't know what's what. We had some testy conversations driving out of San Francisco, but he eventually came around. He seems to trust me. I could've put a bullet in him last night and didn't, so that cemented our relationship."

"Where is he now?"

"Back at the room. And don't say it, Max; I had to take a chance and leave him alone. These are desperate circumstances."

"Alright, pal, I'll defer to your judgment. I just hope he's there when you get back."

"He will be. He has nowhere else to go. The people he trusted couldn't protect him, so I'm all he has."

"Do you have supplies?"

"I had some leftover fast food that we ate for breakfast. I'll pick up some more on the way back to the motel. Other than that, the cupboard's bare."

"I'll get you something on my way over."

"That's well and fine, Max, but what's the plan of action? We can't sit this out forever."

"I hear you. I just had this dropped on me by Cox this morning and I'm still spinning. He and the FBI are gunning for you. If Cox shows up in your vicinity, I suggest you run."

"So what exactly am I doing, Max?"

"Sit tight for now, give me a chance to figure the angles. We can't go to the feds; they're the root of the problem. City and county law enforcement are compromised, so that leaves us with the state. The governor and president aren't the best of friends lately, so maybe we'll find a safe harbor with the local Department of Justice."

"What if that doesn't work?"

"Then we're out of options. We won't cross that bridge until we come to it. Let me put out some feelers and see what kind of reaction I get."

"I have some of my own. I'll do the same."

"Be careful until we produce something conclusive. Play your location close to your chest."

"You don't have to tell me that, Max, not after last night. Right now, you're the only one in the world I trust."

"Wouldn't have it any other way, buddy. We'll get out of this. I promise."

Siegel returned to the car and dropped the slip of paper on the center console before driving away. Irina eyed the paper in silence while Siegel piloted the car out of the city. He was distracted, Irina noticed, his mind juggling a multitude of thoughts. After a while, he spotted the paper and snatched it off the console, crumpling the tiny sheet and stuffing it into his shirt pocket.

CHAPTER 33

———◆———

"THANK YOU FOR TAKING this meeting," Jinnah said. It was late afternoon and he and Siegel were standing next to a fenced play area in a Las Cruces park. Not far away, runners passed on a dirt track that encircled the perimeter. Siegel scrutinized each runner who drifted by. "It's good that you trust me," Jinnah continued.

"I don't trust you, Mr. Jinnah. I came to listen to what you have to say, so make it fast."

"Your attitude is unfortunate. I thought recent events in the Bay Area would bring us closer together, not drive us further apart."

"How do you reason that?"

"You have possession of my comrade. Now you don't know what to do with him. You can't turn him over to the authorities, because they want to harm him. Keeping Raheem safe is a goal we share."

"You keep assuming I have him."

"That you have Raheem is no longer an assumption, Mr. Siegel. You wouldn't be here otherwise."

"What do you want, Jinnah?"

"To help." Jinnah reached into his jacket and removed a thin, manila envelope, which he held out to Siegel.

"What's that?"

"Take it, Mr. Siegel. It's money, a few thousand dollars."

"Why do you want to give me that?"

"To help Raheem get to safety. You must be short of funds. This will help. It's approximately twenty-five hundred dollars, scraped together from contributions within the community. Please take it."

Siegel studied the envelope, debating whether to accept the money. He was unsure of Jinnah's motives, what game he was playing, but the funds could come in handy. He hesitantly took the offering, as Jinnah smiled contentedly.

Half a block away, Agent Frazier also smiled, watching the transaction through a zoom lens attached to a video recorder and parabolic microphone. He sat discreetly in his car, the subjects of his surveillance oblivious to his presence. Picture and sound clarity were outstanding. Ross was going to be pleased.

It was early evening when a joint task force of officers from Clay County, the Las Cruces Police Department, and the FBI descended on the Rio Rancho Motel, a drab, L-shaped facility in a weed-infested clearing. Ross and Detective Cox had made contact with the Indian couple in the front office, confirming that the occupants of Room 3 were in and that no other guests were about.

Before going in, officers in the entry team noted the bullet-riddled car outside Room 3 and ran a check to confirm that the license plate matched Francis Rappaport's county-issued vehicle. There was a light on in the room, although the shades were drawn and a visual of the interior wasn't possible.

Cox hung back in the parking lot with Ross, grinning with delight when he gave the final signal for entry. Immediately, a heavily armed officer pounded on the door to Room 3 while two other officers stood ready to either side of the door jam. "Police, open up!" he shouted.

Barely a few seconds passed when another officer carrying a metal battering ram charged the door and slammed the object into the knob, causing the door to fly open with a resounding bang. A team of armored officers moved in, weapons drawn, shouting for the occupants to surrender.

Rappaport awoke with a start, as did Khan, who was asleep in the next bed over. Rappaport heard the commotion outside and saw the red and blue lights flashing against the window shades. "What is it?" Khan asked as Rappaport rushed to the window and peeked outside.

They were in a room at the tip of the L, giving Rappaport a perfect view of Room 3, which was toward the other end of the motel. What he saw shocked him: a swarm of officers and police vehicles surrounding the room. "They found us!" Rappaport announced. "Get your shoes on. We have to get outta here!"

As Khan scrambled off the bed and did what he was told, Rappaport ran into the bathroom. There was a small, square window in the shower area and he slid it open and pushed out the screen. "Raheem, come in here!" he shouted. Khan appeared in the doorway, his expression panic-stricken. "Come on," Rappaport urged. "We're going through the window. Follow me out."

"We won't make it," Khan protested.

"Yes, we will. They don't know we're here, not yet. We can get away if we go now."

Rappaport didn't have time to brook any further protest. Ignoring the pain in his limbs from his injuries, he hoisted himself through the small window, squeezing past the opening to the waist, and then grasping the sill and planting a hand against the wall as he drew his legs free. His feet clunked awkwardly onto the ground outside and he staggered away from the wall to reconnoiter the area. Once he saw the coast was clear, he helped Khan out, then pulled hard on Khan's coat when he heard approaching footsteps. Running in a low crouch, the two managed to make it down a slight slope to a grassy ravine, barely having time to dive in before two armed officers rounded the edge of the building.

Rappaport and Khan lay flat on their stomachs on the cold, damp ground, their faces pressed into the grass as the officers skirted the rear of the motel. One of the policemen had a flashlight that he clicked on, shining it about, the white beam passing just above Rappaport's head. The investigator squeezed his eyes shut and fought to control his breathing, hoping the team members wouldn't notice the open window, or the screen on the ground.

The officers eventually moved on and continued to direct a beam of light into the field while they walked toward the end of the building. They were about to round the corner when Khan clasped both hands to his nose and grunted, stifling a sneeze.

"Did you hear that?" a voice asked.

Rappaport and Khan froze.

"Hear what?" another voice responded.

"I heard something over there," the first voice said, the beam of his flashlight playing through the grass over Rappaport's head.

The men remained deathly still in the thin ravine, aware that the slightest movement would give them away. A cold breeze blew across the ground, making them shiver with anxiety. It seemed an eternity before the light flickered out.

"It was probably nothing," a voice said dismissively. "Let's finish our sweep."

Footsteps moved away, followed by silence. Rappaport waited a few moments before getting to his feet. When he saw that the officers were gone, he helped Khan up. "Let's go," he said. Breaking into a limping trot, Rappaport ran deeper into the darkness of the field, Khan following obediently behind.

Nearly five hours elapsed since Rappaport's flight and he felt exhausted as he limped along the shoulder of the freeway, following the off-ramp to the Rio Rancho Motel. It was close to two in the morning, and Rappaport hoped he wasn't crazy, returning to the same place he'd fled from earlier in the evening. He was taking a big gamble, but after he'd gotten to safety and cleared his head, it seemed the most logical move. With Khan secured and out of the way, it was time to call the bluff. Rappaport prayed he wasn't miscalculating the depth of determination by his pursuers. Would they risk murder under the circumstances? Rappaport bet he was safe so long as Khan wasn't with him.

The red and yellow neon sign announcing the motel flickered pathetically in the darkness, a beacon to the lowest of wayfarers. Rappaport saw his county car in its spot near the room, two other civilian cars accompanying it a short distance away. It was too dark to see the interiors, but he assumed they were occupied.

The night clerk, a dark-skinned Indian woman, peered nervously at Rappaport through the tiny check-in window when he strode past. Rappaport paid little notice, focusing on the door to Room 3, which appeared slightly ajar, light escaping unnaturally through gaps in the frame.

Prickly hairs stood on end at the base of Rappaport's neck. He sensed he was being watched. Nonetheless, he moved confidently forward, pushing at the door, which easily swung open.

"Hello, Franny," Cox said from a chair facing the door. The deputy beside him sprang to his feet.

"How you doing, Dale?" Rappaport casually replied, leaning against the splintered doorjamb. He heard the pitter-patter of running feet, but didn't bother to look back.

Cox raised his hand against the deputy's chest when the deputy started to move forward, stopping him. Rappaport felt hands roughly grasping his arms and made no attempt to resist.

"Hold off," Cox ordered. "Let him go."

The hands released Rappaport and the three officers accosting him stepped back. Rappaport gave them a casual look before returning his attention to Cox. "Thanks," he said. "Now, would you mind explaining what this is about? Why are you in my room?"

"Where's Khan?" Cox demanded.

Rappaport shrugged. "Your guess is as good as mine."

Cox stood up. "Don't get cute. You're harboring him in this room."

"I am? That's news to me. Whatever put that idea in your head?"

"I'm leading a task force that tracked him here … with you. He's a fugitive and you're holding him."

"Yeah? How'd you come to that conclusion?"

Cox's eyes shifted nervously and his cheeks flushed. Rappaport had caught him off guard. Cox wasn't sure how to respond.

"If you have proof of what you're accusing me of, then arrest me," Rappaport said, his confidence growing. "But before you get that circus started, you better be able to back it up. I'm a peace officer, remember?"

"Where is he?" Cox blurted angrily.

"Beats me, detective. All I know is that I'm working a case, and that I needed a place away from home to get some sleep, so I rented this room. Why you're tossing these accusations at me is a complete mystery. If you have a move to make, make it now or get out of my room. What'll it be?"

"What should we do, Detective Cox?" the deputy beside him asked.

Rappaport could see the gears in Cox's oversized head spinning. He'd been thrown a curve ball and didn't know how to respond. Without Khan, there wasn't a legal basis for Rappaport's arrest, unless the task force had managed to tap Rappaport's call with Max Siegel earlier. If so, then Cox had to lay those cards on the table now, otherwise, he had bunk, because the feds weren't about to acknowledge what happened in San Francisco. Rappaport held his breath waiting for Cox's response. If Rappaport guessed wrong about Cox's case, he'd be spending the night in jail.

"Detective?" the deputy prodded. "Should we arrest him?"

"No," Cox sighed petulantly. "Cut him loose."

CHAPTER 34

RICH DANKO WAS IRRITATED when his expected guests arrived at the front door. It was early morning and he was wearing a blue bathrobe cinched together over a T-shirt and pajama bottoms, his feet in brown slippers. He conducted Bernie Sims, Dale Cox, and Ross into his den and shut the door. The aroma of coffee drifted into the room, but he didn't offer any to his assembled guests. Moving his bulk behind a cherrywood desk, he slumped into a leather swivel chair and glared at Sims. "Okay, Bernie, we're all here. What's so important that my home's being invaded on a Saturday morning?"

"Sorry to bother you like this, boss," Sims apologized, "but this can't wait. "You'd wring my neck if I let this sit until Monday."

Danko turned his glare on Cox. "You look like shit," he declared. "Don't smell too good either. Been sleeping in those clothes?"

Cox gave Danko a tired, tight-lipped grin and snorted, not sure how to take the remark.

"We'll make this quick," Ross said. He was the only person in the room dressed in a suit. Danko saw that he cradled a small video camera, a tiny screen protruding from its side.

"What do you have there?" Danko inquired.

"A present," Ross replied. Without further prodding, he circled around the desk and pressed the play button before handing the device to Danko.

Danko watched the meeting between Max Siegel and Ahmed Jinnah with great interest, his bushy eyebrows rising as the video progressed. By the time the image on the screen flickered off, his expression had softened, transforming into a mirthful countenance. "The date and time on the picture says this encounter happened yesterday."

Ross was beaming. "Yes, the resolution and sound are excellent. Your man, Mr. Siegel, is quite photogenic. Don't you agree?"

"Yes, he is," Danko said, nodding. "How'd you get this incredible footage?"

"We have our ways," Ross replied, hovering over Danko's shoulder.

Danko leaned back and gave Ross a wary look. He was creeped out by the man. "Yes, I'm sure you do," he said.

"We tried to arrest Siegel's boy, Franny Rappaport, last night," Cox said. "We gotta tip he was holding Khan in a sleazy motel outside town. I took a task force over there, but Rappaport was alone when we kicked down the door. He got wind we were coming and managed to stash Khan someplace before we could find him."

"What are you telling me?" Danko asked. "Rappaport's mixed up in this?"

"To the hilt," Cox replied. "Only we had to let him go, because we didn't have anything to pin on him."

"That will change in time," Ross pronounced, snatching the camera from Danko's hands and strolling around the desk. "It shouldn't take long to find Khan and implicate your investigator in aiding his flight. The only question, Mr. Danko, is what you're going to do about it? Max Siegel has been a thorn in the side of this case from the start. Now that you have the goods on him, what do you plan to do?"

"Siegel, that's easy," Danko responded, almost ruminating to himself. "But, Rappaport, he's a good man, a topnotch investigator. He's a war hero for chrissakes. It'd be a shame to take him down."

"He's joined at the hip with Siegel since the beginning," Cox said. "There ain't no separating one from the other. If one goes, the other has to follow."

"I almost couldn't have said it better myself," Ross added smugly.

Danko nodded as he took in what was said, his thick brows knit firmly together. "Mmm," he said, breathing heavily through his nostrils as his mind churned. He snapped out of his contemplation after a bit and fixed his beady eyes on Sims. "I'm not going to tolerate any deputy under my command going outside the law to handle a murder case," he said firmly. "By not sharing his knowledge regarding the whereabouts of a wanted killer, and accepting money to aid the suspect's flight, Siegel's broken not only the law, but his sworn, ethical duty as an officer of the court."

"I agree totally," Sims said.

"This pains me, but I have no choice. I have to take action in this matter," Danko continued. "Bernie, I want you to haul one of the secretaries into the office this morning and have her type the paperwork for an arrest warrant on Max Siegel."

"I'll get right on it," Sims said.

Ross and Cox were visibly ecstatic.

"After it's done," Danko continued, "I want you to personally carry it to the home of the on-call magistrate, along with an affidavit from Detective Cox that gives the particulars for probable cause, and get a search warrant for Siegel's home, cars, and office. When that's done, I want Max Siegel arrested and every piece of evidence we can find on him dug out of whatever nook it's buried in. I want it done today. If Max Siegel's not in jail by tonight, you're out of a job, understood?"

Sims took a breath and blew it out. "That's a tall order, boss, but you can count on me to get it done," he said.

"What about Rappaport?" Cox asked. "We can't leave him walking the streets; he knows where Khan is."

"What do you want me to do?" Danko asked rhetorically. "We don't have anything to hang him with, you said so yourself."

"He's as dirty as Siegel," Cox pouted.

"Maybe so, but until we can prove it, he stays out of the lockup."

"We may not be able to arrest him, but he's still your employee, Rich," Sims ventured.

"Yes, he is. What's on your mind?"

Sims removed his round glasses and began polishing the lenses with a handkerchief he pulled from the pocket of his Docker slacks. "We can't arrest him, but you can suspend him on suspicion of complicity in a criminal act. Maybe that'll shake him up a bit and convince him to rethink his loyalties. You never know, he might come around after he's had a scare."

"I doubt it," Danko retorted. "Franny Rappaport's one of the few people working under my administration that's actually got a set of balls. A suspension won't impress him."

"Maybe not," Sims said, putting his glasses on and stuffing the handkerchief back into his slacks, "but with free time on his hands, he'll also have plenty of opportunity to lead us to Khan. If he's truly aiding the fugitive, he'll eventually show us where the little bastard's hiding."

"I like the way you think, Mr. Sims," Ross coolly interjected. "That's an excellent idea. We could arrange full-time surveillance of Rappaport."

"There you have it," Danko said. "We're all together in a grand spirit of cooperation. This love fest is making me feel all warm and fuzzy inside. Is there other business to take care of before I kick everybody out and return to enjoying my weekend?"

"We covered everything on the agenda," Sims said after scanning the others. "Sorry to bother you, boss."

Danko rose from his chair and trailed his guests to the doorway. "No bother at all," he said as he saw them into the foyer and let them out, grabbing Sims by the shoulder and putting his mouth to his assistant's ear. "Make sure the press covers Siegel's arrest," he whispered. "I want it splashed across the front page of the morning paper. The voters of Clay County need to get a good look at the man who thinks he's taking my job next November."

Rappaport dozed off at his desk in his cluttered office. His feet were crisscrossed on the desktop, arms folded beneath his chest, head leaning back against the top of his chair, mouth slack. When Siegel arrived, he saw his friend clad in beat-up blue jeans and a gray hooded sweatshirt. He could have mistaken Rappaport for a street thug if he hadn't known better. Rappaport was snoring contentedly while Siegel watched. The attorney felt a touch of guilt as he prepared to wake up his friend.

Three knocks on the wall snapped Rappaport's head forward, eyes blinking in momentary confusion before he gathered his senses together. "You finally got here," he said in mid-yawn, stretching his arms.

"Soon as I got your call. Why aren't you at the motel?"

"Interesting question," Rappaport responded groggily. "Maybe you can help me answer it."

"What's that supposed to mean?"

"We had a visit from Dale Cox last night, along with a team of uniforms, a whole squadron of Rambos."

"How'd they know where to find you?"

"Exactly. We're at the location for half a day. I fudge my ID with the desk clerk and sign in under an assumed name. Then I pay cash so there's no blip on any computer that might pinpoint my location. Other than me and Khan, who never left my sight, you're the only other person that knew we were there."

Siegel sat down. "I don't get it. They couldn't have tapped the payphones that fast. We were too quick."

"They didn't hear our conversation," Rappaport stated pointedly, his eyes locked steadily on Siegel. "If our talk was monitored, I'd be in jail now. The contents would've been all the excuse Cox needed to slap the cuffs on. And let me tell you, Max, Cox wanted to bust me in the worst way. It practically killed him to let me go."

"I don't get it," Siegel uttered, perplexed. "How did he get word of your whereabouts?"

"Short a geopositional device planted on my county car—and I checked for that—the only way they could have known is through you."

"But I didn't say anything to anybody," Siegel said, his confusion increasing.

"I'm not saying you did. In fact, I know you didn't."

"Then who?" Siegel cut his own question short as the implication of Rappaport's steadfast, unwavering gaze finally hit him. His befuddlement evaporated, replaced by a cold, gelling anger. "What are you trying to say, Franny?" he inquired icily.

"Does Irina know what's going down?" Rappaport asked.

"Careful," Siegel warned.

"Did you tell her, Max?"

"She's in the dark. I never said a word to her about anything. Now back off."

"Was she with you when you called yesterday?"

"Franny..."

"Was she?"

"She was in the car. She couldn't hear a thing I said."

"Did you write down the address?"

"Yes. She didn't see it," Siegel insisted. But as the words came out of his mouth, the memory of setting the slip of paper on the center console flashed through Siegel's mind and he felt sick.

"Max?"

"I laid it on the console for a few seconds," Siegel responded blankly. "She might have seen it then." His vision had drifted somewhere over Rappaport's shoulder, but now Siegel's eyes honed in on the investigator with laser sharpness. "What if she saw it, Franny? What do you have to tell me? Stop playing games and give it to me straight."

Rappaport watched an ugly transformation come over Siegel as Rappaport spilled his guts, telling Siegel about Irina's clandestine meeting with Cox at the truck stop motel. As much as Siegel tried to maintain a stony exterior, pain was etched all over his features. The news that Irina was cheating on him with, of all people, Dale Cox was an impossible pill to swallow. Rappaport felt his words tearing Siegel apart and he hated the pain he was causing his friend.

"Why didn't you tell me this before?" Siegel asked, barely contained rage simmering inside him. "You had this information for a while. Why am I only hearing about it now?"

Rappaport shrugged helplessly. "How do you broach this kind of subject with a good friend?"

Siegel's taut jaw muscles were flexing. "I don't know if I'll forgive you for this, Franny."

"Don't kill the messenger, Max. Don't blame me for Cox's indiscretion."

"Indiscretion? You mean fucking my wife?" Siegel's lids squeezed shut and he brought a balled fist to the bridge of his nose.

"Sorry, Max."

Siegel unclenched his hand, dropped it to his lap and slowly opened his eyes. "It's not your fault."

An awkward silence ensued. Rappaport kept still while Siegel gathered his thoughts. "Where's Khan?" Siegel asked.

Rappaport stood and limped to the door, scanning the outside corridor before closing it. "He's stashed in a closed cement factory about five miles from the motel. It's the old Tungsten plant. Know what I'm talking about?"

"Yes. Is it a good idea to leave him there alone?"

"Had no choice. I needed to contact you and I wasn't about to trust the phone again. I also had to get some supplies."

"I have a trunkload that I was going to hand over to you this morning."

"Good, I'll put them in my truck. How long do we have to keep Khan underground, Max? We can't stay in a holding pattern indefinitely."

"No more than a few days at the most. Let me contact people in the state. We should be able to arrange some kind of safe harbor no later than Wednesday."

"What if nothing pans out by then?"

"You got me, Franny. I guess we'll go to Plan B."

"Which is?"

"Beats the hell outta me. We'll have to improvise."

"I better get moving, Max. I've been staying mobile since leaving the motel, but it's only a matter of time before I pick up a tail. They know Khan's in my care."

"Okay," Siegel said, rising from his chair. "Give me a ride to the parking garage and we'll transfer the supplies to your truck. Let's hope Khan didn't sprout wings in your absence."

"Don't worry, Max. He's more paranoid about who to trust than I am. Getting raided last night helped us bond. If I was gonna give him up, I would've done it then."

"Which brings to mind the big question, how the hell did you avoid capture?"

Rappaport grinned. "I may be getting on in years, but my instincts are still sharp. I got worried after we hung up yesterday. What if somebody managed to listen to our call? The dump of a motel we were in was deserted, so I figured what the hell? The facility was shaped like an L, with our room near the tip of the stem. So I broke into a room at the other end, confident that nobody would check in anytime soon. I sneaked over there with Khan and left the car parked by the old room. We had a nice view of the original digs from our new position and I thought I'd be able to spot anybody who came snooping around."

"Great thinking. That foresight helped you dodge a bullet."

"Maybe literally. We flew out the rear window when the raid began and never looked back until we came to Tungsten's."

"Hopefully you won't have to hang around that place much longer."

"I'm with you."

The two men left the DA's offices and walked to the elevators, Siegel lapsing into a moody silence while they waited for the doors to open. "You okay, Max?" Rappaport asked with a touch of concern.

Siegel's eyes were downcast and he was slow to raise them. "I don't know, Franny. We'll see."

CHAPTER 35

IRINA WAS PACKING HER belongings in the apartment when Siegel came through the door. Right away she knew something was wrong. Her cheery greeting met a searing look, followed by a stony silence. "Max, what is it?" Irina asked. He said nothing in reply. Instead, Siegel went straight to the bathroom and turned on a faucet, splashing water on his face while Irina stood in the doorway.

When Siegel finished soaking himself, he twisted the knob off and remained bent over the basin, watching the water swirl down the drain while droplets poured off the tip of his nose and chin. He appeared oblivious to Irina's presence. When she touched his back with her fingers, Siegel flinched with unexpected violence and Irina gasped.

Siegel grabbed a hand towel off the nearby rack and briskly wiped his face. Eventually, his hands ceased their motion, but his face remained buried in the cloth.

"Max," Irina ventured, "what's wrong?"

Siegel lowered his hands, slowly withdrawing the towel from his face and turning a chillingly hostile look toward Irina. "We're wrong," he said in a low voice that was more like a growl.

Irina felt the first twinge of panic. "What do you mean?"

"You know exactly what I mean," Siegel sneered, the volume of his voice rising slightly. "This marriage is a joke. I gave you my trust and you tore it to shreds."

Irina felt the floor giving way under her feet as she realized that Siegel knew something. Reaching out a tentative hand, she attempted to press it against Siegel's chest, tears welling in her eyes. He roughly brushed the hand aside. "Don't touch me!" Siegel barked.

He raised his palms to his throbbing temples and squeezed his eyes shut in an attempt to calm himself. Siegel's heart was pounding, complex emotions swirling inside his mind. "Why did you do it?" he asked in a strained voice. "Why did you tell Cox where to find Khan? Why are you with him?"

Irina shook her head, her mouth hanging open. "Max, I ... I don't know what you are—"

"Don't lie to me!" Siegel demanded, grasping Irina firmly by the shoulders, almost lifting her from the floor. "You're sleeping with him."

"What?"

"You met him at a truck stop motel."

"How could you know that?"

The question was like a dagger that sliced through Siegel's chest. He let go of Irina and turned away in pain, bracing his palms against the edge of the sink.

"Max, it is not what you think," Irina said desperately. "Let me explain."

"There's nothing to explain!" Siegel roared, hanging his head low. "Of all people, how could you have an affair with a piece of scum like Dale Cox?"

"Max, I am not having an affair. He is disgusting! I would never let such a man touch me. You have to listen."

Siegel heard the vehemence in the words and they seemed sincere, even if they didn't make sense. He wanted to believe, but he wasn't stupid. He wasn't going to let Irina play him for a fool.

"Max, you must hear me," Irina pleaded. "I love you and would never betray you, my darling. There is a secret between us. I have always had it since we met, but it is not what you think. Please hear me out and I will explain everything."

Siegel calmed down somewhat, a part of him clinging to Irina's denials. He turned and peered into her blue eyes, sparkling with moisture from falling tears. Leaning weakly against the sink, Siegel folded his arms under his chest. "Okay," he said, "I'll give you a chance. Talk to me. Tell me what the hell is going on."

"I ... I don't know where to begin."

"Try the beginning."

"Okay." Irina took a deep, shaky breath. "First off, you have to understand that I am not doing anything with Dale Cox. He is a pig."

"But you met him in a motel room."

Irina put a hand up. "I am not who you think I am, at least not my name. I am the same person, but my name is different."

"What are you talking about?"

"Please let me tell you this. My real name is Svetlana Korchnoi. I came to the United States under an assumed name. Irina is a lie."

Siegel felt as if Irina, or Svetlana, had hit him with a bombshell. Her blue eyes looked at him imploringly while he tried to process what she'd said. Her breathing was nervous. Siegel could see her breasts heaving rapidly as she studied him. "I was a young and stupid girl in Russia," she began, her voice cutting through a vacuum that had developed between them.

"When was that?"

"About ten years ago when I was still a teenager in Moscow. So many changes had come to my country in such a short time. Everything was chaos and the atmosphere of our society infected all who were young. I was, what you say, wild."

"Alright, what did you get into during this period of exuberance?"

"I fell in love with a man. He was Russian, of course. Dmitri Polakov was his name, a businessman, or so I thought. I was a middle-class girl, living with parents of modest means. Dmitri was rich, from what I could see. He was young, only twenty-eight, but he wore designer clothes, lots of gold chains and gold rings, and he only drove Mercedes cars. We met in the clubs and his flash swept me off my feet, as you say."

"What was he into?"

"I did not know at first. I only knew him as an entrepreneur, a man who had lucrative business dealings and lots of friends that contacted him at all hours, night and day. He told me he was a commodities trader and a stockbroker. I believed him for a while. But then, one night when we were out on the town, a car full of men attacked him. They chased our car through the streets of Moscow and Dmitri shot a gun at them. I could not believe what happened. We barely escaped with our lives. It was only then he told me the true nature of his business. He was a criminal in the Russian underworld."

"You've got to be kidding."

"No, it is all true. There were many people making a living in such a way back then, and still now, though not as much. To be associated with such a person in Moscow was not uncommon."

"You stayed with him after he confessed he was a criminal?"

"The answer is not a simple one. It's very complicated."

"It's either yes or no, Irina, or Svetlana, or whatever your name is."

"Please don't talk to me like that, Max. Don't judge me until you hear the whole story."

"Go on."

"I wanted to leave Dmitri; that's the truth. But we were dating for more than a few years and my feelings were invested in him. I was a foolish young girl in love and it is not easy to let go when one is in such a state. My emotions were like—how you say?—a roller coaster. I tried to pull away, but my feelings held me back. It was during this time that the situation between Dmitri and his associates deteriorated. Matters became worse and there were more attempts on his life when I was not around."

"What a parallel," Siegel remarked, noting the irony with grim humor.

"Max, will you let me finish?"

"Yes, I'm sorry. Continue."

"One day Dmitri came to me at my parent's flat. He was disheveled, nervous, and paranoid in a way I never witnessed before. Usually he was cocky and self-assured, and now he was scared. He had dark circles around his eyes, as if he had not slept in days. He told me his time in Russia was over, that he had to flee or he would die. People were out to get him and he could no longer keep them away. When he told me I had to travel with him, I was shocked."

"Did he force you to go with him?"

"No, nothing like that. Initially, I told Dmitri I would not go anywhere with him. But he insisted. He said men that were after him were ruthless, that they would stop at nothing to learn his whereabouts. They thought Dmitri had embezzled millions of rubles, although Dmitri never told me why they had this idea. He said I was known as his girlfriend. When he left, these men would come after me. They would have no mercy. Not only me, but my whole family would be murdered."

"And you believed him?"

"Yes, Max, of course. Russia was a very dangerous place at that time, especially Moscow. Russian gangs were abundant, established in every level of society. They were fighting vicious turf wars to establish dominance over the economy. Murders were rampant, and the government was too corrupt to do anything to stop the bloodshed. The threat to my life and my family was real, something I took seriously. I finally decided that what Dmitri said was right and that I had no choice but to join him when he fled the country."

"Don't tell me you married him."

"No, he wanted to but I could not bring myself to do that under the circumstances. Dmitri had friends in the government that secured the proper documents for a trip to America. Dangerous people were trying to capture us, so it was necessary to assume false names. Dmitri's contacts in the ministries helped accomplish that.

"We immigrated to Sacramento because it has a large Russian

community and Dmitri had connections there. We thought it would be safe and that Dmitri could find work."

"That makes no sense. You leave Russia because the underworld is hunting you and then plant yourselves in the middle of a migrant population that has ties to the motherland?"

"You're right, Max. I can see now how foolish it was. Dmitri didn't want to leave his lifestyle. He promised he would find legitimate work, but in reality, all he did was continue his criminal endeavors. I was already wanting to break free from him when the past caught up and he did not come home one night.

"The police found his body four days later on the banks of the American River. He was tied up and killed in a very brutal manner. The authorities wanted to talk to me about what happened. Because of my false immigration status, I avoided them at all costs. I was desperate to get away. That's when my sister, who was already here in California, suggested I move to Las Cruces. There are few Russians in the area. It is a small town away from the turmoil plaguing my life, or so I thought. As it turns out, it provided only a temporary reprieve to my problems."

"How did you meet Dale Cox?"

A shadow of disgust flitted over Irina's expression. "I met him when I started working at Starbucks. He came in all the time and talked to me, flirting. I never thought much of him. Then he asked me out on a date ... not a date really. We just went out to dinner and then to drinks afterwards. I did not even know at the time, but I found out later that he was married."

Siegel winced.

"It's not what you believe," Irina said quickly. "I was lonely and bored and it was just something to do on a Saturday night."

"What happened?" Siegel asked grimly, preparing to hear more upsetting details.

"Nothing, I swear to you, Max." Irina's face contorted as she relived the memory of her time with Cox. "It was a horrible evening. Dale was arrogant and conceited. He bragged about how great he was and kept speaking to me like we were already a couple. He was what you say ... delusional. I did not want to have drinks with him afterwards, but he made me. He picked me up at my apartment and I did not have a choice but to go with him to the bar.

"He became more intoxicated as the night progressed, and he made passes at me. I rebuffed him every time, kept insisting he take me home. But he would not stop making the play for me. I was at the end of my wits. When I finally decided to call a taxi, he relented and drove me home. He wanted a kiss, but I said no. That's when he put his hands on me, groping me every place on my body. I screamed and fought him off. When I got out of the car, I could not believe he was chasing me to my apartment. Luckily, he was drunk and fell on the lawn. I got inside my place and locked him out. He pounded on the door until I threatened to call the police. Then he left."

Siegel was off balance, not having heard what he expected. Confusion began to creep into his tormented mind. "Did you see him any more after that?"

"Never! I was disgusted. What was I thinking ever going out with him in the first place? But he was very persistent, always showing up at the coffee shop and speaking to me like we were lovers. Even after I met you and we began dating, he would still come and talk to me like we had a relationship. Always he is asking if you know about us. There was nothing to know except the fantasy that he has built in his mind. I wanted for so long that he leave me alone, but he would not go away."

"What about the motel?" Siegel asked, his balance becoming worse, his head spinning slightly. He wasn't sure if he was hearing the truth or an elaborate lie, what he should believe. "You met Cox at a motel and you never told me."

"Yes, I met him there, but it was not for the purpose you think. Somehow, Dale uncovered the secret of my past. I don't know how he found out, but he has all the details about my life here and in Russia

"Dale called and confronted me about what he knew. I was surprised. That's when he demanded I meet him to discuss the situation. I did not want to see him, Max, but he insisted. He threatened to tell you and the INS. He said he could have me deported to Russia. All he had to do was snap his fingers, he said. I felt trapped. That is why I agreed to see him. The motel was his choice. I did not want to go there."

"What happened at the motel?"

"More of the same. He delighted in showing me how he knew everything, kept repeating over and over how he had power now. That's when he said he wanted to have sex."

Siegel felt his heart thumping in his chest. "Did you?" he pressed. He saw Irina's blue eyes brimming with tears that rolled down her cheeks and felt a sinking feeling as he anticipated the ugly response.

Irina raised stretched fingers to her eyes and swiped the tears away, defiance suddenly overtaking her expression. "No, I did not sleep with him," she said, her jaw stiffening. "I said he was a disgusting pig and that I would rather die first. My resistance shocked him. I remember the smug grin fading from his lips. He believed I would bow to his desires because of what he knew, but there was a limit to what I would do to buy his silence. Dale tried to make me change my mind, but I refused.

"Finally, I left. I stormed out of the room and told him to do what he wished. If he told you, then fine. If I was deported, so what? I made it clear that he would never have me. I was frightened after that, Max. Since then I have lived like a condemned person, waiting for the execution to be carried out. That is why I'm in such a depressed mood lately. I was filled with anxiety, wondering what would happen when you found out the truth.

"Then he called and said he would keep quiet if I kept him informed of where you were at all times. He said if I did this, he would say nothing." Irina bowed her head in shame. "I agreed to those terms," she whispered.

"Why didn't you just come to me with the truth?" Siegel asked angrily.

"I wanted to, but I couldn't. I was afraid you would not understand. My biggest fear during all this time is that I will lose you."

"What kind of marriage is this?" Siegel asked in disgust, his anger rising. "It's all based on lies."

"Don't say that."

"For chrissakes, Irina, or Svetlana…. What do I call you?"

"Call me Irina, darling."

"But that's a lie. What you're telling me now, everything you've hidden, could have been told before we got married. Did you think I was incapable of dealing with the truth?"

"I had no way of knowing—"

"Where's the trust? That's one of the foundations of a marriage. It's not just love, but trust. If you couldn't trust me, then we had no business joining our lives together. The whole structure of our relationship is a sham."

"Please don't say that!" Irina pleaded. She tried to place her hands on Siegel's shoulders, but he knocked them away. "Don't be like this, Max."

"Be like what?" Siegel almost barked, slapping a hand over his eyes and slowly drawing it to his chin in an exasperated manner. "I can't believe I'm hearing any of this," he said, turning his back to Irina and starting to walk away.

"Max, don't go," Irina begged, grabbing Siegel's shoulder, only to have her hand shaken off.

"Leave me alone," Siegel demanded, heading for the door. "I need to process this. I need time alone, away from you."

Irina began to weep, tears streaming freely from her swollen eyes. Seeing Siegel open the door, the hurt and anger in his expression made her break inside. This was the moment she'd dreaded happening since Dale Cox tried to blackmail her. It was all out now and her worst fears were coming true; she was losing Max. He paused in the doorway, turning slightly, but not looking directly at her.

"My world's coming apart at the seams lately," Siegel said quietly, his voice fraught with tension. "People are dying, our lives are threatened, and everything I believe in has turned upside down. I'm not sure where I stand anymore, or what I'm doing, but I always thought I had us. It's the one thing I put my faith in and now that's shot to hell, too."

"Don't say that, Max."

"How can I say otherwise, Irina? This relationship was based on deceit from the start, built on sand. We have nothing but lies between us."

Irina attempted to respond but Siegel proceeded out the door and slammed it shut.

CHAPTER 36

"Y‍OU WANT ANOTHER ONE of those?" the bartender asked after he finished rinsing a tray of glasses.

Siegel looked at the thin glass containing the remnants of his rum and coke, lifted it and drained the contents, sucking a sliver of ice into his mouth and crunching his molars on it. "Yeah, give me a double," he said. "And let's forget the ice this time."

The bartender paused and studied Siegel dubiously, until Siegel took notice. "I'm okay," Siegel said. "Don't worry I'm not close to my limit yet."

"You been puttin' 'em away pretty good, pal. Maybe you should slow down some."

"I will, soon as I finish the double. My tab's good, so hurry up. There's a big tip in it for you."

"What the hell," the bartender shrugged. He prepared the drink and set it by Siegel. Then he snatched the empty glass and moved away.

Siegel had a faint dizzy feeling swirling inside his head. Numbness had crept into his limbs and there was a hollowness in his gut, despite the booze that was sloshing around in there. He hadn't meant to get drunk; it just happened while he thoughtlessly downed drinks in an attempt to drive away the feelings that were tearing him apart. Siegel had finally realized the culmination of his fears. The uneasiness that had perched on his shoulders during his relationship with Irina had sprung talons, reached into his chest, and ripped his heart out. In a way, Siegel knew it was coming. He'd always harbored doubts in his subconscious, noted inconsistencies, discerned discrepancies that he swept aside whenever they cropped up. If he was brutally honest, Siegel had to admit that Irina's revelations didn't come as a complete surprise. Somehow, though, having his long-term suspicions confirmed didn't help cushion the impact. In a way, Siegel had clung to the feeble hope that he was wrong, that he was being too suspicious. He never wanted to be right.

Siegel couldn't decide if he believed Irina about Dale Cox. The thought of the detective banging away at his wife was more than Siegel could bear. Irina seemed sincere in denying an affair with Cox. Her disgust at every mention of his name appeared genuine. With all the other lies floating around in Irina's life, however, Siegel couldn't be certain she was telling the truth about the disgusting little pig.

Sipping his drink, Siegel smiled grimly. How silly he must look, sitting in a dingy bar, wallowing in self-pity while major events of national significance engulfed his life. He was in the middle of a political shit-storm, a possible illegal cover-up being perpetrated by the highest levels of government. He'd had attempts made on his life, as well as his friends, and now an attorney connected to his case had mysteriously died. Siegel was facing a tsunami of adversity that was on the verge of rolling over him, and all he could think about was whether his wife was fucking another man. If he saw someone else in his same situation, Siegel would shake his head and wonder how petty and myopic that person could be. Events were slipping out of control and the problems with Irina should be the least of his concerns.

A heavy hand landed on Siegel's shoulder, rudely squeezing like a clamp until he felt pain shooting through his deltoid. Siegel swiveled on his stool to brush the hand away and came face to face with Dale Cox. Cox was beaming in Siegel's unsteady vision, grinning gleefully. "Here you are, counselor," he announced. "We been lookin' all over for you."

Siegel pushed his hand against Cox's chest to back him off and slid off the stool. "We who?" he asked.

"Me and the boys here," Cox replied, indicating the two uniformed officers behind him.

The cops seemed to be distorted in Siegel's eyes, like they were under water. Siegel couldn't understand why he hadn't noticed them until Cox pointed them out. To the rear of the officers, a multitude of red and blue lights flashed against the window of the establishment. Siegel couldn't see clearly because of the writing on the glass, but he had a sense that numerous patrol cars were parked on the street. Other patrons in the semi-crowded bar fell silent, their attention riveted on Siegel.

"We had a hard time finding you," Cox said. "You usually don't come to places like this. Luckily, one of our off-duty guys spotted you and phoned it in."

Cox's smugness was irritating Siegel. That feeling came on top of the growing hatred Siegel felt as Irina's words replayed in his head. *He kept repeating over and over how he had power now. That's when he said he wanted to have sex.* "What the hell do you want?" Siegel demanded.

"I have a warrant for your arrest," Cox responded joyously. "It hit the system about an hour ago. We're gonna take you in."

"Is that right?" Siegel asked, setting himself.

"That's right."

"On what charges?"

"Obstructing justice, accessory after the fact to murder; you know, when you took that bribe from Jinnah to aid Khan?" Cox replied airily. "I'm sure we'll think of more, along with a few enhancements after we arrest you. You're going away for a long time, counselor."

"What about battery?" Siegel asked.

"Huh?"

"You didn't mention battery as one of the charges."

"What battery?"

"This one!" Siegel replied, hooking a right fist into Cox's jaw. It was a perfectly timed, perfectly executed punch that knocked Cox to the floor. The detective groaned incoherently, his head twisting slowly from side to side, before the uniformed officers registered what had happened and set upon Siegel. They wrestled him roughly against the counter, spinning him around, pulling his arms back, and squeezing a pair of handcuffs on his wrists. Siegel complied without a struggle, grinning drunkenly. "Did you see that, officers? I'll admit that one," he mused as they hauled him upright and pushed him toward the exit.

Cox was half unconscious on the floor when the officers conducted Siegel out the door.

Siegel spent the night in a holding cell in the administrative segregation unit at the county jail. He was so intoxicated that he slept the entire night on a metal cot that was barely cushioned with a thin, foam mattress, a threadbare blanket providing him his only warmth. When he awoke the following morning, feeling like a ball peen hammer was slamming around in his skull, he had no idea the splash he'd made in the Sunday news. The local paper talked about the latest, shocking development in the Khan murder case, calling it bizarre that the lead prosecutor was now alleged to be in league with the suspect, who was still at large. The wire services picked up on the story and it was national news before noon, about the same time Siegel was allowed to make a phone call.

Siegel managed to reach Irina, who sounded as befuddled about what was happening as he was. They had a strained conversation in which she agreed to go to their bank first thing Monday and cash certificates of deposit in order to make his bail. The issuing magistrate had set it at a half million, which meant Siegel had to raise fifty thousand dollars to get out. Irina kept pressing Siegel to make sense of it all, but he couldn't oblige her. He was confused himself by the latest events. Siegel felt as if he was caught in a net that was hauling him in for the kill. Matters were coming to a head and he needed to get free if he was going to make things right.

Siegel spent Sunday in his cell, visited informally by officers he'd worked with over the years. Some were friendly, some hostile, all baffled by the situation. Slowly, Siegel became aware through his conversations that reporters were clamoring for an interview. His incarceration had created a media storm that Siegel wanted to avoid. Khan was still in hiding, a status that couldn't last indefinitely. Khan had to be plugged back into the system, in safe hands, so that the wheels of justice could continue to turn. But Siegel had to get out to facilitate that.

Siegel's second evening in jail was a long one. He spent most of the night in an anxious state, waiting for daylight, haunted by images of what had gotten him locked up. After an agonizingly slow progression of hours, morning came and Siegel was pulled from his cell, shackled and loaded onto a courthouse bus.

Siegel received hostile stares from the other prisoners. Some swore at him and hurled insults. One even spit, after proclaiming that Siegel had once put him in the joint for five years. Other prisoners whooped and laughed at the spectacle, while the sheriff's deputies behind the steel screen at the front of the bus ignored everything.

Siegel sat quietly through his ordeal, his mind too preoccupied to worry about the morons surrounding him. He expected an attack when the prisoners were led along a stark corridor in the basement of the courthouse, but—surprisingly—he was left alone. Although the inmates were aware that they had a deputy district attorney in their midst, and each thirsted to avenge past convictions, they were put off by Siegel's size and the fitness he exuded in his orange, jail-issue clothing. The truth was, Siegel was a hulking figure and he towered over most of the prisoners. It made them wary.

Stepping into the courtroom, Siegel was hit by the brightness of camera lights shining from the jury box. Squinting, he attempted to avoid the glare while shutters clicked like machine gun bursts. When he was finally able to focus, Siegel saw that the courtroom was packed, many of the onlookers being staff from his office. Even Rich Danko was there with Sims at his side, standing in the center of a ring of sycophantic deputy DAs by the lawyer tables. The fact that he'd left his exulted perch on the seventh floor, deigning to show himself at the arraignment, signaled the seriousness of the charges being brought against one of the office's own. Danko locked gazes with Siegel, glaring sternly at his fallen deputy while cameras blazed away. It was Danko's moment of triumph and he gloated shamelessly.

The judge couldn't bring himself to look at Siegel while he read the charges off the complaint. Siegel pleaded not guilty to the allegations in a strong, resolute voice and brushed aside questions relating to whether he required a public defender. As expected, the judge didn't reduce bail, given the highly charged political implications of the case. Siegel was relieved, however, when the judge didn't raise it either. What he had socked away in CDs was the limit of his finances. Any further increase in bail would result in Siegel remaining locked up. The judge set a preliminary examination date a month away after Siegel waived time, and the matter was concluded.

While being led from the courtroom, Siegel scanned the audience for Irina, but she wasn't there. He hoped she was busy securing his release. After their previous episode, he wasn't sure where they stood, although he'd find out soon enough.

Siegel breathed a sigh relief when his cell door opened during the night and a jailer told him he could go. His bail had been made. Irina was waiting in the parking lot, standing next to her Lexus in semidarkness beneath the light of a pole lamp, looking fragile and shrunken. She wore a pair of blue jeans and a white, cotton sweater that she clutched together with folded arms.

Something broke inside Siegel at seeing Irina appear so small and vulnerable. Wordlessly, he walked toward his wife, and they embraced. Siegel could feel Irina's thin arms holding him tight, her hands desperately clutching his back. She cried, smothering her face in his chest, her body quivering.

"Shhh," Siegel soothed. "It'll be alright," he whispered. "We'll make everything right, honey."

"I wanted so long to tell you," Irina sniffled.

"I know, sweetheart," Siegel said, cupping Irina's head in his hand and stroking her long, dark hair. "I believe you. Everything you told me was true."

"But ... but how can you trust me after all the lies?"

"You lied because of circumstances, things that were out of your control. How can I judge you for that?"

"I love you so much, Max. I'm so scared about losing you."

"I love you too, sweetheart. We'll get through this. We'll get past the turmoil."

They kissed passionately, melting into each other's bodies while standing in the cold, dark lot. "Save some for me," a voice called out. Siegel broke away from Irina's lips and saw two Okies strolling past, lascivious grins planted on their mouths.

"Keep moving," Siegel growled.

The Okies snickered belligerently, but kept walking until they faded into the darkness.

"Come on," Siegel said. "Let's get out of here."

CHAPTER 37

——◆——

THE FREEWAY OUT OF Las Cruces was sparsely trafficked and Siegel easily spied the distant headlights quickly gaining on them. He watched the lights weave past the few vehicles dotting the road and converge on Siegel's car. As they got closer, Siegel saw that the lights were attached to a pickup, a single shadow in the cab compartment. Remembering Langerman's accident, Siegel felt the first tentacles of panic creeping through him. His speedometer indicated eighty miles per hour. He stepped harder on the gas and it jumped to ninety.

"Max, what is it?" Irina asked nervously.

"Maybe nothing," Siegel replied, eyeing the rearview mirror. The pickup was still gaining.

The nerves in Siegel's gut tightened as the danger looming behind him grew more certain. His heart began to race and his palms became moist as he gripped the steering wheel like a vice. Siegel pressed harder on the accelerator and the speedometer needle reached one hundred.

"Max?" Irina said.

"Hold on, I think someone's after us."

"Oh no!" Irina gasped, shooting a look over her shoulder. "Who is that?"

"I don't know. Whoever he is, he's closing the gap." Siegel's scalp was tingling with nervous tension at the same time a burst of angry defiance raced through his body and limbs, empowering him. He refused to be a victim, or to let Irina be harmed in any way. He'd die first! Despite his rapidly pounding heart, a strange, deadly calm descended over Siegel, borne by the steely determination to fight the danger coming at him with every fiber of his being. "Slide down in the seat, in case he has a gun," he told Irina.

"But—"

"No buts! Just do it!"

Irina complied immediately, thrusting her hips forward and lowering her head below the edge of the seatback.

The pickup kept closing until it wasn't far behind, but Siegel couldn't make out the driver. Bracing for the inevitable crash, Siegel saw Langerman in his mind and pictured the same fate as his friend, but the impact never came. Instead, the lights of the pickup flashed and the horn blared repeatedly. Siegel peered closely into the rearview mirror and saw the shadowy arm of the pickup's driver waving at him. That's when he realized to his sudden relief that it was Rappaport in the truck. The tension drained out of Siegel as if a plug had been pulled and his insides quivered as the horrendous strain he'd been under only moments ago broke.

An exit led to a desolate farmer's field. Siegel took it and the pickup followed. The thin, paved road was dark and lonely, dirt paths peeling off into blackened fields. It was an access road for farmers, unlighted, in the middle of nowhere. Siegel braked to a stop near a set of metal mailboxes on wooden posts and the pickup did the same.

"Why are we stopping?" Irina asked from low in her seat, her expression petrified.

"Don't worry," Siegel said, unbuckling his seatbelt. "It's only Franny. Stay here while I talk to him."

"You scared the hell outta me," Siegel said as he and Rappaport came together. Rappaport appeared tired and unkempt, his limp more pronounced than usual.

"Sorry for the drama, but it's the safest way to make contact. I picked up a tail when I went to my place tonight and I had a hard time losing it."

The two men shook hands and embraced warmly. Rappaport smelled like he hadn't showered in days.

"I see Irina bailed you out," Rappaport said. "I was on my way to do the same when I saw her going in the jail. Is everything okay with you two?"

"Yeah, we talked and cleared the air. There's a lot going on, but it's not what we thought."

Rappaport appeared doubtful.

Siegel lifted his palms. "Trust me, it's a long story that we can discuss another time. Let's get to the business at hand."

"Okay, but it's not looking good. Do you know that Danko's been all over the airwaves spouting off about what a disgrace you are?"

"No, I wasn't aware of that. They've had me locked in ad seg for the past couple days."

"Yeah, well, he's poisoned the waters for your credibility. I can't see how you'll ever convince your contacts in the Department of Justice to get on board with us. You're radioactive."

"It was a good move on Danko's part. Anything in the news about Jinnah? He's the other part of the so-called conspiracy I'm supposed to be involved in."

"Not a peep. Far as I know, they're leaving him alone."

"Why? The money came from him."

"Don't know, maybe they want to keep the spotlight on you alone. If it's any consolation, I did some checking around town today. Jinnah's dropped out of sight. They might be trying to run him down."

Siegel's brows furled and he felt throbbing beginning in his temples. "This case is one strange twist after another," he declared.

"Yeah and we're running out of options for what to do."

"How's the kid?"

"Restless, jumpy, tired of hanging around that dump of a factory. It's cold and damp and he's itching to run, only he doesn't know where to. I'm taking a chance leaving him alone."

"Why are you?"

"I wanted to get you out. It's time we change places. You're no good on the outside, and I'm doing squat holed up with Khan. I called in sick at work today, but that'll only hold for so long."

"What do you propose?"

"You babysit the kid and let me check into the office tomorrow. I'll get the scuttlebutt about what Danko's up to, and then I'll reach out to my contacts in the state. Maybe I can score some help."

"You're not worried about getting arrested?"

"They tried that already and it didn't work. They got nothing on me, and can't move unless they catch me with Khan. That's why it's best I get away from him. It'll give me a chance to maneuver."

"Makes sense. I'm already screwed, so what difference will it make if they bust me with the kid?"

"Precisely."

"Okay, give me till morning, and then I'll sneak over and relieve you."

Rappaport put a hand on Siegel's shoulder, deep concern etched in the lines of his somewhat weather-beaten face. "Watch yourself, Max. The people trying to squelch this are playing for keeps."

"Do the same, Franny. You may be a step ahead of the law but that doesn't mean they won't come after you in other ways."

Rappaport's expression was strangely sober. He said nothing more, embracing Siegel and clapping him on the back.

Two enterprising reporters were lurking about Siegel's apartment complex when he arrived, which unnerved him. They'd found his secret location. Siegel brushed past the men, ignoring their questions, keeping a protective arm around Irina. Once inside the apartment, Siegel checked through the blinds and saw that the newsmen were in no hurry to leave. It was comforting in a way. Their presence would act as a buffer against intruders.

Siegel took a shower before climbing into bed with Irina. He woke her from a half-slumber and initiated a bout of lovemaking. Siegel's passions erupted from deep within, coursing through his body and limbs, pouring from every fiber of his being. Time passed endlessly, until the couple reached an explosive climax, collapsing into a sweaty, entangled heap. They lay silently in the darkness, lazily petting and caressing, until Siegel's deep voice sliced through the quiet. "Go to your sister's tomorrow," he said.

"For how long?" Irina asked nervously.

"Until this ordeal is over."

"When will that be?"

"I don't know. I'm going away tomorrow. While I'm gone, you can't be here."

"Why?"

"Because it's too dangerous. It's for your own protection."

"I can't stand this!" Irina exclaimed, her voice breaking slightly as she clutched Siegel with desperation.

Siegel held his wife tighter. "I can't stand it either," he said, trying to soothe her. "The situation won't last much longer. Things are coming to a head. One way or another, we're going to sort this out."

Irina was quivering slightly in Siegel's embrace. "Max, will something bad happen to you?" she ventured.

"You mean worse than what's already gone down? Not if I can help it. I won't lie, baby; there are bad men doing bad things around here. People are getting hurt. Khan's attorney just died."

"Max!" Irina hissed, her nails biting into his flesh.

"Don't get exited, nobody knows why yet. All I'm getting at is that I can't focus on what I have to do if I'm worried about you. It's better if you're out of the way."

"Okay," Irina relented, reluctance in her strained tone, "but you have to keep in touch."

"That isn't a good idea. Chances are I might become a fugitive. You shouldn't know where I am, and then you won't be an accessory. And don't go telling Cox anything more, got it?"

"I'm finished with him," Irina said resolutely. "Now that you have the whole story, that despicable man cannot scare me any longer."

"Good, it's nice to hear you say that," Siegel sighed. Closing his eyes, he drifted off to sleep and didn't wake until just before dawn.

Siegel helped Irina pack her belongings after sharing a quick cup of coffee with her. Dawn was barely breaking when Siegel checked through the blinds and saw that the coast was clear. Carrying an overstuffed suitcase, Siegel hurried Irina down a flight of stairs to the parking lot and loaded the bag into the trunk of the Lexus. He scanned the lot another time as a precaution before kissing Irina on the cheek and gently peeling her arms from around his neck. "You better get going," he urged.

Irina got into the driver's seat and slid the window down, peering up at Siegel with concern etched in her features. "Max, promise you will be alright."

"I'll do my best, sweetheart. I don't have a death wish. Besides, you're too young to be a widow."

Irina smiled nervously, tears brimming her eyes.

Siegel tapped the roof of the car. "Get out of here," he said.

Irina reluctantly complied, watching Siegel forlornly while backing out of her space. She pursed her full lips and blew a kiss before speeding away. Siegel grinned and waved as she departed, the grin fading the instant the Lexus was out of sight.

Siegel got on the road shortly after Irina left and headed for the abandoned cement plant outside Las Cruces. There was a good amount of commuter traffic on the freeway and Siegel kept a vigil on the rearview mirrors to ensure he wasn't being followed. Not long after leaving the city limits, he spied a dark sedan that he thought he'd seen near the apartments. Siegel couldn't be sure whether he was being paranoid, but he took elusive measures anyway, exiting the freeway and driving in circles before returning onto the freeway again. He did this maneuver twice, until the sedan disappeared from sight.

Rappaport had described the general area of the plant and Siegel managed to locate it in the distance when he pulled off the freeway onto a long, empty road. The plant loomed large in the morning sunlight, a ragtag collection of hulking buildings with rusted tin roofs, some skeletal in appearance, with large piping connecting two of the structures. As Siegel drew closer, he saw that the dusty grounds of the plant were littered with rocks, debris, and scrap metal. The place was drab and dreary, resembling ground zero of a bomb site.

The paved road gave way to dirt and gravel when Siegel pulled into the midst of the plant grounds. There were no traces of anyone inhabiting the place, no signs of Rappaport's pickup. The gravelly road crackled beneath the tires of Siegel's car as he braked to a halt, a fine white powdering of dust encircling the vehicle.

Siegel got out and walked around a semi-open building framed by steel girders. There was a chill in the air, a cold breeze blowing, so he zipped the black leather jacket he wore and rubbed his hands together briskly.

Rappaport appeared by a large mound of scrap metal next to some rusted machinery. "You made it," he greeted, his voice echoing in the hollow building.

"This is the heap you're living in?" Siegel asked, walking toward his friend.

"Home sweet home. It's a good location, isolated, not a place anybody has reason to snoop around in. We're staying in some connected offices upstairs in the next building. It's a good vantage point to see the road from. We even have electricity and running water, believe it or not. Come on, I'll introduce you to our boy."

Siegel followed Rappaport through an opening in the rear of the dark building and across a patch of weeds to a smaller corrugated metal structure with a flight of outer steps leading up to a set of spacious, windowed offices. When they opened a creaking wooden door and stepped inside, Raheem Khan immediately materialized in a doorway. He had dark circles around his intensely penetrating eyes. His clothes were dirty and rumpled, but his stocky build gave the impression of immense strength.

"Max Siegel, let me formally introduce you to the man you're prosecuting for murder," Rappaport said. "Meet Raheem Khan."

CHAPTER 38

---•---

AFTER RUNNING BY HIS home and cleaning up, Rappaport drove to the courthouse, grinning at the obvious tail he picked up on the way. It was Dale Cox. The detective's technique was so clumsy it was laughable. He couldn't be more visible. It was like spotting the sun on a cloudless day. Rappaport made no attempt to evade Cox. In fact, he preferred having the attention on him rather than Siegel. It was exactly what Rappaport wanted.

Rappaport passed Sims in the corridor and they exchanged hesitant hellos. Sims stopped and deliberately watched the investigator continue to his office. Rappaport pretended not to notice the scrutiny and shut his door when he went inside. Taking a seat at his desk, Rappaport found a letter of suspension that Sims must have just dropped off. He waited for Sims to pay him a visit, but after a few minutes elapsed without a knock, Rappaport concluded that he was safe from interruption and picked up the phone receiver and dialed his voicemail.

There were eight messages, mostly routine, until the sixth call. It was from his acquaintance, David, with the Department of Justice crime lab. Rappaport leaned forward, intent on hearing what the criminalist had to say.

"Franny, this is David at the lab. About those pills you sent for that hush-hush analysis. I just completed the job. If you're looking to arrest somebody for poisoning that attorney in San Francisco, you're not doing it with this evidence. The pills are composed of sugar, through and through. Unless your guy had a bad case of diabetes, the proof is zilch. By the way, is this a joke?"

Rappaport cradled the receiver and skipped the remaining messages. He'd been thrown for a loop. If all Gul swallowed during his seizure was sugar, then his death was by natural causes. There was no homicide, but did that rule out foul play? The pills weren't poison, but why were they sugar? The secretary told about Gul's mysterious, upsetting phone call prior to the heart attack. Did somebody switch the pills in advance and make the call to trigger an episode? Rappaport shuddered to believe that was the case. If true, then the people behind the plot were diabolical. The sophistication of the plan made Rappaport very uncomfortable.

Filled with a sense of urgency, Rappaport went through the rolodex on his desk and scratched names and numbers for possible contacts on a notepad. His years of service in law enforcement gave him a wide range of acquaintances around the state, all of whom occupied key justice positions. It would take outside help to extricate him and Siegel from the legal mess they were in. Broaching the subject to anyone was a highly delicate matter, given the reams of publicity surrounding the Khan case. Anybody siding with Siegel at the present juncture would be required to make a gigantic leap of faith, and risk becoming ensnared in a criminal prosecution.

After Rappaport composed a list of potential contacts, he sat back in his chair and thoughtfully weighed the pluses and minuses of each individual, gauging the chances for success of getting them to buy into the Khan venture. Merely bringing up the subject was going to implicate Rappaport in the charges leveled against Max Siegel, so he had to be careful. Finally settling on a name, Rappaport lifted the phone receiver and was ready to punch a number on the keypad when there was a knock at the door.

Cox entered without an invitation. "Hi, Franny," he said, a stiff grin planted on his mouth. He appeared wrung out. "Can I come in?"

"Looks like you already have," Rappaport replied.

Cox scanned the outside corridor before entering and closed the door behind him, leaning his back against it. "How you been?"

"Cut the small talk, Dale. I got lots of work to do. What do you want?"

"You've been suspended, Franny. I came to help you get a reprieve. You're siding with Max Siegel. That's admirable, but the truth is his universe is closing in and you're fixin' to get squashed with him."

"You my salvation?"

"That's right. They say you're a Boy Scout, just like Siegel. They say you can't be reasoned with, but I told 'em they were wrong. I said we go way back and that I should have a chance to talk sense to you before anybody makes a move."

"What move would that be?"

"Siegel's destruction.... He's done, a disgrace. His ticket's suspended, he has charges pending, and now he's dropped out of sight."

"How would you know that? Keeping tabs?"

"He's going down, Franny. So is Khan. The ship's sinking and you need to jump off."

"What are you, my life vest?"

"Yeah, that's exactly what I am, your one chance to get with the program. All you gotta do is give up Siegel and that dirt bag, Khan. You know where they are. Make it easy to tie off the loose ends. It's inevitable, with or without your help. Why don't you spare yourself?"

Rappaport stood and circled his desk. Cox's lids widened and he tensed. Bunching his fists, he raised them protectively to his midsection as Rappaport approached.

"Relax, Dale, I'm not going to hit you," Rappaport said. "I just want you to see me when I say my piece."

Cox swallowed hard. "What's that?"

"Max is my friend. It's a concept I'm not sure you understand. You have an emptiness in you, a hole where your humanity should be. You think I'm going to turn on Max because the chips are down? The odds are stacked against him, so I'm supposed to tuck my tail between my legs and scurry to the other side? That's what weasels do, Dale. That's what *you* would do, because you don't know what it's like to have feelings for somebody else besides yourself. I'm no weasel, Dale.

"I love Max like my own brother. No matter what happens, I'm gonna be there for him the same as he would be for me if I was in a jam. I don't know who you're talking to, but you can tell them that I'm not playing along."

"Those are brave and noble sentiments, but stupid under the circumstances. Don't say I didn't try to warn you, Franny. This adventure's getting closed out soon. Don't be one of the loose ends."

"We're done talking," Rappaport announced, lingering a few seconds before returning to his chair. Cox seemed relieved when Rappaport sat down. "You still wear a badge, Dale," Rappaport continued. "You should think about that when you're getting the hell outta my office. It's supposed to mean something. Maybe it'll dawn on you that you're sworn to uphold the law when you and your slimy friends are busy tying off loose ends."

"The law don't abide terrorists," Cox said, pulling the door open. "You're missing the big picture, Franny. I feel sorry for you."

Cox abruptly departed, leaving the door open. Rappaport stared at the empty space beyond it, contemplating Cox's ominous words. "There's a bigger picture, Dale," Rappaport said out loud. "Trouble is you're looking at the wrong one. Nothing worse than a blind man that doesn't know he can't see."

CHAPTER 39

———◆———

SIEGEL HEARD THE HELICOPTER rotors beating somewhere in a cloudy sky and he chanced a look out a grimy window to see if he could spot it. Khan toyed with the dial of a small radio behind Siegel, switching past various stations, attempting to find music to his liking. The helicopter was drawing tantalizingly close, but Siegel still couldn't locate it in the mass of gray and white clouds that were interrupted by occasional faint patches of blue.

"See it yet?" Khan asked.

"No, it's close though. Must be directly overhead."

The radio finally fixed on a station, a rap duet by Jay-Z and Linkin Park. "You think the cops are lookin' for us?" Khan inquired, undertones of tension in his voice.

"Could be," Siegel replied, still searching. "They may be doing a fly over to see if they can locate any signs of us. Good thing my car's covered with a tarp. Then again, it might be nothing."

The chopper moved into Siegel's view, far off to the east. He could make out that it was a civilian craft, but couldn't determine if it had law enforcement markings. The helicopter moved slowly from right to left, eventually disappearing into a cloud of gray mist.

Siegel turned away from the window and saw Khan fiddling with the radio again. Khan was seated on a metal cot that was pushed against a wall, reclining against the wall as he twirled the knobs of the radio with increasing agitation. "This sucks," he declared, suddenly switching off the music and roughly tossing the radio onto a crumpled blanket. "How much longer we gotta do this shit?"

"Take it easy," Siegel said, pacing the cold floor that was littered with paper wrappings, discarded soup cans, and plastic utensils. "I'm not any crazier about this situation than you are. If things go well and Rappaport scores some connections today, we might get out of here by tomorrow."

"Man, I can't spend another night in this dump."

"It's for your own protection, kid. Walk out of here now and you may as well paint a target on your back."

"This is a trip. I don't get nothin' that's happening. I can't believe I'm sitting here with the DA on my case. You're the dude I should be runnin' from."

"Not any more. Given all that's come to pass, I'm recused from your prosecution."

"What does that mean?"

"I'm off the case. I can't go after you now that I'm entangled in events. Somebody else will have to take over the prosecution, probably from the attorney general's office now that I've created a conflict of interest."

"I don't understand anything you're talking about, Max. All the stuff that's gone down all these weeks is just crazy. First those dudes kidnap me, and then I get fucked up in the head and go into a coma. Then I have everybody tryin' to kill my ass after I'm accused of murder. This shit is insane!"

Siegel stopped pacing. "What about getting kidnapped?" he asked. "What's the story behind the night you killed those men? You did kill them, right?"

Khan's dark eyes rolled deliberately up at Siegel, locking on him suspiciously. There was violence in how he looked at Siegel. He appeared ready to spring off the cot. "Why you askin' that? You tryin' to get me to incriminate myself?"

"No, I'd just like to understand why we need to hide out like this. People all the way back to D.C. want your demise, and I'd like to know why. We don't have to talk if you'd rather not, but can you think of a better way to pass the time?"

"You gotta point," Khan conceded forlornly. "Passin' the time, right?"

"Exactly."

"It don't matter at this point, does it? What you wanna know?"

"Why'd you kill those agents?"

"Self-defense, they were gonna do the same to me. Not right then, but eventually."

"What do you mean?"

"They had me for a few days. I was in the alley next to the restaurant where I work when these dudes came outta nowhere and strong-armed me into a car. They stuck a needle in my thigh and injected me with something that put my lights out. When I came to I was in that house in Pleasant Oaks, handcuffed to the bedpost."

"Did they say why they abducted you?"

"I was groggy for a couple days, going in and out because they kept druggin' me. Not with needles no more, but in the food they fed me. I figured that out after I ate a few times. My head was spinning most of the time, and they took turns askin' me a buncha questions about my friend, Tariq, and Pakistan. I had took a trip there not too long before, sponsored by Mr. Jinnah. Those guys said I was a terrorist; that I was in big trouble. They kept saying, 'Why don't you tell us what you people are planning?' They said they knew what we were doing and that I should tell 'em before I got in deeper. I had no idea what they were talking about, bro."

"What about Tariq and Pakistan? Why'd you go with him?"

"Like I said, I got a free ticket. Mr. Jinnah offered to pay my way to Pakistan, a trip to the land of my ancestors, you know? I thought, why not? My parents are Pakistani, but I was born here, total American. I couldn't pass on the opportunity."

"A sightseeing trip, huh?"

"Yeah, that's what I thought."

"What about your friend, Tariq? What was he going to Pakistan for? From what I hear, he was into some things."

Khan cut his eyes at Siegel, shrewdly appraising him. The kid's manner was getting edgy again. "Yeah, Tariq had some wild ideas," he admitted cautiously.

"Like what?"

Khan squirmed. "You know, man, that whole jihad thing. My friend Tariq was into the world politics trip, like the big struggle between east and west. He talked about it all the time, how the Muslims and infidels were at war. He said us young guys were soldiers and that I had to join the struggle."

"So Tariq was a jihadist?"

"You could call him that. He read the Quran a lot."

"What about you? Did you buy into the struggle idea?"

"Not really; I'm a hommie from the hood. Las Cruces is my whole world. All I wanna do when I get older is heating and cooling repair. Politics ain't my bag, but its fun to listen to when you gotta friend who's all passionate about the subject. My pal Tariq had something he believed in and that was cool."

"What did you do in Pakistan?"

"Some sightseeing, I was mostly along for the ride. I never been there before. Peshawar was a trip. They got like millions of people there."

"Tariq doesn't sound like the sightseeing type. Why did he go to Pakistan?"

"Truth, he went to attend a *madrassa*, a place run by this crazy older dude named, Faisal Abdul. That guy's a trip, a real old country person that looks like he still lives in ancient times. He teaches the Quran and spouts off about jihad and the shit goin' down with the west since 9/11. His students are a buncha guys that mostly wear white and have dark beards the way Muhammad did. Tariq went there to have sessions with the old man and I tagged along. It was a learning experience."

"Your story's dubious, Raheem. A young man travelling halfway around the world to spend time with a cleric in a *madrassa*? All for fun?"

"That's what the guys said that kidnapped me. They didn't believe my story either, but it's true. I don't know what Tariq was into over there. I can't speak to that. But I went to Pakistan for curiosity."

"Why did Jinnah pay for your trip?"

"I don't know; you have to ask him, bro. He's like a father figure in the community, you know? Everybody looks up to him. He's a leader and he treats us Pakistanis like followers. Jinnah helps out where he can and that's why he sponsored me on my trip. I love the guy. He's better than my real pops."

"Did you receive any kind of training at the *madrassa*?"

"How do you mean? Like did I get that al Qaida stuff? No, like I said, I may have sat around in a few of those crazy classes and listened to the old cleric rant about how we should hate the west, but—for me—it was a way of killing time while I hung out in Peshawar."

"What about Tariq? What did he get into while you were there?"

"Hey, man, he had his own thing goin' down, you feel me? He was in tight with the other students. They did a lot of secret meetings, stuff I knew nothin' about. Tariq would disappear a lot and leave me on my own, but that was cool, 'cause we weren't into the same things."

"Did Tariq talk about anything he was doing or saying when he wasn't with you?"

"Nah, matter of fact, Tariq changed after a while. He got more serious in his look and he started gettin' tight-lipped around me. He kept secrets. It was nothin' he said exactly, but I hung with him all my life and you get to know a dude after a while. Tariq definitely had something on his mind that he wasn't sharing."

"Then you returned to the United States."

"Right. I was glad to get home, too. Pakistan was interesting and all, but I'm a Las Cruces kid. It was good to set my feet on home turf again."

"How long were you back before you got kidnapped?"

"Not long, bro, maybe a month or so. Everything got strange almost immediately when I got home. Tariq started droppin' outta sight a lot, goin' on secret trips to San Francisco and other places. I tried to tag along now and then, but he wouldn't let me. Tariq said I didn't have the right commitment, whatever that meant."

"Did you know anything about what Tariq was doing during that time?"

"I had my suspicions, but he never told me a damn thing. About a week before I got snatched, Tariq got real nervous. Whenever we hooked up, he thought he was being watched. He slipped once and told me that the CIA was trying to nail him for what he did in Peshawar. When I asked what he meant, he didn't say. I thought he was kidding, either that or goin' crazy. Then he disappeared."

"How do you mean?"

"Vanished, bro, I mean dropped outta sight with no trace. I didn't know what the hell happened. And I didn't have time to think on it either, 'cause that's when they scooped me up."

"The men who took you, did they accuse you of working with Tariq?"

"Of course, man, what else? That's what I'm tryin' to relate; I didn't know shit about what they were asking. Tariq was the one they wanted. When I was captive, I assumed they had him too. That scared me."

"Were you tortured?"

"No, the dudes didn't do nothing but ask stupid questions and threaten me a lot. Other than druggin' me, they were actually pretty decent."

"Why did you kill them then?"

"'Cause they let me know that's what was comin' to me!" A dark shadow crossed over Khan's expression and his eyes became fierce, somewhat crazed.

"Take it easy, kid. Tell me what happened, what they did that made you believe your life was in danger."

"Man, for two days they spun my head around with all their questions and bullshit accusations. I figured out quick that I was out of it because they were druggin' me through my food. It was takin' my will away, making me weak. So I started makin' trips to the bathroom after I ate and sticking my finger down my throat. It was hard to barf without making noise, but I did it, even with a dude standin' on the other side of the door."

"How long did they have you total?"

"Like I said, two, maybe three days in all. After they couldn't get no satisfaction from my answers, they threatened me with a trip overseas. I asked them what they meant and dude told me there was people in other countries that could ask questions in a lot harder ways. They said I could be electrocuted, or have my balls cut off and shoved in my mouth while I was still awake. If they were tryin' to put the fear of God in me, they succeeded, 'cause I was plenty scared."

"What happened the night of the killings?"

"All day long I knew something was going down. These guys were on their cell phones a lot while I was faking bein' drugged up, you know? I heard bits and pieces, like scraps of conversations. I put two and two together and figured out that they was plannin' to move me late that night. They got mad because, for all their threats, I still didn't tell them nothin', 'cause I didn't know nothin'.

"When one of the dudes brought my food tray, it was late, past midnight. I was still acting out of it, rolling my eyes and puttin' on a show. Then I hear him say, 'You're going on a trip, Raheem. We have the plane sittin' on the tarmac on Beale.'"

"The air force base in Marysville?"

"Yeah. He said, 'Eat this, because its gonna be a long trip, my friend.' I was cuffed to the bedpost and he undid me. The guy had a gun in his hand like usual, but it was kinda dangling real loose like, 'cause he thought I wasn't no threat.

"I was scared as hell. After the way those guys talked to me, I knew if I got on a plane I wasn't comin' back. It was life or death; that's how I read it. That's when I snatched a butter knife from the tray and plunged it in the dude's midsection. He screamed something awful and dropped the gun. I couldn't believe it though, 'cause then the dude grabs me and we start struggling. Even after what I did, the man still put up a good fight.

"I don't like to brag, but I'm real strong. Not just 'cause I lift weights, but because I was born this way. In high school I was an all-state champion wrestler. So while I'm hashin' it out with dude in the bedroom, I know his partner's downstairs and it's only a matter of time before he hears the commotion and comes to the rescue. I'm like, I don't have time to keep playing. That's when I gotta surge and picked up the dude and threw him out the window."

"The pavement broke his neck."

"Yeah, that's what I found out later in the police reports. At the time, I didn't know what happened, only that the dude was outta my hair. I lifted the gun from the floor and headed downstairs and caught the other dude coming up. That's when I blasted him, bro. I didn't waste time. If I didn't smoke him, he was gonna smoke me. That's how it went down."

"Then you ran out the front door and met Mr. Harris."

"Yeah, that big ole man walking his little dog."

"Were you trying to attack him?"

"No, man," Khan said, his features twisting in disgust. "I went to him for help, believe it or not. I wanted him to call the police. I was so scared. Next thing I know I get clobbered with some hella hard jack he pulls outta his pocket. That thing knocked me senseless, till the lights went out cold."

"Why didn't you explain this story to my investigator at the hospital?"

"I was gonna, but I got spooked when that detective told me I was getting charged with murder. That freaked me out, so I thought I better shut up till I talked to a lawyer. Later on, after I escaped, that same cop came blazin' through the door at the house I was in and blew my friend away. Man, he had a look in his eyes like he was all about killing me. That crazy cop had a murder hard-on. That's why I beat it outta town and hooked up with Tariq in San Francisco."

"That's right. You said he dropped out of sight. You didn't know where he was. If that's true, how did you manage to contact him?"

"Mr. Jinnah set it up. I called him when I got away. He sent me to that community center where all the shit went down. I didn't know Tariq was there till I walked through the door. It was a surprise, bro. Then your investigator hunts us down and we get shot at from every direction. Poor Tariq got put down like a dog. What's this all about? I didn't do nothin' to nobody, and now I feel like some trapped rat in this dumpy pit.

"I wanna go home, Max. I want my life back. When is that gonna happen?"

"I wish I knew, Raheem. We're doing the best we can."

"What's going on, man? My world is totally upside down."

"So's mine, kid," Siegel said, walking to the window and gazing at the gray sky.

CHAPTER 40

———•———

Rappaport hung up the phone feeling happy for the first time in days. Sitting back in his chair, he blew a breath of relief. His face was still hot from the long, tense conversation he'd had with an old academy buddy, a supervising investigator with the Department of Justice. Len Eddington came from Rappaport's graduating class and they were close. Despite that, the first fifteen minutes of their call was testy, almost combative. Eddington knew bits and pieces of what happened in Clay County. His preconceptions about Max Siegel and the Khan case fairly mirrored reports in the press. It took a lot of cajoling for Eddington to listen objectively to Rappaport's version of events. Eddington knew about Dale Cox and didn't like him one bit. That eventually helped sway him toward a more open mind about the case.

Fortunately, Eddington also knew about the federal probe regarding Rich Danko. He believed Danko was thoroughly corrupt, unfit to hold his exalted office. Slowly, if skeptically, Eddington came to see the light of the fix Siegel and Rappaport were in. He was also cognizant of Rappaport's noble character and pristine reputation in the law enforcement community. For all those reasons, he finally relented and agreed to help his old friend. "You have some can of worms down there," he'd said. "Let me broach this with my superiors and some of the lawyers in the office. This might be something worthwhile for the governor's boys to intervene in. He has designs on the presidency some day. This could be a political feather in his cap if he accepts the risks."

"I couldn't ask for anything more," Rappaport sighed.

"I'll get back to you tomorrow afternoon, Franny. Keep your head down till then."

"I will."

Satisfied, Rappaport completed tasks to reassign his other pending cases, and then cut out to begin his suspension. He wanted to run by the cement factory and give Siegel the good news, but he thought that might risk revealing the location. Rappaport decided to call Siegel with his cell phone, until he realized it was missing. He was so preoccupied all day that he couldn't remember where he left it. Scanning his memory drew a blank, so he made a mental note to search for it in the morning.

Siegel was going to have to tough it out for a night in the abandoned factory. If all went well, a contingent of state police would move in tomorrow evening, take possession of Khan and shift the case to a different venue. Siegel's problems wouldn't be over, but at least he'd have a shot at obtaining some kind of justice that was better than his present options. It was a long shot, but the best they could manage under the circumstances.

Rappaport felt dead tired while heading home. During the drive, he noticed large breaks forming in the clouds, rays of sunshine bursting through in brilliant shafts that touched the landscape. Exhausted as Rappaport was, the clearing skies had the effect of infusing him with energy and he phoned the air club the moment he got home. A jump was scheduled in an hour and Rappaport was welcome to join.

It was crazy, but Rappaport decided a jump was what he needed. Skydiving relieved stress. Leaping out of a plane and plunging toward the ground at incredible speeds was exhilarating, strangely refreshing. What could it hurt? Rappaport wondered. He'd jump, get a bite to eat, go home, take a hot shower, and then tuck himself in for a well-deserved night of sleep.

Feeling a sense of urgency, Rappaport changed quickly into comfortable clothes and headed to the airstrip in his pickup. He had to fiddle with the padlock on his locker at the hangar. His key kept getting stuck and wouldn't twist until he jiggled it a few times, his equipment spilling onto the floor when he yanked the door open.

Other members were already strolling from the hangar as Rappaport hurriedly donned his flight suit and helmet. He strapped the parachute on his back, securing the rest of the harness impatiently so he could join the others. He was still adjusting his gear when he loaded onto a Super Cessna 182 behind two other jumpers. The engine of the small craft revved, its nose propeller spinning, and it taxied for takeoff immediately after Rappaport closed the door.

A brief pause on the runway ensued while the pilot waited for clearance, and then the noise of the engine overwhelmed the tiny passenger compartment and the craft began its run. Looking out his side window,

Rappaport glimpsed a familiar figure emerging from the hangar. The image was too brief for him to connect who it was, but it bothered him for some reason.

Dale Cox strolled toward his car that was parked in the grass near the flight line. He pressed the flat of his hand over his brows to shade his eyes while watching the Cessna's ascent. When he arrived at his vehicle, Cox placed a cloth bag of clinking tools into the trunk, before slamming the lid shut and leaning against the car. All the time, he remained aware of the Cessna's buzz while it climbed ever higher.

Cox grinned, butterflies flickering in his gut. He felt a curious combination of emotions while watching the gleaming speck travel a lazy circle against the breaking cloud cover. Elation mixed with dread, a tingling, enervating excitement swirling against foreboding. Cox felt a curious cacophony of sensations tugging and ramming at one another, leaving him confused. It wasn't what he'd expected. The plane leveled off when it was barely more than a dot in the sky and Cox knew the jumps would soon commence. Lowering his gaze to the dirty patch of grass at his feet, he stomped on a weedy clump and decided to leave. Cox got into his car and drove away without looking back.

It turned cold inside the old Tungsten plant when the sun went down. The only illumination Siegel and Khan had as they hunkered down on their metal cots was a wax candle stuck in the broken bottom of a beer bottle on the floor. The place actually had electricity, but the occupants didn't dare flick on the lights, which could be spotted from miles away. They relied instead on a wisp of flame that provided barely enough light to make out the shadowy features of one another's faces.

During daylight hours the two could move around freely, breaking up the monotony of the place. But darkness restricted their movements, unless they used the flashlight Siegel kept stuffed in the covers of his cot. Their activities were restricted to talking and listening to the occasional, raspy squeaks of marauding rats that infested the building.

The conversation between Siegel and Khan sputtered and eventually died not long after sunset. They spent their quiet time staring at the candle, or watching the faint shadows skipping about the walls and ceiling. Siegel wrestled with a multitude of thoughts involving Irina and the case, and the surreal reality of his circumstances. After a while, Khan's voice cut through his musings. "I'm not takin' this much longer," he said.

Siegel turned his attention on his companion as if emerging from a trance. "What did you say?"

"I can't put up with this no more, Max; sitting around all day in this drafty dump, eatin' meals from cans. This fix is ready to put me over the edge."

"Relax, will ya? We won't be here much longer. I told you that earlier. It'll all be over soon."

"I keep hearing that all the time, and then nothing happens, bro." Khan bolted off his cot and paced in front of the candle. Its flame briefly trailing him each time he passed.

"I don't like it either, Raheem, but there's no alternative," Siegel insisted.

"Yes, there is; at least I have one," Khan replied defiantly, abruptly halting by Siegel's cot. He cast a shadowy, fiery form in the semidarkness. "I can choose to take my chances and hit the streets."

"Too dangerous."

"So you say, but at least I won't be cooped up like no animal. I could roam free, you know? I got friends who'll put me up, watch my back. They'd take care of me."

"Like they did by I-5? Like they did in San Francisco? You were on your own both times and look what happened. Your friends can't protect you. This is your only shot."

"Bullshit," Khan spat, more animated in his agitation.

"No, that's reality. You had two friends killed since you went on the run, got shot yourself. You're being stalked by dangerous forces and I'm right next to you. Hit the streets and you're dead before this time tomorrow. Trust me, Raheem. Give it one more day and let us make something happen."

"Alright, one more day," Khan relented, slumping haughtily onto his cot. "If I'm not outta here by tomorrow, then I don't care. I'll blow and you won't stop me."

"Fair enough," Siegel placated. He'd say anything to keep the kid calm. No sense threatening him and explaining how there was no way in hell Siegel would let him walk away. Khan was still a fugitive from justice and Siegel would do everything in his power to keep him in custody, even if it took physical force. The kid appeared incredibly strong and Siegel didn't relish the idea of tangling with him, but he would if he had to. Rappaport had to pull something off and fast.

"Hey, kid, why don't we listen to the radio?" Siegel suggested. "It'll help pass time."

"Whatever," Khan replied. Moving in a slow, desultory fashion, he reached over and lifted the radio from the end of his cot, extending it toward Siegel.

Ignoring the slight, Siegel stood and crossed over the candle to take it. Returning to his cot, Siegel clicked the radio on and adjusted the luminous dials to an AM setting. Voices rose and fell and melded together as Siegel twisted the dial to a news and talk station. It was the middle of a broadcast that featured local events. Siegel set the radio next to him on the cot.

"Can't we hear some music?" Khan whined. "I ain't into talk."

"In a minute. I want to catch some headlines, see if we're in them."

The announcer's voice cut in: "*And in our wrap-up for the evening news, once again, local law enforcement officer Francis Rappaport was killed today in a skydiving accident when his parachute failed to deploy during a routine jum...*"

"Did he just name your boy?" Khan asked.

"Shut up!" Siegel commanded, reeling from shock. "Let me hear this."

"*...Mr. Rappaport was forty-six. It's not known at this time why his chute failed to work, but an autopsy and full investigation into the tragic incident will soon get underway. In other news coming up in the next half hour...*"

Planting his feet on the floor, Siegel leaned elbows on knees and couldn't hear anything more that the announcer said; the voice fading into a vacuum as Siegel's mind raced through images of Rappaport. His heart beat rapidly and Siegel felt sick. He couldn't believe what he'd heard. Yet a part of him instantly grasped the reality of the announcement and grief took root. Franny, this can't be, he thought. I just talked to you, buddy. You can't be gone!

"You alright, bro?" Khan asked. No response. Siegel bent forward, gazing into the candle flame with unseeing eyes. "Max? Max? You okay, man?"

Siegel stirred. "Did you say something?" he asked, disoriented.

"You alright? They're sayin' Rappaport's dead."

"They said that, didn't they?" Siegel repeated absently.

"Yeah, man, just a second ago. Rappaport died in an accident."

Siegel's vacant expression fixed on Khan, who saw a strange transformation wash over Siegel's features. Confusion suddenly evaporated and was replaced by a hardened anger. "Franny didn't die in any accident," Siegel growled. "Cox, you bastard! You're behind this! They killed him." Siegel sprang to his feet. "The games are over, they want us dead…. They killed Franny, dammit!"

"What are you talkin' about, Max? You're goin' all crazy, dude."

Siegel looked sharply at Khan. "You need to stay here. Don't go anyplace, got it?"

"What's up?"

"I have to go. I'll be back in the morning. One way or the other, I'm taking you out of here."

"I'll go with you," Khan offered, scooting off his cot.

"No," Siegel said firmly. "You're staying. If they see us together, they'll take us both out. If I'm alone, they'll want to hang back until I lead them to you. At least that's what I hope."

"You expect me to stay put in this dump?"

"Please, Raheem, only for another few hours. I need you to cooperate. Can you do that?"

"Okay, a few more hours," Khan conceded reluctantly. "Do what you gotta do, bro."

"Thanks, I'll be back in two or three hours. I'll bring breakfast."

Siegel rushed from the room and into the night, clunking down the outer steps until Khan could no longer hear him. Minutes later, a car engine started and the hum of its motor revved and faded away. The quiet that followed clamped down like a blanket and Khan felt a sense of desolation. Reaching into his trouser pocket, he removed the cell phone he copped from Rappaport when the investigator was sleeping.

Khan held the phone for a long time, debating whether to use it. He'd been okay with Rappaport, though they didn't have the best start. The investigator was like a soldier and Khan was impressed by how he improvised and rolled with whatever circumstances arose. But Siegel was another story, too intense, too highbrow. His education put him out of touch, not down to earth like Rappaport, who knew the streets. Siegel was the prosecutor that charged Khan with murder, and now he was pretending to be a friend. The situation was a trip that Khan couldn't wrap his head around.

Rubbing his thumb against the phone, Khan flipped it open and studied the luminous numbers momentarily before making up his mind. Without further hesitation, he began punching the numbers.

CHAPTER 41

---•---

SIEGEL PARKED HIS CAR a block from Rappaport's home, carefully making his way to the residence. When he arrived, he cut down a side yard and stopped at the back door. He let himself in with a spare key Rappaport gave him years before when Rappaport went on vacation. They'd maintained a tradition of watching each other's homes ever since, part of a close bond that had formed over time.

Rappaport lived in a sizeable home that he once shared with his wife and kids. She took the children after their divorce years ago and went back to Kentucky for reasons Rappaport never shared. He should have downsized when it became apparent that a reconciliation wasn't in the cards. Instead, he clung stubbornly to the place. Siegel guessed Rappaport couldn't shake the hope that his family would return someday.

Emerging into a darkened kitchen, Siegel instantly felt a profound sense of emptiness. Intruding into Rappaport's private sanctuary was a dose of reality, a confirmation of Rappaport's absence. It was a truth Siegel didn't want to accept, but knew he must.

Siegel moved quietly into the room, until it occurred to him that stealth was unnecessary. Flicking on the lights, he walked into the living room and turned on more lights. He proceeded to the end table next to Rappaport's favorite leather chair and sat down. Noticing a scratch pad beside the phone, he paged through it. He'd only scanned a few pages when he stopped and clapped a hand over his burning eyes. The grief was powerful and sudden. Siegel wept, letting out a wracking gasp before clamping control over his emotions again. He put his sorrow in check, sniffled once as he wiped his eyes, and continued flipping through the scratch pad.

"Hold it right there," a voice commanded.

Siegel looked into the barrel of a gun. Though momentarily stunned, he quickly regained his composure when he recognized the face behind the weapon. "Hello, Gordy," he said in as passive a tone as he could muster.

The investigator stepped further into the room, the gun trained on Siegel. He was old, one of the retired guys working part-time for the office. Gordy was pasty white, his face heavily lined and weather-beaten. Age spots dotted his scalp and forehead where thin strands of red hair remained. "What are you doing here, Max? Danko suspended you."

"Could you put the gun down, Gordy? You're making me nervous."

Gordy scanned the room unsurely, returning his attention to Siegel. "First, tell me why you're in Franny's home."

"We were working the Khan case together. It's a long story."

"I have plenty of time."

"Franny was making phone contact with people in the state, trying to arrange an intervention in the case. I don't know if he was doing it from here or his office. I came to search for who he spoke to. Time's run out and we need action."

"What the hell are you talking about?"

"You're Franny's friend, Gordy, you know we were close. Trust me when I say that his parachute failing was no accident. Franny was murdered."

"Come again?" Gordy said, surprise registering in his tired looking eyes.

"I told you it's a long story. If you'd just put that gun down, I could brew some coffee and do my best to educate you."

Gordy looked Siegel up and down and gave the room another scan before slowly, hesitantly lowering his Sig Sauer automatic. "This better be good," he said in a suspicious tone.

"It is. When I'm done talking, I'll be asking you for help."

Gordy's expression was perplexed when he holstered his gun.

Dawn broke as Siegel drove to the Tungsten plant. The sky was pale blue, reddish orange colors outlining distant mountains, while thin strips of pink vapor streaked the stratosphere. As Siegel traversed the gravelly road leading into the complex, he realized he hadn't paid sufficient attention to whether he was followed. The lapse in awareness bothered him.

He hadn't slept a wink all night and his head buzzed with exhaustion. He and Gordy Parks had put away an entire pot of coffee during Siegel's spiel about everything that had occurred since the murders in Pleasant Oaks. Gordy maintained a cop's skepticism during the recitation, peppering

Siegel with questions, constantly doubting the explanations. In the end, Siegel managed to win Gordy over somewhat, or so he hoped.

Rappaport's home bore no indications he'd contacted anybody from there. Siegel concluded that he'd made the calls from the office. Siegel's access to the courthouse was cut off, so he convinced Gordy to search Rappaport's phone records. If he could discern who Rappaport contacted, Siegel wanted Gordy to call that person and give an update. Whoever Gordy talked to, Siegel wanted it conveyed that the time to act was now.

Siegel didn't bother hiding his car when he arrived at the deserted factory. Parking next to the building where he and Khan slept, he trudged up the outer stairs to the adjoining offices. Siegel heard voices and frowned when he went inside. As he crossed the empty room to the sleeping quarters, Siegel almost bumped into Khan and Ahmed Jinnah as they emerged from the doorway. The two men stopped short, Jinnah appearing surprised.

"I didn't think you were coming back," Khan said.

Siegel was almost speechless, bewildered by the sight before him. "How did he get here?" he asked.

"Mr. Siegel, get out of the way," Jinnah demanded with urgency. "I'm taking Raheem to a safe place. He will die if he stays; we all will."

"I called him, Max," Khan stated. "Mr. Jinnah's the only one I trust. I didn't know where you went."

"What do you mean we'll die?" Siegel asked Jinnah suspiciously. "What is it you know?"

"There is no time to explain, Mr. Siegel. All I can say is that we are not safe. I am the only chance Raheem has to survive."

"He's going into state custody today," Siegel countered.

"Huh-uh," Khan grunted. "I ain't goin' in no custody."

"Who said you have a choice?" Siegel asked coldly.

"Mr. Siegel, we don't have time for a protracted discussion," Jinnah interrupted. "Please get out of the way. I saw the newspapers. You no longer have authority to take Raheem into custody."

"That's beside the point," Siegel responded. "The proper authorities are on the way. Raheem's still a fugitive with a warrant. The only way you're leaving is through me."

Khan's eyes took on a defiant intensity and he started toward Siegel until Jinnah held him back. Siegel braced for a violent encounter, but then saw Jinnah's gaze drift over his shoulder. Khan's attention followed and Siegel was turning to see what they were looking at when he felt a tremendous knock against his skull.

Darkness followed.

Rich Danko arrived early at his office and took his favorite perch in front of the bay windows, wanting to watch the sun complete its rise. He'd come extra early to take a call from Ross regarding a deal he wanted struck with the federal government.

Danko's hands were thrust into the pockets of his slacks and he rocked slightly on the balls of his feet, smiling as he took in the panoramic view of Las Cruces. The drab skyline was transitioning from a dark gray mass to the distinct collection of mostly blockish old buildings that he so loved. Las Cruces wasn't a pretty town, but it was his. As the top law enforcement official in Clay County, Danko felt like the city's overlord. His power was almost absolute, and next November would also be unchallenged.

Max Siegel was done as a potential rival in the upcoming election. The Khan case took him down better than Danko could have ever imagined. Siegel had gotten consumed by events, going from a dogged hero pursuing justice at all costs, to a disgraced prosecutor on the wrong side of the law. The taint on Siegel's reputation was too great to overcome, at least before the election. With no other viable candidates on the horizon, Danko was sure to be unopposed.

For all Danko's good fortune, he knew there was more to be milked from the political circumstances surrounding him, particularly with the feds. He had them by the balls. Their dirty shenanigans had knocked them off the high horse they rode while pursuing him on corruption charges. How could they go after him for taking a few harmless kickbacks when they were steeped in officially sanctioned, illegal kidnappings, and possibly even murder to cover their tracks?

Danko occupied a unique position with regard to what the feds were doing in his backyard to hide their dirty laundry. As county district attorney, he could either expose the entire debacle to the world, or clamp a lid on it so that nothing got out He chose to do the latter, but not without a price.

Danko learned long ago to accept the darker side of his nature and embrace it, not to burden himself with unnecessary guilt and remorse. He was proud of his greed and had no problems exercising it to gain concessions from the feds in exchange for his cooperation in their current difficulties. It was good that Max Siegel would no longer oppose him politically and that the corruption probe would be dropped, but Danko wanted more.

The drug trade in Clay County was growing exponentially with the recent explosion of meth labs cropping up in the area. Also, local developers and dairy farmers were willing to be ever more generous to someone possessing the power to keep pesky regulators in check. Freed from the tight grip of regulations, the groups stood to rake in millions in profit. All told, Danko could make substantial gains for turning a blind eye here and there. The only problem he was going to have was in how to conceal the massive amounts of money coming his way.

"I hate to use the term money laundering," he'd told Ross in their meeting the previous evening, "but I can see how the government might construe my investments as such if they wanted to get technical about it."

"What exactly are we talking about?" Ross calmly asked.

"Nothing terribly sophisticated, offshore accounts in the Bahamas, the Cayman Islands, and elsewhere; straw corporations with nice sounding names that do nothing in particular except hide the fact that I'm the man behind them. Your boys have sniffed around a couple of these bogus companies already during your probe. It would be nice if you backed off, perhaps make the IRS go away also."

"Is that all?"

"Not quite. I could use help with money transfers, especially for my accounts in the Bahamas. I'm playing with the idea of low level diplomats with clearance maybe walking a pouch through customs now and then."

Ross's brows rose.

"And maybe you can do something about the DEA in the area," Danko continued.

"Excuse me?" Ross said.

"I'm not saying they should shut down operations in Clay County completely. It would just be nice if they could look the other way from time to time; not always, but whenever I give the word."

Ross's brows were arched as high as they could go, his forehead a mass of horizontal wrinkles.

"I know I'm asking a lot," Danko said, "but I'm also giving a lot. I mean, what's the difference right? You have your shady dealings and I have mine. So we learn to live with each other's faults, right? You look after my ass and I'll watch yours."

"Very reciprocal," Ross remarked, nodding slightly.

"Exactly. Give me the concessions I'm asking for and I guarantee not a peep will escape regarding Raheem Khan and the overly rambunctious agents that kidnapped him and tried to spirit him out of the country. The president and everybody down the line won't have to worry about their reputations withstanding shouts of hypocrisy and cover-up. Careers will stay intact, grand policies can still be pursued, and all for what price? Nothing more than Rich Danko lining his pockets with a little retirement money. It doesn't get any better than that," Danko said with a look of stern belligerence. He was glaring at Ross, practically gritting his teeth.

"You present us with quite a tall order, Mr. Danko," Ross said.

"Not that tall in the general scheme of things. What do you say? Do we have a deal?"

"What you're asking is far beyond the scope of my powers. Processing your request will require me to go through channels, several layers of bureaucracy."

"I surmised that," Danko said with a wave of his hand. "I'm not expecting an ironclad guarantee here and now. This is akin to getting credit to buy a piece of real estate. At this juncture, I only want assurances that I'm prequalified. A lot of the services I'll need concern future considerations that haven't arisen yet. The only commitment I require from you people now is a promise that you'll play along when the time comes."

"I understand," Ross said, stretching his lips and nodding. "You want to be prequalified for our cooperation in future undertakings. I like the analogy. It's very clever."

"Do we have a deal?"

"Even the limited commitment you're seeking will still require approval from persons higher up the chain, but I believe a swift response is possible."

"How long? Things are happening fast. We don't have the luxury of dillydallying over the details."

"Nobody's more cognizant of that than I, Mr. Danko. Time is definitely of the essence in this matter. I should think we could have an answer for you by early tomorrow morning. When will you be arriving in your office?"

Danko had grinned like the Cheshire cat. Watching that smarmy prick squirm was a treat. Of course they were going to give him everything he asked for. They couldn't afford otherwise. Danko hardly believed his good fortune. If the murders had happened anywhere else, he'd still be sweating the federal probe. Now, not only the probe, but all his other problems were solved, and with the added bonus of help coming from the very agencies that sought to crucify him. Life couldn't get any better.

Danko's musings were interrupted by a glint of light that caught his attention from below. He ceased rocking on his feet and squinted, trying to see where the flash came from. Then he noticed it again, a flicker of light from the rooftop of a building a few blocks away. Danko focused on a dark silhouette that slowly took shape. Leaning forward, he could make out the stick figure of a kneeling man with something long protruding from him. Dread seized Danko in the flicker of an instant once he finally realized what he was looking at. Then Danko saw a pinpoint flash erupt from the tip of the figure. There was no time to react when a piece of glass splintered and a bullet slammed into his forehead, blowing out the back of his skull.

Rich Danko was dead before his body struck the floor.

CHAPTER 42

———————◆———————

SIEGEL AWOKE AS IF from a nightmare, a throbbing, pulsating pain in his head, like his brain was ready to explode. He heard groaning, gradually feeling the vibrations in his parched throat that told him the sounds were coming from him. When his lids fluttered open, light slammed into his eyeballs, causing stabbing pains. Siegel squeezed his lids shut, slowly letting them open again. Dale Cox loomed unsteadily before him as twins, both images grinning broadly as they floated and see-sawed and merged into one figure. Cox pointed a gun at Siegel. "Good morning, sleepy head," Cox said. "Have a good nap?"

Siegel groaned and raised a hand to shield his eyes as he feebly attempted to push himself into a sitting position. He was lying on one of the cots, a slight wave of nausea sweeping through his gut while he slowly moved upright.

"What's the matter, Max? That knock on the head a little too much for ya?" Cox asked lightly.

Lowering his hand to brace himself on the cot, Siegel swung his head around and saw Khan and Jinnah sitting on the other cot, which had been pushed next to his. Khan appeared apprehensive, while Jinnah was strangely composed.

Fingers snapped. "Max, hey Max, I'm over here," Cox said.

Siegel turned and fixed his attention on the handle of the sap that protruded from Cox's brown, bomber jacket. "Whatcha lookin' at, Max?" Cox asked. "Is it my little friend in my pocket? Yep. In case you're wondering, that's what I used to put your lights out. Recognize it? Bernard Harris's sap. I love these things."

Siegel gently rubbed the back of his scalp. He felt broken skin, his fingers red with blood when he pulled them away. "Sneaking up on me make you feel proud, Cox?" Siegel taunted. "Not man enough to come at me head on?"

"Shut up!" Cox snapped, raising the gun. "Don't talk to me like that. I won't take your disrespect. Can't you see I'm holding all the cards now? I could kill you right this second if I wanted to."

Siegel calmly leaned back against the wall, his senses quickly returning. He knew he should be afraid, but he wasn't. He had too much contempt for Cox to be scared. "So you're God now, are you?" he said. "If you can kill me, then why don't you? You're the man, right?"

"Why would you suggest such a thing?" Jinnah asked.

"Both of you shut up!" Cox commanded, his face turning red, suddenly shifting his weight from foot to foot, coming unglued. "This is my moment and nobody's gonna spoil it."

"Your moment?" Siegel repeated. "What the hell does that mean?"

"I'm in charge, that's what it means," Cox said, raising the gun higher and stepping closer. "It means you listen and don't speak unless I tell you to."

"You're in charge, huh?" Siegel queried mockingly.

"Yo, Max, back off this guy," Khan cautioned.

"If you're in charge, why don't you shoot?" Siegel pressed, ignoring the warning. "I'll tell you why, because you're not calling the shots. You're just a messenger boy, a lackey for somebody else. Who is it? Ross? Are you holding us for Ross?"

Cox scratched at his neck with irritation, the crimson color of his pock-marked face increasing. "You're so smart, aren't you? Mr. Star Prosecutor, some kind of golden-boy know-it-all. I have a news flash, smart guy. How 'bout your wife, Irina? What if I told you she's got a secret life that you know nothin' about? How would that sit?"

Siegel looked Cox straight in the eyes. "Her name is Svetlana," he said. "She used to be hooked up with a Russian mob guy named Dmitri. She came to the United States under an assumed name and moved to Las Cruces shortly after her boyfriend's body washed up on the banks of the American River. My wife had one date with you before we met and nothing happened because it was a charity event. She thought you were pathetic. You've been chasing her like a lovesick puppy ever since. She's rejected you so many times they don't even have a number for it. Anything else you think I don't know?" Siegel finished with every ounce of condescension he could muster.

The transformation on Cox's face while Siegel spoke was dramatic. The cocky smugness rapidly dissolved into bewilderment. The grin faded and

Cox's jaw slackened until his mouth hung open. The mental advantage he thought he had over Siegel evaporated and turned to humiliation. "How-how could you know all that?" he stammered.

"You have nothing on me," Siegel said confidently. "You have nothing on anyone, that's why you do all your dirty work by sneaking up on people."

"Shut up!" Cox demanded, taking another step forward. "You gotta lotta lip for someone on the wrong side of my gun. I could kill you right now."

"You keep saying that, so why don't you go ahead and do it," Siegel urged defiantly, lifting his back from the wall. Cox was rattled. If Siegel could just get him to move a bit closer....

"Mr. Siegel," Jinnah interrupted, "please stop baiting him. Can't you tell he means business?"

"Yeah," Cox agreed, "listen to him."

Siegel shot Khan a sideways glance. The kid was a survivor, and pretty good in the type of situation they were in. Khan returned the look and Siegel hoped the kid understood what he was planning. "No, he doesn't mean business," Siegel calmly retorted, fixing his gaze on Cox again. "He can't handle doing his dirty deeds face to face like this. It's not his style. He can only come at people when their backs are turned. He's a coward."

"Dammit, you better shut up!" Cox said through bared teeth, the statement coming out more like a whine. His eyes were beginning to water and he was shaking so hard with tension that he was practically vibrating.

Siegel eased imperceptibly forward on the cot. "He killed my friend Franny Rappaport yesterday," Siegel declared, a slight catch in his voice. He turned to Jinnah. "You saw Franny in court during Raheem's arraignment. Franny was a good man, ten times better than this piece of white trash in front of me."

"I won't warn you again," Cox said, his tone tight and menacing.

"Cox couldn't stand toe to toe with Franny because he was scared to death of him, like he is everything else." Siegel returned his attention to Cox, looking him deliberately in the eyes. "So he snuck into Franny's locker at the airfield, like the greasy little rat that he is, and tampered with Franny's parachute. He let gravity kill my best friend because he was never man enough to confront him."

"That's all I'm gonna take from you," Cox said in a shaking voice, unconsciously advancing on Siegel, raising the gun to shoot.

"Now!" Siegel shouted, lunging off the cot and ducking under the gun as it exploded. He wrapped his arms around Cox's thick waist and drove

Cox through the open doorway and into the adjacent office. The gun went off again before they fell to the floor, Siegel landing on top.

Cox swung the butt of the gun and connected with Siegel's shoulder, causing a sharp pain. Siegel rose up slightly when Cox tried to level the gun at him, violently wrestling Cox's hand to the floor with a two-handed wristlock. Cox pulled the sap from his coat with his free hand, but Siegel couldn't respond without releasing his grips on the hand holding the gun. He watched helplessly as Cox raised the sap to hit him.

Khan grabbed Cox's hand and wrenched it down. Cox squealed in pain and Siegel banged the gun hand on the floor, causing the Sig Sauer to skitter away. Righting himself, Siegel was ready to punch Cox in the jaw when the detective crooked his forearm over his eyes and cried, "No!" Siegel checked his swing. Khan had the other hand pinned to the floor and Siegel realized that Cox was helpless.

Jinnah ran to the gun and picked it up. Holding it unsurely, he turned to the others.

"Don't hurt me," Cox moaned.

"He was gonna do you, Max," Khan said. "We should take care of him." He raised a fist and Siegel stuck his arm out to shield Cox from the blow. Khan looked wildly at Siegel. "Why you protectin' him? I'm gonna take his ass out."

"No, you're not," Siegel countered, pushing at Khan's chest and feeling strong resistance. "The fight's over."

"Screw that shit!" Khan fumed, cocking a fist at Siegel.

"Raheem, come over here," Jinnah said.

Khan didn't budge, his features savagely contorted.

"Do as I say, Raheem," Jinnah persisted, his tone unnaturally calm. Siegel saw that Jinnah was still holding the gun at waist level, the barrel trained in their direction. Jinnah kept his attention fixed on Khan, as if Siegel wasn't there. "Listen to me and stop acting like a child!"

The sternness of Jinnah's tone snapped Khan out of his petulance. He got up from the floor and skulked toward Jinnah, taking a stance beside him. Siegel's breathing was heavy and he slowly lifted himself off Cox and got to his feet. The barrel of the Sig Sauer casually remained pointed at Siegel. "What's this about?" Siegel asked warily.

"It is about you staying where you are," Jinnah replied. "Make no sudden moves, Mr. Siegel, or I will be forced to kill you."

"What are we doing?" Khan asked. "Max has been helping me, Ahmed."

"Silence, foolish boy! These men are both enemies. Don't side with the infidel."

"You shoulda left me alone," Cox said from the floor. "I had everything under control."

"Detective Cox, you would do well to keep quiet," Jinnah angrily warned. "I would not mind shooting you. Your talking makes the temptation grow stronger."

Cox's eyes widened with fright and he said nothing more.

"So what happens now?" Siegel asked.

Jinnah was about to respond when the sound of an approaching car came from outside. All could hear tires crunching on gravel, the purr of a big engine as a vehicle slowly came to a halt. Jinnah and Khan looked toward the grimy windows by the door but didn't move. Siegel took it upon himself to walk across the room and peek through the glass. He saw a large, dark sedan next to the stairs. Ross emerged from the driver's side wearing sunglasses and buttoning his suit jacket, while his blond-haired partner disembarked from the other side with a long rifle in his hands. The rifle had an attached scope and Siegel's brows furrowed while the two men conferred. Ross pointed away from the building and his partner immediately walked off in the direction Ross indicated.

"It's the FBI," Siegel announced.

"Ross and Frazier," Cox said. "Ross told me they were coming. It's all over for you, Jinnah."

"I told you to stay quiet!" Jinnah ordered. "Mr. Siegel, back away from the door. Cox, get up and stand with Mr. Siegel."

"What's the plan?" Khan asked.

"We'll go in the other room. Mr. Siegel, stay still. I will keep the gun pointed at you and Cox. Any sudden moves and I won't hesitate to shoot. I assure you, I'm quite proficient with this weapon."

Jinnah moved quickly through the doorway of the adjoining room with Khan in tow. As Cox got up, Siegel heard footsteps climbing the metal steps outside. There was a pause at the door before it opened. Ross stepped onto the threshold, gun in hand, instantly training it on Siegel and Cox while he removed his sunglasses. Cox signaled at the doorway with obvious jerks of his head and Ross's attention followed. Jinnah appeared in the room, as if on cue, and Ross turned his gun on him. Jinnah did the same in return.

There was a tense moment of confrontation and Siegel prepared to react if shooting erupted, but then he saw Ross grin and lower his gun. "So you *are* here," he said. "I wasn't sure."

"I came right after I called you," Jinnah replied.

Siegel was stunned, as was Cox, whose confusion appeared absolute. Jinnah came further into the room with Khan. Ross's grin expanded.

"Ah, the slippery Raheem Khan, you've given us a tremendous amount of trouble with your recent antics. It's about time we got our hands on you."

"Huh?" Khan grunted. "What's he sayin'?"

Deliberately, Jinnah turned his gun on Khan. "Raheem, I need you to stand with Mr. Siegel and Cox."

"What the hell?" Khan remarked, starting at Jinnah.

"Stop there!" Jinnah demanded, raising the gun. "I'll kill you if you don't obey. Get with those two."

Khan stopped short and reluctantly complied with the command, his expression murderous. Siegel was also reeling from the turn of events. "Agent Ross," Cox ventured, "could you tell me what's going on? All this stuff has got my head spinning."

Ross looked blandly at Cox. "I'll have Mr. Jinnah give you clarification," he responded.

"I don't understand," Cox said, stepping forward.

Ross nodded knowingly to Jinnah, as if confirming some course of action they'd previously arranged. "Are you serious?" Jinnah asked.

"Very," Ross replied. He waved his gun at Siegel and Khan as Jinnah edged toward Cox. "Gentlemen, would you mind stepping aside?" he asked, indicating the windows.

Cox's breathing turned labored and he began to pant when Siegel and Khan moved away. Cringing fearfully, he lifted a shaking hand at Jinnah and backed up, a growing wet stain running down the left leg of his faded blue jeans. Jinnah strode forward until Cox bumped into a wall. "No!" he shouted when Jinnah lifted the gun.

The retort of the Sig Sauer sounded like a canon in the small room. A red dot appeared on Cox's forehead as a bright red spray shot onto the wall behind him and his body collapsed, going through a series of gruesome, spastic movements as a crimson puddle rapidly formed about the head.

Siegel watched the macabre spectacle in horror, his ears ringing, not believing what he'd just witnessed. Jinnah lowered the gun and redirected it at Siegel and Khan, his small eyes bugged open with the menacing excitement of someone thrilled by his murderous act and yearning to do it again. Siegel whirled around, wondering what Ross would indicate next, only to see the agent calmly jerking a finger in his ear while appearing mildly irritated. "That was loud," he said. "Did that shock you, Max? You're as pale as a ghost."

"Shall I do the same to him?" Jinnah asked.

"Ahmed, please!" Ross playfully responded. "Stand down. These two remaining gentlemen are going to perceive you as some kind of cold-blooded killer, instead of a patriot, which is what you truly are. Come stand next to me and keep your gun on them. I'd like to have a chat with Max before we proceed any further. May I still call you Max, like when we spoke in the coffee shop?"

"Call me anything you want," Siegel replied, eyeing the weapons. "You will anyway."

"Please, Max, don't think we're rude because of what happened to poor Detective Cox," Ross said. "His time had come. He wasn't of anymore use to this mission. Actually, he'd just become a liability, what with his immaturity and loose lips. Leaving him alive would have trumped all our hard work. He would have never kept our secret."

Siegel looked at Cox's crumpled body with disgust. "You took a man's life for the sake of a secret? Does death come that cheap?"

"Such naivety," Ross said. "People die every day, all over the world, for the sake of some secret or another. I'll bet if you could tally some sort of count, it would top cancer and heart disease as a leading cause of nonexistence. But, I must say, I'm surprised by the sympathy you're showing for what used to constitute Dale Cox. After all, he had nothing but ill will for you and your friends. He was constantly trying to cuckold your wife. He ran poor Mr. Langerman off that deserted highway. And he murdered your best friend, Mr. Rappaport."

That last line struck a nerve and Siegel exchanged steadfast gazes with Ross. There was a cold, sadistic enjoyment in the depths of Ross's eyes, a predatory steeliness usually reserved for nature specials. Siegel also detected something else … madness, a man who was criminally insane. That's when Siegel became certain that Ross intended to kill him.

"What's wrong, Max?" Ross asked. "Does the revelation about Rappaport's death surprise you?"

"No, I already guessed as much, and now I can see that you were behind it."

"Of course I was, Max. I'm the mastermind, after all. Do you believe someone as primitive as Cox could have conceived such a subtle demise for your friend? I told him to do it, and my partner, Agent Frazier, gave him instructions on how to tamper with the chute so it would appear to be an accident. Frazier has a Special Forces background and he's well versed in such matters."

"But why?" Siegel asked, grimacing.

"To silence him," Ross replied, as if the answer were obvious. "Not only did he know too much, but he was ringing every law enforcement agency in the state trying to get them involved in our tiny intrigue. I simply couldn't have it. The same was true for your colleague, Langerman. I couldn't let him write an exposé in the news. He got away, unfortunately, but not for long. The same with your poor Judge Grafton; he's an avid fisherman who'll be involved in a very tragic boating accident in the near future. You and Gul shouldn't have told him so much."

"Is that why you tried to have me killed?" Siegel asked.

"Oh no, that was an accident; one indirectly caused by Mr. Jinnah here. I didn't want you dead at that time. The two attempts came from overly rambunctious zealots who caused too much unwanted publicity with their thoughtless actions." Ross cut his eyes at Jinnah.

"I really must apologize for those incidents," Jinnah said to Siegel. "I was grandstanding about this case in my community to enhance my credentials as an enemy of the government. A couple of my followers took my rantings to heart and made attempts on your life of their own accord. After they tried to kill you the second time, we relocated them to the East Coast, where they are heavily monitored."

"What are you saying, Mr. Jinnah?" Khan asked, his expression twisted with confusion and the dawning of betrayal. "Are you saying you ain't one of us?"

"I'm sorry, Raheem, but I've never been one of you. I'm an agent of the federal government, a mole burrowing into the deepest recesses of the terrorist anarchy that threatens our country."

"But you sent me to Pakistan with Tariq to study with Faisal Abdul. You paid my way."

"Actually, your Uncle Sam footed the expenses," Ross interrupted. "It was all part of Jinnah's cover. Appear to be a radical leader in the community, become more trusted by your people, and gain access to the diabolical plots you Muslims are always hatching against American citizens. You didn't know it at the time, Raheem, but you were sent to Pakistan on a fact-finding mission for American intelligence. You and your friend were dupes."

"That explains Jinnah's prosecution last year," Siegel said. "You fed us a case against him, and then withheld all the evidence we required to sustain a conviction. It was a setup to buy him credibility with the Muslims. You used our office."

"Exactly," Ross replied with an easy grin. "Jinnah shouted to the rafters in the press about the government persecuting him with false charges and rightfully so. The case stirred up a hornet's nest of indignance in the Muslim community and cemented his reputation. We never imagined such a successful outcome."

"I thought you were cool," Khan said to Jinnah. "All this time you were nothin' but a damn traitor."

"That depends on your perspective," Jinnah retorted. "My allegiance has always been with America."

"What about Gul?" Siegel asked. "Did you kill him, too?"

"Ah, that was my doing," Jinnah replied, raising his free hand like he was a student in class. "Although it's debatable whether that was a murder at all."

"How so?" Siegel asked.

"Mr. Gul was very carefully chosen by me. We wanted someone with serious health problems in case it became necessary to get rid of him afterwards. By paying the attorney, I was hoping to exert control over his actions. The idea was either to persuade Raheem to quickly plead guilty to murder because of the overwhelming circumstances, or at least keep the facts from surfacing in court long enough for us to deal with him. We weren't worried about Raheem talking after a conviction. His paranoid rantings after a trial would never be listened to and he'd soon die in a prison attack not long after his incarceration, which would silence him forever. Before trial was a different story. Investigators and the press would probe his claims and unravel the truth."

"Despite his poor health, Gul turned out to be a zealous defense attorney," Ross added. "Once he got Khan's side of the story, he decided to run with it. He was going to make the case more of a spectacle than it already was. That's when we decided to take him out."

"It was quite simple," Jinnah continued. "His heart was in such a weakened condition that any amount of stress would induce an attack. He was very dependent on the medication he took to prevent an episode. He nearly had a seizure when I visited him one night with some of my followers. It was then that I surreptitiously replaced his pills with sugar tablets."

Ross chuckled viciously. "The rest was simple," he said. "We called the next day and peppered him with ominous threats, inducing enough panic to trigger a seizure." Ross raised his shoulders and spread his hands outward. "God did the rest," he said lightly.

"You're a sick man," Siegel declared.

The grin faded from Ross's mouth and he pointed his gun more deliberately at Siegel. "Strange that you should judge me when you're protecting a terrorist. I'm doing what's necessary to save my country. What about you? You can't possibly believe Khan is innocent. Look at him, just a little thug from the streets, jumping on any bandwagon that gives his murderous impulses an outlet."

"I don't know if he's innocent or not," Siegel said defiantly. "What I've done to bring Khan in isn't about him. What's at issue is bigger than that.

It's about protecting the American system. Our country is about laws and justice, with procedures that were honed and handed down for generations. It isn't about rogue agents cloaking themselves in the American flag, playing God, and deciding who lives and dies because of an arbitrary sense of national security. You call Raheem Khan a terrorist, but what you've done in the past few days makes you no better than the men you're hunting. I wonder if you'll ever understand that."

Still clutching his gun, Ross did his best to slap his hands together in mock applause. "That was inspiring, Max. I admire your sense of justice, although I find it wrongheaded and naïve. You're too myopic to ever see the service me and my associates are doing for this country. When battling tyranny, it's necessary to shed the blood of a few innocents. It's an unfortunate sacrifice, but one that has to be made at times."

"What's he gettin' at?" Khan asked nervously.

"That they're going to kill us," Siegel replied, keeping his unwavering attention on Ross, who was smiling again.

"Yes, Mr. Siegel is right, Raheem," Ross said. "But if it's any consolation, Max, you should know that causing your death will give me no pleasure. In fact, killing you is going to break my heart."

CHAPTER 43

———•———

ROSS SQUATTED NEXT TO Cox's corpse and studied it like a child in an aquarium would peer into a fish tank. Looking over every inch of the lifeless body, prodding it now and then, he seemed enraptured by the sight. "Truly amazing," he declared. "Three pounds of pressure on a trigger, a moment's passage, and what used to be a man is reduced to a rotting pile of bone and tissue. From a quivering, sniveling idiot to a mound of worm food in the blink of an eye. What a fascinating transformation."

"May we finish this foul business and get out of here?" Jinnah inquired impatiently.

Ross cocked a look at him over his shoulder. "What are you worried about? We have the situation under control. Why rush?"

"This is gruesome business, Agent Ross. The longer we drag it out, the more unpleasant this becomes. Let us do what we must, and then depart. Every second we linger places us in greater peril."

"Of what? Are you worried about being found out? Relax, my friend. We monitored Rappaport's phone calls from his office. He did a lot of talking, spewed a tremendous amount of information, but he never disclosed this location. The level of trust he formed with some of his contacts never rose high enough for him to feel comfortable parceling out that tidbit of information. We couldn't be more isolated if we were on the moon. Nobody knows we're here."

"All the same, sir, I would like to be done with this matter."

Ross slowly shook his head and rose to his feet, clucking his tongue against his teeth. "Ahmed, Ahmed," he said wistfully, "you have no sense of artistry, no sense of savoring your handiwork. Some matters shouldn't be rushed. It's like cooking a fine stew, you need to bring it to a slow boil, and then let it simmer if you want to attain a flavor you'll truly enjoy."

"You need lots of help," Siegel remarked. "You're a sick man, Ross. Did your mother not hug you enough when you were a kid?"

Ross turned a cold gaze on Siegel and approached him. Siegel tensed, but still wasn't ready for the vicious strike that followed, the gun slamming into his cheek, jarring his skull and loosening a few teeth. The pain was immediate and deep. Ross stepped back and pointed the gun at Siegel's nose as Siegel cupped his face and groaned, the warm, metallic taste of blood flooding his mouth. He spit some onto the floor.

"There's more where that came from," Ross said. "I'd be happy to oblige if you want a repeat."

"I'm good for now," Siegel responded, more blood spilling onto his chin.

The side of Ross's mouth crooked upward. "You certainly are a brave one. I admire that. I never had you pegged as being that macho. I thought the whole boxing gig was just a way of covering over inadequacies."

"Now see," Siegel said, "in psychology they call that projecting."

The coldness came back into Ross and he moved forward. Once again, Siegel had no time to react, a vicious kick hitting his midsection. The strike was incredibly fast and Ross had returned his foot to the floor before the shock of the blow set in. The air went out of Siegel's lungs as a painful cramp crashed into his diaphragm. He bent over and gasped for breath, feeling light in the head as another half-grin graced Ross's mouth.

"Bet you didn't know I could do that?" Ross said with some pride. "You're not the only practitioner of martial arts, Max. I've been into one form of combat or another for years, as long as I can remember. You have no idea how much I'd love to go one on one with you. You're a big man and it would be quite a challenge, but in the end, I'd humiliate you."

Siegel sucked in air. "That's fine by me," he replied, half gasping. "Why don't you and Jinnah put down your guns, and we'll settle this the old fashioned way?"

"You're trying so hard to be clever," Ross said. "You think you can beat me and that getting this gun out of my hand will set you free. You don't know how wrong you are. I don't need a weapon to finish you, Max."

"Prove it."

"Agent Ross, can we stop playing these childish games?" Jinnah cut in. "No matter what test you feel you must set for yourself, I am not relinquishing my gun. We are wasting too much time. Let's finish."

"You heard my colleague, Max," Ross said. "He's decided not to let us play. What a pity. I suppose I should show him some deference."

"Good," Jinnah said. "Shall we shoot them now?"

"I have a better idea," Ross said. "These facilities are still operable, probably because the corporation that owns it is contemplating reestablishing production. Since we're fortunate enough to have working machinery, we should use it."

"What are you getting at?" Siegel asked, dread flooding his insides.

Ross grinned blandly, his gaze sinister. "We're going to take a walk to the crusher," he declared.

"What's that?" Khan asked uncomfortably.

"A crusher is where rocks and boulders are broken to pieces," Siegel replied, feeling unsettled.

"Very good," Ross said. "I see you have a grasp of cement production. Ever wonder what it would be like to pass through such a contraption?"

Siegel felt an icy tingling that went from his scalp to his toes. "You can't be serious," he said.

"Yes, I am," Ross replied gleefully. "I'm deadly serious."

They descended the outer steps with Ross in the lead and Jinnah pulling up the rear, holding his gun on Siegel and Khan, who were sandwiched in between. Ross kept talking as he descended, not bothering to look back. "Don't try to run, gentlemen," he said. "My partner, Agent Frazier, is a dead shot with his sniper rifle. He's watching us now from a secret location. Any false moves and he'll make your head explode."

"As opposed to being ground to mush?" Siegel retorted.

Ross reached the foot of the steps and strode forward a few paces before turning. "Good point," he said. "I suppose it would be more merciful. Feel free to choose your option. You know what to do to earn the bullet." He gestured with his hand, inviting Siegel to make a dash.

Siegel refrained from taking the bait. He halted by Ross and scanned the nearby grounds, trying to pinpoint Frazier's location.

"Just as I thought," Ross said. "Even while facing the prospect of certain death, the condemned man clutches to the slim hope that his sentence will be reprieved. How pathetic. At least if you run, you might have a chance."

Ross led the group to the edge of the plant grounds and onto a platform overlooking a wide conveyor belt that fed into an enormous, open-mouthed steel bin. The drop into the bin was graded so that whatever fell in would slide beneath a giant, corrugated roller that looked to weigh thousands of pounds. The roller was meant to crush and pulverize limestone, bauxite, and other hard materials that would eventually become cement. Today, as Ross explained, it would only have to crush two men. A windowed control booth stood at the far end of the platform and it drew Ross's attention. "That must be where the juice comes from," he said. "I wonder if I have the technical wherewithal to discern its workings."

"Must we play these silly games?" Jinnah lamented. "Why can't we get this over with quickly?"

"Patience, Ahmed. Keep watch on our friends while I see what I can get started. I'll have a clear view from the booth, so let's not have any game playing."

Ross strolled off and entered the booth. Flicking on a light, the others could see him fiddling with the controls. Siegel felt a sense of urgency. Whatever happened, he determined he wasn't going to be squashed like a bug under a crusher. "You're working with a crazy man, you know that?" he asked Jinnah.

Jinnah appeared perturbed. "Maybe so, but I'm not in a position to dictate anything to him. You all witnessed me committing murder. What choice do I have but to get rid of you? I don't approve of Ross's techniques. However, I believe it will all come out the same in the end."

There was a lengthy drop from the platform. Some steps were nearby, but Siegel and Khan would be shot long before they'd get to the bottom. Siegel's heart raced and there was a tingling in his scalp as desperation weighed more heavily on him. "We don't have a choice, Raheem," he said.

"Huh?" Khan replied. He'd been scanning the surroundings, also searching for a way out.

"They're going to kill us no matter what. We have to do something."

"Stop talking," Jinnah commanded, nervously raising his gun. He was about ten feet away.

"We have nothing to lose, kid," Siegel continued defiantly. "If we cooperate, we'll be grease spots in another minute."

"What we gonna do?" Khan asked breathlessly.

"We have to rush him."

"Okay, Max, I'm down with that."

"Stay where you are," Jinnah warned, backing away. He turned slightly and began to call for Ross when his words were drowned out by the deafening sound of the machinery starting.

Cloaked by the noise, Siegel and Khan were both spurred to action, charging Jinnah together. Panic filled Jinnah's features as he shakily raised his gun and fired a shot before Khan crashed into him. Siegel was on him next, grasping Jinnah's wrist before Jinnah could fire again. Khan held the man in a bear hug while Siegel violently twisted Jinnah's wrist and snapped it. Jinnah's cry of agony was muted in the din of the machinery. The gun fell to the platform, bouncing onto the conveyor belt. Siegel tried to retrieve the weapon, but it was swept away, sliding off the belt and dropping to the ground.

Siegel had moved away from Jinnah and Khan. He looked back and saw them locked in a struggle, their hands clasping each other's throats. It was obvious that Khan was hurt. Ross appeared startled in the distance, just noticing the commotion. Springing to the door of the control booth, he dashed out as Jinnah and Khan tumbled onto the conveyor belt. Khan landed on top and seemed unable to move as Jinnah kicked and screamed frantically beneath his weight. Khan managed to look up at Siegel as they passed and feebly reached out a bloody hand. Khan's eyes were half closed when Siegel grasped for the outstretched hand, clutching it briefly before it slipped from his grip. Jinnah let out a terror stricken screech as Khan collapsed and the two were swept into the bin. Jinnah's cry abruptly ceased when their bodies rolled beneath the crushing wheel.

Ross pointed his gun at Siegel and a puff of smoke rose from the barrel, though Siegel never heard the shot. He felt a stinging in his right bicep as the sleeve of his leather jacket tore. Siegel tried to retreat down the steps when Ross charged, but he didn't get far. Ross was on him in no time, pointing his gun at Siegel's temple from a few feet away. "You're not going anywhere," he shouted over the noise. "Get back on the platform or I'll blow your head off."

Siegel hesitated, measuring his options, but Ross had him at point blank range, a fiercely determined look in his eyes, a look that seemed insane. It was certain death if Siegel tried to get away. He had no choice but to comply.

When Siegel regained the platform, Ross kept the gun trained on him and made Siegel follow as he backtracked toward the control room. Ross crossed his free hand over his shooting arm, holding his palm up. When he saw the questioning look in Siegel's expression, he raised his voice and spoke loudly. "I'm signaling Frazier," he said. "He has you in his sights and I don't want him to shoot. He's a crack shot. He proved that to your boss this morning. But I don't want him taking you out. You're my project."

"You killed Danko?" Siegel asked, feeling a chill.

"Does that surprise you? We tried to make him a partner. Unfortunately, his demands were too much. He was a corrupt man. Frazier did Clay County a service."

Siegel shook his head. "It never ends with you guys, does it?"

"Actually, it does end…. Stop there."

Siegel halted in the middle of the platform. Ross also stopped about fifteen feet away. "It does end, Max," he repeated. "In fact, it's all going to end right here. This is where we put a finish to the dirty piece of business that brought me to Las Cruces."

"I'm not getting on that conveyor," Siegel firmly declared. "You'll have to shoot me."

"Oh, you're going on that conveyor," Ross said, squatting and setting his gun onto the wooden planks of the platform. Slowly rising, he stepped over the gun and moved a few paces toward Siegel. "But I'm not going to shoot you. No, Max, I'm going to put you on that conveyor myself. And then you're going into that bin to be crushed to a pulp, just like poor Ahmed." Ross mocked a sigh. "What a waste. We spent so much time building his reputation with our enemies, only to have you flush it all away. Do you have any idea how valuable an asset he was?"

Siegel glanced sideways, estimating the feasibility of a jump. "Don't try it," Ross said, reading his thoughts. "Frazier is too good a shot. You'd be dead before your feet touched the ground. The only chance you have is to come through me."

"Pretty confident in yourself, aren't you?"

"You only had a slight taste of what I can do in that other building. I'm going to give you a lesson in martial arts, Max. Too bad it won't be one you'll remember."

While Ross stretched his neck from side to side to work out the kinks, Siegel slowly peeled off his leather jacket, wincing at the pain shooting through his right arm. A chunk of flesh was blown away, but it didn't feel as if a bullet was lodged inside. Ross registered surprise when Siegel dropped the jacket. "You're bigger than I thought," he said appreciatively

"Being underestimated is the story of my life," Siegel said, steadfastly advancing on the agent. His blood was up and he was ready to fight.

Ross charged, lunging forward with a straight kick that Siegel barely brushed aside while smashing his fist into Ross's face. Ross stumbled backward and fell hard, shock registering on his expression, two streams of red blood gushing from his nostrils. Siegel advanced confidently and felt a sharp pain in his kneecap when Ross unleashed a kick from the floor.

Siegel limped back, his knee on fire. Ross got up and charged again. The two men grappled, each roughly grasping the other's clothing as they pushed and shoved dangerously close to the edge of the platform. Finally, Siegel found enough leverage to free his right hand and he let loose with two chopping punches into Ross's ribs. The agent's knees buckled and he started to go down, but then swiftly pitched forward, wrapping both arms around Siegel's knees and forcing him onto his back.

The conveyor belt was running just to the left and Siegel made the mistake of glancing at it, giving Ross time to rise up and pound him in the jaw with three rapid punches. The strikes were strong, almost knocking Siegel senseless. Before Ross could hit him a fourth blow, Siegel locked both hands behind Ross's neck and pulled down hard, simultaneously butting his forehead into Ross's face.

Ross groaned and Siegel rolled them both away from the conveyor belt. Ross was a bloody mess when Siegel pushed off him and got to his knees. Siegel thought Ross was done, and was surprised when Ross cocked a foot and kicked Siegel square in the chest. The impact sent Siegel onto his back again and both men lay motionless for a few seconds, trying to regain themselves.

The deafening noise of the machinery throbbed in Siegel's aching temples, but he forced himself to rise when he saw Ross doing the same. Just when it occurred to Siegel that the gun was behind him, Ross staggered forward and swung a looping right that Siegel easily blocked and followed through with an uppercut that caught Ross under the jaw, snapping his head back.

Spinning around, Siegel made a loping dash for the gun. He heard the crackle in the distance when he bent to reach for the weapon and saw it disappear in a flash. Before Siegel could straighten, Ross's weight was on his back. An arm encircled Siegel's throat and tightened with a violent jerk, completely cutting off Siegel's air. Siegel tore at the arm, but it only got tighter and spots began to develop around the periphery of his vision. A strange, tingling sensation travelled through his limbs and Siegel realized he was on his way to passing out.

Siegel felt Ross's legs wrapped tightly around his lower body, squeezing Siegel like a python. As Siegel's mind began to fade, he had one last desperate idea. Bending forward slightly, he snapped backwards, flipping himself onto the hard planks. Ross took the brunt of the fall and grunted with the impact, the grip around Siegel's throat loosening.

Using the rest of his might, Siegel blindly drove his right, then left elbow into Ross's midsection, gasping for breath when the arm came loose from his neck. Siegel weakly rolled off his adversary, trying to recover. He sucked in air until his head cleared, but was roughly pushed onto his back by Ross.

Siegel cocked his right leg and his foot pressed into Ross' abdomen as Ross slid Siegel against the planks until his head was hanging over the conveyor belt. Siegel used all his strength to arrest the motion and keep from being pushed onto the belt. Ross pushed a hand against Siegel's chin to force his head back. Siegel did the same, pushing up against Ross's chin to keep him off balance, while trying to get enough leverage to kick Ross off.

"You're … going … in!" Ross grunted, the pressure on his jaw clamping his mouth shut.

"Go … to … HELL!" Siegel responded, kicking with all his might, launching Ross across the platform.

They both regained their feet and Ross rushed Siegel before he could step away from the conveyor. With his back to the dangerous belt, Siegel exchanged a fusillade of punches and kicks with Ross, each landing heavy blows, each breaking down the other in a desperate, bloody struggle. Siegel was ready to collapse, but willpower kept him standing.

Ross attempted a kick to Siegel's side, but Siegel managed to hook his arm around the leg and hold it in place. With Ross standing on one foot, Siegel pivoted and swung Ross around until Ross's back was to the conveyor. Ross perceived the danger and attempted to fling his hands around Siegel's neck when Siegel hauled back a fist and struck Ross in the mouth.

Siegel let go of the leg as Ross sailed off the platform, landing heavily on the swiftly moving conveyor belt, which swept him away. Before Ross could react, he tumbled into the bin and his horrified screech was suddenly squelched beneath the crushing weight of the giant roller.

Frazier couldn't believe what he witnessed through the lens of his McMillan Tac-50 sniper rifle. He was sure his partner could beat the attorney. That's why he didn't interfere in their combat, even when Ross wasn't getting the best of the fight. Seeing Ross fall and get swept away was stunning. Now a bloodied and exhausted Max Siegel stood erect on the platform, centered in Frazier's telescopic sight.

Siegel's chest visibly heaved as Frazier settled the crosshairs on the point where the heart was located and gently began applying pressure to the trigger. Siegel was looking at the bin when Frazier's presence dawned on him. That's when Siegel suddenly stiffened, as if an electrical current were passing through his body, and turned his attention in Frazier's direction.

Frazier grinned as he increased the pressure on the trigger, deriving a sadistic pleasure out of Siegel's realization that he was about to die. Slightly more pressure and the shot would explode, the bullet travelling a trajectory that would obliterate Siegel's heart and tear out his back. Frazier felt a thrill coursing through him, until a lead pipe crashed against his temple. The rifle jerked spasmodically when the barrel crackled and the bullet flew harmlessly into the sky.

Siegel's knees buckled when he heard the shot, and he dropped into a stoop, looking wildly about. At first he thought he was hit and not yet feeling the damage because of shock. But after a few seconds, he understood that the shot had missed. Dazed and confused, he slowly straightened, knowing he was still a sitting duck whenever Frazier chose to take him out. What he couldn't fathom was why the first shot strayed off the mark.

A dark figure slowly made its way to the platform from a distance. Initially, Siegel thought the person limping toward him was carrying a rifle, but as the figure drew closer, Siegel saw that the man was carrying a pipe. "Franny, is that you?" Siegel called. He rubbed blood out of his eyes and looked again at the approaching man, until recognition set in. It wasn't Rappaport, it was Dave Langerman.

CHAPTER 44

---•---

"**T**HIS HAS BEEN ONE hell of a shindig," Langerman said, embracing Siegel after Siegel climbed down from the platform.

"How'd you get here?" Siegel asked, still not believing Langerman was there.

"I couldn't stay away," Langerman replied, looking down and stubbing the toe of his cowboy boot against the powdery gravel. "I made it to Texas for a while, but it felt like abandoning a sinking ship. I couldn't take feeling like some sort of coward."

"Don't say that; you're no coward. After what happened, leaving was the sensible move."

"That's what I kept telling myself, but it never quite rang true. I felt like I was leaving you and Franny in the lurch, running scared and only thinking of myself."

Siegel placed a reassuring hand on Langerman's shoulder. "You're being too hard on yourself, Dave. We're all only human."

Langerman raised his head and stared into the sky where the sun was breaking through a patch of clouds. "Yeah, I guess so," he agreed without conviction. "I thought it would be best to hang in the background when I got back. I didn't want anybody knowing I was here. I tried to follow you once when you left your apartment, but you lost me."

"I remember that," Siegel said. "I didn't know who you were."

"Then when that accident happened ... I mean when Franny passed, I waited for you at his house. I knew you'd show up there. I was going in to make contact when that investigator arrived."

"Gordy Parks," Siegel said, shaking his head. "He and I had a long heart-to-heart. I'm a bit disappointed. I thought I got through to him and he was going to help. I expected a posse of state police to come rolling in here this morning, but I suppose I misread our conversation."

Sunlight glinted off something metallic on the ground beneath the conveyor belt. Siegel walked over and picked it up. "What's that?" Langerman asked, approaching him.

"Jinnah's gun. It fell off the deck during our struggle."

"I saw the whole event. Pretty gruesome if you ask me. Same with your fight. I woulda come to help, but that other man with the sniper rifle distracted me when he shot that gun away. I crept up on him in the upstairs of that open warehouse over there. Lucky I did, because he was lying on a tarp-covered pile and taking a good bead on you when I brained him with this pipe. I don't believe he'll be shootin' anybody again."

"Thanks, Dave. You saved my life."

"Don't mention it. I'm going to get a helluva byline off this story when I get back to the paper. I trust you'll give me a full and unbridled statement about your side of events?"

"You know it, pal."

A shot rang out and Langerman went down. Siegel saw Frazier, one hand clamped against his head, blood streaming through his fingers, attempting to steady his gun hand while wobbling drunkenly toward them. He grimaced with pain, but still seemed determined to pull the trigger of his automatic handgun a second time.

Reacting without thinking, Siegel bent into a crouch and fired his own gun after Frazier's second shot whizzed past his ear. Siegel fired again and again in rapid succession, watching Frazier perform an awkward Kabuki dance as puffs of blood sprayed from various parts of his torso and head. He dropped in a heap after the seventh bullet struck.

Siegel tossed the empty gun aside and squatted beside Langerman, who was fighting for breath. He had a wound on the left clavicle that oozed blood through the material of his blue jean jacket. Siegel pressed a palm against the wound to staunch the bleeding and Langerman winced. "Awe, that hurts!" he complained.

"Hold on, Dave, you'll be okay," Siegel urged. "I'll get help."

"How you gonna do that?" Langerman groaned.

They both heard sirens and saw the flashing red and blue lights of state police cars entering the grounds behind Frazier's body amidst swirls of white dust. From what Siegel could see, there was a host of marked and unmarked vehicles brimming with law enforcement personnel. The posse had arrived.

The weather was warm and the sun shone brilliantly in a near cloudless blue sky as the Episcopal minister delivered a eulogy over Rappaport's casket. Siegel stood next to Rappaport's ex and two small children on the green lawn, his arm encircled about his wife. Dave Langerman stood nearby, his arm in a sling. They were all silent, listening to the minister's sonorous voice wafting through the morning air.

Kate, Rappaport's former wife, was a pretty blond who looked a decade younger than her forty-four years. She was stoic, doing her best to hide her emotions as she cupped the heads of her young children against her waist. Despite her show of strength, Siegel detected the subtle strain in her expression, the tension around her mouth and eyes. Kate still loved Rappaport, in spite of their divorce, and she was feeling every bit of the loss that his death brought into the lives of her family. Siegel always thought they'd work things out in time, eventually reconcile, but that hope was dashed to pieces now.

Siegel only half listened to the minister's summation as memories of his friend flooded his thoughts. Images of past encounters, snippets of conversations, happy and sad, flowed through his mind in an endless tableau. He couldn't believe Franny was gone. Siegel knew it was going to take a long time to come to terms with the reality of Rappaport's absence. As for the guilt of somehow being responsible for Rappaport's death, Siegel knew that feeling would never go away.

When the sermon ended, friends and family contributed comments and remembrances. Siegel spoke, barely cognizant of the words spilling from his mouth. The heaviness in his heart caused the statements he made to feel somehow empty and hollow.

Afterwards, the casket was lowered into the ground amidst tearful farewells. Siegel hugged Kate and the kids, whispering in Kate's ear that she should call him if there was anything she needed. Kate thanked him politely, and then walked away with her family. They were scheduled to catch an afternoon plane back to Kentucky.

Walking across the grass to their cars, Siegel kept an arm around his wife's waist and squeezed her tight. She did the same, while Langerman grinned beneath his mustache. "You two look like you'll make out just fine," he remarked.

"Of course it will work," Siegel's wife agreed. "We love each other too much."

"Lana's right," Siegel said. "Hmph, Lana, I'll need to get used to calling you that. It's always been Irina."

"Saying Lana is easier than Svetlana. You will get the hang of it," Lana said, smiling.

"How's the immigration matter going?" Langerman asked.

Siegel sighed. "It's going to be a long, uphill battle, but we'll eventually get it ironed out. I hope it won't come down to her being deported. I'd hate to relocate to Russia."

"It would not be so bad," Lana said playfully. "There is much that is beautiful about my country."

"All the same, I'd rather stay here."

"That's not such a bad idea," Langerman said, "especially since you're headed toward exoneration for any wrongdoing in the Khan case. The door's open for your run for DA next November against that Sims turkey."

"I owe it all to you, Dave," Siegel said. "Between corroborating my statements and writing those stories in the press, I'm not so sure I'd be doing this well if you weren't around."

"Aw, think nothing of it. I've got enough material off your tale to write a book. Matter of fact, I've already been contacted by some agents and even a few editors. This shindig is gonna make me a pretty penny in the near future, so spare me the sniveling gratitude."

"Well, since you put it that way …," Siegel replied with a grin.

They'd come to the edge of the grass and were going to have to part ways, finding their cars along the narrow driveway. Langerman extended his good hand and Siegel clasped it firmly, throwing his other arm about Langerman and clapping his back. "Are you gonna be okay, Max?" Langerman asked, blinking against the moisture forming in his eyes.

"I'll be fine," Siegel replied, releasing Langerman's hand and pulling Lana into him. "We'll be fine, Dave."

"I know you will," Langerman said, grinning wanly. "We all will." He lifted his face to the sunshine and took a deep breath. "It's a new day, Max. Remember that."

"I will, old friend. Count on it."

CHAPTER 45

THE CHIEF AND HIS counterpart from the other agency met in the bar of a quaint restaurant in Georgetown. Seated in the back room in high-backed, cherrywood chairs, they each nursed a vodka martini, leaning toward each other over the dim light of a votive candle sitting on the edge of the table that cast a faint red glow on their lined visages.

"How can everything have gone so wrong?" the chief mused, taking a lingering sip from his drink. "Our objective was to squelch an indiscretion and, instead, it blew up like a nuclear device."

"The fallout's been toxic on my side. Our director's lopped off a lot of heads. It's his last gasp before the congressional hearings strip him of his position. I hear he's already packing his boxes and lining up engagements on the lecture circuit. How are you faring?"

The chief rolled his eyes and let out a slight grunt before taking another swallow of his martini. "Don't ask. I'm at the center of about three internal probes and I've been subpoenaed by the Senate and the House. It's only a matter of time before I get the axe and kiss my career good-bye. My pension's locked in. We're talking over three decades of committed government service. I can only hope they'll let me enjoy my retirement *outside* the country club, rather than in." Lifting his glass, the chief drained the remainder of his drink.

"Feeling sorry for yourself? That's so unlike you. This whole disaster could've been avoided if your man Ross hadn't turned out to be such a homicidal maniac. He was only supposed to finesse a quiet cover-up, not create the carnage that he did. And you personally selected him for the mission. How did he ever get past your psychological screening?"

"He was a good agent," the chief insisted defensively. "Sometimes the pressures of the field can cause a good man to snap. He wasn't the agent I'd dealt with in the past. I never could have anticipated the deeds he engaged in over in California."

"Is that going to be your defense? What about Truman's insistence of where the buck stops? It was your operation. Everything your man did was your responsibility. It won't do any good to pawn the blame."

"I'm not pawning anything. Don't forget, it was your boys that initiated the whole ball of wax with that stupid kidnapping. We intervened to clean up your mess. If you thought that Arab was truly a threat, you should've made him lie down in the first place, quick, clean, and quiet."

"Perhaps you're right. It's been a folly all around. Perhaps the biggest miscalculation was involving that DA in the matter. What a persistent surprise he turned out to be. The man has lots of innate talent. We could've used him in some of our special ops overseas. I'll have to admit to a certain amount of grudging admiration for the man."

The chief snorted derisively. "Admiration for what? He's a naïve Boy Scout who can't see outside the idealistic bubble he's created for himself. This whole matter would have easily gone away if it wasn't for him and his sickening high-mindedness. I ultimately blame him for the entire fiasco that's unfolded. And I promise you this, if I survive the damage from this operation intact, Max Siegel will have some payback blowing his way. He can count on it."

Manufactured By: RR Donnelley
Breinigsville, PA USA
April 2010